Stealing Henry

Stealing Henry

Carolyn MacCullough

A Deborah Brodie Book
Roaring Brook Press

New Milford, Connecticut

A Deborah Brodie Book
Published by Roaring Brook Press
A Division of Holtzbrinck Publishing Holdings Limited Partnership
143 West Street
New Milford, Connecticut 06776

Distributed in Canada by H. B. Fenn and Company Ltd.

Library of Congress Cataloging-in-Publication Data

MacCullough, Carolyn.
Stealing Henry / Carolyn MacCullough.— 1st ed.
p. cm.
"A Deborah Brodie book."
Summary: The experiences of high-schooler Savannah, following her decision to take her eight-year-old half brother from his abusive father and their oblivious mother, are interspersed with the earlier story of her mother, Alice, as she meets Savannah's father and unexpectedly becomes pregnant.
[1. Runaways—Fiction. 2. Family problems—Fiction. 3. Mothers and daughters—Fiction. 4. Brothers and sisters—Fiction. 5. Stepfathers—Fiction. 6. Interpersonal relations—Fiction. 7. Pregnancy—Fiction.] I. Title.
PZ7.M1389St 2005
[Fic]—dc22
2004017550

ISBN 1-59643-045-1
ROARING BROOK PRESS books are available for special promotions and premiums. For details, contact: Director of Special Markets, Holtzbrinck Publishers.
Printed in the United States of America
First edition April 2005

10 9 8 7 6 5 4 3 2 1

Acknowledgments

Thank you, as always, to my family, but especially to my mother and my sisters for taking these characters so seriously. Thank you, Uncle Charlie, for answering what must have seemed like random questions about police work. Thank you, Denise, for the Florida haven. And thank you, as always, to Deborah Brodie for reassuring me that puzzle pieces will eventually work themselves into a whole story.

For Grandma Jean

Stealing Henry

one

The night Savannah brains her stepfather with the frying pan is the night she decides to leave home for good.

She has already cut lumps of butter into the skillet and set it on an unlit burner. And she has almost finished dicing an onion, when Jack comes into the kitchen. She feels his presence spread in prickles across the back of her neck, and she inclines her head slightly to gauge his mood. He has been drinking after-work beers down in his workshop in the basement, although the term's relative since he lost his job at the garage a while ago.

He takes a long drink from the beer can in his hand, watches her for a minute, asks, "Dinner ready?"

She still can't pin his mood yet, so she doesn't speak, opens the spice cabinet door, begins hunting for the salt and pepper and powdered garlic.

Halfway into her search, he knocks against her head with his knuckles, which makes her tighten her hold on the pepper shaker before setting it down on the counter, then picking up the knife.

The blade sweeps through the last bit of onion. Refrigerator light spills across her hands as he swings open the door. She holds out a foot to keep the door from banging against her hip. The hinge is broken again, eluding Jack's latest repair efforts.

"Godammit," he says, slams the door closed. The rattle of condiment jars and then silence. Savannah tightens the calf muscles of one leg, then the other, over and over. She thinks it's the broken hinge that has set him off, until he says, "Where's the beer?"

"I don't know," she says, feeling safe enough to inject bewilderment in her tone. Four years ago, Savannah remembers, her mother, Alice, got rid of every bit of alcohol in the house. After that night, she had never tried it again.

Now Savannah glances at the blue plastic clock on the wall. As if reading her thoughts, Jack shrugs. "Corner store's closed." He leans against the fridge. "Why didn't you buy any?"

This time the bewilderment is genuine. "I can't? I'm underage?" She reminds him of this like she is reminding him that two plus two equals four. She knows this isn't exactly smart, but sometimes she can't resist flipping a little sarcasm his way.

She can stand a slap or two. She can't stand the idea of becoming like her mother.

"That's bullshit," he mutters, holding his last beer can up against his eye, which is bloodshot. She wonders briefly if he is referring to the law against underage buying, decides she doesn't care, and reaches over to the stove. She lights it, adjusts the flame until it's a steady-burning blue.

Jack is now pressing the beer can against the bridge of his nose and she remembers that he suffers from migraines. When she was little and learning, she used to make ice packs for her mother to take into the darkened bedroom. Those times felt like a vacation because she was mostly left by herself and she could pinpoint exactly where Jack was at all times. "You're telling me you and your friends never drink?"

She blinks up at him, one part of her thankful that she got the chicken out of the refrigerator before he came in so she wouldn't have to reach around him. "I remember you and that boy sitting on the step here, drinking one of my beers."

"Matt?" she asks, then wishes she hadn't. When they first became friends, Matt used to stop by unexpectedly. Sometimes he dropped her off after school, and once he had walked her to the step, then inside. He had ambled through the kitchen in his loose-jointed way, opened the fridge and said, "Mind if I have a beer?" She should have said no; instead, she found herself sitting with him on the concrete steps outside, watching him drink his stolen beer, opening and closing her fingers together until he glanced down at her, told her to relax, and tipped the bottle down her throat. Foam had fizzed over her shirt and they were both laughing when Jack arrived home.

"You probably drank my beer all the time with him."

"He's gone," she says after a minute, because Jack seems to be waiting for an answer. She tilts the cutting board over the pan, begins flicking the chopped onion into the melting butter.

"Yeah? He find another girl?"

"No," she says coldly. "He went to college."

She is careful not to look at him as she lays the chicken flat on the cutting board and begins to cut it into strips. The meat has lost its first vibrant pink shade and she can't remember how old it was when she bought it. It feels clammy against her fingers and she tries not to mind.

Jack grunts. "Found a college girl then."

"Probably," she agrees, attempting a tuneless humming as he searches for another angle.

"*Probably,*" he mimics. He steps forward, cornering her between the counter and the hot stove. "So he left you, huh? Just left you high and dry. What'd you do?" His voice has dropped, softening like the butter in the pan behind her. He runs a hand down her cheek, and she tilts her head away when his fingers reach her lips. She looks at the ceiling as if there is something fascinating in the web of cracked paint. "Such a young girl," he whispers, pushing his tongue against the thin gap between his front teeth. "So young and so bad." He examines her face. "But you're never going to be pretty like your momma."

She's heard this before, but somehow it still finds its

way. “Yeah?” The smell of burning butter fills the air around them. Something is beginning to crack open inside of her. “Look at all the good it did her.”

Jack’s eyes narrow and he leans his head back from hers. “What?” His voice shoots up three decibels and she reminds herself not to flinch. “What the fuck kind of thing is that to say?”

She opens her mouth, feeling a little like the ugly girl in the fairy tale who spewed only toads and worms every time she tried to speak. But instead, a small voice says, “Dad.” Jack’s body is blocking her vision, but she doesn’t have to see Henry to know he’s close to tears. Jack swings around, and now she can see her little brother, standing half in and half out of the kitchen doorway. Henry is flushed and sweating, on the verge of being sick.

“What’s the matter, buddy?” Jack says, his voice still too loud and jarring, but now forcefully bright. He holds out his arms as if waiting for Henry to run to him.

But Henry is digging one toe into the splintered doorframe. “I heard yelling,” he says, and Savannah knows he heard a lot more. Like her, Henry has learned to listen in at doorways before entering a room.

“No one’s yelling,” Jack says, belatedly trying to lower his voice. He advances two steps toward Henry.

“What were you doing, then?” Henry asks. He sounds like he needs to clear his throat.

“Are you crying, bud?” Jack says, and now his voice is

dangerously quiet. Savannah closes her eyes, listens to Henry swallow, knows they are lost.

"No," he squeaks. "I just . . . thought . . ."

"Jesus Christ, what a . . ."

But Savannah doesn't hear the rest. It seems that time stretches and fades, replaced by something cold and hard and crystallized in her mind. She snaps back in to hear Henry sob, to see Jack take another turning step away from her, giving her all the space she needs to curve her fingers around the hot handle of the skillet. She does not feel the now boiling butter foam across her skin, although she will wonder later at the red blisters on her wrist and forearm. Instead, she feels a rush of blank air, of nothing, as she slams the pan up like a tennis racket, through unencumbered space, and into the side of Jack's head.

Beads of butter and onion bits burst across his face and against the red plastic cabinets. Jack grunts, flings one elbow upward. His fingers open and close on air as he stumbles against the table, slides to his knees. Then his head hits the floor and he is out.

two

"Savannah?" Henry says in his small, scared voice. He barely ever speaks any louder than this. "Is he dead?"

"Hopefully," she answers, and then, "No, he's not dead, Henry, come on."

He sucks in his lower lip. "He's going to be so mad at you."

"What else is new?" But she doesn't feel this brave. Jack is breathing heavily, a strange whistling noise coming from his open mouth.

"Why did you do that?" Henry begins to cry. "Why did you hit him like that?"

"I . . ." She looks at her brother, who is scrubbing furiously at one eye. "Henry, try to calm down. It's going to be okay—"

"But what are you going to do?"

"Leave," she answers, the word fusing with movement as she steps hurriedly around Jack. She gives him another considering glance. Given that he had already finished off a six-pack and that she hit him pretty hard, she estimates that she has a fighting chance of getting out of here alive, if she goes within the next ten minutes. She reaches out with one arm, switches off the burner, pushes past Henry into the front hall to take the steps three at a time. "Get your stuff together," she calls over her shoulder, adding "right now" when she reaches the top of the stairs.

Her movements are precise and fluid, as if she has rehearsed this strange ballet a dozen times. She enters her tiny room at the end of the short hallway, pulls her faded maroon backpack off the bed, jams open the zipper and dumps the contents all across the thin, grimy, green wall-to-wall carpeting.

Pens, papers, books, calculator, and wallet. She grabs the last item and throws it back in. Then she pulls it out, opens it, and fumbles for the slip of paper she has tucked behind her driver's license. It is still there, as she knew it would be, but she unfolds it anyway, reads the address. She knows it by heart now, but repeats it to herself as she refolds it along the seams and replaces it in her wallet.

She slips her wallet back into her bag, sits back on her heels. *Slow down, slow down and think a minute*, Savannah tells herself. *Pretend this is a movie—what would you want to take next?* But even as she cautions herself, her hands are moving feverishly. She jerks open the desk drawer, runs her eyes over the items stored there. A Swiss Army knife that Roy gave her years ago.

She had really liked Roy. He was a carpenter and had made her mother a hand-carved mirror for her twenty-fourth birthday. She can still recall her mother's face while she let Savannah untie the ribbon and tear off the brown paper wrapping, excited and eager and finally delighted when Savannah pulled the lid off the box in which the mirror waited. For a long while, Savannah had hoped that Roy would be the one her mother would marry.

Think, she reminds herself, and slides the knife into the small front pocket of the bag. Toothbrush next. She dashes into the bathroom that she shares with Henry, retrieves the blue brush from the holder, knocking over her brother's little Spiderman cup that he sometimes drinks water from at night. She turns and nearly trips over him. Under one arm, he is carrying Bert, the large teddy bear that Jack's mother had sent him four years ago for his birthday. In the other hand, he is holding a pair of pajamas and a clean pair of underwear.

"All packed?"

"Are we going to Marie's?"

"Sure."

"What if he comes there?" Jack had done that once before and Marie had locked the door. Savannah and Henry sat under the kitchen table and listened to Marie speak to the police, her voice thin and shaking a little.

"He won't. Now move." She picks him up by the shoulders, leans him against the wall. Henry is small for eight. Small and slight, and full of angles.

She stops at the doorway of her closet, scans it. Then she pulls on the army jacket that Wade had given her when she was seven. Being a man's jacket, it was a dress for her then and it is still loose on her now. She tucks up the cuffs, remembering that she had liked Wade. Even though he didn't last too long with her mother. Maybe because he was a military man and Alice had always considered herself a pacifist. Savannah can't remember the reasons Alice had given as they were packing the car, but she fervently wishes, not for the first time, that Alice had married him. Really, any of them instead of Jack.

"Stop it, stop it," Savannah whispers, swings her backpack onto her shoulder. Even though it is full, it is undeniably lighter than when she carries it every day to school, stuffed with books. She slides her arms through the straps, steps into the hallway. *Don't look back, Savannah*, her mother says somewhere in her head. When they had a whole string of places to never look back at. *It's bad luck. Never look back.*

But downstairs, she checks to see if Jack is breathing. He is. The gash on his forehead is oozing thickly, but he is definitely still breathing. She doesn't know whether to be glad about this or not.

He is lying half under the kitchen table, one arm touching a chair leg, his mouth agape, snoring. She swings open the door of the narrow kitchen closet where the coats are kept, rifles through a series of slick, worn pockets, her fingers splayed, hating to touch anything of Jack's. But her search turns up the car keys. She looks over her shoulder at her stepfather lying on the floor, wishing she hadn't gone grocery shopping with the money her mother gave her this morning. Especially since no one's eating dinner tonight.

She eyes the front pockets of his jeans. Flat. "Fuck," she whispers and then gingerly, with the side of her shoe, tries to roll him over. He makes a sort of coughing noise in his sleep, but doesn't budge. Nothing for it. She eases down on her heels and with both hands manages to push him over onto his left side. Since he is right-handed, she can only pray he keeps his wallet in his back right pocket. He does. Carefully, she extracts three twenties.

"Little bitch," Jack mutters hoarsely. Her eyes fly to his face, but his eyelids, purpled with veins, remain shut. He begins to snore louder.

"I'll miss you, too," she whispers, and stands up, brushing her hands against her jeans.

"Savannah," Henry says from behind her. She turns and looks down at him. He has put all of his things into his small blue backpack. Bert's head is poking out from the opening and his brown glassy eyes stare at her mournfully. She swallows, feeling sick, knowing that she really should leave Henry at Marie's first and then . . . But she has planned this for so long that she refuses to believe it won't work. Not quite this dramatic an exit, but the whole rest of the leaving part she had already worked out. "Okay. Ready?"

Henry nods. Then he sneezes three times.

"Get your coat."

"I left it upstairs," he whispers, his eyes fixed on hers.

"Run," she snaps, and he does. A minute, two minutes pass. She can hear him scurrying back down the stairs. "Hurry," she calls, keeping her eyes on Jack's body.

Henry reappears through the kitchen door, fighting to fit one arm into his coat, the other sleeve tangling in the strap of his backpack. "Take your backpack off first," she says impatiently. Then, as he starts to comply, "Forget it! Put it on in the car."

She grabs his backpack—it is ridiculously light—and pushes him ahead of her, the springs on the screen door shrilling unpleasantly. "Run," she orders, a sudden, uneasy premonition sparking across her skin, and they dash open the doors of the car and climb in. She jams the key into the ignition, imagining that if this were a bad movie, the car wouldn't start and that Jack would be throwing himself across the hood and that they would never get away. But the car starts beautifully and she sighs once.

"Sav . . . ," Henry whispers, his voice trembling. She looks at him and then back at the house. Jack is standing in the doorway. Rather, he is leaning against the screen door, and even as she watches, he falls through it and onto the concrete steps.

"Ouch." She winces, knowing that fall must have hurt. "Good." And she guns the car backward out of the driveway. A stray pebble pings the windshield, which is already cracked from an earlier accident of Jack's. They roll onto the street and she puts the car in drive and hits the accelerator.

They drive through darkened streets for a few minutes, and slowly the homes become more and more prosperous looking. Houses full of softly lit rooms behind filmy-curtained windows. Rooms where people are preparing dinner or reading the newspaper or talking about their day at school and at work.

When they smooth past the turn to Marie's, Henry sits up and scrunches his legs under him. "Where are we going?"

She looks sideways at him. His little body is twisted in the seat. She reaches over and pushes his head gently until he faces forward. "Don't look back, Henry. It's bad luck."

three

Savannah's first memory is of sitting in the backseat of the Chevrolet. Although she didn't know it at the time, this Chevrolet was to feel like her home for the next five years. But in this particular instant, she was more concerned with searching the backseat for whatever she could find. She can recall running her hands across the sticky seats and dipping her fingers into the cracks of the tan vinyl. Just as her fingers closed around what felt like a quarter, Alice, sitting in the front passenger seat, cried out, "Look! The Golden Gate Bridge!"

There was such an eager joy to her voice that Savannah bolted up to look between the two seats through the front windshield. But she was disappointed to find that the bridge was more of a dull red than the shining gold her mother had promised it would be. But Alice looked so happy and so pretty with her long red hair blowing out the open window, that Savannah could only hold up her rescued quarter between two fingers. She was rewarded when her mother said with the same amount of delight in her voice, "Look what you found, baby!"

She can remember all this, although she can't remember

who was driving the car at the time. There is a constant snapshot in Savannah's mind of her mother, curled up in the front seat, resting her head on someone's shoulder, her hair spread over the back of the headrest so Savannah could braid and unbraid it as the miles passed by outside the car windows. She thinks it might have been Wade who brought them to San Francisco, because she remembers a day trip to Muir Woods where she hid behind redwood trees and waited for either Wade or Alice to discover her. Or maybe Lionel. Lionel came right after Wade. But for the first nine years of Savannah's life, it was her mother and her. And a lot of time in the backseat of a car, reading books that her mother had bought at every bookstore they passed, filling in those "yes and no" puzzles that she picked up at every rest stop, or just staring out the window, watching the scenery like it was her own movie. Starring diner waitresses, tired and beaten down by too many graveyard shifts; gas station attendants who always flirted with Alice and offered Savannah candy; schoolteachers consistently surprised at where she placed on their tests despite her lack of schooling.

For years, Savannah never thought it odd that her mother and she moved so many times. She did know it wasn't quite normal, from watching enough motel TV. But she still didn't think it was "wrong," as Jack's mother later came to term it.

San Francisco, San Diego, LA, Taos, Boulder. One cold winter in Chicago, followed by one warm summer in

Rhode Island. They drifted into towns, stayed long enough for Savannah to learn the street names, and then one day when she came back from school or the corner store or the library, she would find her mother sitting in their temporary trailer or in their motel room, waiting for her. The oversized and overused roadway atlas would be spread out before Alice, and she'd be poring over it with a thoughtful look. And soon enough, she'd start to hum and Savannah knew to pack her things. Sometimes, Savannah remembered Alice telling her to close her eyes and point her finger, and that's where they'd get to go next. They traveled far in that Chevrolet.

Savannah's last memory of that life together happened somewhere in New Jersey when the car died. For a while, before the car had stuttered to its final halt on the side of I-95, Savannah had been noticing that Alice was different. She was quieter, more inclined to long thinking silences and less inclined to talk. She never snapped at Savannah, never really lost her patience, but still, Savannah could tell that Alice wanted less somehow. She didn't want Savannah to read to her nearly as much as Savannah used to, and she didn't care so much about what was playing on the radio. She let Savannah tune it to anything at all and rarely sang along, even when Savannah was certain that her mother knew the lyrics. Her head ached, Alice always offered.

And one November evening, the car broke down again and they were stranded on the side of I-95. The road was busy with other cars whooshing by, but it seemed that no one would stop. It was a little past rush hour, and these people had homes to go to and dinners to prepare.

Savannah remembered that they hadn't eaten much that day. Stale Cheese Bitz from a box that had been wedged under the driver's seat. Since it had been raining for three days, the crackers were moist with humidity and Savannah had thought they tasted liked mouthfuls of salty cardboard. But that was hours ago and she now wished that she hadn't let her handfuls trail out the open window as the car blew down the highway. Without looking directly at her, Alice shook her head. "Well, I hope you realize you just fed the birds your dinner."

But Savannah was used to skipping meals and didn't see this as such a calamity. So when the car ground to a halt and the front hood began to smoke, she reached for her mother's cigarettes in the glove compartment. Alice believed that nothing was as dramatic and awful as it first seemed, and certainly in the time it took to smoke a cigarette, a whole world of things could happen.

But this time, Alice put her hand on Savannah's wrist to stop her from opening the glove compartment.

"No," she murmured.

"You don't want your cigarettes?"

Alice shook her head and, after a second, Savannah shrugged. Her mother was always trying to quit. She reached for the door handle. But this time, Alice spoke.

"Forget it, baby. It's not going to work this time."

"How do you know, Mama?" Savannah asked this not because she doubted her mother. In those days, Alice was the smartest person Savannah knew. If she knew somehow that the engine wouldn't revive, then it wouldn't. But Savannah asked because she was starting to become uneasy with her mother's tone. There wasn't much expression in it and that was unusual for her. Later on, with Jack, it became her normal speaking voice. But now, by the side of the road, Savannah was bewildered.

"Fuck it," Alice said, but quietly, and this was even more confusing since she took care never to swear. That was the one rule Alice imposed on everyone in their lives. She always said that she had been raised to speak properly and that her daughter would be, too. And everyone in their lives had stuck to her rule.

Alice leaned back in her seat and pressed her palms against her eyes. After a moment, she drew in a deep breath. Damp light glimmered over her cheekbones. Savannah tucked her hands under her knees, sat silent, completely unsure of the moment and even of the person sitting next to her. After a little while, she was rewarded when Alice straightened up and sighed. "Okay." She fished by Savannah's knees, came up with the water bottle. "Let's take a look." She got out of the car and Savannah followed more slowly. There was still something not Alice enough about her mother.

And that was when Jack found them. He must have seen Alice leaning over the hood of the car. Savannah reasons that he must have not seen her also, examining a tire. If he did, Savannah wonders if he would have stopped so eagerly. But he did stop. He pulled his car off onto the shoulder, a little ways ahead of theirs, and got out.

If only her mother could have seen that their future was walking toward them. Savannah liked to think that Alice would have politely refused his offer of help if she had known what it would mean for all of them. But instead, her mother must have seen the Marlboro Man himself walking toward her in his faded jeans and hat, with his easy voice and his big hands. And as luck would have it, a mechanic as well.

"Need some help here?" he asked, so polite, so gentle. He saw the water bottle in Alice's hand and laughed. Savannah can recall that laugh, especially since she heard it so often in the following years, but even more, she can recall the single pure way she felt when she heard him laugh like that for the first time. She thinks she hated him from that moment on. "Don't think that's going to do it."

Savannah waited for her mother to respond that they were fine on their own, that they could manage. She knew Alice never liked it when a man treated her like the "little helpless lady." But Alice only smiled and lowered the upended bottle like the bones in her arm had suddenly melted away, and Savannah thinks that, in the first instant when she hated Jack, she came close to hating Alice as well.

There were all the signs Savannah could read so well. Alice tilted her head downward, her right ear presented to the speaker as if everything he said was so important that she wanted to make sure she caught it all, while pulling so slowly on a curl of red hair that just happened to fall on her long, pale neck. Since she was a master at this, most men fell hard within a few minutes. Jack was no exception.

Savannah examined him from around the side of the car. He was talking to her mother easily, freely, and she was laughing as she had not been laughing for a while now. For that, Savannah might have softened. But then Jack caught sight of her peering around the side of the car, from where she had been sitting on cold pavement, running one finger around the battered hubcap.

"Who's that?" he called. "Your little sister?" Savannah rolled her eyes in the dark, waited for her mother to react. That falsely cheerful note to his voice, that obvious line that they had both heard so many times before.

"My daughter actually."

"Your daughter?" He took care to put enough stunned incredulity in his voice and none of the disappointment. Savannah was sure he was wondering *daughter?* and then *husband?* "Well, you don't look old enough to have a daughter."

And of course, her mother laughed again. "Savannah. Come here." For a minute, Savannah thought about refusing. She considered the spindly trees and sparse grass on the side of the highway and then looked at the bleak New Jersey skyline. The dark, frosty November air whirled around her ankles and she shivered a little. There was nowhere else to go.

She got up painstakingly slowly and scuffed over to her mother's side and mumbled something in response to Jack's jovial *hello* and said very little while he arranged for a tow to his station, even when Alice tapped her ankle with the sharp tip of a boot and hissed, "He's nice, so you be nice, too." Savannah said even less when he offered her mother a ride to wherever they were going.

four

Savannah pulls into the hospital parking lot and kills the engine. She thinks about putting her head down on the steering wheel and closing her eyes, but with Henry breathing next to her, she won't.

"What are we doing here?" Henry asks. "Are we going to see Mom?"

"Well, who else do we know here, Henry?"

He shrugs a little. "Will Mom be mad?"

"What for?"

"'Cause you hit Dad?"

"Who the fuck cares!" Savannah explodes. "I mean, did you notice that he was going to hit *you*?" She looks away, leans the side of her face against the cool glass. A breeze sweeps across the darkened parking lot, whistling through the cracks of the driver-side window, which hasn't closed properly for years.

"He hit me once before," Henry says. "But only 'cause I broke the VCR. Only that once."

"Great," she murmurs, her lips half-pressed to the window glass, smudging her voice. "Now you sound like

Mom." A steady mechanical clicking noise fills the car. She looks over to see Henry pulling up and pushing down the door lock.

"Thanks," he says, just as she says, "Stop that."

When he doesn't speak again, she follows up with "Thanks for what?"

"For hitting him. So he didn't hit me."

She shrugs. "Yeah. Sorry I didn't do it sooner." She unlocks her door, slides out of the car. "Come on. Bring your bag," she calls back and starts across the pavement toward the brightly lit hub of the hospital center.

Savannah selects the third-floor waiting room because it is mostly empty and seems quiet for this time of night. A TV set is crackling in the corner and Henry's eyes are immediately drawn to Alex Trebek's face, which is lined with grave disappointment as he informs a contestant that the correct response is "What is the Danube River?" The contestant, a pale, thin woman, moves her lipsticked mouth briefly, repeating the word *Danube* to herself.

It is Henry's greatest ambition to be on *Jeopardy!* one day. Last year, Savannah gave him the set of encyclopedias that Alice had given to her when she was six. For three years, Savannah and Alice would read a page or two together after dinner. They were on the *F*s when they met up with Jack, and somehow that tradition faded early into the *G*s.

Savannah remembers how good-natured Jack had seemed about it at first. He read a few entries with them, but lost interest before they reached the end of the *F*s. Then he just laughed and shook his head whenever Alice flipped open the book and asked him to sit down with them. Soon he started calling Alice to bring him another beer or come rub his shoulders for a minute, and with an apologetic look, she'd go. And pretty soon after that, Alice started off the evenings sitting with him on the couch. Sometimes, the next day, she'd ask Savannah what she had read, and then one day, she stopped asking, and somewhere late into the *K*s, Savannah stopped reading and the encyclopedias got stacked neatly in a corner of Savannah's room.

"Okay, wait here," Savannah instructs, and Henry bobs his head a little, his eyes already scanning the categories of Double Jeopardy. Savannah wraps her fingers around his upper arms, blunders him into a red chair, and he sits. "Are you hungry?" she asks, and then tries to remember what she had been planning to make for dinner. But all she can see is the arc of steaming butter splattering from the pan.

He nods, quick, small motions of his soft chin, so she finds some loose change in the outer pocket of her knapsack, examines the contents of the two vending machines, decides on peanut M&M's, considering that nuts at least have protein. She fumbles through the correct amount of money, retrieves the bag, hands it to him. Since a commercial is playing, she has his undivided attention. "Did you push the buttons twice?" he asks intently. "Because one time, when I did that, another bag of M&M's came out and I—"

She shakes her head at him. "Keep dreaming. Wait here. Don't talk to anyone, okay? I'll be back. Bet you two games of Scrabble you won't get the Final Jeopardy question."

He offers his hand for her to shake and seal the deal. She smiles.

Savannah hurries down the brightly lit corridor, her eyes drawn to random snapshots of rooms sliding by. In one of them, an old woman is reaching out a hand to someone or something unseen, while in another, a large, burly man, dressed in a red plaid shirt, taps at a foot protruding from the white bedsheets.

Two left turns, a short elevator ride, and she arrives at the emergency room. Scanning the scene from the doorway, she decides it is a slow night. Two men are huddled on a corner bench, one of them is holding his hand out before him, grimacing. An elderly man is sitting on the opposite side of the room, patting the arm of a much younger woman beside him. Every once in a while, he stops to wipe his eyes.

A voice over the loudspeaker steadily summons Nurse Witkin to room 229. Savannah lets her eyes rest on her mother, who sits alone behind a long white counter, bookended by two large rhododendron plants, their trailing, deep green leaves a testament to the power of fluorescent lighting.

Alice is sorting papers, her hands flicking through piles, discarding, filing, perusing. She pulls a strand of hair back behind an ear, presses her thumb briefly between her eyes. A woman shoulders past Savannah, who is still standing in the doorway, and hobbles over to the desk. Alice looks up, her face even and composed, turns to her computer monitor, begins taking down the information. She looks away from her screen, tilts her head, gives the other woman a half smile. She opens a drawer, comes up with a clipboard, and hands it to the woman, who seems to be cheerful despite whatever pain she is in.

The *click*, *click*ing of boot heels down the corridor behind Savannah startles her. A woman wearing a leather jacket and too much rouge sweeps down the hallway, her stride assured and defiant, even as she puts one hand up to her nose, which is running darkly with blood. Savannah steps aside, thinking the woman is heading for the emergency room, only to watch her walk off, bearing down on the exit sign.

The door swings, closes out the sound of her heels, and all at once, Savannah recalls the year spent in a tiny apartment on the edge of Santa Fe, listening every night to her mother walking away from the front door that she had so carefully instructed Savannah to lock. Savannah used to tuck herself back into bed to the sound of her mother's footsteps fading down the street.

She always woke before Alice, feeling sunlight slip through cracked and bent blinds. With her eyes closed, she absorbed the rhythm of her mother's steady breathing. Finally, unable to wait any longer, Savannah would open her eyes, roll over, careful not to shift or dislodge her mother's arm, which was invariably wrapped around Savannah's waist. She would study the mascara that had smeared into the corners of Alice's eyelids, the lipstick that had faded into the creases of her mouth, and wonder what new stories her mother had learned.

Until one night, when Savannah surfaced into the still-dark bedroom. She blinked away the insistent edges of a dream to discover Alice sitting on a corner of the thin mattress, one hand pressed to her neck, blood coating her fingers.

"Baby," she said, her voice steady and low. "I need you to help me." She reached over, tossed her purse onto the bed. "In there is a needle and thread. Can you thread it for me?" Savannah nodded, blinked sleep away, poked the thread through the needle on her first try. "Good job," her mother said, smiled. But her smile slipped a little as she stood.

In the bathroom, the sharp smell of rubbing alcohol drove the last bits of fog from Savannah's head. Fascinated, she stared at the pinkish red, soaked wad of toilet paper that Alice was using to dab at her neck. "What happened?"

The outer dark ring of Alice's eyes seemed to have swallowed her pupils as she looked at Savannah. "Oh, just a little disagreement. Hang on. I need to concentrate on this." She leaned her hip against the bathroom counter, pinched the edges of the cut tightly together, slipped the needle through skin with a little gasp. Other than that one sound, Alice was completely quiet. It was Savannah who had to sit on the rim of the tub with her head between her knees, listening to the faint whisper of thread.

After a time, she dared a look to find Alice admiring her handiwork. "Not bad." She held the needle aloft. "Want me to pierce your ears while we're at it?"

That memory dissolves as Savannah enters the emergency room and moves toward her mother's desk.

Alice looks up, expectant at first, then surprised. She half rises from her chair.

"Sav," she begins and holds out her hand. "What are you doing here?" The cords of her throat jump briefly. "Is it Henry? Is something wrong with Henry?"

"Henry's okay. I'm okay. We just had to get out of the house again." Savannah shrugs, listens to Nurse Witkin being paged, the speaker's voice undeniably more irritated this time.

Alice draws in a breath, eases back into her chair. "What did you do?"

"Nothing. Jack's drunk again."

"Where's Henry? Is he at Marie's?"

"No. He's upstairs in the waiting room. He's watching *Jeopardy!*"

But Alice shakes her head. "You shouldn't have left him by himself."

"I didn't want to bring him down here," Savannah gestures behind her. The inner doors of the emergency room open and a nurse appears.

"Thomas Cleary, Thomas Cleary," she announces to the middle of the room. The man who has been holding his hand out before him stands up, starts toward her, and Savannah can see that he is limping. The nurse watches his progress with no expression and then turns to the front desk, looks directly at Alice, rolls her eyes upward to the ceiling.

"Lonnie's on a tear tonight. Watch it."

Alice nods, looks back at Savannah. "Just go to Marie's, baby, okay? I'll be home tomorrow morning." She touches slender fingers to her forehead, as if to smooth away a troublesome thought. "Everything will be okay, tomorrow—you know Jack, how he gets. It doesn't last." She sighs a little, her hands closing over some papers, tucking them out of sight. The computer ticks at her, digesting information. Alice glances at the screen.

"Mom," Savannah begins, the words half-whispered in her throat. "I'm not going to Marie's tonight."

"What?" Alice looks back at her. "Where are you going?"

Savannah lifts her hands, lets them fall back to her side.

"Savannah," Alice begins, dips her head forward, presses her hands against the back of her neck. She holds this pose for a moment, then looks up, her gaze pleading. "I don't know what happened exactly and I don't have to, to know that it's going to work out, okay? You have to trust me on this one. Jack is going through a bad time now, with losing his job and all. It's been pretty hard on all of us. You think I like working so much, these hours?" She swings one hand in a half circle around her. "It's awful. But it's going to get better. You just have to stay away from him."

"Trust me, I do," Savannah says, but her mother continues as if uninterrupted.

"Just keep quiet when he gets in his moods and—"

"That's bullshit, Mom." Savannah puts her hands on the desk between them, leans forward a little. Her right wrist burns against the cool countertop and she pulls her arm back, examines it. A series of red blisters has formed across her skin. She skims a finger over her wrist, registering the bright flare of pain.

Alice slumps back in her chair, presses her bottom lip into her top one until her mouth forms a thin line. Static crackles on the loudspeaker and then another, deeper voice summons Nurse Smithers to room 446. The inner doors fling open again and a large, calm-faced woman sails past Savannah.

"Okay," Alice says, then again, "okay." She looks at Savannah for a long moment, then past her, as if to seek inspiration from the handful of people in the room. "We'll talk about this more. I promise. I have the day off on Friday. We'll do something together, just you and me, after school. Or maybe you can even take the day off from school, like we used to, okay?"

Savannah closes her eyes briefly. After they started living with Jack, the hardest thing was to accustom herself to the endless routine of school, five days a week. She was far too easy with picking up mid-month, mid-year, and moving across the country, where it might take at least a few days after they had resettled before her mother would start inquiring about public schools again. Sometimes, she could convince Alice to let her have a few weeks off before leaping back into the round of school buses, the sounds and smells of the long gray hallways. She says nothing, only opens her eyes, blinks as rings of light spread across her vision.

"So I said to him, Al, if you had stopped smoking like I asked you to, all those years, you wouldn't have lung cancer now. And do you believe what he said to me? To his own wife? He told me to go to hell. Isn't that nice?"

Savannah can hear the woman's voice halfway down the hall and when she slips back into the waiting room, she finds Henry wide-eyed, cornered in his chair. The speaker, an older woman with dyed black hair, is tapping a rolled up copy of a magazine against his small leg for emphasis. "I wasn't raised to speak like that. And you know what?" She leans over Henry and he tightens his shoulders a little. "I certainly wasn't raised to be spoken to like that." She jerks her chin up twice and unrolls her magazine.

"Henry, we have to go now," Savannah says, holds out her hand. Henry peers around the woman's shoulder, unfolds his legs, and practically jumps off the chair.

The woman leans back hesitantly. "Are you his mother?" she asks, regarding Savannah with narrowed black eyes.

"Do I look like his mother?" Savannah answers abruptly, wraps her hand around his, and pulls him into the hallway. He trots awkwardly beside her while, with one hand, he searches through his jacket pocket.

"Here, I saved you some." He holds out the crumpled package of M&M's.

"Thanks." She shakes the contents of the packet into her mouth, bites down.

"Did you see Mom?"

"Yeah. She was busy."

"Did you see anyone without their legs?"

"No, everyone had their legs tonight." She looks down at him. "Sorry."

He shrugs. "I didn't win on Final Jeopardy," he says after a minute.

"Oh, yeah? What was the question?"

He frowns a little. "The first major motion picture to use a rock-and-roll soundtrack and starring Sidney Poitier and Glenn Ford?"

"Beats the hell out of me. What was it?"

"*Blackboard Jungle*?"

"Never heard of it."

"Mom would have known."

"Maybe."

Henry murmurs something too soft for her to catch. She shakes his hand a little, then releases him. "What?" They pass three nurses who are standing close together, examining a clipboard. One of the nurses shakes her head at Savannah. Belatedly, she remembers that visiting hours end at seven.

"Can we still play Scrabble?"

She looks down at him, smiles. "Sure."

He regards her for a minute, then gives a half skip. "At Marie's? Are we going to Marie's now?"

"No."

They come to the stairwell and Savannah ducks into it, holding the door open with one hand until Henry is through.

"Why not? Where are we going?"

Savannah stops. "Henry . . . I can't go back home now. Not after tonight. I don't want to, anyway. . . ." He is nodding, but she knows he doesn't fully understand. "I've been thinking about taking a trip."

"Like a vacation?"

"Yeah. From Mom and Jack." They look at each other for a long moment, until Henry's gaze slides away from her face and lands somewhere along the floor.

"Look. Mom isn't who she should be." Henry looks back at her, his eyes wandering over her face, as if making sure she is still there.

"Who is she, then?"

Savannah shakes her head. "It's hard to explain. You don't know Mom the way I do, the way I used to. I just think that if we got her away from Jack, just away, then who knows? She might come back to being . . . the right person." Her voice sounds light and odd, distorted by the echoes in the stairwell. She clears her throat, shifts backward. "I have an idea. Just trust me on this one, okay?" The sound of wheels squeaking past them, followed by rapid footsteps. All at once, she has an overwhelming desire to leave. But Henry's face is still troubled.

"How long would we be gone?"

"Not long. Look, you don't have to come with me. I can drop you off at Marie's." She makes her voice neutral, expressionless.

"Alone? I don't want to go by myself."

She shrugs, pretends to consider this, even though she had anticipated it.

"Okay," he says finally.

"Okay what?"

"I'm coming with you." He fixes his eyes, moth brown and big with worry, on her face again, but nods.

Savannah tucks herself into the cramped phone booth, gives a quick scan to the nearly empty parking lot. Her eyes pick out only Henry, crouching in the shadows against the closest wall.

She unhooks the receiver, holding it slightly away from her mouth, and slides the quarters into the slot. She presses the numbers, prays that Matt will answer.

The phone doesn't ring, just clicks once and then Matt's voice, unusually deep and smooth, fills her head. "Hi. You may think you're talking to Matt." There is a three-second pause. "But you're not talking to Matt. You're talking to Matt's voicemail. . . ."

She rolls her eyes, waits through the idiotic instructions on how to leave a message. A long *beep* followed by a series of short *blip*s. Then there is an expectant silence.

"Matt. It's Savannah. Ah . . . remember, back a while ago, when you kept asking me to visit you in New York?"

Alice 1986

The door opens and the bells tied to the frame clang out three jarring notes. A man dressed in a police uniform saunters in. He is tall and widely built, the short sleeves of his dark blue shirt banding tightly around thick biceps. His hair, buzzed close to his head, glints blond under the fluorescent lighting of the store. "Hey, there, little bit," he calls to Cindy.

"Oh, God," Cindy mutters, sprays Windex against the ice cream case with extra force, and swipes at the curved glass with wide, careless strokes. "What are you doing here, Mike?"

"What's up, Double A?" Mike adds, looking at Alice Ainswell, clearly unfazed by his sister's lack of welcome. He stretches out his arms, cracks the knuckles of one hand with a loud popping sound.

"And why are you wearing that uniform? You're not even on duty," Cindy insists, all the while scanning the sidewalk with an air of desperation. "I think you would sleep in that uniform if Mom would let you."

Mike reaches out and scrubs a hand across Cindy's

head. "Just finished a long shift and thought I'd come make sure you ladies are keeping out of trouble."

Alice tips her head, lets her hair swing forward, hoping it obscures her face, trying not to look at Cindy, who snaps back, "What kind of trouble could we get into here? I mean, we're at *work*." She stomps behind the counter, brushing Alice's shoulder in passing.

"Well, I don't know now," Mike drawls, gives an elaborate sweeping glance to the premises. Alice can feel his eyes on her as she wads up paper towels, comes out from behind the counter, begins wiping away dribbles of Windex that Cindy has missed. "For example, Alice here is in direct violation of sanitation codes by not wearing her hair pulled back." He waits expectantly as Alice turns slowly to face him.

She blinks up at him, gives him her best deer-caught-in-headlights look. "I thought that would be a job for the Health and Sanitation Department. I didn't know that rated a real, live actual *junior* police officer." She pauses, lowers, then lifts her lashes, lingering on the shiny brass buttons that she is sure he polishes each and every evening. "Wow. I am. So. Deeply honored."

Mike tips his head back as if studying the ceiling, and Alice watches the column of his throat swell wide with bellows of laughter. Already, she can feel irritation prick at her, and so she jerks her head toward Cindy, touches two fingers to her lips, and pivots through the swinging doors to the back room. Mike is still guffawing loudly behind her.

Alice steps through the narrow door leading to the alleyway, fishes through her apron pocket, and comes up with half a cigarette and the glittery pink lighter she found on the sidewalk outside the store last month. She had been smoking the first half of the cigarette earlier in the afternoon, until she heard the cash register ringing open and a loud argument erupting between two customers about who was first in line.

Now that the sun is edging down in the western half of the sky, any heat the day held is gone. Alice leans her head against the split rail fence of the alleyway and draws on her bent stub of a cigarette, the smell of smoke temporarily driving away the odor of frying meat from the diner next door. The back door creaks and air-conditioned air coils around her bare legs. She smoothes down the front of her apron, flicking away stray cigarette ash, before turning to glance at Mike.

"Got a light?" He is fitting a cigarette to his mouth and she hands him hers, shakes her head when he tries to hand it back after lighting his own. She has smoked it down to the filter, anyway. She watches the tip of his cigarette flare brightly, then subside, shakes her head a second time when he offers her a drag.

"You know, you're not really supposed to be back here. Employees only," she says finally, because he is staring too intensely at her through thin sheaves of smoke.

"Why don't you call the cops?" he answers, smiling

slowly, and she looks away, annoyed that she handed him that one so freely.

She examines the wooden fence again, listening to the banjo music playing on the radio from the diner kitchen next door. There is a heavy clatter of pans dropping, then someone shouting unintelligibly. Alice looks back at Mike. Even though he is only twenty-one, he looks much older, his face broad, a thick blond beard covering his wide jaws. Cindy has informed her that he spends two hours a day in the basement on the weight machines that Cindy's father installed four years ago and never used. "So when did they actually let you on the force?"

"When I passed their exam," he answers. "So when are you actually going to go out with me?"

"When you pass my exam."

He steps forward, puts both hands up against the fence on either side of her head. From the corner of one eye, she can see the curly blond hairs growing thick and close on the planes of his arm. "So what's on this exam?"

She turns her head slightly, fits her mouth around the cigarette trapped between his fingers, the edge of her lips barely brushing against his palm. She inhales, exhales, asks, "You mean, like, you want a review session?"

He runs one finger along her collarbone, dips the pad of his thumb into the hollow at her throat, pressing against the pulse. It is lightly uncomfortable. "To start with."

She knows she should consider what she is doing. She also knows that if she does, she will come up with at least three reasons why she doesn't want to encourage Mike. So she tips her chin up, closes her eyes, and lets him kiss his way up her neck to her mouth. She tries not to mind the prickle of his beard against her skin.

"Oh, gross," Cindy says, watching Mike turn and wave at Alice before climbing back into his car. "You and my brother?"

Alice shrugs. "I'm bored."

"So watch TV, for Christ's sake. Don't mess around with Mike. He's . . ." But here Cindy fails to find the word to sum up her brother.

"He's what?"

Cindy sighs, drifts closer, leans one hand on the freshly polished chrome of the ice cream case. "He really likes you. He talks about you all the time."

"Yeah?" Despite herself, Alice is more than faintly interested.

"Just don't get married." Cindy swings behind the counter, ducks into the storage closet, and Alice can hear her scuffling through the bucket of cleaning supplies. "Not that I wouldn't want you for a sister-in-law. That'd be the greatest, but . . ."

Alice waits until Cindy reappears, a bottle of Ajax in one hand. "We just kissed. That's all."

Cindy gives Alice a direct look. "That's not going to be all for Mike. Trust me."

"Change of subject?"

"Happily." Cindy kicks the mop bucket out of the closet and they both watch as it clatters onto its side. "Want to sweep or wash the windows?"

"Gee, what a choice. I'll sweep." Alice puts up one hand, catches the broom that Cindy levels at her like a javelin. She casts a quick look over her shoulder, through the floor-length windows, but the curb is empty of any cars. She reaches up through the shelves to the radio and cuts the classical music tape that has been looping through the afternoon. Their manager insists that they play the three Mozart tapes in the store ad nauseam, and twice Alice and Cindy have been caught by surprise drop-ins. But Alice figures they can play anything they want after hours, and now she spins the tuner until she lands on 96.3, their favorite station. There is an initial buzz of static, an overlay of two songs at once, but Alice is patient, persistently adjusting the broken antenna, and is rewarded by the opening bars of Cyndi Lauper's "Time After Time."

"Nice," Cindy exults, positioning the stepladder by the windows to the left of the door. She begins to spray them with Windex, announces for the third time that summer, "I'm going to start spelling my name like hers. It's so much cooler."

Alice nods, stops sweeping. Leaning into the smooth knob handle of the broom, she begins to harmonize with the chorus. "Suitcase of memories," she says a few beats later. "I always love that line."

"Yeah," Cindy agrees, adjusts the purple bow barrette in her hair before swiping at the windows some more. "What exactly is a 'suitcase of memories,' anyway?"

Alice shrugs. "Probably not something you'd pack after living in Three Springs all your life."

"True. Here comes your chorus."

Alice closes her eyes, giggles, but manages to reach out her hand, dramatically beckoning. She takes a breath.

The music sinks abruptly into nothing. Alice opens her eyes. A boy is standing in front of her, framed by the open doorway, staring. Something shimmers along her skin, gathers in her chest, propels her forward. She looks at Cindy, who has descended from her ladder, finger locked around the spray mechanism of the Windex bottle as if to ward off intruders. But it is the boy who speaks first.

"I'm sorry. I didn't know you were closed." He shifts, puts his hands in his pockets, looks at her so directly that she immediately drops her gaze to his feet. He is wearing black high tops without any socks. His shins are lean, covered with fine black hair. Alice studies the frayed white wisps of his cut-off jean shorts, noting the way they brush against his knees, which are a darker brown than the rest of his skin. She looks up then, meets his eyes, which she decides instantly are the most beautiful eyes she has ever seen, before offering a little ripple of one shoulder.

"No problem." She deepens her smile. "I forgot to lock the door."

five

Savannah is hoping they have tonight and half of tomorrow before Alice realizes that they are not at Marie's. Less, if Alice calls Marie in the morning. But Alice is usually too tired to do much but sit on the couch when she returns from the night shift at the hospital. She stares at the morning television shows, holding a cup of tea, occasionally stirring herself to answer whatever question Henry is asking, before lapsing back into silence.

Henry doesn't complain when Savannah parks the car in the municipal lot near Marie's house and they start to walk. The air is clear and chilled, and Savannah keeps taking deep breaths, trying to slow the shivers that seem to be settling over her arms and chest.

During the dark half-mile walk to the train station, she tries to tell herself that there will be a late train to New York City. It is the only thought she allows to thrum through her head as they clatter up the stairs to the train platform. She veers toward the posted schedule, a piece of paper encased in smudged plastic and mounted on the brick wall. Luck is with her. There is a last train at 9:42 that gets into New York at 10:59. The ticket booth is empty and the platform completely deserted, but still she leads Henry behind the newspaper containers, the darkest part of the station.

"Savannah?"

"Yeah?"

"What if the train doesn't come?"

Since this is precisely the new thought that is now running through her head, she answers, "That's stupid, Henry. Of course the train will come." And in punctuation, a far-off blast sounds; then the bell begins to *ding* down the whole length of the concrete platform. The tracks shimmer in the approaching headlights.

She closes her eyes for one second, letting the noise of the oncoming train rush through her skull and blot out everything. Then she opens them again, to find Henry facing the train, hair blowing off his forehead. She grips their bags tightly. "If anyone asks anything, you keep quiet." He nods.

There are three other people in the compartment she selects. An old man drowsing in the seat across from them, a bowler hat pulled over his eyes, a newspaper piled in sections on the seat next to him. And a middle-aged man and woman, whom she puts down as husband and wife. Although both of them are holding open magazines, Savannah feels the woman's scrutiny thrust toward them, sharp and true.

Savannah lets Henry take the window seat while she settles their bags between them. The train resumes its motion and she stares into the flat darkness churning past.

She looks at Henry. His left sneaker has come untied, and the cuffs of his jeans are edged with grime. One thin-bladed ankle is showing. But he has pressed his face to the glass and is watching the towns whirl by, and she realizes that, before tonight, he had never left Colbank, New Jersey. At his age, she had seen at least a quarter of the country.

"Henry," she says softly, leaning over the backpacks. He turns, and she leans her head down so their faces are close together. "Let's play the people game." He gives her a puzzled look and Savannah remembers that Alice stopped playing this game a long time ago. She and her mother had played it countless times in diners and truck stops, in stores and libraries, in movie theaters, and at parties they had always seemed to arrive at as if by chance. Parties, where Savannah remembers a revolving doorway of names and faces and the inevitable moment when she, dazed by all the smoke blossoming in the air, would fall asleep on yet another worn-out couch.

"What's that?" Henry asks, looking between her and the window.

"This game Mom and I always played. Mom was always really good at it. Okay, we have to guess who these three people are and where they are going and why. And then somehow we have to make up a story that links them all together."

"How come?" Henry asks, doubt lacing through his voice.

Savannah leans back a little. "Oh, never mind." She wraps a hand around a strap dangling from her backpack, looks over Henry's head, back out the window again.

There is an abrupt sliding noise, and then, "Tickets," the conductor announces in a bored voice as he barrels through the narrow train doorway between the cars. Savannah feels in her pocket for the money.

The woman is searching in her bag and, with a triumphant "ah," she pulls out two tickets. She beams up at the conductor, but although he gives her a clipped nod, he doesn't return her smile. She lowers her eyes then, as if searching for another target to direct all this light and love upon, looks around and finds Henry. Unaccustomed to this reaction from anyone, he shrinks into Savannah's side. The woman's smile folds in on itself and she snaps the pages of her magazine open again. Savannah touches the bills in her pocket, unwilling to pull out her money until the conductor is standing over her.

"She's a spy."

She blinks and look down. "What?"

Henry's eyes are hopeful. "She's a spy for . . . the Germans. And that man sitting next to her is her husband, but he doesn't know she's a spy. He thinks she's a . . . nurse."

"A school nurse?"

"Yeah. The ones who make you say which way the *E*s are pointing. For the eye tests."

"Okay. I'll buy that. And the old man?"

Here Henry falters a little. "Another spy?" he offers. He leans across her lap and looks at the old man again. She taps him back into his seat.

"Don't be obvious about it. Especially if he is a spy." He nods, chastened, studies the seatback intently, so she says quickly, "A counterspy. Sent from the German government because they think she's a double agent."

Henry doesn't turn, but she sees the side of his face crook into a smile. The conductor heads their way, stopping first to glance at the old man before bending over and taking the ticket from the pocket of the man's faded sports coat. He punches it twice, shoves it into the holder on the seat. Then he gives Savannah a quick raise of one eyebrow.

"Two for Penn Station," she murmurs, careful not to make her voice too soft.

"Return?"

"No." She is aware of the woman's renewed curiosity, but she keeps her eyes on the conductor's face, studying it as if she might be required to identify him later. This was another game she and Alice used to play, and she concentrates now. The conductor has shaggy blond eyebrows and a moustache to match and one large brown mole to the left of his long nose.

But for all her scrutiny, he barely looks up, clearly not interested in anyone on this train. He makes change quickly, clicking quarters and dimes from the change holder on his belt, punches two tickets, hands her the receipt. He slides back the doors and the train swallows him.

Savannah breathes in and out again, a wonderful lightness fizzing through her wrists and hands. She passes Henry the receipt. He folds the paper carefully three times and then unfolds it again and begins to read it.

"Where's Penn Station?" he asks.

"Where we're going," she answers, fixing her eyes on a streak on the windowpane. Dark, sleepy towns slide past.

"What will we do there?"

She shrugs. "Hopefully, see Matt."

"Does he know we're coming?"

But she has managed all she can for the moment. "Go to sleep for a while, okay? You're giving me a headache." She puts her right hand over Henry's eyes to shut them, but after a minute, he squirms free.

"What will—"

"I mean it."

He leans his head against the window and seems to sleep. She turns her cheek against the blue vinyl seat, but is unable to recapture the sense of well-being. Now she just feels tired. "*Please, please, please,*" she whispers and tries not to think about the fact that Matt may not answer his cell phone all night, that she hasn't heard from him in five months, and that he may be less than thrilled to receive a random visit from her and Henry. Instead, she reminds herself that, at one point, she was pretty sure Matt liked her. A lot. As the train carries them further and further into the night, she lets herself slide into her old pastime, dreaming with her eyes wide open.

* * *

"Hey, trig girl," Matt calls. She nods, brushes past him, feels his fingers clasp her wrist, run up her elbow before falling away.

"He's such a jerk," Carmen breathes, looking over her shoulder as they walk down the hall.

"He's not that bad," Savannah says noncommittally, focusing on the glass doorway ahead. The lines of her reflection shift and distort as she draws near.

"You actually like him?"

"I don't *like* him. I said he's not that bad."

"Rumor has it that he asked you to the prom."

"Rumor has it wrong." Savannah shifts her shoulder under the strap of her backpack. "I wouldn't be caught dead at the prom."

"Did he ask you?"

"No." She puts her hand out to pull open the glass door. "Not exactly."

"So what are you doing prom night?"

Savannah looks up from her notebook to find Matt balancing his pencil on the eraser end. One wrist is braced against the table edge as he tips his chair forward, concentrating, while his trig book lies open to a chapter different from the one they are supposed to be reviewing.

"I'm not going with you."

"Did I ask you?" His pencil bounces onto its side. He immediately retrieves it and tries again.

"I don't know. Did you?"

Matt gives her his slow, lazy smile, which she knows he has been practicing. She rolls her eyes, looks back down at her notes of neatly printed equations.

"Okay, so today I think we should concentrate on the Y equation. If you take Y and you take X—"

"Fuck X and Y. Let's do something else."

"Okay." She refuses to look up again; instead, thumbs through the slick, worn pages of her textbook. She picks up her own pencil and taps it against the table. "We can look at the integers of G and R and decide that—"

With a spinning motion, Matt flips the pencil from her hand. It clatters to the floor, skitters to a stop under her chair at the kitchen table. She locates it with her toe, kicks it out into open space, looks pointedly at Matt, who bends and retrieves it after a few seconds. Their fingers meet and pause as he hands her the pencil.

"Your mother is paying me," she says, but their faces are too close together and when he kisses her, she isn't surprised. After a minute, she leans her upper body away from him, looks out the window at the empty gravel driveway. "You have two weeks to pass this class and—"

"And then I will never need math again." Matt cracks his knuckles, folds his hands behind his head, rocks his chair back at a steep angle. "I am so out of here. I can't wait."

Savannah studies the stretched column of his neck,

watches the easy motion as he swallows, the jubilation of his voice seeping into her brain. She experiences a dangerous urge to hook her foot around his chair leg and pull it hard. "Yeah, well, NYU isn't going to want you if you fail your math class."

Matt thunks his chair back down. "*NYU isn't going to want you,*" he mimics in a shrill falsetto that Savannah is pretty sure she has never used in her life. "Now you sound like my mother."

"Fuck this," she says, stands up, piles her notebook and textbook together on top of her backpack.

"Come on, Sav," Matt says, catches her hand and pulls her down onto his lap.

Her focus narrows to the long, smooth edges of the table. "Let go."

But he tips the chair back so she is thrown off balance, against his chest. In a swift motion, she jams her elbow into his stomach and kicks out wildly with her foot, trying to bring the chair down. She succeeds, shoves herself free.

"Easy." He holds up his hands, and the fact that he is treating her like a wild dog only makes her more furious.

"No! Don't touch me! Okay?" He nods, flushing red to the tips of his ears. "I'm going home," she mutters after a minute, and this time, he doesn't stop her.

Savannah sets a piece of bread down on a yellow-and-white ceramic plate, slathers it with peanut butter, scraping the knife around the bottom of the family-sized jar to get the last crunchy bits. She wipes the knife completely clean with her finger and then dips it into the round glass jar of grape jam. She hates to leave traces of peanut butter in the jam. She folds the bread over in half, making a small sandwich, cuts it into two squares.

Henry is standing on one foot in the doorway, reading a book. "Sit down," she says as he continues reading. Finally, she plucks the book from his hand, careful to keep her thumb inserted in the pages so she won't lose his place. He blinks up at her and then looks at the sandwich she is holding out before sighing and trudging to the table. "Your homework?" she says, holding the book slightly aloft.

"Already did it," Henry mumbles through a full mouth. She looks at the neat compact circle he has bitten out of his sandwich and smiles, handing him back the book after glancing at the title. "*Monsters at Sea*?"

"It's really good. It's all about these different sea monsters."

"I wouldn't have guessed."

But he is already reading again, so she walks back to the counter, fishes out the end pieces of sandwich bread from the plastic bag, and contemplates making herself a sandwich, too. Absently, she scans the countertop, picking up stray crumbs by pressing them into her thumb, then inserting her thumb into her mouth.

"Hello?" Matt's voice calls. Savannah snatches her thumb out of her mouth, spins around, glares through the screen door at Matt, who is standing on the second of three concrete steps.

"Peace?" He waves a white sheet of paper at her, obscuring his face. In the corner of her vision, Savannah sees Henry look up, give Matt a doubtful look before he takes another bite of his sandwich and resumes reading.

"What are you doing here?" She doesn't attempt to soften her tone.

"Waving the white flag of peace?" He flaps the piece of paper more vigorously this time.

"Spruce," Henry announces.

"What?" Savannah looks at her brother, who is holding his book open with one hand and gesturing toward his mouth with the other. She waits through his elaborate chewing and swallowing.

"It's a truce."

"That's right. Thanks," Matt says.

"You're welcome." Then after a small silence, "But it's not usually a piece of paper. I think it's supposed to really be . . . a flag. Like, material."

Savannah raises her eyebrow at Matt, who shrugs. "I know. I didn't think your sister would really appreciate it if I came over waving my boxers. So . . . anyway, this paper is not just any old flag." He puts his free hand on his heart and his voice deepens dramatically. "It's a mark of how truly, truly sorry I am."

"What'd you do?" Henry asks, setting down his book, swiveling sideways in his chair.

"Never mind," Savannah interjects. "So what's the paper? No, let me guess. Your completed math homework?"

Matt comes up the last step and stands just outside the door. "Please. I'm sorry, but not that sorry." And then he gives her a look that she can't interpret, but that makes her suddenly glad for Henry's unsuspecting presence.

She unlatches the screen door. He makes a motion to swing it open from his side, but she holds on to the handle and he shrugs. After a minute, she lets the door widen by an inch and he slips the paper through the space.

It is a drawing of a table. His kitchen table, she realizes after a few seconds, recognizing the inlaid tile pattern on the top. A drawing of his kitchen table and an empty chair and one pencil lying on its side. She doesn't know how he managed it, but somehow the table and empty chair look forlorn and uncertain. She can't stop herself from feeling pleased.

"I just had to draw it," Matt explains.

She looks up at him. "A chair?"

"Not just any chair." He shakes his head at her, looks to his left as if examining the strip of side lawn and the three scraggly begonia bushes for clarity. He cocks his head, looks at her from lowered lashes, and she knows this is another one of his practiced expressions. "Your chair, Savannah. Your *empty* chair." He sighs. "Empty, empty, empty," he sings in a mournful voice.

"Oh, shut up," she says finally, smiling at him fully.

"You'll forgive me?"

"Yeah."

"And you'll still tutor me?"

"Yeah." She waits a beat. "Your mom pays really well." She nudges the door open with her foot.

Matt claps his hand to his heart, but now he is smiling genuinely at her, too.

"And you'll go to the prom with me?"

"What? No! Never. I hate the prom."

"Oh, really? How many proms have you been to?"

"None, but—"

"So how do you know you'd hate it?"

"Because the whole idea is so stupid and because . . ." But here the words stutter and then stop. Over Matt's shoulder, she sees a brown Ford station wagon pull into the driveway. The engine stills and the door creaks open. Savannah focuses on a booted leg emerging from the car. "Hey, listen, Matt. You've got to go now, okay? I'll talk to you in school tomorrow."

Matt glances over his shoulder at Jack, who is now standing beside the car, stretching. "That your dad?"

Savannah reaches out and pushes his wrist off the doorjamb. "Stepfather. Please." He looks back at her, nods.

"See you, kid," he calls to Henry and then swings around and off the porch, his long legs skipping the middle step, landing lightly on the ground. He passes Jack in the driveway, and Savannah hears him say politely, "Afternoon, sir," and Jack's evenhanded, almost friendly response, "Afternoon."

She steps away then, back into the kitchen, screws the red plastic lid back onto the jar of peanut butter. The door bangs, the whisper of the torn screen flapping out of place. Savannah scoops the sponge out of the sink, squeezes it, dirty water trickling over her knuckles.

"Hi, Daddy," Henry says. There is the clank of a toolbox meeting the floor.

"Hey, bud. Whatcha got there?" There is a rustle of pages, then, "*Monsters at Sea*? That for school?"

"No. Just for me," Henry says. "I did my homework already, so this is okay."

"I know, kiddo." Heavy boots tromp into the kitchen. Savannah's eyes follow the motion of her sponge as she wipes the counter over and over in small, interlocking circles.

"That your boyfriend out there?"

Savannah shakes her head.

"Huh?"

"No."

"Who was he?"

"A classmate."

"A classmate?" Jack draws out the word, walks past her, pulls at the refrigerator door. He opens a can of beer, the sound cracking across the still air. "You must really think I'm dumb as shit."

Not a topic for discussion, Savannah reminds herself, grinding the sponge into beige Formica.

* * *

The train jerks once and Savannah swallows a momentary rising panic, her shoulders tightening before she can force herself to relax. Stretches of gray alternate with splashes of harsh light as the train arrives at Penn Station. Savannah pushes out her arms in front of her, feeling the pull of each muscle. Then she stands, letting Henry sleep still.

The woman is also standing in the aisle now, pulling on a long tan coat, staring all the while at them. Suddenly, Savannah flushes through with anger. She directs a hard look in the woman's direction.

The woman turns to her husband. "Kids are out so late these days," she says loudly, and her husband looks up dazedly from his magazine.

"What?" he asks, making a motion toward himself as if he is somehow at fault.

"Kids. They're out so late these days. I don't know why they aren't home with their parents. Especially the *younger* ones." Her husband still looks confused until he sees Savannah standing, halfway down the aisle of the train, and then his forehead smoothes. He shakes his head but offers no further commentary. The woman gives a tight, satisfied smile and Savannah rolls her eyes.

"Get the bag," the woman snaps at her husband, who has gone back to his reading. "We're in the station already!" He leaps to his feet, his shoulders hunching briefly as he takes their bulky plaid suitcase down from the overhead rack.

"Hah!" the old man across from her says loudly, and Savannah glances over at him as he snorts himself awake, knocks his hat off his face, and yawns noisily. He shuffles and reshuffles his newspaper before abruptly dropping it on the floor. The train jerks forward once and then stops.

"Come on, Henry," Savannah whispers, her hand on his arm. He opens his eyes so swiftly and easily that she doubts that he was really asleep after all. He doesn't ask any questions but accepts his small backpack and slings it over one shoulder, letting her adjust it for him. Together they move into the aisle. The woman and her husband have disappeared.

"Listen here, girlie," the old man suddenly says. Savannah looks back over her shoulder. He is still seated, but he is pointing his finger at her. His eyes are intent and narrowed. "I want to tell you something."

"No, thank you," she responds, and pulls Henry off the train after her.

This time, she positions Henry in the phone booth with her, jams sticky quarters into the slot, presses numbers, and prays.

"Speak," Matt's voice answers on the third ring.

"Oh, good," she says.

"Savannah?" His voice slips into a quicker, higher notch. "What is happening with you? It's been a long time, girl."

"Um, a lot. Did you get my message?"

There is a pause. A siren starts up across the street. "No. Should I be asking where you are right now?"

She sighs. "In kind of a bad place. I'm on Thirty-third Street and Seventh Avenue."

"Oh, that's fine. Apparently, this city cleaned up a lot, and in the year I've been here, I've never experienced any sort of—"

"Matt. Shut it. I meant mentally. Physically, I am standing on the corner of Thirty-third and Seventh. With Henry. We need a place to stay for the night."

This time there is a longer pause. The smell of burning sugar winds its way through the half-open door and Henry inhales audibly, appreciatively, looking up at her. Out of the corner of her eye, she watches a man shoving a large cart across the street. The sweet aroma begins to fade.

"Just for tonight," she repeats, hating the pleading tone she has adopted. It feels like someone else speaking.

"What's going on, Sav?" But his voice is strange to her, delayed, reminding her of the one and only time he had convinced her to smoke pot. The way his voice had faded in and out during what felt like hours, as he strung a sentence together.

"I need your help. We have nowhere to stay other than with you. Please do not pull any shit with me because now is really not the time. I left home tonight and I can't go back, for reasons I will explain later, but if you can't help me, then fuck all . . ." Her voice is narrowing into a sharp, high note, but she puts her free hand on Henry's cheek and tries to smile.

"Okay, okay, okay. Chill out, Savannah. Hop in a cab and come here. The address is 113 Avenue C. Avenue C and Fourth Street. Got that?"

"Yeah. Okay." She is trembling.

"See you soon." His voice has smoothed out, reassuring now, and she closes her eyes briefly, hangs up the phone. Matt has always let her be another person.

Alice 1986

It is two days later when they meet again. Having missed the bus, Alice has decided to walk home. She cuts through the cemetery, running her hand along beveled planes of marble and granite and simpler, dark, silvered stone. The late afternoon air is bright and fills her with the sense of expectancy that she always carries at this point in the day. She has just started on the old quarry road when she hears a car slowing behind her. She turns her head, glances over her shoulder, waits as the bright blue Dodge pulls up, idles beside her. And she is not really surprised to see the boy from the ice cream store, now sitting behind the wheel.

"You want a ride?" He palms the steering wheel with his right hand, one finger lifting, falling in time with the music from the radio.

Alice leans over, crooks her elbow through the open window, lets her arm dangle down, fingers just above the door latch. "Depends on where you're going."

He looks at her for a minute, angles his upper body across the unbroken front seat, flicks open the passenger door without touching her hand. She climbs into the car and they move back onto the road.

"This your car?" she asks after a minute.

"No, I stole it."

She can't help it. She gives him a sideways startled flash of her eyes. It is then that she discovers that he has a dimple on the right side of his smile.

His dimple deepens. "It's my uncle's."

She thinks for a moment. The only black man she knows who lives in town works at her high school. "Mr. Castleton? The janitor at Three Springs High?"

"That's right."

"Is that your last name? Castleton?"

"No."

"What is your last name then?"

"Don't you want to know my first name?"

"Okay, that, too."

"Noah."

"Alice."

He takes his right hand off the wheel, extends it, they shake, until the car begins to veer off the road. He takes his hand back, corrects the steering.

"So what are you doing here in Three Springs, Noah No Last Name?"

"Science camp."

"Science camp? In Three Springs?" Disbelief shades her voice.

"No. In Portland. At the college. I'm just staying at my uncle's house."

"Oh." She reaches forward, twirls the scanner on the

radio until she finds her favorite station. "So you're, like, one of those smart guys?"

"Um . . . ," he laughs. "Is that a trick question?"

She slides back against the headrest, puts her hand out in the open air, and lets the breeze of the car's movement blow through her fingers.

"So, what do you do for fun around here?"

"*Fun* and *here* are not two words you can string together in the same sentence when referring to Three Springs," Alice informs him. "And where are you from, anyway?"

"Savannah, Georgia."

"Savannah." She rolls the word around, looks out the window at the houses sliding by. "This is my street." She extends her arm, indicates. "Okay, third house on the left, that's it."

"Wow. Nice." Noah lets the car idle in the driveway.

Alice shrugs. "I guess." She looks at her house critically. The yellow paint has faded in streaks over the three dormer windows and the barn needs a new roof. She turns to him, flashes a smile. "Thanks, Noah No Last Name, for the ride. You saved my feet a long walk. Now I owe you."

Noah looks at her seriously, takes his hand off the steering wheel, puts it down on the seat divider, very close, but not quite touching the inside of her wrist. "So, maybe we can hang out some time?"

Alice shifts so she is facing him. "I—"

"Hello?"

Alice twists, looks over her shoulder at her mother's worried, flushed face peering in through the passenger's window. "Oh, Alice. I didn't know this car. I didn't know it was you."

Her mother's tone is overly confused and achingly polite, and Alice grits her back teeth hard before saying, "Mother. This is Noah. Noah, this is my mother, Mrs. Ainswell."

"Pleased to meet you, Mrs. Ainswell," Noah says, and tries to extend his hand through the window. Alice's mother nods, smiles, but does not move otherwise, and after a moment, he draws his arm back.

"Alice, I need you to set the table now."

Alice looks pointedly at the clock on the dashboard, which reads 4:15. "I'll see you around, Noah," she murmurs. "Mom, you have to move back so I can get out," she whispers, and finally her mother does step back and Alice manages to slide her body sideways through the small opening of the car door. Alice presses the flat of her palm briefly against the window, then follows her mother toward the house. Behind her, the crack and pop of gravel under tires signals Noah's leaving.

"Who is that boy?" Mrs. Ainswell asks so quietly that Alice has to dip her head to hear her mother.

"I told you his name."

"I don't know him."

"He's Mr. Castleton's nephew, visiting for the summer from Savannah."

Mrs. Ainswell shakes her head. "If you needed a ride, you should have called me. Or your aunt."

"I didn't need a ride," Alice replies, making her voice as calm as possible.

"Well, don't take any more rides from strangers." She jerks at her apron as it flutters up in the sudden breeze.

"He's not a stranger."

"Oh, really?" Mrs. Ainswell says, quickening her pace. "Exactly how long have you known him?"

"Mother! He's not a psycho killer. He goes to science camp in Portland, for God's sake! He's probably a science nerd. Okay? *Okay?*"

"You know best," Mrs. Ainswell replies in the tone that clearly indicates she thinks Alice does not. She smoothes down her apron again, retreats into a shroud of silence that nothing and no one can penetrate.

Alice shades her eyes against the sun, squints at the porch. Her aunt, Jane, is sitting on the wicker love seat, smoking. No doubt she has heard the whole conversation between her sister and Alice, but her face remains cheerfully blank, even as Alice stomps up the steps, sits down, puts her chin on her knees. Mrs. Ainswell brushes past both of them without a word, and the screen door squeaks open, then shut. Alice holds out two fingers; Jane lifts her eyebrows toward the kitchen. They wait in silence until they hear the slam of a bedroom door before Jane passes Alice the cigarette. The sky is a hot blue bowl, empty of everything except the early, ghostly presence of the moon.

"By the way, Mike called you," Jane says after a while.

"Great," Alice mutters.

six

The cab smells musty and Savannah rolls down the window. Once again, Henry is holding his face close to the glass, intent on the outside world as they lurch and jerk through the traffic. After a particularly neck-snapping short stop, Savannah thinks about asking how long their driver, Rajeev Kumar, as it says on his name tag pasted to the plastic shield in front of her knees, has had his license.

"What side of the street?" he mumbles, after nearly ramming into the back of another cab.

"The right side?" He immediately swerves over at the corner of East Fourth and Avenue C, amidst a blaring of horns. The fare lights up on the meter and Savannah hands him the money. A girl with three silver hoops protruding from her lip is already waiting impatiently on the sidewalk. She brushes past Henry and, with a flash of bare skin, dives into the backseat. The cab lurches back into the traffic stream.

Savannah steps onto the sidewalk, Henry so close behind her that he kicks the heels of her shoes. She looks up and down the street until her eyes come to rest on a boy sitting on the stone steps of a five-story building. His legs are thrust out before him in an easy sprawl, and he is talking emphatically into a cell phone. She walks closer, noticing under the ample streetlight that someone must have once painted the building red in an effort to make it look like brick. Patches of the original concrete are showing through.

"Is that Matt?" Henry asks.

But she is spared from answering. As if he hears his name, Matt angles his head sideways, catches sight of them.

"Gotta go," he says abruptly into the phone, clicks it shut, stands up, holding his arms open wide. "Sav," he says, pulls her against him, dislodging the backpack from her shoulder. She bumps her cheekbone against his shoulder, rests it there for a minute, then they both step back. Matt looks down, gives Henry a light slap on the shoulder. "Hey there, man."

"Hi, Matt," Henry says, and then begins examining the sidewalk.

"So," Matt begins, reaching out his hand, as if to help her readjust her backpack, then thinks better of it. "You look good."

"Yeah, well, running away really agrees with me. Can we go inside? Henry's going to fall over."

"I'm okay," Henry says, but she ignores him, watching Matt's face as he gives a sideways glance up at the building. Several of the windows do not have curtains and rectangles of light are scattered here and there.

"Listen, Sav, I need to tell you . . . things have changed."

She snorts. "No kidding?"

He looks back at her, clearly irritated. "Be serious. I live with my girlfriend now."

She nods. She expected this. It still hurts. "Look, I don't care, Matt, who you live with. We just need a place to stay for the night."

"Okay, okay." He holds up his hands in a peace gesture, and she lets him take her bag because he seems to want to. She wraps her fingers around Henry's damp hand, feeling his head bump against her elbow. They follow Matt into the building. The foyer smells like mold, and Henry sneezes repeatedly as they trudge up the stairs. Matt lopes ahead of them, his legs taking several steps at a time, spinning around the banister before stopping at a nondescript brown door. All of his motions slow, he knocks on it once, politely. Savannah swallows, tries to catch in her breath as the door swings open. A girl poses gracefully in the backlight that now floods the dusty darkness of the hallway. For one instant, she is so still that Savannah can only think of a painting.

She is tiny, delicately built, and completely exotic looking. Unlike anything in Colbank, New Jersey. Beautiful dark eyes slanted with thick, long lashes flick toward Savannah and Henry, then away. One small hand smoothes hair that is a rich, shining black. Gold glints in her nose and in her navel, revealed by a thin, brightly printed shirt. Savannah rolls up one sleeve of her army jacket, exposing a pale, sturdy wrist, and sighs.

"Kurti," Matt says, and even his voice is different when he speaks to her. "This is my friend Savannah, and this is her brother, Henry. Sav, Henry, this is Kurti." He sounds as if he is trying to pretend that everything is normal. Kurti and Savannah regard each other for one minute, long enough to seal their mutual dislike.

"Come in," she says, and her voice is low and soft. She retreats, almost swaying, backward into the apartment, and as she follows, Savannah has time to note bare feet and dark red toenails.

The air in the apartment is heavy and sweet like pipe tobacco. Kurti leads them into what seems to be the living room, complete with a flat wool rug in bright blues and reds and a long, low table, its dark wood gleaming with polish. Red cushions are placed precisely at opposite ends of the table. There seems to be no other place to sit, but then Savannah recognizes Matt's cracked leather armchair. He had carted it from home, and it has now apparently been quarantined in the corner, away from the rest of the decor.

Henry wanders over to the two dark bookshelves flanking another doorway, and Savannah trails him awkwardly. Two-thirds of the shelves are stacked with college textbooks while the last third is a haphazard collection of art books and Japanese poetry. Savannah touches the spine of a thick poetry volume, runs her forefinger across the top of the pages, feeling the tiny ripple of paper. She tries not to remember that Alice used to love poetry.

"Kurti's studying psychology," Matt announces behind Savannah, and she turns, attempting to smile and appear interested.

"Child psychology," Kurti corrects gently, and her eyes fasten on Henry. Savannah moves closer to Henry, takes his bag from him.

"Sit down," she whispers, and he looks away from the books dubiously. Savannah nods toward the armchair, watches him climb into it. As if this is a cue, Kurti sinks down onto one of the red cushions and crosses her feet into some complicated-looking position. Then she busies herself arranging the folds of her skirt. She looks as if she might start meditating. Savannah crosses one foot behind the other, starts to tilt off balance, adjusts her posture, and remains standing. So does Matt.

"Can we get you anything?" Kurti asks, and Savannah suddenly feels as if they just crashed a party.

"Water would be nice," she tries.

"Maybe some milk for Henry," Kurti counters, regarding him with concern. He blinks and looks down at his shoelaces. Both of them are now untied and he begins to correct this with painstaking precision.

"He hates milk." Savannah comes up with this too abruptly, because Matt looks at her, surprised. Henry pauses, looks up from his loops of shoelace, but doesn't contradict her.

"Orange juice?" Kurti persists.

"Sure," Savannah answers, matching the other girl's pleasant tone. "He hasn't reached his vitamin C quota today. We've been a little distracted."

Kurti's face remains expressionless as she gets up and walks the three steps into the kitchen. The refrigerator clanks and hums, glasses clink.

Savannah can feel Matt looking at her, but she pretends to examine three framed pictures of Buddha on the far wall.

Kurti returns with two glasses of orange juice and a plate of something. Somehow she manages to carry all of it without spilling or dropping anything. She sets everything down on the coffee table and hands Henry a glass of orange juice. "It's freshly squeezed," she says, and he nods, giving her a shy smile.

"Thank you," he says, begins gulping the juice, then pauses, wary, and takes a smaller sip. Kurti watches him for a minute, then hands the second glass to Savannah.

"Thanks," Savannah says to Kurti's shoulders. She is already whirling back, as if dancing, picking up the plate and offering it to Henry. Six apple and pear slices slide across the plate toward Henry's reaching hand.

A crunching sound fills the room before Matt sits down on the second red cushion. Savannah watches him fold his legs under himself, bump one knee on the coffee table, and stretch them out instead. When he is settled, Kurti sinks down beside him, winds one arm through his, and leans against him. She does this without taking her eyes off Henry.

"So," Matt says. "Things got pretty rough at home, right?"

"Yeah, kind of," Savannah says. She realizes she is in a half crouch, and sits back on her heels.

"And what are you going to do?" Kurti asks her after a moment.

"We'll be fine."

"And what about Henry? Doesn't he have to be in school tomorrow?"

"I think he can miss a day." She digs her fingers into the soft crease of her inner elbow and tries not to scream.

Henry looks up. "I miss school sometimes," he says earnestly to Kurti. "It's okay."

Kurti tightens her lower lip. "I really think that—"

"Listen," Matt breaks in.

"That you should call your—" Kurti continues unflappably. Matt puts a hand on her knee, fingers flexing. As if this is some special signal, Kurti falls silent.

"It's really late," Matt begins again. "I have an 8:30 class in the morning, and so do you, Kurt." Now he is rubbing his fingers over her knee. Savannah looks down at her wrists, presses her thumb across her blistered pockets of skin. "So, why don't we all get some sleep now and we'll figure out what you're going to do tomorrow, okay, Sav?"

She lifts her head. "Yeah. Sure."

Kurti rises, brushes past her through the doorway to what must be the bedroom. Savannah pins her eyes to Matt's face.

"We're not going back there. No fucking way."

Matt raises his shoulders, lets them sink. "We'll think of something."

Kurti reappears, carrying a pile of blankets and one sleeping bag. "We only have one extra pillow. I'm sorry."

"No problem." And then before Savannah can stop herself, "Henry doesn't really need a pillow, anyway."

Kurti stares at her.

"It was a joke, Kurti." Savannah takes the sleeping bag. It is thick and lined in bright green flannel. She spreads it on the floor, puts the pillow at one end.

"Am I sleeping there?" Henry asks, eyeing all three of them.

"Yes, you're sleeping there," Savannah answers, and as he begins to crawl into the bag, adds for Kurti's benefit, "Your teeth." She watches him burrow back out and unzip his backpack.

"The bathroom's this way." Kurti indicates the narrow door next to the kitchen that Savannah had mistaken for a closet.

"Thank you." She and Kurti look at each other for a minute. "Well, thanks," she says again, and to Matt, "Good night, I guess."

"Yeah. 'Night, Sav," Matt says. "Henry."

"Good night, Henry," Kurti says and a little warmth enters her tone. To be abandoned almost immediately. "Good night, Savannah."

Savannah nods, steps out of her shoes by bracing one heel against the other. The bedroom door clicks shut, and Savannah reaches up to dig her stiffened fingers into her shoulders.

"I forgot it," Henry whispers, looking up from his bag. He seems close to tears. "My toothbrush."

"Who cares?" And then when Henry doesn't answer, she rolls her eyes at him, unzips her bag, and tosses her toothbrush at him. It falls into the folds of the sleeping bag. He retrieves it, pads into the bathroom.

Savannah shakes out the rest of the blankets, the smell of perfume suddenly choking her. She shrugs out of her jacket, rolls it up, fits it under her head. She lies on her stomach, the buttons of her jeans pressing into flesh.

Over the sound of running water in the bathroom, she listens to Kurti and Matt's voices. The wall between rooms blurs the words, but Savannah picks out Kurti's tone, even and persistent, with Matt's voice punctuating hers intermittently. Savannah drifts for a few seconds until Henry comes back, tucks himself into the bag. Once in, he seems to fall into a coma, breathing deeply within a minute. She rolls onto her back, eyes burning.

Right by her head it seems, she hears Matt laugh once and say, "Not really," and then Kurti murmuring to him again. A window slides shut, the bedsprings squeak. Savannah begins to recite random names in her head, something she used to do long ago when she was awake for too long at night.

She can hear someone opening and shutting a door repeatedly in the apartment below. A steady banging sound that begins to reverberate behind her eyelids.

"Baby, get the door, would you?" Alice implores as she slips from the bathroom into the bedroom she and Savannah are sharing. "Tell him I'll be out in one minute." Savannah listens to something fall against the dresser that Alice found at the Salvation Army last week. As if in response, the knocking at the door grows louder.

"Savannah," Alice hisses from the doorway, and Savannah catches a glimpse of her mother's face, pink and freshly scrubbed from the shower, her hair hidden in the thin blue towel she has wrapped around her head. Around her body, she has knotted their only other towel, and now Savannah thinks how the two towels will stay limp and mildew-smelling for days in their damp closet of a bathroom that never seems to dry out.

Savannah trudges to the door, tripping over the trailing ends of the red scarf that Alice has draped over milk crates to make a coffee table. She reaches up, turns the knob, inches the door open, regards Jack silently. He is leaning forward a little, on the balls of his feet, one fist raised in the air. Now seeing her, he drops his hand, uncurls his fingers.

"Well, hello there, little lady. I was just about to really start pounding on this door." He shifts forward one step. The crease in each leg of his khaki pants has been ironed into a knife-sharp pleat.

"Hi, Jack," Savannah answers, hooking her left foot behind her right ankle and scooting over to the side because Alice always told her it was rude to turn her back on someone in the doorway. Jack brushes past her, the edge of his short-sleeved shirt just flicking her ear as she turns and shuts the door. Then she folds her hands behind the small of her back, her elbows forming right angles to her waist. She leans against the wall, watching Jack crane his neck to scan the confines of the living room. "Mom will be ready in a minute." There is the huff of the blow dryer from the other room.

"Well, okay. But it's you I wanted to talk to first," Jack says, with a solemnity that makes her want to run. "I heard it was a special day today for you," he begins, raising his thick, straight eyebrows for emphasis on the word *special.* She wishes he would just come to the point and announce that he heard it was her tenth birthday today. She knows Alice told him, and she also knows that Alice told him that it might be a really nice idea if he got her a little something to open while they had cake at the apartment. She helped Alice go shopping for balloons and party hats earlier that afternoon.

"What's special?" Alice asks now and both Savannah and Jack turn. Alice is silhouetted artfully in the arch between the living room and the hallway. She is wearing her new yellow dress and her arms hang gracefully by her sides as if, at any second, she might pick up her skirt with both hands and twirl across the room. Her red hair is worn the way Savannah loves it best, long, loose curls, and each freckle on her face is glowing, like chips of golden fairy dust.

"You are," Jack says simply after a moment, and Alice smiles too brightly. Savannah drops her eyes as they kiss their hellos.

"Is that for me?" she hears her mother ask, and Savannah raises her eyes again to note, for the first time, a square of dark green in Jack's hand.

"No." Jack draws the word out into a drawl that makes Alice laugh and Savannah cringe. "This is for the birthday girl." He turns. "Happy tenth birthday, honey."

"Oh, Jack," Alice says before there can be even a second of silence. "That was so sweet of you to do that." She touches his shoulder lightly, moves past him, signals Savannah with her eyes. But Savannah stays mute. "Well," Alice says after a second. "Let's all sit down at the table. And eat cake. And open presents!" She claps her hands together until both Jack and Savannah move forward on cue.

Alice whirls into the kitchen and Savannah hears her mother scrabbling around in a drawer, opening and closing the refrigerator. She knows that her mother snuck out earlier that afternoon and bought a cake, because she was lying on the couch when Alice returned, half asleep. She had opened her eyes just wide enough when the front door clicked shut to be able to define the outline of a bakery box in her mother's hands.

Now Alice steps carefully out of the kitchen, holding aloft a chocolate cake covered in pink sugar roses and unlit pink candles. "Happy Birthday, sweets!" she singsongs, and sets the cake down on the table. "Well, presents first or cake?" Savannah blinks, feels them both looking at her. Her mother has planted eleven candles deep into chocolate frosting—ten for her years, one to grow on.

"How about cake?" Jack suggests.

"Presents," Savannah returns.

"Presents it is," Alice says, and produces a small box from her skirt pocket. She nudges it toward the center of the table, to the left of the cake. Finally, Savannah sits, reaches out one hand, then withdraws it in confusion when Alice says, "How about you open Jack's first?"

Jack's chair creaks. "No, no, let her—"

"No, really. Jack's first," Alice insists, and she is not smiling now.

Savannah turns to Jack, studies the way the folds of heavy skin under his brown eyes deepen as his face spreads into a smile.

"Your mom told me you really liked books. I hope I picked out something that you haven't read already. If you have, the guy at the store said we could take it back and exchange it, no problem."

Savannah nods, waits, and finally, Jack holds out the package to her, his hands trembling slightly. She swallows, drops her eyes, unable to bear the way her mother is leaning over Jack's shoulder now, one long-nailed hand caressing the back of his neck while she waits for Savannah to open the present.

The gold ribbon is curled expertly, the way they do it in the stores, and the package is sealed with a matching bright gold sticker bearing the name of a popular chain of bookstores. She tears the crisp, dark green paper neatly, quietly, and slides the book free from its wrapping.

"Oh, how wonderful," Alice rushes in first. "*Black Beauty*. I loved that story when I was little." Savannah looks up. Alice has never claimed this before when Savannah brought the book home three times from various libraries.

"No problem if you want to exchange it," Jack announces again to the air above her head. Alice's eyes are sharp on Savannah's face, and so Savannah clears her throat, says politely, "Thank you, Jack. It's great. I can't wait to read it."

She puts her hands out for her mother's present, knowing that it doesn't matter what it is, that no present, and no chocolate cake, no matter how many sugar roses she will be allowed to eat, will sweeten the moment when Alice decides to tell her that Jack is staying, that he will become a part of their lives.

* * *

When she next opens her eyes, it is to the sound of a large, rumbling engine, glass breaking, and someone shouting. Halfway up into a crouch, she is convinced that Jack is somewhere in the room. Slowly, she places the sound outside the window. Garbage trucks on the street below, hauling away the night's trash. She puts one hand out, touches the soft mop of Henry's hair, listens to the whisper-quiet pulse of his breathing. With her fingers still pressed against Henry's skull, she eases back on her elbows, remains that way for what feels like a long time.

seven

"Wake up, sunshine," Matt says, even though she is awake. He is standing between the bookshelves. Behind him, through the open door of his bedroom, she glimpses a red-and-cream bedspread on the double bed, pulled neat and tight. There is no other sign of Kurti.

Savannah reaches over, touches the tips of Henry's hair that are sticking out from the opening in the sleeping bag. Matt walks a few steps into the room, nudges at her blanketed foot. "Let's go get some breakfast."

"Don't you have a class?"

"Skipping it."

She rolls up on both elbows, smiles lazily at him. "What would Kurti say?"

"Hey." He kicks at her foot a little harder. "Don't start with any shit, okay?"

She kicks back. "Fuck off." Then she sits up, stretches. "Glad we're so back to normal."

He doesn't answer as she peels back the layer of sleeping bag to find Henry. He is awake, watching her with wide eyes. Even when he was very young, he always woke quietly, without fuss. Now she smiles at him. "Want to eat some breakfast?" He nods. "Okay. Get your clothes on."

"I already have them on."

"Oh. Good job then." He sits up, still half in the sleeping bag.

"You do, too," he points out.

"True."

Henry rubs his eyes and then looks at Matt.

"Hey, man," Matt says.

"Hi."

"Sleep okay there?"

He nods.

"He's not very talkative in the morning," Savannah offers, stands up, begins to fold the blankets into neat squares.

"I'll show you," Matt says and steps forward, and she gives him a look, only to realize he is offering to help Henry with the sleeping bag. She leaves them to it, goes to find the bathroom.

The bathroom is a labor of love. Painted pale green and white, with scrollwork shelves holding several bottles of lotion and pretty colored soaps. Savannah wonders if Matt ever even tried to leave some of his *Simpsons* comic books on the back of the toilet like he used to at home, smiles to imagine Kurti's reaction.

"Should I take my bag?" Henry wants to know, as she comes out of the bathroom, running quick fingers through her hair. She forgot her hairbrush, but doesn't dare use Kurti's silver-backed one on the shelf by the bathroom sink.

"No. We're only going across the street," Matt says,

although Henry casts a worried look at his backpack.

"Your bag's not going anywhere," Savannah says, handing Henry his jacket. She steps close to Matt, slides her hand into his back pocket, closes her fingers around his comb, and pulls it up and aloft. He gives her a look she can't read, and she says to Henry, "Brush your teeth before we go, okay?" Henry nods, slips into the bathroom, and the sound of vigorous brushing follows. Savannah raises the comb to her hair, knowing its fine tooth edge won't be much help. "Nice place here, Matt. Did you do *any* of the decorating yourself?"

The silence between them stretches, snaps as she looks up at him. Matt clears his throat, mutters, "God, I had forgotten how beautiful your hair is."

She flips the comb back at him. "Whatever. Can we go now?"

The Triangle Diner is crowded and noisy, but there are two tables open and they head for the one near the back of the room, passing a glass case crowded with slices of cake and pie. Savannah and Henry both pause, study the contents.

"Banana cream pie?" Henry asks hopefully, and she points toward the back, then inhales the smell of sweet syrup and fried food. Diners never fail to remind her of her mother, considering they spent enough time in them. Sometimes, all Alice had was enough change for coffee and a glass of milk for Savannah in the early mornings. If the waitresses knew them, or if Savannah asked sweetly enough, they might sometimes come up with a basket of rolls left over from last night's dinner. If this was the case, then Alice told Savannah to make "pies." To do this, she smeared the packets of jam that came free with every table into the center of the stale rolls, flattened them thoroughly with a fist, then drizzled them with syrup.

Later, when they moved in with Jack, Alice made so many real pies that Savannah could usually find one waiting on the kitchen table, next to a can of Reddi-wip, when she returned from school. She loved these times in the kitchen with Alice, the late afternoon settling in around them as they crammed pie into their mouths, faces covered with sticky-sweet goo.

"The chocolate cake is really good," Matt says, close to her ear, and then, "I come here all the time," as she and Henry slide into the red vinyl booth.

She settles her legs under the table, surreptitiously scraping a palm across the edge of the sticky seat. Spilled Coke from the last occupant is her best guess, judging from the paper straw wrappers scattered across the seat. "Nice place," she says, since Matt seems to be waiting. Henry has disappeared behind the thirty-page menu and Savannah barely flips hers open before a youngish woman, streaked blond hair skinned back from her face with two barrettes, glides to a stop at the table.

"Hi, honey," she oozes at Matt, snapping her pen once against her notepad.

"The usual, Marlene," he says in a suddenly deeper

voice. Savannah resists rolling her eyes, looks at the waitress instead.

"Can I have an omelet with cheddar cheese and mushrooms and a side of hash browns and a chocolate milkshake and coffee?" She smiles sweetly, nods her head in Matt's direction. "Since he's paying."

Marlene arches an eyebrow but writes it all down, swivels to Henry. "For you, baby?"

He looks up at her and then back at the menu. "What's a *sm*?" He points to the plastic page coated with glossy pictures. "See, *sm orange juice*."

"Small," Savannah whispers.

Matt laughs loudly. She darts a look up at him. He stops.

"Get whatever you want, Henry. Get the most expensive thing on the menu."

"Can I have pancakes?"

"Short or tall stack?"

"Short. No, um . . . tall."

"Syrup? Jam? Whipped cream?"

"Okay."

Marlene smiles. "All set, dolls." She clicks her pen again and moves off.

Another waitress passes their table, her walk loose and aimless, carrying coffee pots in both hands. She glances over at them dreamily, then steps closer, smiling solely at Matt. Savannah turns over her coffee cup, pushes it closer to Matt, watches the girl fill both cups, slopping some steaming brown liquid on the table in the process. "And what about you, little man?" She looks at Henry, but he shakes his head vehemently, so she drifts away.

Savannah raises an eyebrow at Matt, who is watching the girl weave her way through the diner. She clears her throat, his gaze jumps back to her face. "Friend of yours?"

"Bella? Sort of." He leans forward a little, drumming two fingers on the red Formica tabletop. "So. What are you going to do?"

"I don't know. I thought Henry and I could stay in your living room indefinitely, driving Kurti insane, until finally one night, Kurti and I rip each other's throats out in a mad fit of passionate jealousy over you."

"Be real, would you, please?"

"But that does appeal to you, right? Kurti and me fighting over you?" She rips open a series of half-and-half containers, watches the cream sink into her coffee. "I used to watch a lot of late-night TV with you. I know the kind of shit you like. And by the way, you owe me thirty dollars."

Before he can answer, Bella reappears. She has lost the coffee pots, but now comes bearing Henry's orange juice, which she deposits on the table with a beatific smile. With a flourish, she pulls a straw from somewhere inside her apron pocket, then wanders over to the next table, an inquiring look on her face. Henry fiddles with the straw, peeling back the wrapper slowly.

"We could get jobs," he offers.

Savannah looks at her brother. "Doing what?" She looks at Matt. "And I'm not kidding about the thirty dollars."

"I don't remember owing you—"

"I do." She turns back to Henry. "What kind of jobs, Henry?"

He shrugs. "Selling newspapers. Or . . ." He squirms in his seat, the straw hanging from his fingers. "We could steal."

Matt is nodding. "That's a good plan."

"Yeah, we're off to a terrific start here," Savannah interjects. "Henry, what are you talking about?"

"We could pick pockets for a living."

"Oh, really? Maybe we could get together a whole gang. Like, maybe we could free a bunch of kids from an orphanage and then we could find this secret hideout? And then we could all go out and pick pockets and sing songs." Henry's bright expression fades. "Yeah, and we could rename you Oliver Twist." The musical had been playing almost constantly on the Family Channel about two weeks ago. Henry had watched it over and over.

"Ease up, Sav," Matt says, and the food arrives.

"Keep thinking, Henry," she says, and starts to eat.

"Don't worry," she begins again, after they have all chewed in silence for a few minutes. "We're not going to stay with you for long. I do have a plan." She drags a piece of omelet to the side of her plate, feeling Henry's eyes suddenly swivel to her face. But she is reluctant to say too much because things have a way of sounding really wrong once they're spoken out loud.

"Okay," Matt says encouragingly.

She takes a deep breath. "Ever been to—"

"Hey, man," a voice cuts across hers. A boy is standing in the aisle between the tables. He slaps Matt's shoulder. "Missed you in class."

"Yeah." Matt shrugs. "Did Ellen care?"

"Oh, boy. She seemed really off, crying and all, every time she looked at your empty seat." The boy grins.

"Yeah, I bet," Matt says, and then to Savannah, "My professor."

"He looks kind of young to be a professor."

"What? No, Ellen is. Not this dork."

"Oh." She smiles up at the boy and he smiles back, before saying to Matt, "but I need those two books, seriously, right now. My paper is due at the end of the week and I haven't even read them."

Matt holds his hands up. "No problem, no problem. We're on our way back to my place. Come with us and I'll get them. Anyway, Savannah, this is Holt. Holt, Savannah. Wait here, I got to go pay." And Matt lurches out of the booth and ambles over to the register. A line is forming there, due to the fact that Bella, now behind the counter, seems to be more interested in chewing her nails than in ringing anyone up.

Savannah pushes her plate aside, looks at Matt's friend, who has sat down in Matt's seat. He inserts a coffee stirrer into his mouth, chews on it for a few seconds, examining her all the while. He seems happy not to speak. She shifts her legs, brings one up under her. "*Holt*?" She says this politely, with just a lick of disbelief.

"*Savannah*?" He mimics her tone perfectly and she grins.

"Yeah, right, okay, but . . . *Holt*? Was your mom reading a bunch of Harlequin Romance novels?"

"It's a family name, okay?" He pauses for a moment, fixes her with an intense look. "Unlike *Savannah*, I would guess. Let me see, you were born in Savannah, right?"

She sighs loudly. It is her real name and not some nickname, as everyone usually thinks. Alice, eighteen at the time, claimed she wanted something different and was hazy on any of the supporting details. When asked about that time in her life, she always answered, "Savannah is where the party came to a halt for a while."

"We have a winner," Savannah informs her brother, and Henry smiles uncertainly, then knocks over his glass of orange juice. The remaining liquid trickles across the table and meets the napkin that Holt already has in hand. "And this is Henry," Savannah adds.

"Henry. Nice job here." But he says it so cheerfully that Henry ducks his head, smiles a little, as if to ward off a true compliment. "So, Henry and Savannah, visiting Matt in the big, bad city?"

She nods.

"Are you thinking of going to NYU?"

"That's right."

"Well, I can tell you it's the best school."

"Oh, really? What other schools have you attended?"

He shrugs, looks abashed for a second, and she is suddenly sorry. "Well, we're having a great time, aren't we?" she says for Matt as he comes back to the table, peels off a couple of ones for a tip.

"Oh, yeah, the best. Savannah and I go way back."

"Two whole years," she adds, ducks away from Matt as he tries to rub his knuckles across her head. "And where are you from?" she asks Holt.

"Oh, he's not from around these parts," Matt answers for him.

"Neither are you," she reminds him sweetly, looks back at Holt, waiting.

"Iowa," he answers, dividing a smile between her and Matt.

"Oh? Nice place."

"You've been?" Matt says to her. "Jesus, where haven't you been?"

"Really?" Holt asks. "You've been to Iowa?"

"Well, it's not like it's Tibet. Yeah, I've been. Ames, Iowa City, the Amana Colonies."

Holt laughs. "Oh, God, not the Amana Colonies."

"Yep."

"What's the Amana Colonies?" Henry asks. He is collecting all the empty straw wrappers in a pile on the table.

"A wacky place."

Savannah nods. She remembers a wine tour, Alice slipping her a thimble-sized cup of something fiery and sweet. Dandelion wine she thinks, remembering the gold and lavender plaque outside the building touting this delicacy. The tour guide poured her mother seconds and even thirds, and finally bored, Savannah went out into the hot sunshine to look at the sheep.

"Wacky," she echoes, nudges Henry to slide out of the booth. The diner is still crowded and a group of four college girls are eyeing the emptying table.

"So what were you doing there?" Holt asks, holding the door open for her and Henry. She steps through, looks back over Holt's shoulder, spots Matt, who has stopped by the dessert case to talk to a girl with short, dark braids and a guitar case slung over one shoulder. He looks up, catches Savannah's eye, nods, then touches his fingers to his lips before pressing his hand to the girl's forehead.

Savannah looks away, pushes her sleeves up, feeling Matt swing through the door behind her. He wraps an arm around her waist, as Holt asks her, "Do you have relatives there?"

She shakes her head. "We were just passing through. When I was eight, I think. Or maybe seven. Can't remember now." She tips her head up to him. "I do remember miles and miles of cornfields, though. My mom used to say that one of the most beautiful sights she ever saw was the sun setting every night over all those fields of corn. I also remember trying to eat some of it."

"But it's the wrong kind. The kind they feed to cows and horses," Henry reminds her because this is his favorite part of her story. Holt looks at him with surprise.

"Henry knows a lot of things," Savannah says, noting that her brother is nodding solemnly.

"So you were just taking a vacation? In Iowa?" Holt persists.

"Savannah and her mother did some traveling when she was little," Matt fills in.

"For about nine years," she adds, unwinds his arm from her waist.

"Wow, that's pretty cool." Holt is nodding at her in a thoughtful way. "Nine years, huh?"

"Give or take a little. We stopped at a few places for a longer while."

"Have you been to California?"

"Oh, yeah." Wade, Lionel, Rick. Although she always called Rick "Redwoods Man" because it made her mother laugh. Alice met Rick when he was leading a tour called Friends of the Redwood Forest. She went to the tour three times, claiming her daughter just loved it. Savannah supposes there is some truth to this since she had tried to convince her mother that they could live in the treetops.

“Colorado?”

“Yeah.”

“Montana?”

“Yeah, for about three months, when my mom was in her cowboy phase.”

Henry is watching her, and she wonders if he is trying to reconcile their mother with the woman Savannah is describing.

“Damn.” Holt whistles. “We never went anywhere when I was little. Except to DC once. School trip.”

Savannah looks at him with pity.

eight

Kurti, wearing another beautifully patterned skirt and her usual neutral expression, opens the door after Matt knocks.

"Hey, baby." He holds his hands out from his sides. "Forgot my keys, again!" She turns her cheek to the side as he leans in to kiss her. One hand reaches to curve around his shoulder. In her other hand, she is holding a lint roller. She and Savannah acknowledge each other with a brief glance before Kurti's eyes rest more closely on Henry. He gives her a small smile and goes back to worrying at a smear of syrup on his shirt. Her eyes flick over Holt once.

"Hi, Kurti," Holt says pleasantly enough.

"Good morning," Kurti replies, looking at the lint roller in her hand as if addressing it as well.

Savannah shifts, puts her hand between Henry's shoulder blades, and guides him into the apartment, feeling Holt follow close behind her. Once inside, she notes that the pillow and blankets have disappeared from the corner, where she folded and stacked them earlier that morning. Some sort of smoky scent hangs heavily in the air and Savannah looks around, finds the tall stick of incense protruding from the mouth of a brass-colored Buddha.

"Where's my bag?" Henry asks. Kurti, who has begun lint-rolling the red cushions, turns, her skirt swishing out around her legs.

"Oh! I put them both in the bedroom to get them out of the way while I was cleaning."

As she moves toward the bedroom, Holt catches Savannah's eye, gives her a half smile, before asking Matt, "So, you got those books?"

"Yeah," he answers distractedly, his hand hovering over the books on the shelves. "They were right here . . . wait, here's one." He pulls a thin blue book out from the shelf. "Catch," he says, and Frisbees it across the room, narrowly missing Henry's head. Henry flinches aside.

"Matt," Kurti says, her tone full of quiet reproof. Savannah bites her lip to keep from agreeing with Kurti. Henry's stuffed bear, Bert, is hanging out of the bag balanced in the crook of Kurti's arm.

All his first year of school, Henry wouldn't go anywhere without Bert. This habit seemed to embarrass Jack more than anything else about Henry, and once, her stepfather hid the stuffed animal. Savannah remembers every place they looked in that house. For three days, Henry, normally so quiet, threw screaming, raging fits that left their mother shaking until Alice finally found the bear shoved behind the washing machine in the basement.

After that, Henry started having nightmares that Bert was lost again. So Alice sewed a red-ribbon collar and name tag into the brown fur of the bear's neck. The image of her mother's needle trailing red in the kitchen after dinner burns briefly in Savannah's mind.

A name tag with their address and phone number so anyone could call if they found the bear.

Acting on instinct more than anything else, Savannah looks hard at Kurti. The older girl meets her eyes for a second, then crosses the room, sets the bag down in the corner. Savannah follows her progress, tracks her slight, settled movements, then says, "You called, didn't you?"

"Here's your other book. I forgot I left it here," Matt says, snaking one long arm under his leather armchair. He retrieves a thick black-and-white book and slides it across the rug to Holt. Then, as if noticing the sudden silence, Matt looks up, a frown beginning to crease his forehead. "What's happening?"

"Your fucking girlfriend called my house. Did you know about this?" Savannah demands of him.

Matt gets to his feet slowly. "What are you talking about, Sav?"

She holds his look with one of her own for the space of four boiling seconds, long enough to know that he has no idea what Kurti has done. She doesn't answer, shifts her focus to Kurti's face instead, feeling Matt do the same.

"You called who?" Matt asks her, and his voice is still blank, still willing to produce the best from this situation.

Kurti twists a fold of her skirt in her hands, looks

directly at Savannah. “Do you realize how much trouble you’re in?” she says. Contrary to her words, her voice isn’t spiteful at all. “You’ve kidnapped a child. You’ve taken him across state lines. That means the FBI will probably get involved. I didn’t call the police. I called your house. Just to talk to your mother. I thought she should know that you are both safe and that maybe, if she talked to you, you would come home.” Her words tumble faster and faster now.

Savannah closes her eyes briefly, opens them, looks at the ceiling, anywhere but at Kurti. Matt is staring at his girlfriend with a frightened expression.

“I had to.” Her voice is soft but still firm, as if she alone is unshaken by what she has done, and right then, something inside Savannah burns, wishing for another frying pan. “For his sake.” Kurti indicates Henry, as if there is another child in the room, and puts her hand on his shoulder. Savannah can feel her brother looking at her, but she can’t tear her gaze from Kurti, watching with fascination as composure slips back over the other girl’s face. She seems satisfied that she has considered all the facts and has made the right decision.

“Who answered the phone?” Savannah asks, but she already knows. By now her mother would have been curled up in bed with her cup of tea. She would have switched off the ringer on the bedside phone, prepared to sleep until the afternoon, sure in her assumption that Marie had sent her children off to school that morning. “What did you say to him?" Her voice is rising, but she can't seem to control it. Kurti moves closer to Henry and wraps her arm around him.

"You'll only make things worse," she says softly.

"I think you've done a really good job of that already, Kurti," Holt says from the corner.

"He thanked me for calling, and said that he'd send someone over to pick you both up."

"Holy fuck! When did you call him?"

"He sounded quite calm and reasonable—"

"He sounds that way for about three days after he sleeps it off! Then he forgets everything he—"

"When?" Matt cuts through.

"About an hour ago."

The words fall calmly, quietly into a close silence, broken only by a wheeze from Henry.

Savannah looks at her brother, who has one hand twisted into the material of his T-shirt. He is half kneeling and his other hand is opening and closing on his kneecap. "Bathroom," she snaps at him, and he runs for it but doesn't quite make it. Well, another thing for Kurti to clean up, Savannah thinks as she ducks into the bathroom, finds a blue towel bordered with white flowers. She twists open the taps, runs the towel under the faucet, watching the white petals darken under the weight of water.

Returning to the living room, she kneels next to her brother. His back rounds under her hand. "Come on," she whispers, lifts up his face and tries to smile at him while skimming the cloth across his mouth and his neck and his forehead. She stands up and pulls him with her.

"I didn't think he . . . ," Kurti begins and ends.

"Do you have any concept of what you've done? Do you even know what life is like with my stepfather when he's drunk? Which is, like, every night practically. Do you know how many times he's hit me? Do you know exactly how much help my mother is? Zero, zilch, nada. You know absolutely nothing about our lives and who we live with. But, wait, I'm sorry, I forgot that you've taken some fucking child psychology courses. You must obviously know more than I do."

Naturally, there is a silence. Savannah feels the breath circle in and out of her lungs, but she is having troubling swallowing. And there is no crack in Kurti's impassive face, but then she bites her lip and looks away. "Matt," she whispers.

"I can't believe you did that, Kurti," he says slowly, looking from her to Savannah.

"I can't believe I ever came here," Savannah says to the ceiling. At this, Matt turns, his face wounded, his mouth open, but she is not remorseful. "I don't want to hear it, Matt. We're leaving. Have a nice life here with Kurti." She snatches at the bags, taking a second as she jams them shut to wonder if Kurti combed through both of them or just Henry's after she found what she wanted.

The buzzer sounds once, sharp and imperious.

Savannah's hands still. She thinks for a moment of the clean-shaven, heavy-eyed face Jack will present to everyone in the room. She looks at Matt. He shakes his head. "I don't know. That's pretty quick. But it could be him . . ."

"What if it's the police? What if he called the police?" No one seems to be able to speak. She tries to reason that the police wouldn't ring the buzzer, would they? All the cop shows she has seen indicate no; they weren't usually that polite.

Savannah curls the fingers of her left hand, digging the nails into the center of her palm, an old trick to wake herself from nightmares, one that is unsuccessful most of the time.

Then Holt moves. "You can't go out the front door," he advises, nods his head toward the hallway. He swings around and pushes Henry in front of him. "Come on." Savannah experiences a brief, widening flash of relief.

"What should I say?" Matt asks.

Holt shrugs. "I don't know." Then he raises his eyebrows in Kurti's direction. "But I wouldn't let her do the talking."

"Sav," Matt says as she moves away from him.

"Tell him, or whoever it is, we went home on the train, okay? Can you manage that?" she snaps at him, wanting to claw at the forlorn expression on his face.

"Oh, God, I am really sorry—" Matt begins.

She opens her mouth, but Holt replies, "Save it for later," and then, "Are you coming?" He and Henry disappear into the next room. Oddly blank, Savannah follows.

In the bedroom, Holt pushes aside the curtains—more Indian-print tapestries—yanks open the one window, and steps through it. Beyond looms the fire escape. She throws one leg out the window.

"Um, won't they check the fire escape?" she asks, and looks down. The inside of her head whirls until she focuses on the windowsill, solid and unchanging. She reaches for Henry's arm.

"We're not going down this way, Savannah."

"What?" she says, pulling Henry through the window. He bumps his head on the frame and gives a yelp. She puts a hand over her brother's mouth, leans more weight on her left leg, and steps out onto the metal platform. "Please tell me we're not going to climb up, are we?"

"Why? Scared of heights?" Holt flashes a look at her, as if daring her to make him laugh. Not up to answering, she watches as he leans over the edge of the fire escape and raps on the window of the adjoining apartment. After a minute, he pounds on it harder. Just like the police are going to be pounding on Matt's door in a minute. The neighbor's window creaks, and Savannah manages to stop herself from following that thought. The window rattles open after a minute, and a guy, wearing a blue-and-white bandanna, thrusts his head out.

"Oh, hey," he says to Holt. He yawns, looks at the sky, shields his eyes, even though it is completely overcast.

"Jeremy, these are friends of mine—"

"Damn, it's fucking early."

"Yeah, sorry about that. Can we come in?" There is no urgency to Holt's voice, but Savannah bites her nails and looks back through the pane. She thinks Matt has shut the bedroom door and for that she is grateful. She swallows a sliver of torn-off nail, pulls her fingers from her mouth, squares her hands on Henry's shoulders. She can feel how thin and crunchable his bones are.

"Oh, sure, yeah." Jeremy yawns again and slides the window open farther. "Hop over."

Holt throws one leg, then the other over the railing with an ease that lets her know he has done this before. For one second, he is standing on the slender outside edge of the fire escape. Then he is safely over on Jeremy's side. She moves forward reluctantly, studying the gap between the fire escapes, knowing enough to not look down the four-story fall. Then she looks anyway.

"Um . . . ," she says, one syllable of panic.

"You want to explain everything to the police?" Holt offers her.

"Police?" Jeremy says. "Fuck, not again!" He withdraws his head and begins to rummage noisily within the apartment.

"He's cleaning up for the guests," Holt explains. "Are you coming or what?"

She shakes her head, fastens her gaze on a vine growing up the side of the building. The leaves shiver and scrape at the dirty gray wall. Henry slips his cold, sticky hand into hers. Her fingers close around his palm once, then she lets go.

"Hand him across," Holt says as she looks down at her brother. She hopes Henry is not comprehending much of what's happening, and she leans down and picks him up. It's been a long time since she held him, and he is surprisingly light. She shifts him in her arms, edges closer to the rail.

"Be brave," she whispers when he won't unlock his arms from her neck. She bends the upper half of her body as far across the three-foot gap as she can, thinks of gym class, and pretends that this is no different from the hurdles or the rope climb.

Holt meets her halfway and somehow she manages to pass Henry through empty air. His eyes are squeezed shut and for some reason, this makes her want to cry. *I'm sorry.* But Henry's feet touch the metal fire escape on the other side, and he wraps his fingers together and looks at her across the gap. The sun is behind him and his face is still.

"Don't think about it, Savannah," Holt advises.

"Easy for you," she mutters. "You're on the other side." But there is a slight noise to her left, Matt's voice lifting into a question, and she swings one leg over and then the other and clings with her fingertips to the railing. The metal bites into her skin.

"Good, now turn around and climb over," Holt's voice

encourages. Edging her feet around so they are facing forward, she pries one hand off the railing, reaches out. Holt leans over, grabs her upper arm and pulls, his grasp so tight that it hurts, but she steps into it and wedges her foot firmly between the rails on Jeremy's side.

For one wavering second, she straddles the gap between the two fire escapes before Holt pulls again, causing a burn to slice through her elbow and upper arm. Then she is leaning forward, the front of her body pressing into the railing, at her heels a wedge of pure, blank space. With his help, she climbs over.

"Not so bad," he says, smiles at her. A long strand of her hair rises and falls rapidly over her left eye, in time with her breathing. He pushes it aside and she shifts a little. There is a fine tremor beginning somewhere behind her eyelids.

Alice 1986

Alice can wait only one day, one hot, on-the-knife-edge-of-her-seat kind of day, and when Noah doesn't appear in the store or on her walk home, she decides to find him.

She waits until she hears the suck and pull of the kitchen sink emptying, then her mother's brisk footsteps and the living room TV erupt into polite laughter, before she walks out the front door. Behind her, she can feel the lit windows of the house like so many eyes.

She walks down the edge of the street, her footsteps muffled by the clumps of grass bursting through cracked pavement. Occasionally, the road brightens as cars gleam past, full of her classmates. Former classmates, she corrects herself, since she graduated a month ago. Most of them will still be here in the fall, a very few, like Cindy, are headed to the college in Portland.

But fall seems far away now as the summer darkness brushes sweet and cool against her skin. And right now, she knows exactly where she is headed, since she looked up Mr. Castleton's address in the phone book. All through dinner, she swung her legs under the table, pushed her peas to the side of her plate, and drank three glasses of water until Jane asked in her usual dry voice if Alice had a fever. Her mother looked up sharply at that, and for the rest of the meal, Alice could feel her mother's glance resting on her thoughtfully.

Alice crosses the street, steps over a child's tricycle left on the sidewalk. A small gray shadow comes to rub inquiringly at her ankles and she stops to pet the cat for a minute before continuing on. At last, she turns down Still Pond Lane, wondering why it's named this since there isn't a pond in sight.

Mr. Castleton's house is the third one on the left, and Alice begins to think that Noah is not home since she doesn't recognize his car among all the others parked along the curb. But there is one light shining from a first-floor window and an instant later, Alice sees Noah cross the room within. She traces through dry summer grass.

"Hey," she says softly, then louder, "Hey."

Noah turns, comes to the window, leans down and peers through the screen, disbelief shimmying across his face. "So I don't think we got to finish our conversation," she says, as if they are standing in the street in broad daylight, having just bumped into each other again.

She waits while he flattens his elbows against the sill, rests his chin on folded hands. "You came all the way here to tell me that?" He snorts a little. "What, did your mother drive you over?"

"Actually, I walked."

Now he straightens up, regards her with even more disbelief. "Are you crazy? You walked through the dark like that? I know a girl who got knifed pretty bad one night doing that."

Alice steps back a little. "Where? This is Three Springs, Noah. I told you, nothing ever happens here." But he is staring at her, unconvinced, and she scrapes the heel of her sandal against her ankle, refusing to look away.

Finally, he smiles. "You're kind of crazy, Alice. Lucky for you, I happen to like crazy."

She grins back. "Are you going to let me in?"

In response, he pushes the screen up as far as it will go and she places her palms flat against the sill. She flexes her legs, gives a little jump, wedges one knee up and over, and tumbles more or less gracefully through the open space, onto the floor. She straightens up, looks at her surroundings, her eyes skipping over the unmade bed, then turns.

"Bet you never had a girl come through your window before."

He grins. "You'd bet right."

"I love this one," Noah says, fingers spinning the volume way up. They are sitting on opposite ends of the pullout couch that Noah had hastily reassembled while Alice had flipped through his tapes.

Now she listens for a second, recognizes "Tangerine." "You like Led Zeppelin?" When he nods, she smiles, softly hums a little of the refrain. "This song is so sad."

"Yeah," Noah nods, holds up one finger. "Listen to that guitar," he says, closing his eyes. Alice sighs, wondering why guys are always saying things like *listen to that guitar.* She leans back in the chair, dabs her foot along the floor. She lets her gaze drift from Noah's ankles to his calves, studies the shape of his fingers splayed out on his knee. The tape clicks loudly, silence abruptly replacing the music. She looks up to find Noah's eyes are open, that he is looking steadily at her.

"Well, anyway, I should be going."

"If you wait till my uncle gets back, I'll drive you."

"No, that's okay."

He stands up. "Then I'll walk you back."

"You don't . . ." She shrugs then. "Okay." She watches Noah yank up the screen again.

"Um . . . we're not going to walk out the door?"

He shakes his head. "It's more fun watching you climb out the window."

nine

When Savannah climbs through the window, she finds Jeremy whirling through the rooms, clothes, books, papers, pens scattering in a trail behind him. She guesses that they are now in what must be his bedroom, because he is freely emptying drawers. "I can't find my other pipe. You know, man? The one I never use."

"That's probably why you can't find it," Holt ventures. Henry looks at Savannah, opens his mouth. She shakes her head, puts the tip of her thumb against his lips. "Anyway, Jeremy, this is—"

"Louise. And my little brother, Paul."

Henry looks at her again, doesn't attempt to speak this time, clearly mulling over his new name.

"Yeah," Holt finishes easily, "these are some friends from back home."

"Oh, yeah? Visiting the Big Apple? That's nice." Jeremy says all of this in a rush, his head halfway under the bed. Meanwhile, Henry has wandered over to the open closet and is peering in.

"Hey," he says excitedly. "There are plants in here."

Jeremy emerges from the bed, scraps of dust in his long brown hair. His bandana has disappeared from his head. He scrambles over to the closet and reaches in. "Think I should flush them?" he asks no one in particular, holding up a spindly plant in a white plastic planter.

"Isn't that your college tuition?"

"Yeah, but if it's a raid, they'll be coming over here."

"No they won't," Holt says. "Trust me."

"You sure?" Jeremy asks, one thumb stroking the leaves protectively.

"Yeah. It's cool. Seriously, just trust me on this one, okay?" Holt meets his eye for a minute, and they hold glances before Jeremy sighs, slumps a little. He looks at the plant in his lap, then up at Henry, who is still standing by his shoulder. He holds it up so Henry can take it carefully into his hands.

"Great," Savannah whispers to Holt. "I can just see Henry's future evolving right before my eyes."

"Paul's," Holt whispers back.

"Right."

"Want the tour?"

"Ah, sure," she says, stepping over a small, upended table and a clock radio.

"Just to warn you, it's not up to Kurti's standards, but we like it."

"Naw, see, when the flower buds, you just want to pinch them off gently . . . ," Jeremy is explaining to an intent Henry.

"Come on, Paul. *Paul*," Savannah says.

"He's okay with Jeremy," Holt suggests from the doorway. “So, here’s the kitchen.” She walks three steps into a small alcove, complete with a doll-sized stove and refrigerator. Crumbs and wrappings litter the countertops and the floor is a dingy shade of bluish gray. The cheap plastic tiling is peeling back in one corner under the window, revealing another nondescript layer of floor covering. Three paintbrushes soak in murky liquid in an old peanut butter jar.

“Let me guess. You do a lot of cooking here, right?”

“Oh, yeah. I know about fifty-one creative uses for Ramen.”

“Impressive.”

Holt grins, moves a few steps down the hallway. “Bathroom on the left. Probably don’t need to see that. Living room here.” They step into a smallish room. One wall is brick and the other three are painted red, white, and blue. “I was feeling patriotic.”

“Weird.”

He shrugs. “Just felt like painting nothing. You know? Something that didn’t have to mean anything.”

“Yeah. You’re in Matt’s art classes? You’re a painter, too?”

He nods.

“Did you always want to do that?”

“Yeah. I was painting on the walls with my watercolor set when I was three.”

Savannah runs one hand over the nearest wall. Its surface is unevenly textured, slashed with visible brushstrokes. “Bet your mom loved that.”

"She didn't care. She hoped I would turn into another Picasso."

"Did you disappoint her?"

"At least once or twice by now. And this is my room." On the far side of the living room, he indicates a half-open door, knocks on it. "Don't want to startle the paintings," he whispers.

"Are you serious?"

"Do I seem serious?"

"You seem like a nutcase."

He laughs. "I'm joking with you. Trying to take your mind off the situation next door."

"Not possible. But thanks." She crosses the living room floor, follows him into his room. And blinks. Three walls are covered in swirls of multicolored paint while the fourth bubbles over with tiny, precise blue-and-white polka dots. She turns in a circle, feels dizzy with all the color. "Wow."

"It takes a second to get used to." He is standing by the window, watching her. "So, how come you never visited Matt before?"

She shrugs. "I don't know. I didn't think he wanted me to. Out of sight, out of mind is pretty much how he operates."

"I don't see how he could. With you, I mean."

She stops turning, polka dots popping in front of her eyes, but he looks away from her. After a moment, the colors settle, so she begins to examine the rest of the room. Besides the double bed, a dark wooden door rests on top of two sets of wooden sawhorses. It is covered with sheets of half-finished sketches, thick ink pens, and wide charcoal pencils. She reaches across the pages, picks up a wood-framed sketch that is sitting off by itself on one corner of the desk. It is a pen-and-ink drawing of a little girl, her head turned away from the viewer, one shoulder raised.

"That's my little sister," Holt explains.

She nods, fumbles in her bag, fishes out the photo that she always carries in the inner pocket, holds it out to him. She had wrapped it in a Ziploc bag and the plastic tears a little as she pulls it free. "That's me and my mom." Savannah holds out the photo, looks at it with him, even though she knows the scene by heart.

She is five and standing side by side with Alice, both of them smiling widely at the photographer, although Savannah has forgotten, or maybe never even knew, who had clicked the shutter. Alice's hair is wound into two braids and she is dressed entirely in dark green. There is a wide belt clasping her slender waist, and she is holding a green felt hat with one hand. The other hand is resting on Savannah's shoulder. Savannah is dressed in gold tights and a pale yellow skirt. A large, flat piece of cardboard in the shape of a pot is hanging around her neck. Several green dollar signs and round gold coins, all made from paper, are pinned to her clothing.

"Halloween," she explains to Holt.

"Figured. Your mom was a leprechaun?"

Savannah nods. "And I was her pot of gold."

He touches the ragged corner of the snapshot. "You should have a frame for this."

"I know. I always meant to—" But she stops, watches his long fingers unhook the backing of the little drawing. He slides the piece of paper out from behind the glass, sets it down on his desk. Taking the photo from her unresisting fingers, he tucks it in, closes the frame fastenings. He holds it up.

"It's a little small for the frame, but it'll do." He hands it to her.

She examines the photo, now caught behind glass, runs one finger over the wood, smiles at him.

The phone rings, jarring them apart. "Hang on," he says, exits the room. She remains motionless until he comes back. "It's Matt."

Savannah steps out onto the fire escape, ducking under the clothesline that Jeremy has rigged up. Matt is already waiting on his side and they look at each other across the gap in silence. Savannah shivers a little as a faint breeze leafs through her hair.

"Hi," Matt says, all jauntiness and swagger gone from his voice for the moment.

She doesn't answer, just folds her arms, watching as he puts his hands in his pockets, takes them out again, places them on the rail.

"Look, I'm really sorry about what happened. I didn't think—"

"Who was it? At the door?"

"Oh," he shrugs. "Just some friend of Kurti's."

She absorbs this but can't decide whether to be relieved or not.

"Can't you call your mom?"

"And say what?"

"I don't know, Sav. Your mom was always pretty cool. Maybe she would listen this time. It sounds like it's gotten worse."

Savannah shrugs. "Yeah. Because he lost his job. He's been around a lot more."

"When did he lose his job?"

"Two months ago." Two months of trying to stay away if she saw the car in the driveway, and if that was impossible, two months of studying the floor whenever he entered a room. "I've stayed away for a night or two before."

"Yeah, I know, but not with Henry. Maybe she'll know you're serious now."

She chews at her thumbnail, splitting off a piece. "I don't know."

"Well, . . ." He looks worried now. "Where are you going to stay?"

She looks directly at him. He looks down almost immediately. "Thanks, Matt," she says softly, a full weight of bitterness in her voice. "Don't worry. I didn't even want to stay with you. Not with Miss Speed Dial in there." She lifts her chin toward his bedroom window.

"Kurti's been crying all day," he offers.

"Good." There is enough snap behind the word to make him swallow.

"I explained some stuff to her about . . . Jack . . . and your life back home. She's really sorry and she wants to help."

"I think I've had enough of her help. What are you doing with someone like her, anyway? I can't even believe you."

"What do you want me to say, Sav? That I'm sorry it didn't work out with us?"

"What are you even talking about? There never was any 'us.' Six months of me tutoring you in trig and watching a lot of bad movies together does not make any 'us'!"

A door slams below and Savannah looks down, through the gaps between the metal bars. A large man hauls a bag of trash to the rusted metal cans stacked in one corner of the back lot. He is whistling as he pulls off a lid, lets it clatter to the sidewalk, fits the bag into the garbage can with some effort. The song sounds half familiar to Savannah, and she stares harder at the man, studying his bald head as if it holds the answer. But abruptly, he stops whistling and, without replacing the lid, walks away. Although he does not look up, both she and Matt are silent until the man disappears through the door.

"Look," Matt begins, awkwardness written in the way he holds his arms at his side, in the way he averts his eyes.

"That's not what I meant, Sav. I meant, I'm sorry that I didn't call more, that I wasn't around more this last year. I didn't know things had gotten so bad."

"You couldn't have done much," she says, pleased that this seems to hurt him.

"Yeah, maybe not."

She blinks, studies him in the dusk. His face is blank and she shivers again, wondering at the time when she thought she knew him. Five months apart, though, and he is gone.

"So . . . you going to stay with Holt?"

"Why? Jealous?"

He leans across the railing, lowers his voice. "Is that a good idea, really? I mean, you don't even know him."

"He's been a hell of a lot nicer than your girlfriend."

He shrugs painfully at that. "Yeah. Look, here's the money I owe you." He stretches his arm out, offers two folded bills. She takes them, their edges damp against her palm, and studies Andrew Jackson's somber face. "I owed you thirty. Keep the rest for the taxi ride last night."

She starts to shake her head, but he stops her with, "Please. You're going to need it."

"Okay."

There is a slight sound from inside his bedroom. Although he doesn't turn to look, he shifts his weight from one foot to the other. "Take care of yourself, Savannah."

"You, too." The words are polite and cool and plain.

There seems to be nothing else to say, even though she finds herself searching, guesses he might be, too. In the end, she reaches her arm out, they touch their hands together once, briefly, across the railing. Then she climbs back through the window.

Alice 1986

"I can't believe I'm going on a double date with my own brother," Cindy moans, her words garbled as she applies another layer of lip gloss to her already vibrantly colored mouth.

Alice looks over her friend's shoulder, fluffs her hair up with quick fingers, then changes her mind and smashes it back down.

"And Peter," Cindy wails. "Peter Shuemocker, who used to put glue in my hair."

"That was in fourth grade, Cindy. And besides, I think he always liked you." Her fingers slip through tubes of lipstick, flat discs of eye shadow, eyeliners. "Where's my blue mascara?"

"Not the blue one," Cindy admonishes. "You have brown eyes. You look better in brown mascara. Seriously."

"I always wanted blue eyes."

"Mike has blue eyes. Maybe you'll have blue-eyed children," Cindy says straight-faced. The two girls regard each other in Alice's bedroom mirror solemnly, until Alice's mouth trembles and she starts laughing. Once she starts, Cindy begins howling, too, until they both slump down with their backs against the dresser.

"Oh, crap, now my makeup just ran all over the place," Cindy says, swiping under her eye.

Alice examines her friend's face, tries to rub away the gray-black trails of mascara. "Yep. You're a mess."

"Ladies," Alice's mother says from the doorway, and both girls jump. "You two were making such a commotion, you didn't hear me. Your dates are downstairs." She regards them thoroughly. "That's a very nice blouse, Cindy," she comments.

"Thanks, Mrs. Ainswell."

Alice stands, holds out her hand for Cindy. They take a last look in the mirror, Cindy repairing the damage as best she can, before they file downstairs.

Peter is sitting at the kitchen table, drumming three fingers on its surface, a beat to a tune only he is hearing. Mike is standing by the sliding glass door, hands in the pockets of his khakis, looking out over the lawn. Through the window, Alice can see bright flecks of light wink low in the bushes.

"The fireflies are out early," she murmurs, going to stand next to him. Mike turns, looks down at her. A pinpoint of blood in the skin between his nose and his upper lip testifies to the fact that he has recently shaved.

"You look beautiful," he says, too low for anyone else to hear, and she blushes, suddenly somewhat intoxicated by the mixed scents of hair gel and shaving cream.

"Hey, Pete," Cindy throws out and gets an equally lukewarm "Hey, Pierson" in response.

"Well," Mike suddenly booms. "Is everyone ready?" Alice steps back, looks at her mother standing by the kitchen sink. One hand is poised above the dishes, and Alice suddenly experiences a winging feeling of remorse. She steps over to her mother, puts her arms around the older woman's shoulders. She can feel her mother's surprise in the brief clasp of arms around her waist before they both move away from each other.

"Okay, Mom, I won't be too late. I think the movie's over at eleven. Okay?"

"Everything will be fine, Mrs. Ainswell," Mike says, even though Alice's mother appears unworried. Alice looks at him with irritation. Pete and Cindy are already down the porch steps and are arguing.

"Now, no funny stuff back there," Mike warns, craning his neck and shooting a look into the dimness of the backseat.

Alice can't resist and she turns around, too, glares at Pete and Cindy, who are sitting at opposite ends of the car. "Yeah, or your father and I are turning this car right around and going home." She catches Cindy's eye and they start giggling in unison until Mike pulls her to him, his arm anchoring her to his side. The seat belt buckle is pressing into her hip and she shifts a little, letting Mike's hand slide over her bare knee.

They are at the Three Springs Drive-In and, even though it is a notorious place for teenagers, Alice figures that not even Mike can make much happen with his little sister Cindy and Pete in the backseat. Now she just has to decide if she is disappointed or relieved.

Halfway through the movie, Alice curls her legs under her, tries to stretch out a kink in her shoulder, passes the tub of popcorn back to Cindy, who has moved exactly three inches closer to Pete.

It is then that Alice spots the blue Dodge a little to her left, one row behind them. She doesn't even pause to consider. Leaning over, she puts her lips to Mike's ear. He squeezes her knee, shifts his leg closer, but then she whispers, "I have to go to the bathroom. I'll be right back." He nods. Alice slips out of the car, closing the passenger door quietly, moving away quickly before Cindy can offer to come with her.

She winds her way through the parked cars, careful to keep her eyes on the invisible path she is walking. When she nears the blue Dodge, she tightens her shoulder blades, pressing them toward each other across her back. As she is passing the driver's-side mirror, she lets her left arm swing away from her side just enough so that her fingers fly free through empty space, skim parallel to the side of the car. She is rewarded by the briefest of touches against Noah's elbow, before she is past the car and gone.

Behind her, a loud explosion blows across the giant screen, the audience stirs, a girl shrieks and is shushed almost immediately afterward. In the temporary and relative silence that falls, Alice hears a car door creak open, close. She smiles, heads beyond the concession stand to the empty bleachers.

She watches him approach her but says nothing, not even when he brushes her hair off her shoulders, slides callused palms down her arms. He pulls her to him with a kind of force she appreciates, and there, in the deep, popcorn-scented darkness, they kiss. Her hands fall down his back, catching where the edge of shirt meets skin.

She twists away a little. "I have to go," she whispers, but he touches his tongue to her ear. She grinds her fingers into the base of his neck. "I have to go," she says more urgently, pulling back.

"Don't leave me like this," he mutters, but she flits sideways, her lower lip between her teeth.

"Tomorrow. Night. At the old stone quarry, near the top of the waterfall. You know the place?" After a minute, he nods. "Eight-thirty?"

"I'll be there."

She walks away without another word. At the edge of the field, she can't help it. She looks back.

ten

"These are pretty good," Savannah says, settling herself cross-legged on the floor of Holt's room. She is flipping through his portfolio with one hand, trying to eat from a carton of Chinese food with the other. She gives up, begins munching a spring roll that Henry left behind when he moved off to the living room. From the sounds of it, he is either watching or playing a video game with Jeremy. She listens for a minute. A loud and noisy video game complete with squelching sounds every time someone dies. "All drawings? No paintings?"

"Oh, you're going to be sorry you asked," Holt answers, gets up from where he has been sitting, goes to the corner of his room, pulls out three oversized black portfolios. Obligingly, she sets the drawings aside, slides a few feet over, and opens a new portfolio, only to be confronted by a half-size nude painting of Kurti. Her features are completely recognizable, although the watercolors have given her a softer look.

"Oh, sorry," Holt says over her shoulder. He reaches across her right arm, flicks the page. "I forgot that one was still in there."

"I can't believe she took her clothes off for you."

"Oh, it wasn't only for me. It was a class."

She nods. Then she stops nodding to consider this. "Oh, God. Please don't tell me that's how she and Matt met?" One look at Holt's face to confirm this. "Oh, Jesus. Let me guess. Matt decided to make his move when she had a break, right?"

"Pretty much."

"What was this, the first week of class?"

He shrugs. "Second."

After a minute, she manages to smile, flips another page. "Thanks for letting us stay the night." She doesn't look at him as she says this, but stares down at a watercolor of three brown buildings. The sky behind them is a soft smudged blue.

"No problem. What happened with Matt?" He had not asked her that when she came back through the window, just mentioned that they were ordering Chinese food and what did she want. She was grateful for that. Now she says, "Not much. He asked me what I was going to do." Holt is flipping through a thin black book full of drawings, stick arms and legs pirouetting through the pages. "And I didn't tell him."

"Because you don't know," he finishes for her, but she shakes her head.

"I'm going to call my mom tomorrow. Right now she's at the hospital. I don't want to call her there."

"She's sick?"

"No, she works there. Night shift." She pulls her hair back out of her face, loops it around her wrist, ties it in a slippery knot. "How come you're helping us so much?"

Holt shrugs, closes the sketchbook, runs his finger down its spine. "I'm just a nice guy from Iowa," he says finally, giving her a wide smile.

"Yeah, right," she answers, closing the portfolio in her lap, crunching through the last of Henry's spring roll.

"I don't know. Maybe because I've never been anywhere, never did anything like this."

"Like running away? Well, lucky you." He doesn't answer. "Oh, come on. You've done stuff in your life. You must have."

"Nah. Not really. Life was pretty ordinary where I grew up. My parents are still married, I've got two older brothers, one sister, and now two nephews. We get along. All pretty tame."

"Oh. Well, you got yourself to college at least. That's something."

"Yeah, but everyone does that."

She laughs, looks sideways at him. "Oh, really?"

He looks abashed. "Maybe you'll go, one day."

She shakes her head, feels her hair come loose across her neck, decides it is not worth debating.

"I just meant that I feel like I never did anything in my life, anything exciting."

She pauses to wipe her fingers on the stack of napkins by the food carton, before picking up the second portfolio. Turning the pages randomly, she stops at another cityscape. "You're not finished, are you?"

He gives her a quizzical look, puts one hand out to the picture, examines it.

"No." She is sure he understood her the first time. "I mean your life. You're not finished with it yet."

"Oh, right. No, hopefully not yet. I always wanted to travel, like you did."

"Maybe you will someday."

"Maybe. Maybe if you get this . . . straightened out, we could take a trip somewhere? Sounds like you know a lot of cool places." The skin over his cheekbones is turning a faint pink.

She smiles. "Yeah, sure. Why not? And by the way, how did you become an expert at climbing fire escapes? I mean, your building does have stairs, right?"

He laughs. "I did a lot of rock climbing."

"Rock climbing? What the hell can you climb in Iowa? I remember it being pretty flat."

"Water towers."

"Isn't that illegal?" There is a sudden random image of flashing blue-and-red lights illuminating a figure at the top of a tower, a crowd of people thickening at the base. *Oh, what an idiot*, she can hear her mother saying, but what is that in Alice's tone? Affection? Amusement?

She struggles, but the *who* and *where* slide away from her.

Holt shrugs. "Yeah, but only if you get caught. My brothers and I used to do it all the time."

"I see." She sets the portfolio aside, careful not to smear grease on it, devotes her attention to the remaining container of fried rice. Somehow, the smell of hot cardboard is only making her more hungry.

Holt pushes his sketchbook out of the way, shifts forward so that his knees almost touch hers. "Listen. I do have one condition for helping you. You think—"

The phone rings. Savannah's chopsticks freeze in midair. One grain of rice falls to the floor.

"What's up? No man, that's not cool. I didn't say that to her." The video game sounds are abruptly extinguished as Jeremy's voice filters through the cracked plaster wall. "You tell her, I smoke that shit all the time. I'm not selling any old ditch weed." Then the sound of a phone being bounced back into the cradle.

Savannah breathes again. "Your condition?" She sets the chopsticks down, arranges her face into neutral lines, already forming replies to whatever he will ask.

"Can I draw you?"

"Can you what?"

"I have to draw three people for my art class on Monday. I can't draw Jeremy's face again." Holt raises his voice on this last part.

"Hey," Jeremy calls back in protest.

Holt laughs, kicks the door ajar with his foot, leans out into the living room. "Sorry man, what can I say? You're pretty ugly."

"Fuck off!"

Savannah peers over Holt's shoulder. Henry is sitting with one leg folded under him, a control in his hand, staring straight ahead at five gold coins dancing on the television screen.

"Come on, please?" Holt says.

She looks back at him, twitches her mouth to one side. "I'm not taking my clothes off."

He grins. "Do you think I made Jeremy take his clothes off?"

Holt taps the end of a pencil against the page and the soft drumming noise fills the space between them. "Okay, I'm making some quick sketches of your hands first."

"Why?" She resists the surging impulse to fold her hands under her knees.

"Because the assignment is to capture the center of someone. It doesn't have to be a full-on drawing of the person."

"And my hands are my center? That's definitely weird."

"Art is weird." He swoops his pencil across the page, pauses, looks hard at her hands for a minute. "Perfect." She looks at her hands, doesn't think he is talking about them. Careful not to move the lower part of her body, she eases her head back against the cool plaster wall, polka dots stretching to the left and right of her peripheral vision.

There is a hacking noise, Henry yelps, then Jeremy says, "Naw, you're the thief. I'm the Elven warrior lord. Check out my stats in the corner of the screen there. And see my heavy crossbow? It has awesome damage point value. Shoots acid green fire bolts. Anyway, let me handle the troll here. While I'm distracting him, you go in and steal everything he's got. Okay man? You clear on that? Can I unpause it now?"

"Okay. I'm ready." Henry sounds determined and brave.

Savannah closes her eyes. *You're never going to be pretty. Not like your momma here.* Her eyes dart open, light blending with dark across her field of vision. Jack's voice fades from her head. Holt is looking at her, his pencil still again.

"What? I didn't move my hands."

"No, I was looking at your hair. It's beautiful."

She looks down, focuses on a paint drip on the baseboard. She hears him clattering through his pencils.

"So, you got that from your mom, I guess."

"Yeah. She has the same hair."

"You should never cut it."

"I know." And her mother's voice echoes Holt's words. *Never cut this.* Brushing Savannah's hair one night. Then, as a surprise, Alice held out a closed fist, let Savannah pry it open to find two matching rhinestone star barrettes, the very same barrettes she had been admiring that day when they stopped at Wal-Mart for Alice to fill out an application.

"But I don't look anything else like her," Savannah feels compelled to explain now.

"You look like your dad?"

"Probably." He doesn't comment, so she adds, "I never knew him."

He stops sharpening a pencil, looks back at her. "Wow. How come?"

Savannah flexes her toes, her foot is falling asleep. "I think my mom just wasn't too sure."

"Who your dad was?"

"Right."

Holt doesn't say anything, the reaction she is most used to. He taps his pencil a few times vigorously against the spine of his drawing notebook, curves his shoulders back over the paper. "So you can't go to him, then?"

"Oh, you mean now? No. No idea where to start looking. I don't even know his name."

"Do you have any other family?"

She nods. "Yeah. My aunt in Maine. Where my mom is from. Actually, she's my mom's aunt, so she's my great-aunt. She was my grandmother's younger sister."

"You close with her?"

"My mom was. At one time. The last time I saw Aunt Jane was at my mom and Jack's wedding." Jane had arrived in a blue suit and had brought her mother a pair of gold earrings, insisting that Alice wear them since she needed something old to fit part of the wedding rhyme. Savannah always remembers this because she had never seen a pair of earrings that weren't for pierced ears.

Alice clipped them to her earlobes and then, looking into the bathroom mirror, she had burst into tears. She wouldn't or couldn't tell Savannah why she was crying, so finally Jane leaned over and whispered that the earrings belonged to Alice's mother and were the very same ones she had worn on her wedding day.

And because Holt has been so nice, Savannah is prompted to confess, "I haven't spoken to Jane in seven years."

"Um?"

"I know. But she's all I've got. And I have to try."

"You think she'll take you in?" She doesn't answer, but he continues. "You might want to call her."

"No."

"Why not?"

"Because it's way easier to say no over the phone." This was one of Alice's rules.

"Good point."

"I found her already." And now she reveals the secret that she has told no one else. "She used to send cards every year for my birthday and for Henry's. My mom never saved the envelopes. But once, when I was at school, I used the computer in the library to look her up. I found this article on her. She opened a vet clinic in her barn. It gave the address—42 Linden Road, Three Springs, Maine." The words loop through her head over and over.

Holt looks thoughtful. "So, you're going there?"

"I want to. Depends on . . ." She raises one shoulder, lets it fall. "You think I'm crazy?"

"A little. But that's not always a bad thing." He hesitates, then, "And there's no way to go back again?"

She shakes her head, gives up, moves her leg, and begins to flex her toes more seriously. His next words frighten her. "My uncle's a cop, you know."

She half startles to her feet before he understands. "No, no, no," he says, dropping his pencil. "I'm not going to call him or call the police or call anyone. Come on. Wouldn't I be your accomplice by now?"

Savannah takes a small breath, settles back on her heels, wraps her hands around her elbows since the drawing is clearly on pause. "So why tell me about your uncle?"

Holt leans back a little, too. "Because he used to deal with a lot of stuff. Like yours."

"Stuff like mine?" Her words are precise, expressionless.

"Like your stepfather. If you get in trouble from all of this, taking Henry, like Kurti said, you could make a case, too. With the Department of Social Services, I think. That's all I wanted to say."

She shrugs. Her only experience with Social Services was when a nice lady wearing pink-orange lipstick showed up on their porch one day when Savannah was nine. She sat with Alice in the makeshift living room of the trailer. Alice made fresh coffee and showed the lady all of Savannah's artwork tacked up on the wall, and the lady left, smiling. Alice claimed not to have any idea who might have alerted DSS, but she washed the dishes with a vengeance that night and they moved the following Friday. But Savannah knows that is not all Holt wants to say, so she waits.

"Did your mom know? About him . . ."

"No. Not really. I don't know."

"She must have," Holt says softly, and suddenly she is angry.

"She didn't, okay? She's always working. We see her for, like, an hour when we come back from school before she's gone again." She senses that he is not convinced. "I just can't believe she ended up with someone like him." She rubs her palm against her knee. "There's no one in my life right now who could understand that she used to be a different person."

Alice 1986

When Alice and Noah are finally alone, without fear of being interrupted, without any chance of being seen, they are strangely quiet with each other, holding themselves stiff and separate.

She realizes he is nervous and she reaches out, rubs the back of her wrist against the edge of his cheekbone. He turns his face, kisses her fingers, the offhand gesture gallant and awkward.

"Let's go skinny-dipping," she announces abruptly, begins to unlace her sneakers. She can feel Noah's surprise as she unbuttons her jean skirt, shimmies it down her legs, kicks it away from her with one foot. "You don't have skinny-dipping in Savannah?" Alice asks, but his answer is indecipherable as she strips off her shirt. She tosses it aside, looks at him.

"What did you say?"

"I don't think I've ever gone skinny-dipping with a white girl before."

Alice considers this. "I think it's probably not all that different." And with that, she scoots to her feet, pirouettes lightly to the lip of the quarry. She swings her arms through space, feeling the air stir past her elbows. Then she steps off the ledge.

Alice loves those three seconds of free fall before her pointed toes slice through the dark surface of the quarry. The water shatters, shivering into widening circles as she sinks. She registers the slowing of movement as gravity shifts and morphs and then, when her chest is blazing, she kicks upward, lets her head break free.

Noah is standing on the ledge, watching her. He is now wearing only boxers, and she studies his long legs and arms in the light, his skin a darker shadow against the rock outcropping behind him. She opens her mouth to call him, but before she speaks, he flings his body into a perfect dive. The impact sends the water slapping against her chest and throat, and she scissors her legs, turning in a slow circle, waiting for him to emerge. But he does not. Not for a while. Longer than she would have thought possible. And when he does, he is nearly at the far end of the quarry. She waves one arm, sure that he sees her, but he ducks under again.

This time she waits patiently, knowing that he will make a grab for her legs. It still comes as something of a surprise, though, when she feels his two hands brush up against her knees. He pulls lightly, not enough to make her go under, but enough to make her resist by churning her arms harder through the water. Then, just as suddenly, the pressure is gone and he surfaces close behind her.

He wraps his arms around her waist and treads water for both of them as she leans her head back, resting it between his neck and shoulder. They stay that way for a minute before she twists her body around, winds her legs around his waist, feeling his hipbones press into her thighs. He stands then and she realizes he is tall enough to touch the bottom where she can only tread. Water sheets off their shoulders and backs and arms as he carries her to the shore.

"Wait," he breathes, sits up abruptly, leans away from her. Pale moonlight plays down his hipbone, crosses the long line of his waist. He is searching through the pockets of his discarded shorts and she hears the *snick* and crinkle of foil. "Got these today," he tells her.

"Way to have faith," she says. His teeth flash briefly in the dark. She removes a pebble embedded under her thigh, settles back, looks expectantly at him. "You want me to put it on?" Inwardly, she is singed with gratitude for the day that she and Cindy stole the box of condoms from Cindy's older cousin. They had spent an hour locked in Cindy's bathroom, practicing with two bananas Cindy lifted from the fruit bowl and the six condoms the box contained.

"Thanks, but I think I got it," Noah tells her now. At one point, it begins to rain. One of those brief summer showers, the kind that lightly speckles their arms and legs but is gone before the ground has time to grow damp. Alice closes her eyes, watches swirls of gray and white chase across the backs of her eyelids.

Afterward, she lies on her side, her shoulder pressed into warm stone, his hand resting on her hip. She waits him out, lets him speak first.

"Are you . . . ?" He stops, starts again, "Was it . . . ?"

She decides to put him out of his misery. "Yeah. *A* for effort."

"For effort? *Only* for effort?"

She laughs soundlessly, knowing that he can feel the vibrations traveling through her rib cage. "Okay. *A* for preparation, *A* for effort, *A* for completion. *A*s all around." She shifts onto her back, points one toe toward the sky, begins tracing the outline of the Big Dipper. "So, you ever done this with a white girl before?"

He snorts. "No." Knocking one knee into hers, he asks, "You?"

"Me? No, I've never been with a white girl."

He leans over and bites her shoulder just hard enough to make her yelp. She lets her foot drop back to earth. "No. I've never done . . . this . . . at all. Before." She rolls back onto her side, presses the length of her body into his, her eyes wide open.

After a minute, she feels him put his mouth up against the top knob of her spine, blow breath across her skin in the lightest of kisses.

eleven

Savannah lies awake in Holt's bed, Henry curled against her left side, breathing evenly. A siren wails steadily in the distance. She presses her thumbs lightly to her eyes, blinks, looks at the clock. It is 3:42. The streetlight is slanting through the blinds and blue-and-gold-edged stripes line the walls. Henry kicks out his leg with a sudden movement, then rolls away, his head wedged between the bed and the wall. Savannah reaches out one arm, eases him back, slides the pillow they are sharing under his head. She had given the other pillow to Holt, who had insisted on sleeping on the futon in the living room. She waited until he came back from the bathroom, feeling suddenly awkward.

"Thanks," he had said, taking the pillow from her, setting it down at one end of the mattress. "You want some water?"

She shook her head. "Thanks again for letting us stay the night."

He nodded. "Do you need me to take you to Port Authority tomorrow? You know where it is?"

"No. And yes." She smiled at him. "I mean, no, I don't need you to take us, and yes, I know where it is. Thanks."

She wondered if she could find anything to say besides *thanks*, then stepped back, her hand reaching for the sliding partition that divided his room from the living room. Behind her she could hear the small rustling sounds of Henry settling down to sleep.

"Sav," Holt says, then, "it's okay that I call you that?"

She looks directly at him. "Matt and I were never together. We were just friends. I mean, I was his trig tutor. Then we were just friends." She hurtles to the end of the sentence, pauses.

Holt raises his eyebrows, nods. "Okay."

"Okay, good night."

Now, Henry rolls back toward her, one hand comes up sharply, then drifts down to cover his exposed ear. Savannah closes her eyes, tries to keep them closed.

"California clouds, baby." Alice pushes her black sunglasses farther onto the bridge of her nose, leans back on her elbows. "Don't you just want to take a nap in them?"

Savannah looks up from burying Alice's feet in the sand and stares into the sky. She knows exactly what her mother means.

"Hmmmm?" Alice murmurs, tying her hair into a knot on top of her head. "Aren't you glad we came here?" She arches her foot so that her toes appear through runnels of sand.

"Yeah." But she is thinking about the Oregon Trail, and

how at her last school, they had been doing a project about the first settlers of the West. Sara Cho had been her partner and together they had been making a series of dioramas about the pioneers' journey. *But why*, Sara kept asking her when Savannah told her she was moving again. *Who will be my partner now?* Savannah had shrugged, unable to explain, but inside, she was already stretching beyond the classroom and its construction paper–covered walls.

Now she begins outlining her mother's feet with tiny bleached white shells. "I really want to see Oregon, though."

"We'll get there, we'll get there," Alice promises. "We have time."

In the morning, Savannah wakes to Holt's footsteps fading down the stairs. The apartment air settles around them, heavy and still. She rolls over, pretending to smother Henry in the blankets. He struggles and kicks but emerges with a tentative smile. "Well," she says. "What should we do?"

A concentrated frown crosses his face and then he blurts out, "Can we go see the dinosaurs?"

"What dinosaurs?"

"You know, the ones I was supposed to see on the trip?" He sits up on his heels, bounces a little. "But I got sick, remember?"

"On your field trip?"

"Yeah. Mom was going to take me, but can we go now since we're here?"

"Sure. Why not?" She looks at the alarm clock by the bed. "We have time."

"The Museum of Natural History," Henry informs her, drawing out the word *history*. "How will we get there?"

She considers this. She knows she should conserve their money, even with the forty dollars Matt gave them. "We might have to walk, okay?"

Henry looks doubtful.

"Come on, it won't be that bad. And there are lots of things to see on the way, probably. I might even buy you a hot dog."

"Okay." He nods. "Should I take—"

"Yeah." She looks over at his bag in the corner. Bert has been tucked inside it and it is neatly zipped together.

"I packed it while you were brushing your teeth last night," he informs her. "And I took this off." He opens one hand and holds out the red scrap of ribbon and the address tag. Some dark synthetic fur is clinging to it.

"How did you get it off?" she asks, peeling the scrap from his hand. The edges are frayed and she wonders if he ripped out each stitch with his teeth.

"That knife on his desk." Henry points to the X-Acto knife now lying on the floor.

Savannah raises her eyebrows. "Nicely done."

He shrugs, pleased.

"Okay, scoot off the bed here. I'll make it. You shower. Fast, okay?" Henry disappears down the hallway. She snaps out the comforter, folds it twice, leaves it draped at the foot of the bed. It is extremely thick and overly warm, accounting for last night's dream of being boiled in a red-and-blue soup of paint. She scans the rest of the room, to see if they have left any traces of themselves.

Holt's sketchbook lies open to the drawing of her hands. The right hand is unfinished, while the left one is sharp and clear, down to her bitten nails and the crescent-shaped scar on her thumb where she burned herself making pancakes when she was eight. She traces the actual scar, remembering how Alice had admired it, pronouncing that it was the exact shape of Australia and how not everyone could say they had a continent in their hand. She smiles, pulls the page out, folds it twice, and shoves it into her backpack.

Savannah holds the building door open, letting Henry scoot under her arm and out into the bright sunlight. She blinks as the glass door suctions closed behind her. The morning is warm and she busies herself tying her jacket around her waist. It is only when she looks up that she sees Jack, standing on the opposite street corner, in profile to them. He is holding the newspaper that he has just bought from the nearby corner stand and is accepting his change from the vendor. Her mind registers all this, while her hands are already in motion. She swings Henry around by the shoulders, puts him in front of her.

"Walk," she hisses, and frightened, he complies. They walk down the street, his progress awkward in front of her. They make it two blocks, her eyes searching the sea of traffic before she finds what she is looking for. She puts her left hand on the back of Henry's neck, keeping him in line, and with her right hand, she hails the cab. It pauses beside her, she opens the door, they duck in.

"What is it?" Henry whispers.

"Port Authority, please," she says in her best grown-up voice, trying to sound brisk but not frantic. "Keep your head down," she murmurs to Henry as the cab begins to move. She ducks her head, too, pretending to search for something in her bag. Meanwhile, she keeps one eye on the approaching light. *Stay green, stay green.* It doesn't. It turns yellow.

The cab shoots through it anyway and the street corner vanishes behind them. Only then does she allow her hands to still and fall into her lap. After a minute, she looks over at Henry. "The dinosaurs might have to wait."

twelve

Savannah scans the waiting room area with its dirty cushioned chairs. Finally, she selects a woman who is sitting close to the ticket line and who appears to be alone. She is youngish, somewhat overweight, with thin blond hair, and is wearing a short-sleeved yellow sweater and a denim skirt.

"Sit here," she instructs Henry. "Don't talk to anyone. Pretend that woman is your mother. If she moves, though, don't you move." Savannah surveys the woman again. She is reading a thick paperback novel with a torn cover, and several Macy's brown paper shopping bags are arranged in a neat line at her feet. Savannah gives Henry a light push forward. He goes silently, but he has been silent since the cab ride.

As he sits down next to her, the woman, without looking up, nudges the bags over to one side. Henry touches his toes to the gray linoleum floor, swings his feet a little, and tries to look normal. He does not look at Savannah and finally she goes to join the ticket line.

A large group of people have planted themselves around an electronic message board. Every once in a while, the board flickers, the lettering changes, and part of the group rushes off in one direction, only to be replaced by more and more people.

Savannah waves at Henry; this time, he acknowledges her, raises his hand, waves back. Savannah smiles, then gives an exasperated glance at the woman, as if for failing to respond. She knows this whole charade is ridiculous, but she can't stop herself.

Finally, it is her turn. "How many tickets?" the teller begins. Her eyes seem focused on the collar of Savannah's jacket.

"Three for Three Springs, Maine. Two adults and one child. My mom and my brother," Savannah adds, making a quick motion over her shoulder. "And I'm a student."

"Do you have a Student Advantage card?" the teller asks, neon blue fingernails arrested in mid-flight across her keyboard.

"I forgot it today. I go to NYU?" Savannah offers hopefully.

"No card, no discount." She resumes her typing.

"Fine."

At this, the teller looks up, as if hoping for further argument. "It's the rule. No proof, no discount."

"Okay," Savannah answers.

The teller sighs, looks back at her computer, names the fare. Savannah keeps a pleasantly bored expression on her face while she is desperately subtracting. They will have seven dollars left.

She slides the bills under the glass partition, the teller's fingers flash, and the money is gone. "Bus leaves at nine-fifteen. Gate six. Change in Portland. The local to Three Springs leaves every half hour."

The printer whirls out the tickets.

"Henry?" Savannah says, focusing on the top of her brother's head. He has been arching his neck to read every exit sign and billboard that flashes by. Now he looks at her briefly before leaning his cheek against the window. "That window's dirty," she comments. He shrugs, stuffs Bert under his head, turns his face into the bear's plush fur.

Savannah looks away, begins studying her fellow passengers, surprised at how crowded the bus is for a weekday morning. Diagonally across the aisle from her is a large man overflowing his seat. He has taken off his blue sweater and has spent most of the first twenty minutes of the bus ride arranging and rearranging it around his shoulders, then tying it around his waist before untying it and draping it back over his shoulders. Now he seems to be sleeping, although every so often, he opens his eyes, glares at the seatback in front of him, and gives it a kick.

Farther up front, three little girls and one boy are playing their version of musical chairs, until a man sitting behind them, presumably their father, half stands, catches one of the girls by her arm, gives her a little shake, muttering something into her ear. Immediately, her face assumes a frozen blank expression, her eyes locked on her father's shirt.

Savannah dips her head, fishes in the plastic bag by her feet, comes up with the jar of peanut butter and the crackers that she bought at the drugstore just outside the Port Authority. She avoids looking at the front of the bus, concentrating instead on opening the jar, dipping a cracker edge into the peanut butter. Silently, she holds it out to Henry. He takes it immediately, stuffs half of it into his mouth. Cracker crumbs rain down on Bert's head. She hands him another one.

"It's a seven-and-a-half-hour bus ride to Portland. I hope you're going to talk to me at some point."

Henry finishes crunching and the corners of his mouth turn down.

"What?"

"I have a test on Monday. I'm not supposed to miss it. It's for that advanced math class. Remember?"

Briefly. She remembers a month ago, at dinner, Henry telling her and Jack something about this class, how if he passed the test, he would get to be on next year's accelerated track. She remembers Jack nodding, telling Henry that he took after the old man, had a head for numbers, and she remembers kicking her bare foot into the table leg so she wouldn't be tempted to remind Jack that she was the one who checked Henry's math homework every night.

"It'll be okay," she says now.

"No, it won't, Savannah. Mrs. Kohler said that we had to be there to take the test."

"Well, when Mom gets to Maine, we'll have her call and talk to your teacher."

"And tell her what?"

"That you still want to take the test, but that you had to miss it this time." She injects the most reason that she can into her tone.

"But. . ." He is quiet for a minute. There is a smear of peanut butter on his upper lip and she reaches over and rubs it off. He touches the same spot after she takes her hand away. "What if Mom doesn't come to Maine?"

"She'll come, Henry."

"How do you know? Does she even know where we are?"

"We'll call her when we get there." The cracker in her fingers snaps. She pokes out the pieces, eats them so rapidly that the half-chewed edges scratch the back of her throat as she swallows.

"Baby, I'm home," Alice sings, her voice lifting on the word *home*, making it into two syllables. "And I've brought dinner."

Savannah lifts her head from her book, bursts out laughing. Alice is still wearing her work uniform, a red-and-yellow sombrero and a bright yellow T-shirt that says *Mama Mexican* in cactus green, curvy letters. "What do you think?" She twirls dramatically, the braid of her hair looping over one shoulder with her movements.

"Will you get in trouble wearing your uniform home?"

"No. But I did get a few stares. Are you hungry?" She sets down a paper bag on the rickety table they have wedged into the corner of the trailer's front room, lets Savannah remove the cardboard take-out container.

"What is it this time?" Savannah asks, her eyes closed. She inhales the familiar aroma of rice and beans, but she waits.

"Tonight," Alice intones, "we will be dining on grilled rock shrimp and snow peas as a starter. For our main course, we will be having fettuccine Alfredo, and for dessert, we will be enjoying—"

"Flambéed bananas," Savannah suggests, then opens her eyes as Alice laughs.

"Where'd you get that? You've never had flambéed anything in your life, baby."

"I read about it in a book," Savannah informs her mother, unfolding a paper napkin and spreading it across her lap like Alice taught her.

"Okay, flambéed bananas. With whipped cream and caramel sauce and rum."

"Mmmmm," Savannah says, too hungry to wait anymore, forking rice and black beans into her mouth. After a while, she looks up to find Alice folding and refolding the paper bag that the food came in. Her mother's fork lies still on the table, its clean white plastic tines pointing in Savannah's direction. "Aren't you eating, Mama?"

"I'm saving my appetite for the dessert. You go ahead." Alice winks at her.

Savannah nods, but slows her mouthfuls, begins taking half bites. After a few minutes, when she thinks she is in the clear, she puts down her fork. "I'm full," she announces, pushing the container away.

"Well, don't announce that, silly. That's not polite table talk," Alice reproves, but her tone is so gentle that Savannah is not deterred.

"I am so stuffed. I can't eat for another week." And her reward is Alice's smile as she begins to eat what Savannah has left for her.

"Savannah?" Henry whispers, and Savannah jerks one shoulder, opens her eyes. The bus has stopped in a parking lot and people are shuffling past her as they exit. "We could see if that man has anything in his suitcase." He flicks his eyes up to the luggage rack, then lowers them back to her face.

"Like what?"

"Money!"

"What do you think this is . . . a video game? We get caught and we're off this bus, stupid." She settles back down, watches their fellow passengers stretch out their arms. The three little girls in pink jackets immediately start hopping across the parking lot, until their father calls something in their direction and they stop, turn, walk slowly back toward him.

Two men search through their pockets, each producing cigarettes and lighters at the same time. They stand next to each other, looking off in opposite directions. The rest of the passengers head for the swinging glass doors of McDonald's.

"Have another cracker. Don't think about Happy Meals." Savannah hands Henry their second-to-last packet of crackers, leans her head back, closes her eyes again. "Besides. You should never steal from a person. A corporation is okay. Not a person, though."

"Who told you that?" Henry asks.

Savannah opens her eyes as a few people begin thudding back onto the bus, the intoxicating smell of salty grease wafting in with them. Henry chews on a cracker, regarding her with a skeptical expression.

"Mom did. It was a big belief of hers, once." Savannah watches as the large man lumbers back to his seat, holding aloft a bag marked with the familiar yellow arches.

If this were a movie, Savannah thinks, he would open the bag and hand Henry a box of french fries. She wills this to happen as the man hunches one shoulder away from them and stares out the window, steadily cramming food into his mouth.

She shifts her body in the seat, leans on her side, smiles

at Henry. He is running his finger along the window track and then tracing designs on the pane with one dusty finger. "Want me to write letters on your back?" she asks, and after a minute, he nods, scoots down in the seat, presents her with the back of his neck and sweatshirt.

She traces a shape over his shoulder blades

"*H*," he says immediately.

"Yep. And this one?"

"*R*?"

"Right again." She tries *T* and then *X* and then *G*, which he confuses with *C* at first.

"Now words?" he suggests, so she draws three slow, large letters, one overlapping the next on his shoulder.

"*You*?" he guesses.

"Right. And this one?"

"*Are. Getting. Sleepy.*"

"Oh, you are? Me, too." She spreads out her five fingers, drums them lightly on his temple, in time with the rain that begins to smear down the windows. She watches the gray, wet asphalt of the highway slide by, listens to the faint hiss of tires as they slick over with water. The soft rhythmic squeaking from the front of the bus is now the only other sound.

"Did you and Mom drive in the rain?" Henry asks after a minute.

"Yeah. A lot. I loved waking up to rain. The whole world was all gray, and we were inside the car, and Mom would wrap me up in blankets because the heater never worked. I loved driving in the rain."

"Do you think Mom will ever take me on a trip like that? Like yours?" His eyes are closed; he is speaking mostly into Bert's fur.

"Maybe one day."

"Will you come, too?"

But she doesn't want to talk anymore, so she presses her palm lightly against his mouth, then arches her wrist, begins tracing aimless patterns across the knots of his spine.

"Mom used to do this for me when I couldn't sleep. Circles on your back," she says after a while, but he is breathing slow and deep.

She leans her head back again, trying to get more comfortable as the rain steadies into a downpour.

Alice 1986

"Ali?" It is Jane's voice and Jane's hand smoothing across her forehead. "She's crying," she hears Jane whisper, and Alice opens her eyes long enough to locate her aunt and her mother standing over her with worried faces.

"What happened, honey? Did you have a fight with Mike?"

Alice rolls over, nudges her face farther into the pillow, the cool, crisp material temporarily soothing to her hot cheek. "I'm okay," she says, her words muffled by sun-smelling linen.

Her mother smoothes a wrinkle from the sheet, tucks it closer around Alice's neck, repositions a glass of water on the night table. Alice knows her mother is deeply uneasy with any bout of tears, always has been, so Alice makes a concerted effort to stop crying. She fails.

"I'll sit with her," Jane says in her firm voice. After a moment, Alice hears a soft brush of cotton and then her door gently shutting.

"Now," Jane says, untucking the sheet from the stranglehold that Alice's mother has imposed. "What's wrong? Is this really about Mike?"

Alice shifts, looks up at her aunt, shakes her head against

the pillow. "It's Noah. He's gone. He left. He didn't even say good-bye." Her voice breaks on the last word, trails off into a squeak as she begins to cry harder. After a while, she blots her face with the corner of the sheet and watches a small black fly zoom endlessly across the white ceiling.

"Alice," Jane begins, and her voice is very soft. "Maybe it's for the—"

"No, it's not for the best," Alice interrupts.

"But it wouldn't have worked out for you two."

"Why? Because he's black? And I'm white?"

"That, and he's not from here, and so he would have left anyway."

"But . . ." Alice crumples and uncrumples the corner of the sheet in one fist. "Why didn't he even say good-bye?"

"I don't know," Jane answers, shaking her head. She strokes back the hair on Alice's forehead. "The older I get, the less I seem to know about men." She gives a little huff of a laugh, which, halfway through, turns into a sigh. "Want me to write letters on your back?"

Alice nods, scrunches onto her side, waits for the dizziness in her head to fade. Jane's touch is light across her shoulders, looping and swirling letters across her spine. But their shapes remain mysteries to her skin. It is only Noah's face she sees when her eyes are closed. Dark eyes and white teeth and delicately shaped ears. His features dip and circle, refusing to reassemble themselves into a coherent whole.

Noah, who must have decided to walk away from her without looking back.

thirteen

At the next rest stop, halfway to Portland, Savannah steps off the bus into a fine, soft drizzle. Henry hops along beside her as they hurry under the shelter of the bright yellow bus station awning. The driver stretches out his arms, yawns until his jaw cracks audibly, then warns them that they have only ten minutes before the bus departs again. "Don't go wandering now," he cautions them, smiling at Henry.

Savannah pushes her hair, already damp, off her neck, notes the bank of telephones positioned at one end of the lot, across from a pair of Coke and Pepsi machines.

"Go check the vending machines for change, okay?" She expects Henry to resist, but this mission seems to brighten him up considerably. Still hopping on one foot, he sets off. Briskly, she heads toward the phones, selects one, shoves the door open with her foot, picks up the receiver. The dial tone is abruptly silenced by the click of quarters. She punches in the number, waits.

"Hello?" Alice answers, her voice breathless. And Savannah finds she cannot speak. "Hello?" Alice says again in the same exact voice, and then, "Savannah?"

"Hi, Mom," Savannah whispers.

"Oh, my God. Where are you?"

"We're okay." Savannah runs her thumbnail down the metal phone cord, listening to the zinging sound it makes.

"You're both okay? Where's Henry? Is he with you?"

"Yeah, he's fine."

"God Almighty, what have you done?" But her mother says this like a prayer.

"I told you I wasn't going home."

"You went to Matt's. Are you in New York City still?"

"No."

"Where are you then? I swore to Jack you'd come back by now. I swore you would do the right thing, act responsibly." She keeps her voice low and Savannah realizes then that Jack must have returned from the city and is somewhere in the house.

As if he can hear her, Savannah lowers her voice, too. "We took a bus."

"Where?"

"To Maine." She catches her lower lip between her teeth, worries at it. "It's really nice here, Mom."

There is a pause. "Maine? Are you . . . how do you . . . are you going to *Jane's*?"

"I looked up the address online. She's a vet now."

"I know that," Alice snaps, and Savannah stops speaking. "Now do *you* know how angry Jack is? It's all I can manage to keep him calm. He wants to call the *police*." She hisses the last word, so that it cuts into Savannah's ear.

And she is suddenly more furious than she has ever been with Alice. "Let him call the police. I'll call the Department of Social Services. Let him explain a few things. You, too. I'm sure they'd love to talk to you."

"What are you even talking about? Department of Social Services? You think the Department of Social Services is going to step in whenever a teenager decides she hates her stepfather? You think they don't have enough to do? Trust me. I work in an emergency room. I know."

"I know where you work," Savannah says tightly.

The thinness in Alice's voice hurts. "For a really smart kid you've just gone and been incredibly stupid. I mean, what did you hope to accomplish with this little stunt of yours? Taking an eight-year-old like that?"

Savannah stares at the window opposite her, pictures herself smashing the receiver through it, if only to silence her mother's insistent voice. There is a short burst of static crackling over the line, and Savannah leans her head away from the phone. Through the rain-smeared Plexiglas, Savannah watches Henry thrust his hand into the last of the vending machines, an expectant expression on his face. Then he steps free of the machine, turns in a complete circle, scanning the lot. She kicks at the door, waves her arm to alert him to her presence. He holds up one hand in return, running toward her.

"Are you still there? Savannah?" Her mother's voice has dimmed a little. "You've put me in a really bad place."

"Yeah? Well, now you know how it feels."

She listens to her mother breathe on the other end of the line, taps her fingers in time to the seconds she is now counting in her head. She is up to sixty-three before her mother speaks. "Okay," Alice says, and now her voice is calmer. "Come back and we will work this out. You don't have to stay here if you don't want to. I'll figure something out. Please. Just bring Henry back."

"Do you think that—"

There is a faint humming on the line and then a very sharp click.

"Savannah?" At the same time that Savannah says, "Mom?"

On the other end of the line, Savannah hears Alice draw in a deep breath, then say, "Jack? Jack? *Wait* a minute."

"Oh, God," Savannah mutters. She drops the receiver into the cradle, turns, looks at Henry crouching on the low stone wall. He has pulled his hands into the cuffs of his jacket until only the tips of his fingers are visible. His head is hunched down between his shoulders, reminding her of nothing more than a baby turtle, half-submerged in his shell. She emerges from the phone booth, walks over to him, holds out her hand. After a minute, he takes it.

"I'm sorry," she says to her brother because he is crying.

fourteen

When the bus finally pulls into the Portland station lot, Savannah is unsurprised to see the police car waiting in the rain. A man, wearing dark glasses even though the sun has not appeared once today, gets out of the car. Savannah studies him from the window, all of her options flitting through her head. The last of the passengers are streaming off, and she sees the cop look hard at a girl roughly her own age before stepping up to the bus.

Quickly, she shakes Henry awake, pulls him down to the floor with her as she ducks and gathers their things. "Excuse me," she hears the cop say to the bus driver. "I'm looking for two runaways, ages . . ." The men confer in lowered voices as the radio on the cop's belt emits Morse code blips of sound followed by long waves of static. Beside her, Henry squirms, peers through the gap in the seats, and then shrinks.

"Savannah," he begins.

"Henry, whatever happens, don't say a word. Let me talk. Please?"

He nods.

Alice 1986

"Your boyfriend's back," Cindy sings under her breath. Then announcing in a much louder than necessary voice, "I think I'll go have a smoky treat outside," and with a dramatic flip of her apron, she vanishes through the swinging doors.

Alice doesn't bother to run her hand over her hair or bite her lips to give them some color. Instead, she selects an ice cream scooper, rinses it under tap water with extra care, before turning slowly, languidly, and regarding Mike, now standing a few feet away from her.

"What'll it be?" She leans across the counter, her whole body curved like a question mark. She watches him pretend to study the flavors, his eyes darting back up to hers every few seconds.

"Mint chocolate chip and—"

"Cookies and cream, I know. You're predictable." But she says this with the smile that she knows he is waiting for. He spreads his hands wide across his side of the marble countertop, his face glowing with sudden color.

"Hey, I like what I like."

"So, I gather," she murmurs, looking up at him, her arm digging into the container of bright green ice cream. The silver scoop grows cold in her hand as she scrapes up a clump of chocolate bits. She has decided that it doesn't much matter what a girl says to a guy as long as she says it the right way, and Mike, so far, is not doing much to prove her wrong.

"So?" he says, putting his fingers over hers when she tries to hand him his cone. "You busy tonight?"

She shrugs. "Maybe." She watches as the cone, already listing to the side under the weight of the ice cream, begins to drip onto her wrist.

"So, I'll pick you up at eight?"

She pulls her hand free, licks the chocolate off it. "No chaperones this time?"

He shakes his head. "Just you and me."

"Do you have a—"

"Yeah, yeah, yeah. I got it right here." He indicates his discarded shorts. "But just let me do this for one minute, okay? Just like this one minute, all right?"

She twists her face away from his, stares through the gap in the backseat to the clock on the dashboard. "One minute." The metal part of the seat belt is pressing into the last knob of her spine and she shifts her hip, kicking one leg free to wrap around Mike's waist.

"Put your leg down," he whispers against her neck, but she can only push sideways again, the twitch of his lips against her skin suddenly unbearable.

"Mike," she says after a minute, then thumps him on the shoulder. "My foot is cramping. Ow—"

"Shit, shit, shit," Mike huffs, rearing off her.

Her bones, suddenly free of his weight, feel solid again and she sits up. She rearranges her dress, pressing out the worst of the creases with flattened fingers. Inside the car, Mike is breathing as if something has torn in his throat, while she stares through the windshield at dim outlines of the trees that dip and sway in the encroaching breeze.

"I'm sorry, Alice. I'm so sorry. This never happens to me. I just . . . it felt so good there . . . I—shit!" With a stiff jerk of his arm, he tosses the still wrapped condom onto the dashboard.

"It's okay, Mike," she says. "Don't worry about it." She leans back against the seat, closes her eyes. If he would just shut up, she could pretend for one minute, one swift, sweet, stolen minute, that it is Noah in the car with her.

fifteen

All throughout the ride to the police station, Savannah and Henry hold hands.

At one point, she leans over and whispers, "Remember, you have done nothing wrong, okay? You are not in any trouble."

Henry looks straight head, chews his lower lip miserably. "But what about you?" She shakes her head, concentrates on the back of Officer O'Brien's neck. He appears to have some sort of rash because he keeps snaking his hand back and scrubbing fiercely at the pink skin.

"Ah, here we are in Three Springs," Officer O'Brien abruptly announces, his voice shaking a little. "On your right is the statue of our founding father. He came to Three Springs in 1770." Savannah turns her head, looks out the window, a flash of a bronze figure making a quick and jumbled impression. "And this here is our local drive-in theater. It shut down back in the 1990s. Shame."

Savannah meets his eyes in the rearview mirror, realizes that he is only a few years older than she is. This fact helps to keep her from throwing up.

"Okay, here's the police station." The car slows, stops. Officer O'Brien becomes abruptly businesslike, ushering them out of the car and walking closely behind them as they shuffle into the police station.

Inside, they file past a woman behind a desk who is talking into the phone. She winks at Henry, smiles at Savannah, and puts her hand over the receiver, whispers, "Honey, your mom called. She wants to know what you want for dinner." Savannah stares at her until Officer O'Brien clears his throat, mutters something indecipherable, and then Savannah realizes that the woman is not talking to her.

"In here," Officer O'Brien says, and leads them into a windowless room, complete with a table and four chairs and not much else. "Um, Chief Pierson will be here at five." He checks his watch, then taps the face repeatedly. "That's not too long. He'll want to talk to you. Get your statements."

Savannah looks at him. "Thanks?"

He smiles, relieved, walks backward, exits.

"Was he a cop?" Henry asks her.

"I think so."

"I don't know," he says doubtfully. "He didn't seem like the ones on TV."

Savannah walks to the corner of the room, peers out through the cracked door. The woman at the desk is now leaning across it, speaking to Officer O'Brien, who is flushed. He is twirling a pen in his fingers and, as Savannah watches, he tosses it up in the air, tries to catch it, fails. It bounces across the woman's shoulder.

The outside door swings open again and an older man walks through, carrying two Dunkin Donut bags. He is tall and heavyset, widely built. He stops mid-room, sniffs the air, once, twice.

"Gladys!" he booms out, and the woman, who has sat back down at his arrival and is clicking keys on her computer, looks up brightly, as if surprised to see him in front of her desk. "What is that smell?"

"Do you like it? It's Sea Mist."

"I hate it. No more of that aromatherapy shit, I mean it."

Savannah whirls back, away from the cracked door. "Okay, Henry," she warns, and he nods.

They are seated, facing the door when it opens and the heavyset man walks through, still carrying the pink-and-orange bags. He nods at them but doesn't say anything as he sits down, studies them in a silence that stretches and stretches.

Beside her, Henry swings his legs soundlessly under the table, until one foot accidentally knocks into a chair, making a dull thud. Savannah puts her hand on Henry's knee.

The cop raises his eyebrows, looking only at Henry. "You like fried-egg sandwiches?"

Henry considers the potential in this question. "Yeah."

The cop flicks one bag across the slick surface of the wooden table. Henry catches it, opens it, removes the foil-wrapped lump inside.

"What about you?" the cop asks Savannah as Henry, unable to resist, peels back the foil, wraps thin fingers around half the sandwich, and begins to eat.

"No, thank you," she answers.

"Hmmm. Manners. Don't often see that in kids today."

Savannah leans back, waits for the diatribe about how this generation is so irreparably worse than the last one. But the cop pulls a large-sized coffee from the other bag, takes a sip. "Well, now that your little brother is eating my dinner, maybe we can talk."

Henry looks up, a scrap of egg clinging to his cheek, ducks his head again.

"I'm Chief Pierson."

Savannah nods, thinks of the futility of introducing herself, since he obviously knows who they are.

"Do you want to tell me what happened?"

Savannah shakes her head. "I'd like a lawyer," she offers, only to regard him with bewilderment as he laughs up at the ceiling.

"Do you think you need a lawyer?"

"Maybe. Don't I get one?"

"Kid, you watch too much TV."

"We get a phone call?" Henry whispers, wiping crumbs from his lip. Then he looks at Chief Pierson. "We get a phone call."

Chief Pierson nods. "Is there anyone you want to call?"

Savannah thinks about this. "No."

"Okay." Chief Pierson gathers himself, leans toward them, thumps his knuckles down. "Here's what I know. Your stepfather called us about four hours ago." He looks pointedly at Savannah. "He claims you attacked him, kidnapped your younger brother, and stole the car."

“She didn’t attack him,” Henry insists. “He fell and hit his head.”

“Henry.” Savannah digs her fingers into his knee.

“Oh, really?”

Savannah regards Chief Pierson silently, until he sighs.

“Officer O’Brien says your mother is on the way. As of about three hours ago. I’d say, since she’s going to hit rush-hour traffic, she won’t be here for another six hours. Maybe seven. That’s a long time not to talk.”

Savannah focuses on the space over his left shoulder.

“Just tell me where you were headed. At least that much?”

“To our aunt’s.”

“And she lives in Maine?”

“Yes. In Three Springs.”

Chief Pierson frowns at her. “No kidding. What’s her name?”

Savannah considers this, decides it doesn’t matter now. “Jane O’Rourke. She’s a vet.”

Chief Pierson is looking at her. “Jane O’Rourke is your aunt?”

Savannah shrugs. “Great-aunt.”

“What is your mother’s name?”

“Alice. Why?”

Chief Pierson sets his coffee down, pushes it away from him as if it’s gone cold, although Savannah can see the steam still rising through the slitted lid. Abruptly, he leaves.

* * *

When Chief Pierson enters the room again, Savannah wonders what has happened beyond the closed door. He stares at her for a long time, until she shifts on the hard wooden seat, drops her eyes.

"What?"

"I . . ." He sits down. "Look, why don't you wait in my office? It's more comfortable." He waves his arm behind him, his hand brushing past the dull metal doorknob. "Go on."

Savannah stands up slowly, trying to stretch her legs unobtrusively, watches Henry slowly slide his arms through the straps of his bag. They make their way across the main outer room, where Gladys is stroking the leaves of a large rhododendron plant on her desk.

"All set?" she asks brightly, smiling at Henry.

"Actually," Savannah begins, trying not to stare at Gladys's long, incredibly scarlet fingernails, "we're supposed to wait in his office?"

"Oh, of course." She bustles out from behind her desk and opens a door on the opposite side of the room. She scrapes her hand along the wall and fluorescent lights flicker to life. "Here, dolls." Just then the phone rings. "Oh!" Gladys gives a little jump, hurries back to her desk. Savannah steps inside the office, Henry's head knocking into her elbow. She turns then, looks across the outer room, letting her gaze rest on Chief Pierson's back.

He has not moved except to put his face into his hands.

Alice 1986

Alice picks her head up off the closed toilet lid, clamps her teeth down hard against the heaving waves rippling up her throat. She eases back on her heels, then lowers herself very slowly so that her cheek is resting against the pristine blue tile floor. The chill of the ceramic squares feels good against her overheated skin. She presses her hand against the fuzzy white bath rug, rubs her fingers against the edge of the nylon matting. Staring at the space directly under the claw-foot tub, she focuses on a stray red hair and a long-lost cap from a toothpaste tube.

"Alice," her mother's voice calls from outside the bathroom door.

"In a minute, Mom," she tries to say in a normal voice. She braces her hand against the cool porcelain lip of the tub, arches her back, and without looking at the toilet, she manages to flush it. "Please, please, please," she whispers under the cover of rushing water. She splashes her mouth out with half a capful of Listerine and looks at herself in the white-framed mirror. Her eyes are bloodshot and her hair has straggled loose from its ponytail.

"Alice, are you all right?" Her mother punctuates this

question with a soft tap on the door. "Are you sick?"

Alice opens the bathroom door, steps into the hallway. She leans back against the wall, aligns her head between two large yellow roses blooming on the cream-colored wallpaper. Jane is standing directly behind Alice's mother, motionless, as if, while passing through the hallway, she was arrested by this small scene.

"Yeah, something I ate, I think."

Her mother leans forward and puts one square, capable hand on Alice's forehead. "A little warm, but no temperature." She tilts her head back. "There's that stomach flu going around. Maybe you should lie down. I can call the store for you and tell them you're not coming in."

"Maybe," Alice murmurs. Her eyes travel to the two windows on the opposite wall. A lawnmower is whining insistently. The urge to be sick is gone, as if it never happened. Instead, she feels empty and light. As light and clean as the frilled white curtains that flip in the sudden breeze traveling in through the open windows. "I'm okay, Mom. Don't worry."

And over her mother's head, Alice encounters Jane's cool and knowing gaze.

sixteen

"Alice," Chief Pierson says simply.

"Mike," she answers, and somehow Savannah gets the impression that she and Henry and the whole room have disappeared.

"Alice Ainswell," he murmurs.

"Not Ainswell anymore," she reminds him, smoothing Henry's hair down, cupping his ears lightly, then smiling at him. Over Henry's head, her eyes freeze Savannah into her seat. Dropping her gaze to the floor, Savannah examines the tiles, trying to rearrange the streaks and splotches of gray in the linoleum into patterns that make sense.

"Right," Officer Pierson says, and Savannah hears pencils clinking against a jar, the sound of paper tearing from a pad. "I need an official statement from you. I know what you said on the phone, but—"

"Of course." Savannah hears the hitch in her mother's throat as she tries to clear it.

"Now, your husband, Mr. Rydell, says that his stepdaughter ran away with the boy here, took the car, and—"

"There was a misunderstanding." Savannah lifts her head. Alice has turned Henry's face into her waist, is holding him firmly, one hand wrapped around the back of his neck.

Officer Pierson presses the tip of the pencil into his thumb as if testing for sharpness. "As of five hours ago, your husband wanted to press charges against your daughter."

"No," Alice says simply. "As I said, there was a misunderstanding. I arranged for my children to visit their great-aunt for a weekend. Savannah stopped by the hospital where I work this past Wednesday evening and I gave her my permission to do so then. You can speak with Jane. She'll verify this."

From where she is sitting, Savannah can see that Alice has closed the skin of Henry's neck between her thumb and forefinger, lightly, like a mother cat will do to her kittens.

"Alice," Mike says, and there is a sadness in his voice that makes Savannah blink. "You're telling me your husband, who called us five hours ago and wanted to press charges, simply forgot that you told him that you sent the kids, *by themselves*, a seventeen-year-old and an eight-year-old, up to Maine, to visit their great-aunt?"

"That's what I'm telling you." Alice's voice is steady, flat.

"Is there any reason I should believe any of this?"

"Yes," Alice says softly. "I think you know one reason."

For a long moment, Alice and the policeman stare at each other, and it is Mike who looks away first. He sets the forms down on his desk, scratches an eyebrow with one finger. "I'll need your husband to make a separate statement."

"He will," Alice says in such a way that Savannah is surprised to find that even she believes her mother. "Now, if you'll excuse me, Mike. It's been a long, long day. I need to get the children to Jane's house tonight. We're leaving in the morning." Her mother's eyes find her face again, and Savannah stumbles onto her feet, more tired than she realized. Alice shifts toward the door and Mike speaks again.

"These are my three boys," Mike says, picking up a picture frame off his desk and holding it out to Alice. After a minute, Savannah watches Alice take it, study it carefully.

"You have a beautiful family, Mike. Good-looking boys."

He bends his head over hers. "Yeah. This is Charlie, my oldest. He wants to be a cop, just like me. And these are the twins, Timmy and Will. They're their mother's delight." He waits a few seconds, takes the frame from Alice's trembling fingers, puts it back on his desk. Still looking at it, he says casually, "You know, I always wanted a daughter." He looks at Alice. "I think I would have made a good father. To a girl."

Alice leans back a little. "I never doubted you'd be a good father." She puts her free hand on top of Henry's head, guiding him toward the door. "Come on, Savannah," she murmurs. Savannah regards Alice's straight back, the bare nape of her neck as her hair swings forward.

"Take care, Savannah," Mike says. "It was a pleasure to meet you. At last."

Savannah realizes he is holding out his hand, and she takes it. He grips her hand with both of his, gently, then releases her. "You call me anytime, if you need anything."

She nods, looks down, realizes that he has closed her fingers around his card.

Alice 1986

"Alice!" Headlights splash over her arms and legs as a car turns into the parking lot of the police station. She doesn't check her pace. "Alice, Jesus, wait, will you?" She whirls so suddenly that she accidentally jabs her elbow into his midsection. Mike gives a grunting whoosh of breath, steps back.

"Don't lie to me. Did you have anything to do with Noah's leaving? Anything at all? You tell me, because I swear to God, I will find out the truth. One way or another." There is a weird hitching feeling in her throat, making it difficult to breathe. Mike stares at her for a long moment. A cool breeze slips through the parking lot, pulling goose bumps from the skin over her collarbones.

"I made it worth his while to leave," he finally grates out, the words biting one at a time into her head.

"You *threatened* him?" When he doesn't answer, doesn't change expression, she doesn't check the scream rising in her throat. "You threatened him! I can't believe you!" She closes her eyes for one second, feeling nausea crowd hot and thick into her chest.

"Whatever, Alice. He's nothing. He's not from here. He's not like us, he's—"

She slaps his hand away from her waist, the side of her palm slamming into his thick forearm. A dull shock tremors through her wrist. "I'm not like you. Don't *ever* think I'm like you in any way."

"No, I guess you're not." His voice has softened and then he steps forward swiftly, digs his thumb into the soft skin under her chin so that her head tips back hard.

"Just tell me one thing, Alice." She feels a faint twinge between her shoulder blades, but she doesn't move away from the pressure. "Is it mine? Say it is and we'll . . . I'll do the right thing, Alice. We'll get married. I've got my eye on a place. We'll fix it up any way you want to. If you want, you can work until the baby's born . . . anything you want. You could take classes or—"

She closes her eyes, expects to see her whole future in Three Springs in a fixer-upper of a house wash over the backs of her eyelids. But there is only a soft, blank screen, stretching as far as she can imagine. She opens her eyes, says with a certainty she knows she has no right to use, "It's not yours, Mike."

He pulls his hand away from her face.

seventeen

On the ride to Jane's house, where Alice has announced they are staying for the night, Alice and Savannah do not speak one word to each other. Henry, sitting in the front seat, keeps twisting back and forth between them as he recounts their adventures for their mother. Savannah slumps against the window, letting her head bounce against the glass each time they hit a pothole in the road. She looks up only when Henry says, "Is this where you grew up, Mom?"

"Yes," Alice replies. "This is it. It hasn't changed much."

The porch light is on and a white van is parked in the driveway. When she gets out of the car and walks closer, Savannah can make out the words *Three Springs Veterinarian Clinic* written in black block letters on the side of the van. Jane is standing on the porch and, as they approach, she unwinds the cellophane wrapper from a pack of cigarettes she is holding, shakes one free from the pack, lights it, and without a word, gives it to Alice. Then she looks at Savannah, one eyebrow raised. Savannah shakes her head at the same time that Alice says, "No, she doesn't smoke." She looks at Jane, sighs. "At least I did one thing right." She coughs.

"Mom," Henry says, still clinging to Alice's hand. "You quit."

"Well, this one doesn't count," Alice answers, pale smoke leaking through her lips. In the weak porch light, Savannah studies her mother, notes the grayish purple circles under her eyes, the deep grooves bracketing her mouth.

"Come on, Mr. Man," Jane announces briskly, looking directly at Henry. "How about you and I go in and put together some dinner? Or maybe just dessert at this point, since it's so late?"

Henry scuffs the toe of his sneaker back and forth along the wooden porch floor. Alice puts the cigarette in her mouth, reaches out with one fingertip, smoothes away the worried frown that is creasing the thin, pale skin of his forehead.

"Go on, Henry," she says, her cigarette bobbing in time with her words. "I'm not going anywhere. I'm just going to finish my smoke and have a talk with your sister. Okay?" Henry reaches around, scratches the back of one leg.

Savannah shrugs. "It's okay, Henry," she says, watches Jane hold the door open for him.

Alice makes a loose gesture at the wicker love seat behind them, and she and Savannah walk slowly toward it, sit in silence. The sharp, sour smell of burned tobacco rises as Alice crushes her cigarette with the tip of her sandal. She locks her ankles together and swings her feet slowly. She does not look at Savannah.

"So what now?" Savannah asks finally, and Alice slows, then completely stops the movement of her feet.

"I think you should stay here. For a little while. With Jane." Alice curls her fingers together in her lap. "I talked it over with Jane already. On the phone earlier today. God, it feels like forever ago already. Anyway, it's okay with her. For the summer . . . or maybe . . . I don't . . ."

Savannah studies Alice's profile. The porch light is shining directly down on her bowed head, splashing over the pale gold freckles, the pink scar on her neck.

"I can't take you back with me." Alice's voice is subdued, flat.

"Me? Or me and Henry?" Savannah knows the answer somewhere but waits anyway.

"You. It's the deal I made with Jack. He won't press charges, he won't . . . he won't say I lied. As long as I bring just Henry back. I can't take you back with me, baby."

Savannah stares at Alice's face, watching her mother's mouth crumple downward. She continues to stare until Alice presses her hands into the sides of her cheekbones, effectively shielding her face from view like the games of peek-a-boo that Savannah remembers her mother playing with Henry when he was a baby.

They are both silent for a long time. Savannah looks up at the swollen moon, hanging heavily in the sky. "Why did you marry him, anyway?"

Alice flutters the fingers of one hand, as if to stop further words, but Savannah persists. "I mean, I never understood it. Why did you decide to marry *him* and not someone else? I remember you had other boyfriends, I remember—"

"None who wanted to marry me." Alice's eyes are still closed. "No one wanted a single mom. At least not for keeps."

"But . . ."

Alice pushes her fingers into her hair, holds it off her forehead for a minute, giving Savannah time to note the smeared dye marks at the edge of her mother's hairline. "Savannah, I know you don't understand. But I was scared and I was alone—"

"You weren't alone. I was with you."

"That's my point. I was barely making any money. I was in debt. Don't you remember some nights we just didn't eat?" Alice's voice rises, cracks on the last word. She turns sideways on the bench, smoothing her skirt over her knees. "And I swear, I didn't know that it was going to be so . . . hard with you and Jack. I just thought that it would take a little time before you two got used to each other. But . . ." She lifts her hands from her lap, as if seeking words from the air between them. "By the time I realized it wasn't going to get much better, there was Henry to think about. And there's no way I could have made it with two kids if I couldn't make it with one on my own." She shrugs. "I guess I spent ten years looking for something . . . for someone who didn't exist. So I gave up."

Savannah feels as if the sky is spinning above her, that

she is the only still thing in the universe, and so she looks down, studies the shape of her sneakers against the porch floor. Next to her, Alice is crying.

And finally, Savannah knows that she has lost her mother. The person she adored for the first ten years of her life, the person who has been fading all along, has vanished. Savannah knows that, no matter how many times she closes her eyes and spins and spins and lets her finger land on the map, she won't be able to find Alice anymore.

And knowing this somehow enables Savannah to turn her head and promise softly, "I am never going to be like you."

"I know you won't." And Savannah feels Alice touch her shoulder so lightly, lighter than a dandelion puff.

eighteen

Savannah knows there is nothing she can say to her brother at this moment that will make any sense. So she leans down, puts her fingers behind Henry's earlobes and tickles them. This was the way she had first made him smile when he was a baby. But now he shrugs his shoulders, dislodging her hands. She lets her arms fall to her sides, and they regard each other as the car idles patiently behind them.

"Where will you be?" Henry asks finally.

Savannah shrugs. "I don't know. Here for a little while, I guess." She looks at Jane and Alice, who are standing a few yards away, their heads inclined toward each other.

"But how will I know what . . ." Henry's voice trails away, lost, as a motorcycle suddenly whips down the street before making a sharp right turn and vanishing.

"You have Jane's number, right?"

He nods, pats his front right jeans pocket.

"Listen," she says fiercely. "Memorize the number, okay?"

Henry gives her an inscrutable look. "I already did."

"Good. And I'll be calling you, too, okay?"

"Okay."

She pulls him to her for a minute. He wraps his arms around her waist, she bends down, her hair falling across his face. His body feels completely still and stiff as she lets go of him.

Henry climbs into the car, closing the door with a small, inconsequential *thud.* Savannah crosses her arms over her chest, hunches her shoulders. Dimly, she is aware that her mother is walking slowly away from Jane, crossing Savannah's field of vision. Then Alice is standing before her.

Savannah lets her mother press her forehead into hers, stands still as stone when her mother whispers, "I love you." Then Alice leans back. "Listen, I forgot to tell you last night. Since you're sleeping in my old room. Look under the windowsill."

And with that, she slips into the driver's seat of the station wagon and the sunlight falling across the windshield makes it impossible for Savannah to see her mother's face anymore.

She wonders if Alice will play *I Spy* with Henry all the way home. She wonders if they will make strawberry pies with truck-stop rolls and packets of jam. She wonders if Alice will sing out the billboard signs as they flash by on the highway. She wonders if Alice will stop anywhere, take a detour, and let Henry see something besides miles and miles of highway. She wonders if Alice has bought a new atlas and will ask Henry to navigate for her. She wonders if Henry will make any mistakes when map reading, like she, Savannah, often had, and if they will end up someplace far from where they expected to be, as she and Alice so often had.

The car pulls out of the driveway, sails down the empty street.

"Don't look back, Henry," Savannah murmurs, hoping he will anyway, her hand poised to wave the second he does.

Alice 1986

Alice drifts through the predawn kitchen and is almost at the door when she hears a soft stirring behind her. She leans her forehead against the doorframe, takes a breath, turns. Wearing a long cotton nightgown, her mother is sitting stiff-backed at her usual place at the kitchen table.

"Are you going to him? To that boy?"

"Noah," Alice murmurs. "His name is Noah. And he lives in Savannah. And I am going to find him."

"And how were you planning to get there?"

Alice pauses, confused at this tack, but sees no reason to lie now. "Hitch to the bus station. There's a bus that leaves at 5:30. The early bird bus, I think they call it." She tries to smile at her mother, who only nods thoughtfully.

"I'd say that's pretty early." She stands up, opens the drawer built into the kitchen table. There is a click of metal, then Alice's mother presses something into Alice's hand. The car keys. "I was going to give it to you anyway." She hesitates, tucks her now empty hand under the opposite elbow. "In the fall. After you had decided what you were going to do . . ." She waves her hand rapidly through the air. "About everything."

"Mom, I—"

"It's a good car. It's got another ten years in it. I just imagined you driving somewhere else in it." She sighs, runs her hands over the curved high wooden back of the chair, then glances at the framed portrait of her husband, hanging on the wall. "He was so proud of you. Thank God, your father isn't alive to see . . . all this."

Her mother is standing close enough now that Alice can breathe in the faint sweetness of her hair. Close enough to watch the lines in the older woman's face sag downward. "You would have broken his heart."

The radio speakers give a short blurt of music, then lose the signal, and the rushing blur of static fills up the small space. Keeping her right hand on the wheel, Alice eases her foot off the gas pedal, letting the car roll slowly toward the yellow *Yield* triangle that presides over the junction at the edge of town. She glances at the green-and-white sign to her left that broadcasts a cheerful *Welcome to Three Springs, Maine.* To her right, the road stretches and winds toward the still-distant lights of the highway. Since no one is behind her, since she is the only person awake enough to leave town at this time of night, she lets the car stop completely and leans her head back on the seat.

Alice takes a breath, feeling the seat belt press and give

against her stomach. It is too early to show, too early to even feel the first flutterings that she has read about in the musty dimness of the Main Street library. But she taps two fingers against her stomach, trying to simulate a baby's kick, trying to remind herself that she is not quite alone.

Applying a steady pressure to the gas pedal, Alice guides the car through the empty junction. The road to Three Springs smoothes away, the letters on the town sign dwindle into unrecognizable shapes, until at last, they are lost to her sight.

nineteen

In her mother's old bedroom, Savannah sleeps all afternoon. It is a sleep broken by frequent wakings and half-remembered images, but each time, she manages to close her eyes and drift again.

Later, after she has refused Jane's offer of dinner, of a cup of tea, Savannah sits on the edge of the rumpled bed in her mother's old room and runs her fingers along the windowsill. On her first attempt, she feels only the sweep of smooth painted wood. But on her second pass, she is rewarded with the discovery of small, gritty-feeling shapes in the left underside corner of the windowsill.

She lies on her side and cranes her neck upward, but has to switch on the large brass bedside lamp before she can make out letters. Slowly, she traces the first carved shape, a flamboyant *S*, its tail looping and curving back in on itself. She closes her eyes and lets her fingers spell out the rest of the letters of her name, written the way only Alice ever wrote it, with the consonants and vowels all leaning into each other as if being blown by a strong wind. After a time, she reaches for her bag at the foot of the bed, rifles through it until she finds her knife. She flicks it open, touches the point to the wood. She wraps her free hand around her other wrist so that the letters will be as steady as she can make them. When she is finished, she forces the blade closed, sets it down next to her, blows the finely curled peelings of paint off her hands.

"Savannah." Jane pokes her head around the half-open door, and Savannah jerks up halfway, pressing her knife into the mattress with her hip.

"Yeah?"

"You have a phone call. The phone is out in the hallway here." Her head bobs out of view.

Savannah frowns.

"It's a boy." Jane's voice floats back and there is an odd note in her aunt's voice that Savannah can't quite pin down. After a second, she decides it might be amusement.

Savannah stands up, nearly falls as one foot catches in the ruffles of the white spread. She recovers, moves toward the door. The hallway is empty except for a little yellow table. The phone sits on top of two soft-cover books. She listens for her great-aunt as she picks up the phone, carrying it as far as it will go. Just inside the bedroom, she feels the slight tension in the cord, so she sets the cradle down on the floor.

For one second, she closes her eyes, pretends that she is a normal girl who lives in this pretty white bedroom and that her only wish in the world is for a little privacy to talk on the phone.

"Hello?"

"Sav." It is Matt, and she opens her eyes.

"How did you get this number?"

"I have my ways." When she doesn't respond, he continues. "Look, I know you probably don't want to talk to me, maybe—"

"You're right."

"But I just wanted to call and see if everything was okay."

"I'm fine."

There is a small silence and she flexes her feet, tracing a swirled pattern in the quilt with one heel.

"Yeah? That's good. So you're in Maine, huh?"

"Holt told you."

"Yeah. He didn't want to, but . . . is your Mom coming there?"

"She came already."

"Is she gone?"

"Yeah. She's gone."

"And did she—"

"I don't want to talk about it, okay? How come you called?"

"Okay, okay. I called because I wanted to tell you about a plan of my own."

"That's typical of you." But she is listening.

"Finals are done in a couple of weeks, and this job I was supposed to have sort of fell through because, well, we don't need to get into all that right now—"

"You got fired."

"And I thought, hey, why not take a trip cross-country with my favorite friend who knows all about this kind of stuff? So, what do you think? Want to come along?"

"You and me? Where's Kurti this summer? Helping out needy children in China?"

"Ah, we're not doing the couple thing this summer."

"So you guys broke up."

"Yesterday."

She doesn't want to ask, but she does anyway. "Are you doing okay?"

"Yeah, I'm okay." His words are quick and sure and she knows that he is lying. "So, listen, talk to Holt for a minute, okay?"

"Holt? He's there?"

"Yeah, I'm at his place for now."

"Oh." She pictures Matt sleeping on the faded futon couch in the living room, playing video games with Jeremy all night while Kurti moves through their ordered apartment next door. There is a slight fumbling noise, muffled conversation, and then Holt's voice.

"Hi, Savannah. Are you okay?"

"Hi. Yes. I'm okay. You?" Her words pick up speed, she rearranges her legs under her.

He laughs a little. "I'm fine. So, what's Maine like?"

"Quiet."

"And your aunt? I mean great-aunt."

"She seems . . . really nice."

"Yeah? You thinking about staying?"

"Well . . ." But she doesn't know what she can hope for, so she says hurriedly, "So what's with this plan of Matt's?"

"Actually, it was my plan."

"Oh?"

"Yeah. Remember I told you I always wanted to see more of the country?"

"Yes, I remember since it was two days ago."

"So, anyway," Holt continues, although she can hear the grin in his voice. "Meeting you made me start thinking about it a lot these past few days. And Matt just kind of jumped in when he and Kurti—"

"Yeah, he said they broke up."

Holt lowers his voice. "She broke up with him."

"Oh."

"So, anyway, I think he kind of needs to get out of here, and I thought maybe if you're free?"

Savannah sits up, folds one leg under the other, puts her left hand on the windowsill. She presses the phone between her ear and shoulder, lets her fingers wander onto the fresh marks she has carved into the wood beside her name. Slowly, she lets her finger climb the point of the *A* before sliding over the *l* and the capped peak of the *i*, the double curves of the *c* and the *e*. Then she runs the tip of her finger over the letters that Alice carved so long ago, before coming to rest in the small but definite space between the end of her name and the start of her mother's.

She wonders if Alice was admiring the same evening shade of endless sky when she made her plans to leave this place.

about the author

Carolyn MacCullough says, "This story began with a single word. I was traveling through the city of Savannah when the idea for a character of the same name came to me. Why she was given that name swiftly wove itself into the plot. After that, it was a matter of listening to who she was: a determined survivor."

Carolyn MacCullough received her MFA in Creative Writing for Children from New School University in New York City. Her first book, *Falling Through Darkness*, praised as "a promising debut" *(The Horn Book)*, was a New York Public Library Best Book for the Teen Age.

Currently, she is enjoying something of the nomadic life herself as she wanders up and down the East Coast.

PRAISE FOR *SIMULATIONS AND THE FUTURE OF LEARNING* BY CLARK ALDRICH

"****" (out of four)—*Training Media Review*

". . . Riveting."—*Training & Development* magazine

"Two polygonal thumbs up."—Slashdot.net

"Advice to Chief Learning Officers: Read Simulations and the Future of Learning"—*CLO* magazine

"Subversive writing at its finest."—On The Horizon Special Issue. *Second Generation e-Learning: Serious Games, 12*(1), 14–17, 2004.

"If this is the future of learning, then I want to be there. Go, Aldrich!"—*Training* magazine

"Clark Aldrich . . . has written a book that will revolutionize e-learning in both education and industry."—*Human Resource Development Quarterly, 15*(2).

About This Book

Why is this topic important?

The interest in simulations at corporate, government, military, and academic levels has grown year over year. In part, this is because students are increasingly pragmatic, craving interaction and personalization, highly visual problem solvers, averse to reading, and computer-savvy. Meanwhile computer games, leveraging new technology, continue to set expectations and impact our culture and even skill sets. Finally, early examples of simulations are creating massive increases in the productivity of and knowledge transfer to students and employees.

Yet confusion over different types, in fact different genres, of simulations persists, dragging down effective short-term action and long-term strategies. Computer game advocates are both exciting us and muddying the conversation. This book provides critical differentiation between simulation types today and critical success factors for all simulations going into the future.

What can you achieve with this book?

This book, based on hundreds of new interviews with practitioners, as well as new analysis of best practices and trends, will help anyone better plan, manage, and execute simulation deliverables. This includes today's four proven models, as well as the emerging, more computer-game-like next generation simulations. It will also help strategists understand simulations in a greater context, build consensus among stakeholders, and understand where the field is going.

How is this book organized?

In Section One, Building and Buying the Right Simulations in Corporations and Higher Education Today, we will look at the computer-based simulations that are proven and established. If you are conservative and want something predictable, here is where you go. We will highlight their appropriate uses and defining components.

In Section Two, The Broader Opportunities of Simulations, we will discuss why these first models are not sufficient, either in capturing others' views of current simulations or in sufficiently providing an evolutionary foundation to next generation sims. We will formally examine three content types, linear, cyclical, and systems. And we will begin to tease apart the conflicting elements of simulations, games, and pedagogy.

Then we will look at other types of tangential simulations, including non-technology simulations at one extreme and computer games and military flight simulators at another.

In Section Three, Next Gen Sims, we will look at innovative simulations that are breaking new ground. We will look at role models that contain lessons learned that will become increasingly dominant in the decade to come and at some of the challenges these models have highlighted and overcome.

In Section Four, Managing the Simulation Process, we will look at the planning and implementations of all different types of sims in the real world. This includes the identification and balancing of simulation, game, and pedagogical elements, as well as their deployment and measurement. To paraphrase an old programming axiom, the creation of the core of the simulation takes the first 90 percent of the project. Building sufficient support material takes the other 90 percent.

Finally, in the Appendices, we will shoot the breeze about what the impact of the Next Gen Sims could have on all of education.

LEARNING BY DOING

A Comprehensive Guide to Simulations, Computer Games, and Pedagogy in e-Learning and Other Educational Experiences

Clark Aldrich

Pfeiffer
A Wiley Imprint
www.pfeiffer.com

Published by Pfeiffer
An Imprint of Wiley
989 Market Street, San Francisco, CA 94103-1741
www.pfeiffer.com

For additional copies/bulk purchases of this book in the U.S. please contact 800-274-4434.

Pfeiffer books and products are available through most bookstores. To contact Pfeiffer directly call our Customer Care Department within the U.S. at 800-274-4434, outside the U.S. at 317-572-3985, fax 317-572-4002, or visit www.pfeiffer.com.

Pfeiffer also publishes its books in a variety of electronic formats. Some content that appears in print may not be available in electronic books.
ISBN 10: 0-7879-7735-7
ISBN 13: 978-07879-9735-1

Library of Congress Cataloging-in-Publication Data

Aldrich, Clark
Learning by doing : the essential guide to simulations, computer games, and pedagogy in e-learning and other educational experiences / by Clark Aldrich.
p. cm.
Includes bibliographical references and index.
ISBN 0-7879-7735-7 (alk. paper)
1. Education—Simulation methods. 2. Computer-assisted instruction. 3. Computer games. I. Title.
LB1029.S53A42 2005
371.39'7—dc22 2005002491

Acquiring Editor: Lisa Shannon
Director of Development: Kathleen Dolan Davies
Production Editor: Dawn Kilgore
Editor: Rebecca Taff
Manufacturing Supervisor: Becky Carreño
Editorial Assistant: Laura Reizman

Printed in the United States of America
Printing 10 9 8 7 6 5 4

CONTENTS

LIST OF FIGURES AND TABLES

To Slater and Lisa

ACKNOWLEDGMENTS

THE BOOK WOULD have been much less interesting, and perhaps not possible, without the contributions of Darius Clarke, John Curran, Bill Ellet, Gloria Gery, Abhas Kumar, Peg Maddocks, Lyn McCall, Andy Snider, and The Serious Games Community.

PREFACE

FIVE BLIND PEOPLE were walking down a path. They stumbled upon something that none of them had ever experienced before, an educational simulation. They each tried to describe it to the others.

"It is a class. People sit down and learn important ideas," said the first.

"I don't think so." said the second. "It's a computer game. It moves quickly, it involves a mouse, and requires my complete attention."

"No," said the third, "It can be used with a class, but it's more like a book. It can be sold anywhere in the world. It is scalable—hundreds of thousands can engage it at the same time."

"What are you talking about?" asked the fourth. "It is like a pill. It is a compact package of intellectual property that improves quality of life."

"I beg to differ," said the fifth. "It is more like a gym. It requires the users to work hard and sweat and put in hours to tone themselves."

Tragically, a consensus was never reached. At just that moment, an elephant came running down the path, trampling them all.

'SPLAINING SIMULATIONS

I spent over two years leading a team determined to build a concept car of simulation-based education. That journey resulted in SimuLearn's *Virtual Leader,* which was honored in 2004 with the award of Best Online Product of the Year by *Training Media Review* and *Training & Development* magazine. And the inward journey of the development of the simulation was the centerpiece of the book, *Simulations and the Future of Learning* (Pfeiffer, 2004).

After that, I came out of my self-imposed exile and re-engaged the outside world. Part of that engagement was exposing *Virtual Leader* to others. More importantly, part of that was trying to help in the creation and success of other educational simulation-based initiatives.

This second part was harder than it sounds. I found a lot of frustration on the part of enterprises looking at using simulations in their curricula. Case studies were simply not comparable with each other. Advocates used overly fuzzy, academic, and optimistic terms. e-Learning "gurus," like eight-year-olds, were demanding attention without actually saying anything. Conversations between different people from different parts of an organization, or the dreaded research communities, almost inevitably seized up and became intractable.

I directly worked on a few dozen simulation projects. I consulted for about a hundred others. I also talked to thousands of designers and implementers, customers and associates. (I could rely on very few second-hand sources for help with client projects, or for this book. Most of the quotes here have been taken from one-on-one interviews.)

I realized that most people had very different and often conflicting views of educational simulations. Often, what seemed like one conversation about simulations was actually fragments of dozens of different ones.

The vendor community was partially to blame. They also had similar confusions, but that did not stop them from blaring out half-truths and hyperboles like, "learning by doing," "a safe environment to practice skills," or "a flight simulator for business skills."

There was a lot of frustration.

And yet. . . .

And yet something wonderful was happening.

There were some great, and historically important, educational simulation models being implemented. There was incredible value being delivered. People were learning in different ways than ten, even five years ago. And these new ways were working.

Mostly in isolation, and mostly misunderstood in a greater context, but designers were building *structures to significantly augment education.*

This book is a summary of what I have learned. Where *Simulations and the Future of Learning* was a map of a small town, complete with sewers and brothels, *Learning by Doing* is an atlas of the world (and maybe the moon). Where *Simulations and the Future of Learning* focused in on the almost completely misunderstood *deep simulation* aspect of an educational experience, *Learning by Doing* looks at both more accessible simulation models and the *game* and *pedagogical* elements of all simulations (Figure F.1).

One request from my clients is *to understand the tapestry of simulations available today, to understand when, where, and why they make sense.* That is here. Short-term planners and implementers of simulations will be more confident and capable and can avoid costly mistakes by reading this book.

A second goal is to *understand next generation educational simulations.* Many increasingly want to know what kinds of educational content should, can, and will be created within our planning horizon.

Figure P.1. Ideas (Mine and Others) in This Book.

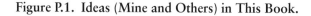

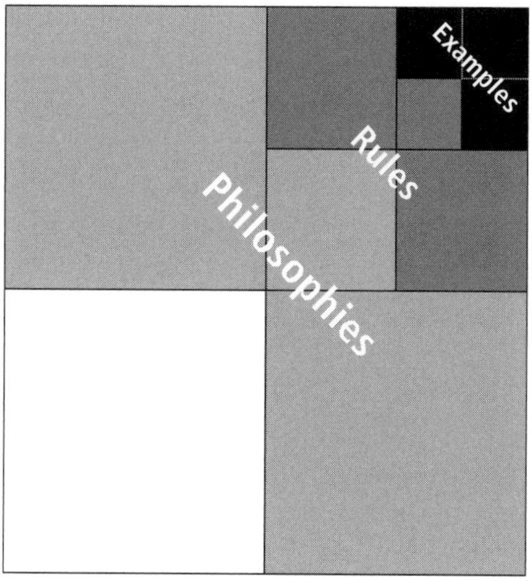

That is especially exciting. This field is wide open, ready to be influenced. At least a handful of people reading this book will, through their work, define the future of learning, just as absolutely as Shakespeare defined drama, Eastman defined photography, the Beatles defined modern music, Ford defined automobiles, Hitchcock defined modern cinema, and Beethoven defined, well, Beethoven.

Regardless of your interest, commitment, or resources, however, everyone who is involved in education will get something from this book. Because even if you never plan to use, build, or procure a simulation, the techniques here will improve *any* educational experience or program.

We are at a time in the history of education when everything can change. Our minds can be as well-developed and nurtured as our bodies. Productivity and the corresponding standards of living can be raised to the next level. The work of a few people will echo through the ages, changing the very wealth of nations.

It won't be easy. And the bumps in the road ahead are, ah, nontrivial. But it will happen. And the perspectives in this book, mine and mostly others, will help.

CLARK ALDRICH
February 2005

INTRODUCTION I

THE CHALLENGE—A CONVERSATION WITH THREE GAME GURUS

There may be a shift in the skills valued by an organization that computer games, more than classes, develop and reward.

—John Seely Brown

STUDENTS ARE CHANGING.

They are increasingly pragmatic. They crave interaction and personalization. They are highly visual. They are problem solvers. Often they are averse to reading. They want more material in less time. And, hardly worth mentioning anymore, they are very computer-savvy.

So it is worth talking to some of the people who helped them get that way. I met with computer game designers *Jane Boston* from Lucas Learning Ltd., *Warren Spector* from Ion Storm, and *Will Wright* from Maxis. What follows is what they said about educational simulations. And their words and ideas introduce a series of challenges that will be addressed in the pages, and years, to come.

CLARK: What is best taught through simulations?

JANE: From my perspective, simulations are best used in four ways. First, they are ideal for developing an understanding of *big ideas and concepts*—those things for which experience alone can deepen understanding. It is one thing to memorize a definition of nationalism or to read a passage describing the brittleness an ecosystem; it is quite another to enter into an environment where those ideas play themselves out based on your own actions and ability to identify and solve problems.

Second, I believe simulations are great for dealing with time and scale. The computer gives us an opportunity to speed up results of an action that might actually take several lifetimes to play out. This allows players to see the potential impact of decisions made now on the future.

Third, I think simulations are good for situations where it is important to give people *practice in decision making before it is faced in a dangerous or critical, real-life situation.* Some of the simulations used for emergency personnel provide an opportunity to experience "life-like" situations and react to unexpected and challenging problems.

Finally, simulations are wonderful resources for taking us to a time or place that we are unable or unlikely to experience directly.

CLARK: What are the elements that make a simulation immersive?

WARREN: What you want to do is create a game that's built on a set of consistently applied rules that players can then exploit however they want. Communicate those rules to players in subtle ways. Feed back the results of player choices so they can make intelligent decisions moving forward based on earlier experience.

In other words, rather than crafting single-solution puzzles, create rules that describe how objects interact with one another (for example, water puts out fire, or a wooden box dropped from sufficient height breaks into pieces and causes damage based on its mass to anything it hits) and turn players loose—you want to simulate a world rather than emulate specific experiences.

WILL: The more creative the players can be, the more they like the simulation. This might be giving them a lot of latitude. People like to explore the outer boundaries. There is nothing more satisfying than solving a problem in a unique way.

Another derivative: being able to describe yourself to the game, and the game builds around you. It also helps if a player can build a mental model of what it going on in the simulation. This has more to do with the interface. Most of my games use an obvious metaphor and a non-obvious metaphor. They think *SimCity*™ is a train set, but they come to realize it is more like gardening. Things sprout up and you have to weed.

CLARK: Can games change the behavior of players outside the game?

JANE: I've facilitated simulations in which some participants exhibited extreme forms of emotion and carried feelings from a simulation into their relationships with others for months, even years, later.

I believe the transferability of game-learned experiences can be maximized by being clear about the purpose of the simulation before using it and by thinking of it as one tool in an overall learning experience. Setting an appropriate context with the players in advance is important, as is making sure that the players understand the rules and roles. In some simulations, guided practice may be needed before starting the actual game.

From my perspective, the most critical elements of a simulation come after the game itself. Debriefing what has happened—what a player experienced, felt during the simulation, and is feeling afterward; what strategies were tried and what happened; what other strategies might have been applied; what else the player needed to know or be able to do; analogies to real-life situations; how the players' own values and experiences influenced their actions—are all important items for discussion.

CLARK: How accurate does a simulation have to be to be a valid teaching tool?

WILL: In most interesting fields, like weather modeling, predictive simulations are very difficult or impossible. However, the property of weather being unpredictable can be a property of a good descriptive simulation.

Say you put the ball on the tip of a cone and let it go. A perfect predictive simulator would tell you exactly which side of the cone the ball would fall on for the exact condition set up. A descriptive simulator, like *SimCity*™, would probably use a random variable to decide down which side the ball would fall. While that simulation would fail at being predictive, it would teach both the range of possibilities (that is, the ball never falls up), and also, from a planning perspective, it teaches that you can't rely on predicting the exact outcome and how to deal with the randomness.

I have seen a lot of people get misled. I see a lot of simulations that are very good descriptive (like *SimCity*™), but a lot of people use them predictive (like a weather model).

CLARK: What makes a simulation rewarding?

WILL: In *SimCity*™, you can go for happiest people, or biggest city. Give them strategic decisions. Give the people maximum creativity.

There is never one way. One way kills creativity. New ways of solving problems drives people in wanting to share experiences.

The photo albums in *The Sims*™ are also important. We have to create new ways for users to share. Getting people to engage other people with what they learned is critical. If you can get people to talk, it creates a snowball effect. You have to create glue. The community becomes the effective tool for learning.

For the complete interview with these people, head on over to Appendix 8.

COMING UP NEXT

Is the time right for educational simulations? Yes, and no. And yes again.

INTRODUCTION 2

TECHNOLOGY AND SIMULATIONS: WHY TIMING MATTERS

TECHNOLOGY—A DOUBLE-EDGED SWORD

Technology is about more than technology. It is about experience, expectations, value, even delivery models. Discussing any technology in mid-evolution, as we will do with educational simulations, requires comfort with the patterns of technology.

Some of us remember the advent of a typical example of new technology: microwave ovens. These were oversold, not well understood, and too effective at capturing the imagination of consumers and futurists. We were told of a day when Christmas dinner could be cooked in less than five minutes.

We collectively got over first our rapture around this technology, and then our subsequent frustration. We shared stories and samples. Cooking magazines evolved; pre-packaged food evolved. We grew our understanding, and we now are closer to using microwave ovens for when they actually are the best solution.

Microwave ovens, like most new technology, turned out to be only a partial solution. They were three steps forward, two steps back from conventional ovens.

THE ROCKY ROAD OF TECHNOLOGY

Most technologies go through this volatile yet predictable six-step process. (It would go a bit smoother if each started the process with the admission that, "my name is . . . , and, I am an emerging technology.") They are conceived as *theory,* are created by *innovators,* become seen as *magic bullets,* fail causing mass *confusion,* become reinvented to become a *strategic advantage,* and then mature into *infrastructure.* Understanding the risks and opportunities in each stage is critical to almost any successful use of technology, and *Learning by Doing* initiatives are no exception.

Theory: Wouldn't It Be Great?

New ideas first tend to bubble up in academic papers, magazine columns, web logs, or conference panels. Those who introduce the emergent idea are *very detailed* in critique of the last generation, *very vague* in their descriptions of what the actual solution would look like, and *very enthusiastic* about the promises of what the technology will accomplish.

A lot of history analogies are brought in (we all get to learn about Dutch shipping patterns or the advent of the abacus), as well as out-of-context quotes. There is often some graph of how large *something* is (dot-com companies loved showing how fast Internet access was growing as a justification for their own business model), no matter how indirectly related. The technology tends to be described in a pure environment, one without legacy systems.

As far as the theory goes, it sounds good. And almost all who hear this new theory nod and think, "This makes a lot of sense. This could be big." But there are *no* examples of it working the way it is described. At best there are precursors that are "sort of" similar. Or a wild success in a different industry is held up as a model.

For example, "Schools and classes are so bad that computer games, popular entertainment with deep, inherent learning, will provide a much better model for formal education." Theorists would defend this claim by focusing on examples of bad classes and on the success of the computer game market.

Maybe instead of ideas in the "theory" stage, we could call them wide-ranging hypotheses, organized pre-proof, established by reason. That would be WHOPPERs for short.

Having written academic papers, magazine columns, and web logs, and been on plenty of conference panels, I have spouted my fair share of WHOPPERs. And so keeping in character, this book will end with some unsubstantiated but very exciting visions of the future. To foreshadow my argument, I will suggest that simulations will do no less than break down the artificial barriers between *what we learn and what we do,* between *learning in business and learning in academics,* and between *understanding history and controlling our future.* I'm serious.

Innovator: Imagine This Were Everywhere!

Then comes the innovator stage. Somewhere a few teams, independently, pour blood, sweat, and tears into the theory to make it work. They blow through evenings and weekends, do not accept defeat, and beat the odds, building a model of the new technology roughly as described, and either used internally or sold externally. They create real value.

We will read later on in this book about some examples of next generation simulation efforts that fall into this category. They include *Virtual University, First Flight,* and *Full Spectrum Warrior*™.

Examples of innovation *can* be ugly if judged by the limited and focused standards of the previous generation (the early Palm Pilots® had black and white screens when all PCs had color). There is often something not quite right about them, like an actor after bad plastic surgery.

There are strongly mixed reactions about the new technology. Some end users like it (and some love it), but professionals who built a lifetime of skills around the old technology are very suspicious, often undermining it. Even the advocates admit the technology often has to be cajoled into working.

The old guard (who, in all fairness, tend to be judged by us on running a smooth, cost-effective, ubiquitous infrastructure rather then on creating value) balks at its price, its unfair distribution (some members of a community will have it and some will not), and unpredictability.

The good news is that the people who pulled off the miracle now have the opportunity to become gurus. They are pushed to the front of conferences, given book deals and higher organizational authority, even the ability to funnel large amounts of cash into new projects through venture organizations. When they travel, they stay in places like The Bellagio or Amangani, rather than Embassy Suites.

Magic Bullet: Look! A Paradigm Shift

The technology is then widely perceived as a magic bullet. Many organizations form committees to figure out how to procure and implement it. We apply high-profile resources, expecting fast-tracked results. The technology becomes a solution looking for a problem. The amount of money each company spends in this area spikes.

Vendors and consultants, lured by the open purse strings, stoke the excitement, widely advertising the vision (rather than the reality) of what can be done. They talk in strong, confident tones. Each has one or two case studies of pilots, relentlessly milked.

Naysayers, even if they are later vindicated, are viewed as obstructionists. They are told that they "don't get it." This is as true of honest vendors and magazines as of internal experts. Many suffer permanent wounds to their reputations.

This was where e-learning was in the year 2000, and computer games (witness Atari and Coleco) were in 1980. The industries around the magic bullet technology are perceived as an endless opportunity to create (and reap the rewards) of a new type of value.

Confusion: Why Did We Think This Would Work?

In the traditional technology adoption curve model shown in Figure I.1, there is a smooth ramp-up of demand. Feng-shui-like, the graph seems very soothing, capturing the optimism of the early computer pioneers.

Venture capitalist and author Geoffrey Moore introduced a chasm to the model (Figure I.1). He noted that there is a break between the *early adopters* (a kinder term than *geeks*) and everyone else that must be successfully navigated.

Despite these nice models, Gartner Group's observation is more useful: often, the technology just crashes. At some point after the initial excitement, finding new successes becomes quite difficult. Even some of the early examples of success no longer seem quite so successful. Failures start building up, first privately, and then in the press.

Figure I.1. A Traditionally Modeled Technology Adoption Curve.

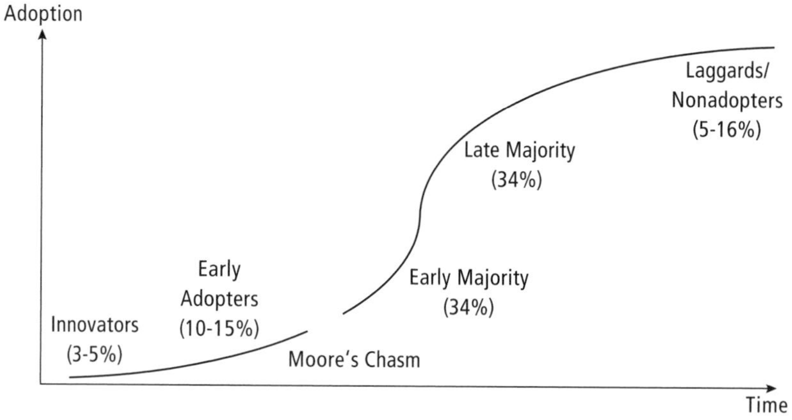

Invariably, people just did not realize how hard it was to pull it off. What seemed easy and obvious is in fact quite daunting. Staffers just could not replicate the success of the revolutionaries who were willing to do whatever it takes.

Or else the technology was high on novelty and low on functionality. And when everyone started doing it, nobody cared anymore.

In the same way that markets overreact to financial news, enterprises overreact to technology trends. Those responsible for the investments either wisely moved on to a new position or were caught in the downdraft. There is a collective "What were we thinking?" Even saying the name of the technology becomes highly distasteful, like having to recount the details of an ill-fated fling.

One current example of an idea in disrepute in "school reform." Most people believe that education reform is simply impossible.

Strategic Advantage: Here Is the Business Case and ROI

The story should end here. The technology should just die. But then something happens. Just what is hard to say. But somehow, like a made-for-TV movie or a favorite sports team in the ninth inning, the technology comes back from the dead.

Groups from all over, independent of one another, recommit to the original, but modified, vision. No longer naïve, they are both buoyed and sobered by the amount of real industry knowledge that now exists.

By changing a few of the premises, often incorporating emerging technologies from other areas, they make it work. These new groups are pragmatic. They sacrifice some of the artistic and philosophical purity, even some of the quality, distancing themselves from the first batch, to make it work in a way that is repeatable, scalable, and predictable.

Now the technology has significant value with minimal risk. More importantly, the value is differentiating because competitors and magazines have often given up on it.

When a technology enters the strategic advantage stage, this is when even conservative business leaders should jump on the ship. There is resistance because of the past, but the payoff is significant. Successful implementers should at least expect a promotion, although not industry acclaim. They have bought their organization some time (anywhere between six months and many years) of competitive advantage. Successful vendors generate family money.

Quite a few early simulation models have matured nicely and are just becoming well-understood and garnering predictable results. We will start this book by discussing examples that fall into this marvelous combination of being relevant, predictable, and cost-effective. Analysts, as I will do here, can finally talk about rules and processes, not just isolated case studies.

Infrastructure: Turn It On, Would You?

Finally, the technology evolves into being part of the infrastructure. It is no longer differentiating; everyone has it. Competitors flood in. Brute force and scale, be it marketing or technology implementations, wins over elegance. The price for the technology plummets, often bankrupting the organizations that championed it and are publicly identified with it, as they built a cost structure around a consulting model, not a commodity. The *half-as-good solution for a quarter-as-much price* wins. Designers and early advocates stop caring.

No one will get promoted for implementing technology at this point. But they very well might get fired for *not* implementing it.

There are some e-learning examples here, although no simulations. I recently helped in a merger where the training managers from the smaller company gained control of the joined group because they had experience in using new technologies. The managers from the larger organization (but with the more traditional experience) were asked to leave.

Where there is money to be made outside of a few monolithic vendors, it tends to be at the *people services* side of highly leveraging the technology.

A Brutal Path

As brutal as this path is, not all technologies even have the opportunity to traverse it. Some technologies, including knowledge management and artificial intelligence, never seem to get past the confusion stage. Spinoffs succeed, but the discipline constantly goes back to theory where every leap year it is reinvented and relaunched.

An Inevitable Path

Does it have to be this rough? Does innovation have to come at such a steep personal and business cost? Mostly, the answer is "yes." The best tool for smoothing out the road, at least a little bit, is good reporting and analysis. When magazine reporters do their homework, when analysts deflate the false expectations, when authors avoid hyperbole like "the future of learning" in their titles, the process is smoother. But it may not be in any of their best interests to do that.

BOOK SECTIONS

This book will increase your ability to develop a productive educational simulation strategy across the entire rocky road of technology. It is focused on helping you meet both short-term and long-term needs. You will understand what the different types of simulations are, what the appropriate use is of each, and how to plan their development. It will also help you *improve* any content by modifying the appropriate simulation, game, and pedagogical elements.

To accomplish this, *Learning by Doing* is divided into four sections.

In Section One, Building and Buying the Right Simulation in Corporations and Higher Education Today, we will look at computer based simulations that are proven and established (Figure I.2). These are the simulations that are at the strategic advantage stage.

If you are conservative and want something predictable or if you actually want to eat and pay your mortgage, here is where you go. We will highlight their appropriate uses and defining components. If you want to think about the glorious, gleaming potential of simulations, rather than the dirty reality, skip this section at all costs! Go straight to Section Two. But return to it at some point. The information will still be surprisingly helpful for any development project.

In Section Two, The Broader Opportunities of Simulations, we will discuss why these first models are not sufficient, either in capturing

Figure I.2. The Four Traditional Corporate and Higher-Ed Simulation Genres.

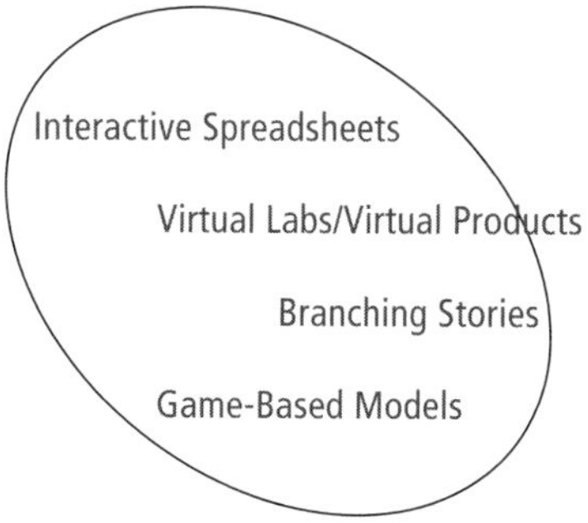

others' views of current simulations or in sufficiently providing an evolutionary foundation to next generation sims. We will formally examine three *content* types, *linear, cyclical,* and *systems*. And we will begin to tease apart the *three elements*: *simulations, games,* and *pedagogy.*

Then we will look at other types of tangential simulations, including non-technology role plays at one extreme and computer games and military flight simulators at another (Figure I.3), that are all driving the expectations and providing critical, if incomplete, models. We will also dig more formally into the concept of *genres* and think why, for a simulation, they are as important as subject matter for teaching anything.

In Section Three, Next Gen Sims, we will look at innovative simulations that are breaking new ground. We will look at these potential role models, including some of the challenges these models have highlighted and, in some cases, overcome.

In Section Four, Managing the Simulation Process, we will look at the implementations of all different types of sims in the real world. This includes the identification and balancing of simulation, game, and pedagogical elements, as well as their deployment and measurement. To paraphrase an old programming axiom, the creation of the core of the simulation takes the first 90 percent of the project. Building sufficient support material takes the other 90 percent.

Finally, in the conclusion, we will discuss what the impact of the Next Gen Sims will have on all of education.

Figure I.3. The Many Facets of Educational Simulation, with the Traditional Corporate and Higher-Ed Genres in the Middle Circle.

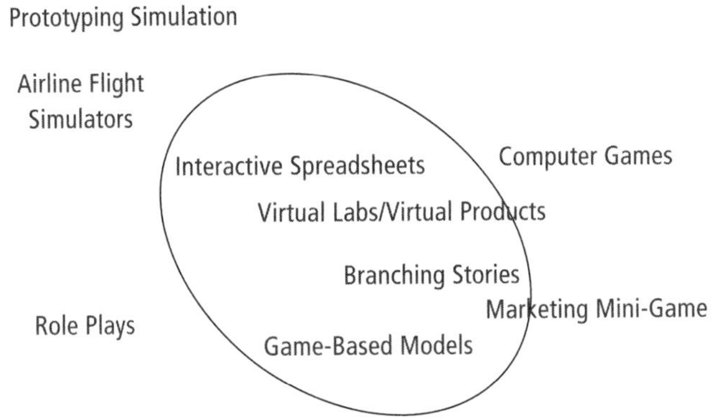

WHY A BOOK?

Anyone who talks about simulations and interactivity in general has a bit of a problem when it comes to books. If simulations are the way to learn, why should I write this book and, much more importantly, why should you read it? Books are background, what we will later call "slate one content." It is not enough for you to achieve your goal by just reading this. But like a good lecture series, it is critical background, a comprehensive set-up that will prepare you to move forward quickly and with minimum false paths.

COMING UP NEXT

Simulations are impossibly complex and expensive, right? Not necessarily. Here are four types of simulations that are relatively easy to build, will get great results, and not break the bank. You've probably used several of them yourself.

SECTION ONE

BUILDING AND BUYING THE RIGHT SIMULATION IN CORPORATIONS AND HIGHER EDUCATION TODAY

1

FOUR TRADITIONAL SIMULATION GENRES

As anyone who's been to a "corporate training" conference can attest, that industry is a festering sty of bad design and shovelware, procured by pinheaded HR bureaucrats and produced by the lowest bidder. It makes the K-12 educational multimedia sector look like a hotbed of cutting-edge innovation.

—J. C. Hertz, author of *Joystick Nation*

PEOPLE ARE *TALKING* A LOT about simulations. There are thousands of teams, task forces, dissertation committees, and ad hoc groups going on *right now* discussing simulations.

Over the last two years, I feel like I have addressed them all. The conversations range, from

- Extolling video games to
- Passing around vendor brochures about "learning by doing" to
- Recounting people-based role plays or early computer simulations from decades ago that have stuck with the participants

Take my word; we will need *all* of these perspectives before this journey is over.

THE FOUR TRADITIONAL SIMULATION GENRES

But let's start with where the early action is. Across corporations and universities, *four* different genres of computer-based simulations (Figure 1.1) cover most of what organizations are *actually implementing today.*

These *were* all innovative, groundbreaking, unpredictable approaches *five or ten (or even twenty) years ago.* And they have all evolved into safe, recommended, stable genres today.

That does not mean that vendors or implementers are using my labels. In fact, many champions will fight these descriptions as not capturing the beauty, the majesty, and the "simulation-ness" of their approaches. These labels are a bit more sober, a little less "magic bullet-esque" and I hope more useful.

Branching Stories

In *branching stories,* students make multiple-choice decisions along an ongoing sequence of events around what to say to another person in a given situation. The decisions impact the evolution of the story, ultimately terminating in either successful or unsuccessful outcomes.

Their ease of use, ease of deployment, and content style make them highly appropriate for entry-level salespeople, call center representatives, freshmen, customer-facing retail positions, and entry-level managers. *Any* high-turnover position should be trained, although not exclusively, using branching stories.

Figure 1.1. The Four Traditional Simulation Genres.

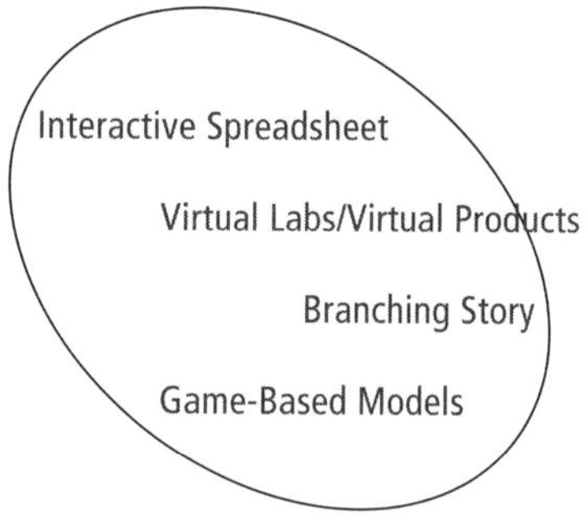

Interactive Spreadsheets

Interactive spreadsheets focus on abstract business school issues such as supply chain management, product lifecycle, accounting, and general cross-functional business acumen. Students allocate finite resources along competing categories at successive turn-based fixed intervals, and each time they watch their results play out on dense graphs and charts. This is often done in a multi-player or team-based environment and often with facilitators.

The subtlety, unpredictability, and variability make them appropriate for training b-school students and high-potential supervisors through the direct reports to the CEO. They are often the cornerstones of multi-day programs to align a fractured department or organization by building shared knowledge and understanding.

Game-Based Models

With the goal of "making learning fun," students engage familiar and entertaining games such as *Wheel of Fortune®*, solitaire, or memory, with important pieces of linear or task-based content replacing trivia or icons. More diagnostic than instructional, game-based models nonetheless might be the technique of choice by traditional educators and training groups looking to quickly goose their reputation, student satisfaction, and even effectiveness. Game-based models also introduce, in the purest possible way, game elements that all educational simulation designers will need to understand in the near future.

Virtual Labs/Virtual Products

Virtual products and virtual labs focus on equipment, as straightforward as a camera, as complicated as a human body, or as immersive as a smoking car pulling into a dealership.

With *virtual products,* students interact with visual, selectively accurate representations of actual products without the physical restrictions of the reality. The interface aligns with the real function of the objects represented. Clicking the graphical "on" switch results in the lights turning on.

Virtual labs forsake some of the fidelity of virtual products. They focus instead on the situation where the product is being used.

The rigorousness, kinesthetic properties, and ease of deployment make virtual products and virtual labs perfect for a range of tasks, from giving a potential customer or salesperson a feel for a product, to a lab, to an all-out, no-kidding, verifiable, comprehensive hardware certification program.

THE RIGHT ONE

Each of the four traditional simulation genres is a valid, important model of educational content. Each works.

But they are very different, with often opposite strengths and weaknesses, and therefore have different roles. They are far from interchangeable. Expecting one, and getting another, can cripple a learning program.

I can say at least two things about all four of these genres:

1. Almost any given teaching program would benefit from using *at least one* of the four genres described. I have not seen any exceptions.
2. Any organization with a significant internal or external teaching capacity *should be using all four frequently* and easily. If they do not, they simply no longer have a significant internal or external teaching capacity.

Finally, let me issue a perspective. These models, while surprisingly flexible and often remarkably subtle, are simple compared to what we will later discuss.

Again, if you want to think about the potential of simulations, rather than the dirty reality, skip this section and go straight to Section Two. But c'mon back. The most impressive next generation educational simulations will use techniques from these four traditional simulation genres. Knowing them, appreciating their appropriate use, is essential background for everyone who wants to shape the future.

Let's explore the four genres in depth.

COMING UP NEXT

What children's book series has inspired easy and accessible simulations, perfect for entry-level employees all over the world? And might people be the easiest thing to simulate?

2

CONTROLLING PEOPLE WITH BRANCHING STORIES

Three roads diverged in the forest, and I—I took the one best calculated to give me a successful outcome. That made all the difference.

—With apologies to Robert Frost

I SPENT MANY HOURS BETWEEN the end of classes and the beginning of sports in pre-computer game bliss when I was younger with the *Choose Your Own Adventure*® books. I read all I could find both at the Fenn school library and the public library in my hometown of Concord, Massachusetts.

The plots were that of grade-C movies, but the fun part was that you were involved actively in the story. I remember situations like this:

> A large strange man with a scar approaches you menacingly. Do you:
>
> (A) Run into the nearby culvert? (turn to page 19)
>
> (B) Throw a rock at him? (turn to page 139)

The books had dozens of endings, some short, some long, a few happy, most grim. I became good at "gaming" the books. I could tell, for example, by the page number links which option had the brightest future (hint: page 139 in option B doesn't look good—the back of the book had most of the ending scenarios).

The first genre of popular simulations could be called, "*Choose Your Own Adventure*®" simulations, but let's refer to them as *branching stories.* The student engages a highly defined scenario where, at defined intervals, he or she makes multiple-choice decisions that branch the story down different paths.

Branching Story Example

A typical decision in a story-based sales simulation might be

> You are now sitting in front of a direct report to the key decision maker. What do you say?
> (A) Is your boss available? I really need to talk with her.
> (B) What do you think of our proposal?
> (C) Do you have any suggestions for me?

Then students choose and immediately see the results of their actions in a video or text-based response. The direct report might smile, shoot you down with a sarcastic quip, or ask you for a job. For the sake of visualization, let's draw that example (Figure 2.1).

Figure 2.1. A Visualization of the Structure of the Branching Story Example (or an X-Ray of a Duck's Foot).

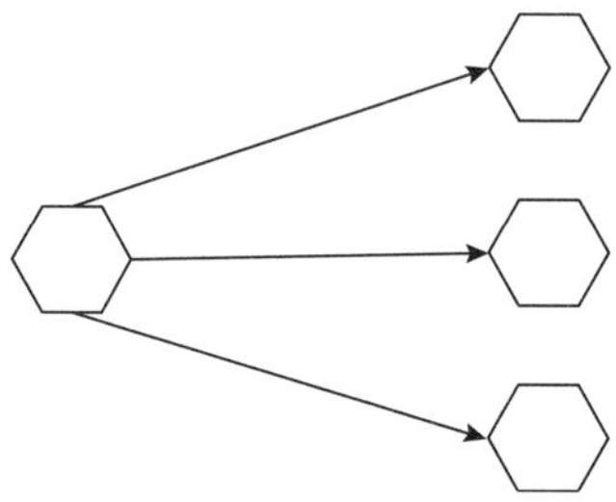

MODELS

A Perfect Tree

Then comes another multiple-choice decision point, and another result.

Theoretically, a branching story (or a *Choose Your Own Adventure*® book, I suppose) could provide multiple distinct paths from each state, creating a very diverse experience. Here is a model of that "perfect" structure would look like (Figure 2.2).

Figure 2.2. A Pure Branching Story Model.

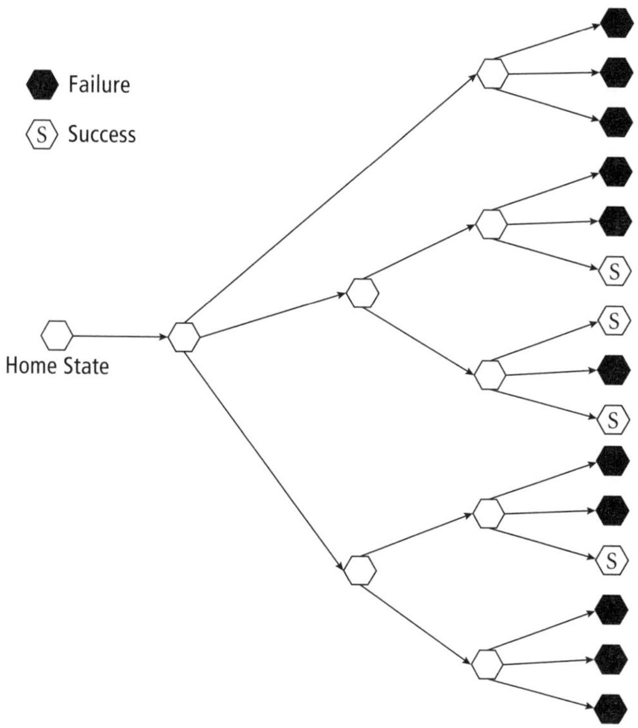

The problem is that either the simulation would be very short (only three or four decisions), or the tree would be very, very large. A second problem might be that any two users would have too different an experience. It is all nice and well to talk about customization and "you are in control," but at some point the experience can become almost too divergent from other learners' experiences, especially if there is a specific teaching objective. Students can actually feel cheated if there are too many dramatic moments that they missed altogether.

A More Common Model

Therefore, for numerous practical reasons, most branching stories are not quite as open-ended. They have more economical structure (Figure 2.3).

"Coaching"

There is one other defining characteristic of branching stories. Most share a property that other simulations envy: *The simulation knows exactly where the student is on the tree.* That means that if a student asks for "help" at any moment during the experience, he or she can get a specific, targeted, appropriate response (Figure 2.4 and Figure 2.5).

Figure 2.3. A More Common Branching Story Model.

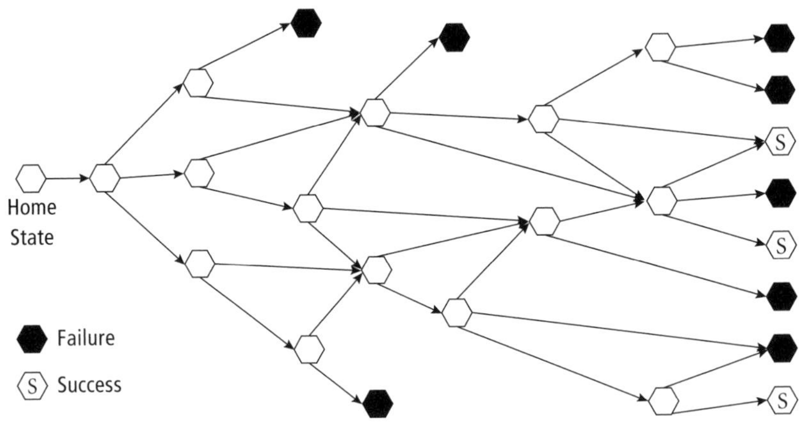

Figure 2.4. The Right Advice at the Right Time.

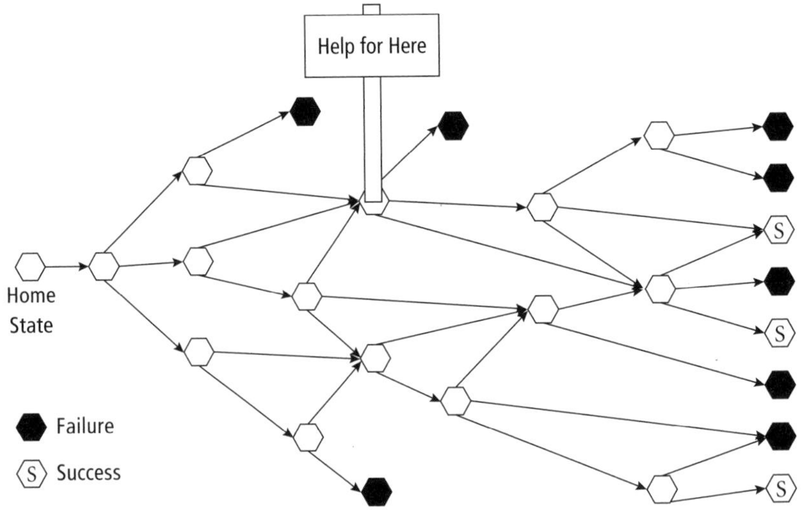

Figure 2.5. A Retail Moment from a Branching Story Simulation.

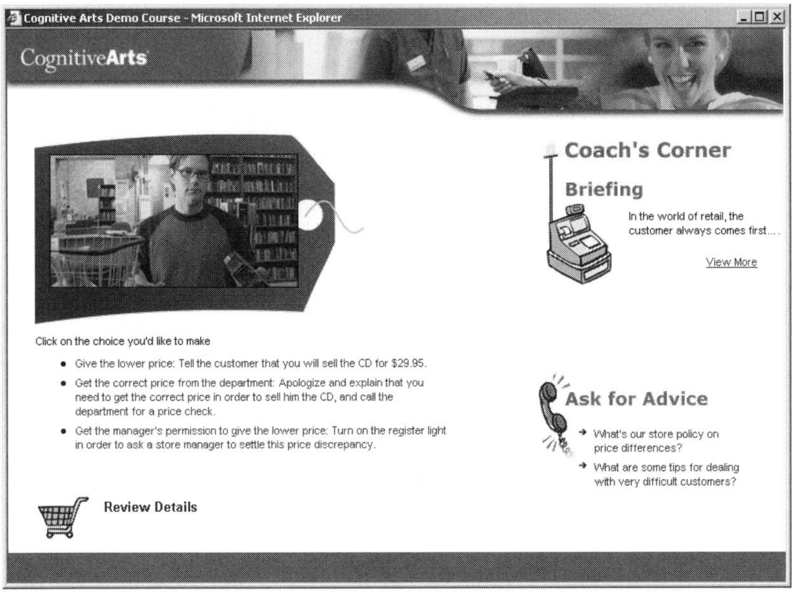

Source: Screen Shot Reprinted by Permission from CognitiveArts, a Division of NIIT.

(Vendors love using the word "coach" to describe this feature. They want to summon the image of a life enhancement specialist from Tucson's Canyon Ranch Spa. The reality is closer to a helpful toll collector.)

Still, some trees even have multiple help files for the same spot, determined by the level of difficulty selected. And when learners reach a final success or failure point, the simulation can make accurate statements about why they ended up where they did.

Non-Branching "Interactive" Stories

There is an area similar to branching stories, but different. WILL Interactive, a simulation vendor, sometimes uses this simple technique in addition to their full branches. They present a situation that is interrupted with a multiple-choice question. The question might be in the form of "How would you respond to this person's issue?" or "Who is the right person for them to call?" The answer given by the student prompts a coaching response. Then the story continues regardless of the input, leading to another multiple-choice question.

APPLICATIONS

I have some quick questions. Which of the following are true for you?

- I have used a branching story in a course I have taken.
- I have used a branching story in a course I created.
- I have a strongly favorable impression of branching stories.
- I have a mixed impression of branching stories.
- I have a very negative impression of branching stories.

If you have an opinion about branching stories, it often reflects how appropriately they were used. By the way, if you were frustrated because the options were not exactly what you wanted, welcome to the user side of any branching interface.

Branching stories can expose employees to first-person scenarios, preparing them for common situations that they might face in the course of a new job. They provide highly specific advice and templates, build confidence, and let students make common mistakes in a safe environment, minimizing the chance that they will make the same mistake in a "real," high-pressure situation (Figure 2.5).

The sweet spots for the applications are training programs for entry-level salespeople, unmotivated students, call center representatives, customer-facing retail positions, and entry-level managers (Figure 2.6). They do very well at modeling conversations between people. Vendors often use terms like "role play," "interactive scenarios," "stories," "situations," or "interviewing techniques" to describe branching stories.

Although often dealing with interpersonal situations, branching stories can highlight other types of decisions (Figure 2.7). Having said that, branching stories are not as good for more subtle or sophisticated manager and supervisor training, an area on which some early interactive story vendors had focused.

The framework traditionally is fairly rigid. This rigidity is a common complaint from students, designers, and implementers. More sophisticated students are often not satisfied with their limited numbers of options ("But I don't want to do any of these options.") or resent their forced march through what can feel like a predefined maze. Still, they might at least provide an introduction to the more subtle material.

Media

Branching stories can use full motion video at one production extreme and text at the other. Many vendors had used video exclusively (the model

Figure 2.6. Traditional Branching Stories Vendors.

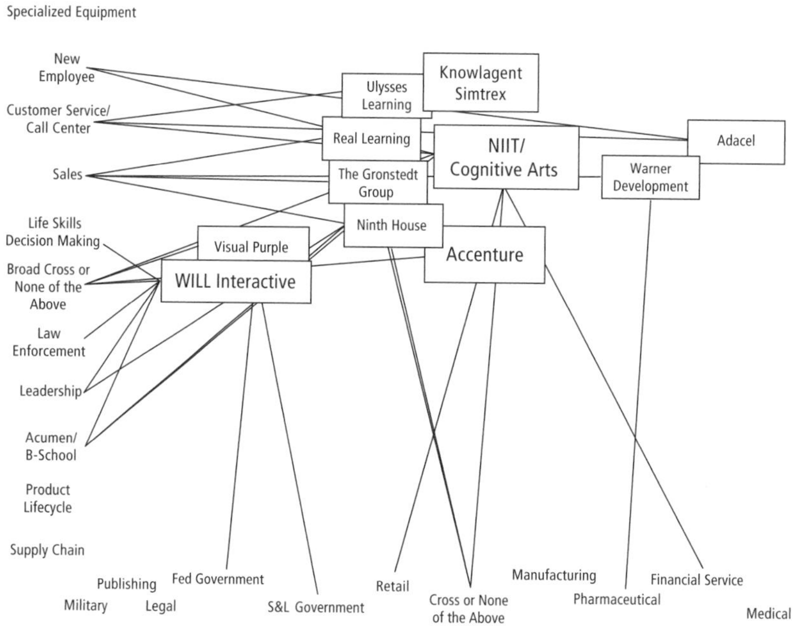

Figure 2.7. A Strategic Branching Decision.

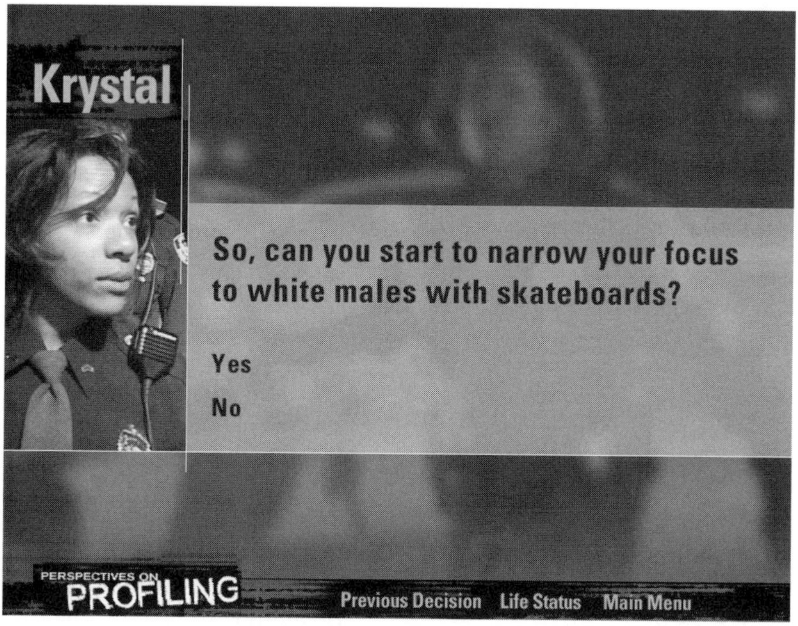

Source: WILL Interactive. Used with Permission.

was pioneered to take advantage of videodisks), but moved, reluctantly, to static pictures to facilitate Web delivery. Despite pushback from clients, I still strongly recommend video as often as possible, and especially when teaching entry-level employees who have to demonstrate a highly specific skill, such as parking cars, greeting guests, and preparing food safely.

Deployment

One of the greatest strengths of branching stories is that they are very easy to deploy. This is for several reasons.

The multiple-choice format requires very little set-up prepping. Everyone knows how to select an A, B, or C (or even D, E, F, G, and H) option.

In fact, branching stories are often self-contained learning experiences that do not require any trained human support. The simulations themselves can do all of the work, including embedded lecture-style content at the front to explain theories and interface, the story, navigation tools, and assessments at the end as well.

They are almost always single-player experiences, although teams can make decisions, if desired. The single-player stand-alone nature means that it is easy for a student to "play" a story in small pieces; designers should put in natural start and stop points every twenty or thirty minutes.

Meanwhile, a single branching story typically takes between ten minutes and several hours to complete.

- At the ten-minute end, the simulation would probably be replayed several times to practice different approaches, and would be just one module of a larger program.
- At more than forty minutes, students are much more reluctant to start over. As we said, these longer branching stories should have natural break points so users do not have to go through them in one sitting.

Architecture

Branching stories tend to be delivered over the Web, launched by a learning management system (LMS, pronounced L-M-S). If they use dense media such as video, they may be distributed either partially or completely on a CD-ROM or increasingly DVD directly to the desktop (Figure 2.8).

Figure 2.8. Branching Story Architecture Considerations.

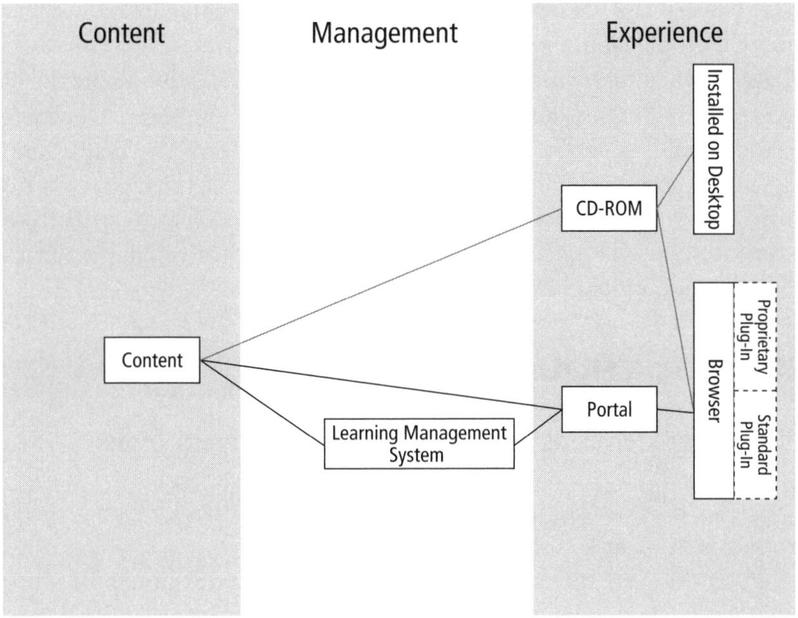

Development questions around branching story-based content include:

- What media options are traditionally used? Video? Static pictures? Audio? What are the selection criteria for each? What are the costs for each?
- What are the ranges of coaching available? How are they activated?
- How long does a story take the average user?
- How thick are the branches on the tree? What is the cost per segment?
- What is the delivery method? If web-based, what are minimum client-side requirements? What is the bandwidth required?

OTHER RESOURCES

- Schank, Roger. (1995). *Tell Me a Story: Narrative and Intelligence.* Evanston, IL: Northwestern University Press.
- Schank, Roger. (1997). *Virtual Learning: A Revolutionary Approach to Building a Highly Skilled Workforce.* New York: McGraw-Hill.

A Place to Practice

Use PowerPoint® to experiment with the basics. Use the linking ability to tie multiple-choice answers to next slides.

Meanwhile, *Scenariation* is a Web application used by instructional designers and subject-matter experts to build branching stories. Designers create scenes—a screen that poses a situation and provides images and sounds to accompany this information. Learners select several alternative reactions to the situation posed. These selections branch the learner from scene to scene and path to path until he or she has resolved the problematic situation. (Link: http://www.scenariation.com)

A FINAL THOUGHT

Branching Stories as a Smaller Piece of a Larger Whole

Complex experiences, including computer games, use branching stories to augment on at least two levels.

First, they use this technique for almost all conversations between characters. Depending on the conversation, the player might earn bonus items, turn an enemy into a friend or a friend into an enemy, or open up or close down broader paths to victory.

Second, branching stories can shape high-level strategic decisions a player makes. Should we invade country A, B, or C? Should we move to facility B or C or stay in A? This adds replayability and strategy to the rest of the interactions.

COMING UP NEXT

A Final Branching Example . . .

To go into much more detail about branching stories, go to Appendix 4: Advanced Techniques for Branching Stories.

To review this material, go to Chapter 2: Controlling People with Branching Stories.

To see a case study, go to Chapter 25: One Branching Story Business Model.

To learn about customizing an existing simulation, go to Appendix 6: Getting What You Want: The Black Art of Customizing the Four Traditional Simulation Genres.

To learn about another traditional model of simulation, go to Chapter 3: Introduction to Systems Thinking: Interactive Spreadsheets as Simulations.

To learn more about some conceptual models about advanced simulation content, go to Chapter 6: A More Complete Perspective: Looking to the Broader World of Educational Simulations.

To maintain your credibility at the club, never wear black socks with sandals.

To learn more about how computer games have introduced new models and elements, go to Chapter 13: The Most Popular Simulations: Computer Games as Expectation Setters and Places to Start.

3

INTRODUCTION TO SYSTEMS THINKING

Interactive Spreadsheets as Simulations

GRANDPARENTS ARE WONDERFUL. They are vast, often untapped resources of this great nation. They can bring us back to days long ago, unimaginable by today's standards. If you have a quiet moment with one of them, maybe on the porch drinking some lemonade, ask him or her to delve back. To melt away the years, to go back before Excel®, even back before Lotus 1–2–3®. Ask about VisiCalc®.

The original spreadsheets were sold, in part, by a wondrous "what-if" capability. You can imagine the early salespeople.

"If you want to see how much you would save by lowering the interest rate half a point," they must have explained, "all you have to do is change this one number, press recalculate, wait for the computer to update the cells, fix any circular errors, and then you would see the new number here, which you can compare against the old number that you had written down."

Well, it might not have been exactly how the salesperson said it. But looking back, I am pretty sure that was the operation he had to explain.

The second popular genre of corporate and higher education simulations is the *interactive spreadsheet.* It takes the early, integral *what-if* ness to a new extreme.

Across a bunch of turns, the student decides how to allocate resources. After each decision, the simulation generates graphs that show a bunch of results (for the more literal reader, "a bunch of" is usually between three and twenty).

Let's look at a simplified example, where you run a start-up *gaufres* shop (*gaufres* are those waffles often sold by French street vendors, enjoyed with powdered sugar or strawberry preserves)—and I quickly must add that I have made all of these numbers up. The only research I did was to actually eat a few *gaufres.*

This might be the interface:

> Your shop has been built just off of the sun-drenched beaches of Key West. You have $50 in the bank. A pair of gaufres cost 50 cents to make and sells for $1. For this simulation, every customer buys one pair of gaufres.
>
> Every day, you have to decide how much you want to spend on advertising, and how much gaufres batter you want to prepare (you can never sell more gaufres in a day than batter you prepared).

Here's how I allocated my resources for the first four turns (Table 3.1). I decided to put a lot into advertising up-front, but then slowly tapered it off. Meanwhile, I start off by only producing a few gaufres, but slowly bring the number up.

Let's say the impact of the decision might look like this (Figure 3.1).

OK, things are looking a little grim. After four days, my bank account has dropped pretty significantly. My accountant is getting concerned. This venture is dangerously close to falling into the "write-off" category.

But there is some good news. The number of customers is increasing steadily.

If you didn't believe in systems, you might strongly suggest I try something different. But I do believe.

And if I continued the strategy of decreasing advertising and increasing my daily inventory over eleven more days, my play would end up like this (Figure 3.2).

That is the intrigue of systems and interactive spreadsheets—and real life, of course. Strategies take time to play out, and local minimums can be necessary for long-term maximums.

Table 3.1. An Example of Allocations over Four Days.

Day 1	*Day 2*	*Day 3*	*Day 4*
Advertising: 20	Advertising: 18	Advertising: 16	Advertising: 14
Inventory: 10	Inventory: 10	Inventory: 15	Inventory: 22

Figure 3.1. An Example of Changing Key Metrics in an Interactive Spreadsheet.

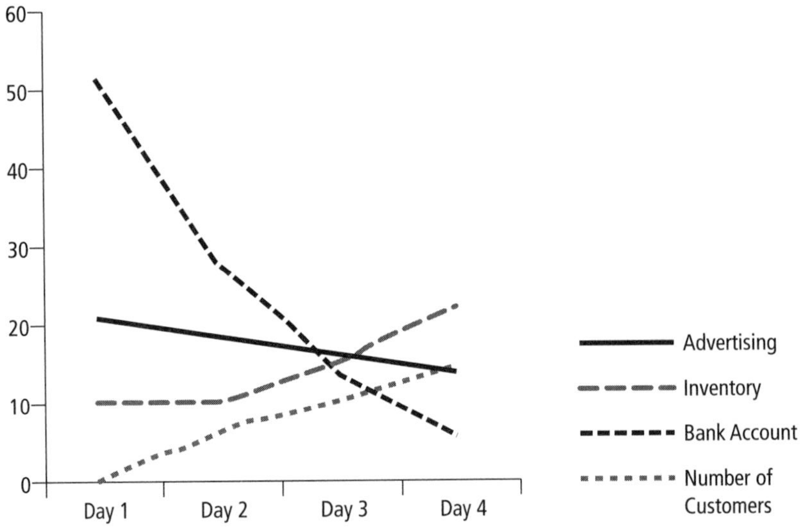

Figure 3.2. An Example of Changing Key Metrics in an Interactive Spreadsheet.

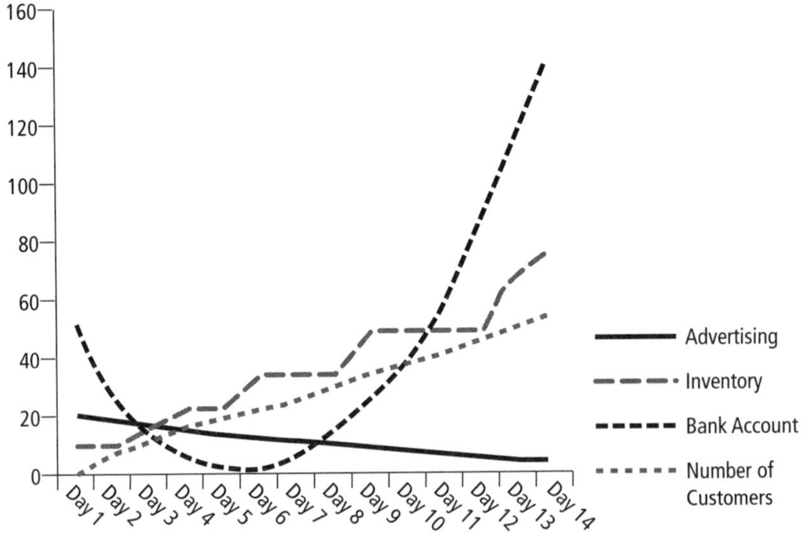

The business-focused people should be imagining what those graphs feel like in real life—the hustle and bustle of a shop, rats getting into the thrown-out batter. And I am impressed if you are.

But the designers should be wondering what calculations I used. They are very, very simple.

Here are the only other relationships and assumptions than those I was given when I started (and again, I made all of these up):

- It takes $3 to attract one new customer through advertising.
- Through word of mouth (for you see, I make very tasty *gaufres*), my number of customers grows by 5 percent every day.

Yet even these simple assumptions still display somewhat interesting patterns. I could play several different ways, and get very different results.

Depending on the learning objectives, we could add many layers to our scenario.

- Advertising dollars spent could still increase customers entering our store, but over a period of time, not immediately.
- The player could change the price of *gaufres,* altering demand, or offer more varieties, as well as some *glaces* perhaps.
- The overall economy could improve or worsen.
- The player could move to a higher rent, higher foot traffic location.

As shown just a bit in the *gaufres* example, variables are tightly connected. In a well-designed interactive spreadsheet, any decision impacts the entire system.

DEEPER INTERACTIVE SPREADSHEETS

For real interactive spreadsheets, each turn would vary in complexity, but centers around inputting allocations (Figure 3.3). The entire simulation experience might take between half an hour and multiple days.

Goals in interactive spreadsheets often include reaching a certain high point in one or more variables within a given time frame. We might have tried to reach a certain volume of customers or revenues, or make the most profit. The mathematics tend to be a lot more sophisticated as well.

Figure 3.3. A Spreadsheet Input Example.

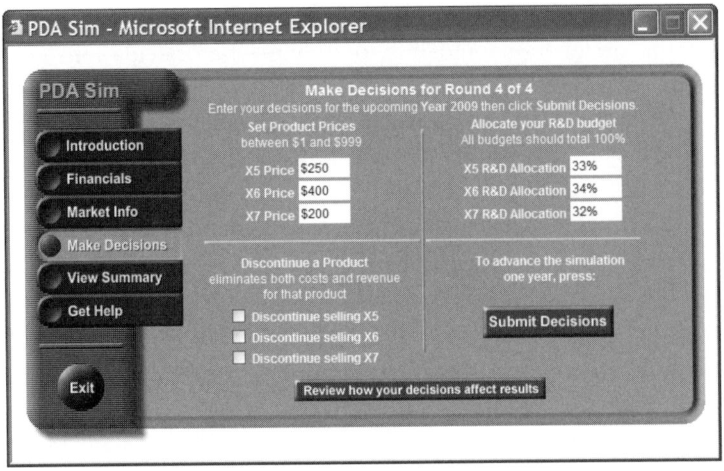

Source: Forio Business Simulations. Used with Permission.

More Discrete Interactions

Some interactive spreadsheets have more discrete interactions. Instead of allocating funds, for example, a learner may have a list of, say, twelve initiatives. They can only do a few each turn.

Now it is truly a case of strategic timing. I could give another business example, but this might be more fun.

> You are going on a date with the most charming person in your apartment building.
>
> It is the first date. Due to time (and other arbitrary) constraints, you can only choose three of the following "investments." Which do you make?

- Buy a cheap gift.
- Buy an expensive gift.
- Buy great tickets to a show.
- Buy ingredients for a nice dinner to be prepared at your home.
- Buy new sheets.
- Buy ingredients for a nice breakfast to be prepared at your home.
- Clean out your apartment.
- Clean out your car.

- Find out what time a cheap restaurant opens.
- Get a haircut.
- Get Botox injections.
- Buy new clothes.
- Make reservations at an expensive restaurant.
- Make reservations at a bed and breakfast.
- Offer the person a job at your company.
- Take out friends and get more information.

After the event you get some feedback as to how it went, and (assuming you chose appropriately) now there is a second date. You have the same list available to you. Now which do you choose? The cycle could continue through six dates.

There is a tighter focus on timing in the discrete input model. But the calculations and feedback are not inherently less complex than the more subtle allocation-based models.

Visual Front and Back End

Dense graphs and equations are the native outcome of interactive spreadsheets. Users watch very carefully to see whether the lines they care about trend upwards or downwards (Figures 3.4 and 3.5).

Figure 3.4. A Spreadsheet Graph Output Example.

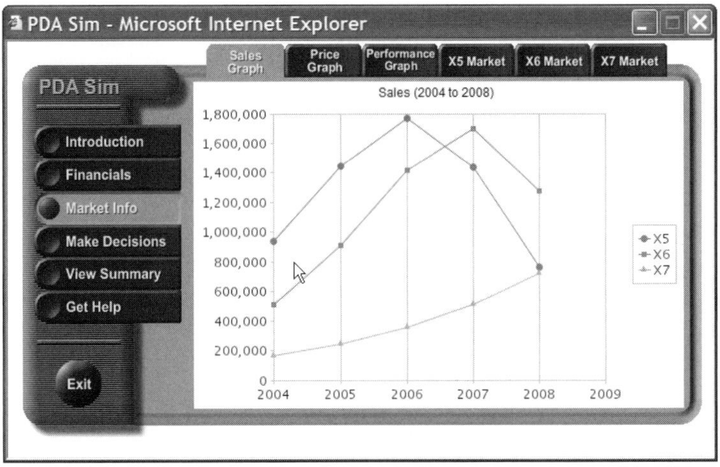

Source: Forio Business Simulations. Used with Permission.

Figure 3.5. A University of Phoenix/Tata Interactive Input/Output.

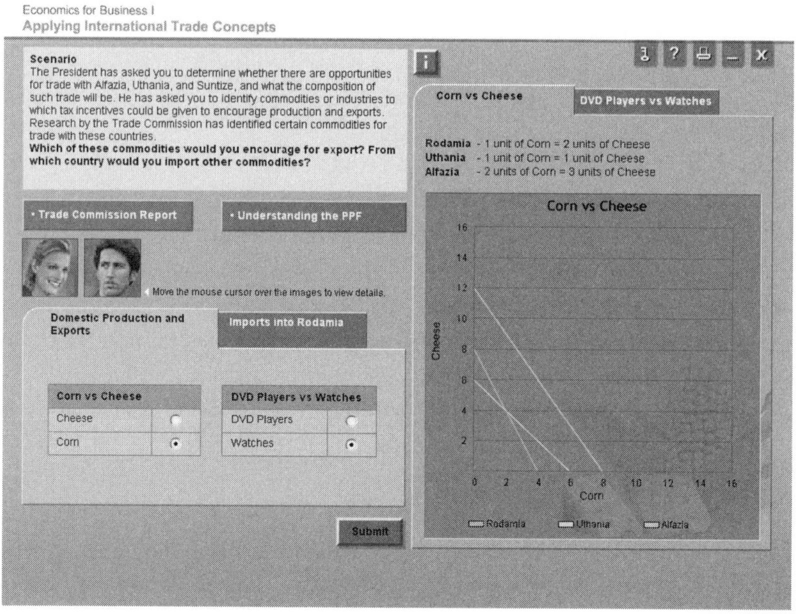

Source: Tata Interactive Systems. Used with Permission.

Trigger-Based Feedback

But interactive spreadsheets can do more that just show graphs twitching up or twitching down.

At pre-determined times, many interactive spreadsheets will look to see how a player is doing. The program would play an appropriate, pre-rendered media clip.

Recall our *gaufres* example. After Day 12 the simulation showed a graph for feedback. It could also have shown the *medium* bank account video, with a nonchalant visit from the bank's vice president (Figure 3.6).

If we had more money, the bank officer might be a bit happier, and may have bought some *gaufres* herself. If we had less money, she might close us down, ending the simulation.

For a practice exercise, think of various triggers and media for the date simulations. What would you show if, after the third date, things were going badly, well, or really well.

Figure 3.6. A Trigger at Bank Account, Day 12.

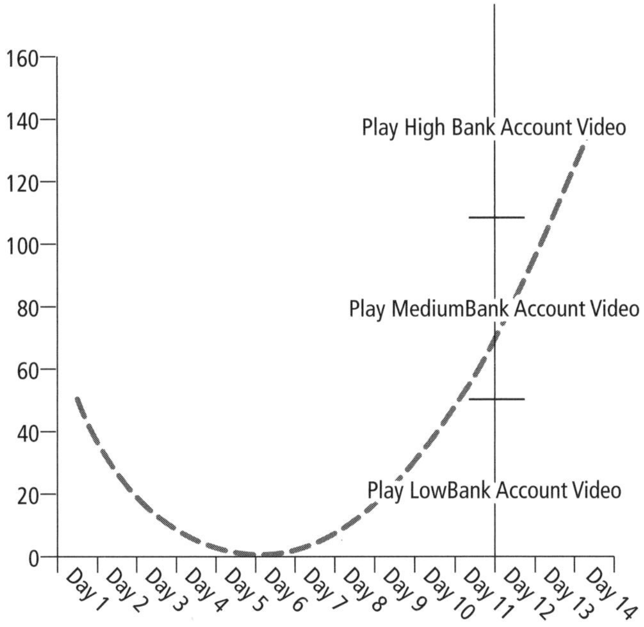

While not as targeted as the "coaches" in branching stories, trigger-based feedback lets learners know what is going on more vividly than graph ticks and forces them to reflect on their decisions. Gary Klein has suggested that players can only really keep track of three causal factors through six states, so advice and framing should happen at least that often. (Klein, Gary. [1998]. *Sources of Power: How People Make Decisions*. Cambridge, MA: MIT Press).

A trigger can look at what *actions* the player has taken. For example: *if* the player has spent less than 10 percent of available funds on advertising *and* volume of customers is below thirty people/day *then* the player would see a clip saying something like: "One of your friends suggests to you that the local paper is a pretty good way of getting your message out. It may be time to spend some advertising dollars."

Tata Interactive's Rupesh Goel and others also use these trigger-based techniques to make the experience more immersive. "It is an opportunity to wrap a story around the situation, and to add characters. The goal," he explained, "is for people not to even think they are interacting with a spreadsheet."

APPLICATIONS

I have two quick questions.

1. On a scale of 1 to 10, with 1 being the most negative opinion and 10 being the most positive opinion, and decimals are allowed, what was your opinion of interactive spreadsheets before you read this chapter? And what is it now?
2. Given the last ten classes that you have taken or given, what percentage should use:

    Branching stories?
    Interactive spreadsheets?

Similar to branching stories, interactive spreadsheets need to be used in the right place. There is an unquestionable "business school quality" to interactive spreadsheets: academic, intellectual, distant, yet subtle and mind-expanding. Some people thrive in these environments, and some do not.

Interactive spreadsheets compress time, allowing students to see quickly the results of their actions. They present a somewhat complex system, allowing individuals to better understand how specific actions affect the organization. They surface hidden assumptions, allowing significantly richer and more aligned conversations between decision makers.

Interactive spreadsheets also allow participants to try allocations they would not want to do in real life to see how they evolve, although most designers are quick to say they are not accurate or complete enough to be fully predictive.

Because of the open-ended and systems-based content of most interactive spreadsheets, students can have a hard time articulating what they have learned. The learning still exists, but its non-traditional nature compared to other types of more linear learning can create a frustration in the student if proper debriefing isn't conducted.

Focus on Lifecycle

The traditional use of interactive spreadsheets is by b-schools, manufacturers, and retailers, and the focus on lifecycle/supply chain types of issues (Figure 3.7). These are places where relationships are highly

Figure 3.7. Traditional Interactive Spreadsheet Vendors.

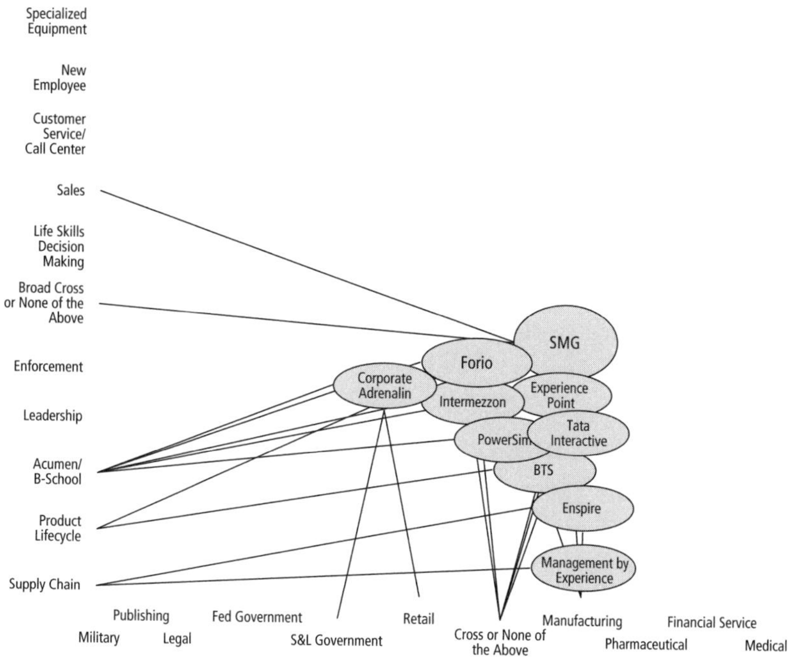

defined and play out over time. They are also topic areas where small decisions early on are magnified through the system.

Interactive spreadsheets have been a good choice for higher-level management training, especially cross-functionally. They are not very good for less experienced or less motivated students, who often get confused and even bored.

Development

Unlike building an interactive story, building an interactive spreadsheet involves dealing with building systems. Rupesh Goel explains Tata's development process: "Together with UOP academic affairs, we poll the faculty and the students at the University of Phoenix." They ask them what concepts they thought were difficult to understand. Out of those concepts come the learning objectives. "We find public domain or expert content. We make up a fictional case. We start modeling and adding characters, continuing to do research at each stage."

Rupesh continued, "We aim for one learning objective per cycle, with each simulation representing three or four cycles. The learning objective in each cycle is either a slice of an overall objective for the simulations or integrally related to the learning objective of the adjacent cycle."

They make the first cut into a Word document. Then they create a fully working Excel spreadsheet, using Visual Basic.

"It is very interactive at that point," Rupesh explained. "This allows you to begin to play the spreadsheet." Tata's tools import the Excel sheet and export a Flash action script. It is around this that they go into the final parallel visual development (Figure 3.8).

Deployment

As with branching stories, these interactive-spreadsheet-based simulations are traditionally turn-based. The simulation waits for players to

Figure 3.8. An Interactive Spreadsheet Development Process.

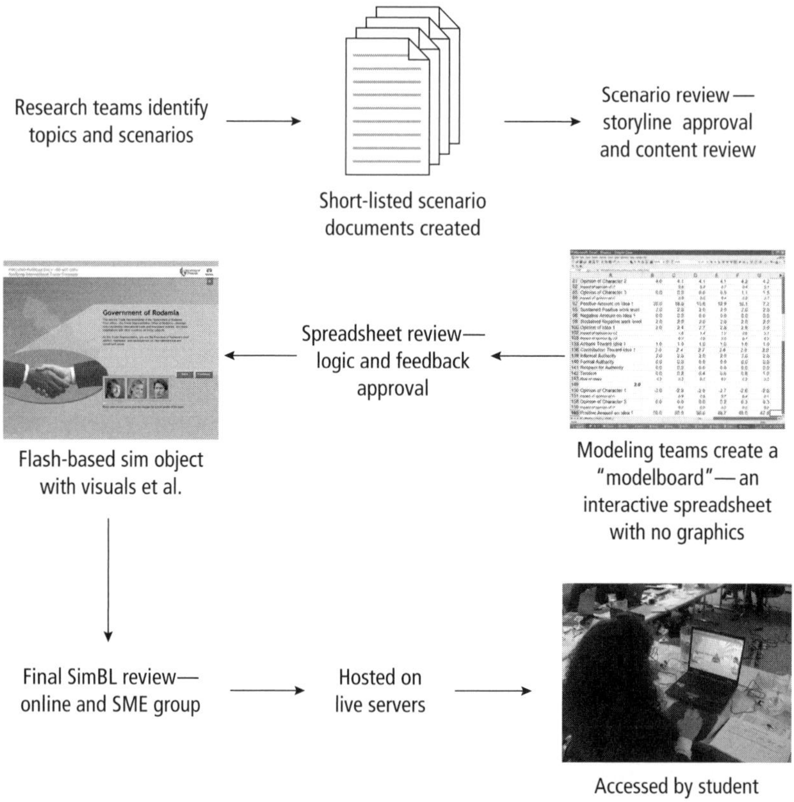

Source: Tata Interactive Systems. Used with Permission.

complete their turn, providing them the opportunity for thought, reflection, research, coffee, and/or a ball game.

Unlike branching stories, interactive spreadsheets *tend* to be instructor-supported. *Instructor-supported* models use trained people to introduce, facilitate, and debrief the learning. At one extreme, it might take two instructors to support just one student, such as in a senior manager role play or coaching session. More often, I have seen and used instructor-supported ratios around one instructor per six to twelve students. Instructors may not even be in the same time zone, involved from afar.

A typical business use of interactive spreadsheets would be to gather supervisors or officers for a week-long strategy retreat. For two of these days, the group would form teams and play against each other, battling for profitability, using tools such as market share, pricing, and sourcing. As we saw in our early example, the tides of battle can switch quickly.

In many cases the learners would not interact directly with the interactive spreadsheet. (Considering the unevenness in computer literacy among senior managers, that is a good thing.) Instead they use the facilitator to both capture their inputs and to present and explain the outputs.

A SECOND LAYER OF LEARNING FROM COMPETITION With interactive spreadsheets, students spend time constructing knowledge of the system with which they are interacting. But when competition is involved, the learning goes to a second layer.

Suppose four companies are battling in the high-end automobile industry. Every turn, the teams submit their plans and then collectively receive the results.

Here, each team is impacted by not only its own strategy, but the strategies of the other three teams as well. Soon, each team is thinking not just about understanding the abstract system that the interactive spreadsheet represents, but also about how to out-maneuver the other teams.

In short, students go from learning about rules and systems to learning about exploiting rules and systems. If you are thinking this sounds like Congress, you are absolutely right. If you are thinking that rules should be followed, not exploited, you need to get out more.

SHARED REFERENCE The rest of the off-site (or course) would use the shared experience as a reference point. The individual players would better, and sometimes viscerally, understand the issues.

Architecture

Stand-alone (non-instructor-supported) interactive spreadsheets tend to be delivered over the Web, launched by a learning management system (LMS). If an instructor supports them, they may reside solely on the instructor's PC, or they are delivered via CD-ROM (Figure 3.9).

Development questions around interactive-spreadsheet-based content include:

- What are the relationship models that are/have been used? What are the key variables? How were they determined?
- Will this be a custom, modified off-the-shelf, or straight off-the-shelf simulation?
- What is the delivery method? If Web-based, what are minimum client-side requirements? What is the bandwidth required?
- How many calculations per turn are traditionally used? (The more calculations per turn, the more divergent and open-ended the content can be.)

Figure 3.9. Interactive Spreadsheet Architecture Considerations.

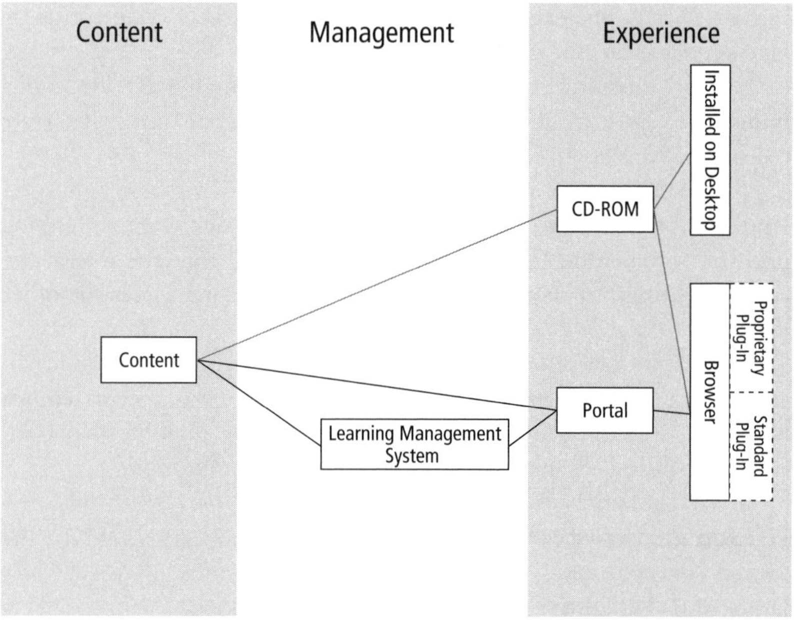

- Are instructors used to deliver the simulation? What is the ratio of students to instructors? Is there a train-the-trainer option, to bring the facilitation in-house? What does that entail?
- What different assessment models have you used in the past?

But wait there's more!

If you want to learn more about interactive spreadsheets, go to Appendix 5, Advanced Techniques for Interactive Spreadsheets. If you don't, I understand.

OTHER RESOURCES

- Schelling, Thomas. (1978). *Micromotives and Macrobehavior.* New York: Norton.
- Schrage, Michael. (2000). *Serious Play: How the World's Best Companies Simulate to Innovate.* Boston: Harvard Business School Press.
- Sterman, John. (2000). *Business Dynamics: Systems Thinking and Modeling for a Complex World.* Boston: Irwin/McGraw-Hill.
- Wolfram, S. (2002). *A New Kind of Science.* Champaign, IL: Wolfram Media.

A Place to Practice

Build a simple model using Excel®. Practice playing around with just a few interacting variables.

Meanwhile, Forio Broadcast is a Web application used by instructional designers and subject-matter experts to build interactive spreadsheets. Designers create systems and results. Learners make allocations and see the results of their decisions.

(Link: http://broadcast.forio.com)

A FINAL THOUGHT

Interactive Spreadsheets as a Smaller Piece of a Larger Whole

Complex experiences, including computer games, copiously use interactive-spreadsheet-type models, especially where long-term resource management comes into play. Players build or capture buildings (or geographies) that add resources, or convert a lower-value resource to a higher-value resource. At the same time the buildings (or geographies) might have to consume other resources (material, electricity, people, vodka) to work productively. They also might have to be defended. Finally, buildings (or geographies) can have unwanted byproducts, from pollution to the generation of negative will from neighbors. These attributes are at the heart of management games, but also real-time-strategy games, even action games such as those in the Grand Theft Auto™ series.

COMING UP NEXT

Can you learn from a game? Do *Jeopardy!*® and *Wheel of Fortune*® have a place in classes? Can learning be made more fun? Should learning be made more fun?

4

MAKING THE BORING FUN

Game-Based Models

A lot of corporate executives think that "game" is a four-letter word.

—Matthew Sakey, e-learning designer

BEFORE WE GO ANY FURTHER, let's review some of the material so far. See how well you do in this self-evaluation.

Make sure your answers are in the form of a question. The category is "Things That Start with B."

[For $100] A magic one of these solves all of our problems.

[For $200] The only early simulation genre to be in this category.

[For $400] Something you might want to inject before a date.

[For $800] A repository for linear content.

[For $1,600] A breeding place for interactive spreadsheets.

GAMES AND SIMULATIONS

In game-based models, students engage simulations of a familiar and entertaining game in which educational content is embedded. *Jeopardy!®*, *Wheel of Fortune®*, and *Solitaire,* even computer game genres such as adventure games or first-person shooters, provide templates.

The reason for using game-based models is simple. Matthew Sakey, e-learning designer, calls it the rule of high school English: "People learn better when they don't know they are learning. People hate being told what to learn, even if it is useful."

Said a different way: taking a test is no fun. Being a contestant on "Who Wants to Be a Millionaire?" or "Jeopardy!" is (Figure 4.1). Go figure.

A typical game-based question might read:

> For a chance to solve the puzzle, where is the first place end-users should go if they need help?
> (A) The Help Desk
> (B) Their Department Coordinator
> (C) The Person Next to Them

Figure 4.1. A Game-Based Simulation from Games2Train.

Source: Games2Train. Used with Permission.

GAME TEMPLATES

Game templates, both commercial, freeware, and home built, come in several forms. But they all are familiar and easy to play. These include:

- Game shows, such as "Wheel of Fortune"[1,2], "Jeopardy!"[1,2,3,4,5], "Who Wants to Be a Millionaire?"[1,2,3,4,5], "Family Feud"[1,2,3,4,5], and "Hollywood Squares"[1,2,3]
- Word games, such as Hangman[1,2,3] and Word Jumble[1,2,3]

[1]Names; [2]Jargon; [3]Acronyms; [4]Facts; [5]Charts

- Card games, such as Solitaire[1,2,3,4] and Memory/Concentration[1,2,3,4,5]
- Board games, such as Trivial Pursuit®[1,2,3,4,5], Monopoly®[1,2,3,4].

Adventure Games

Some game-based models use adventures games, a genre popularized in early computer games. Students traverse maps, either from a first-person or top-down perspective, looking for pieces of information or performing small tasks to unlock new parts of the map.

This was the model for much of the early "educational" software. ("Sure Miss Squirrel, you can come into our clubhouse filled with toys and friends. But you have to identify these right four physics laws to get the key." There are also corporation examples, that might read, "Sure Mrs. Squire, you can come into the executive board room filled with stock options and great contacts, but you have to identify the right four ethics policies to get the key.")

SIMPLE PROGRESSION

The constant emphasis is on a *quick moving, quick reward, and enjoyable* experience. There is typically less contemplation than in the other traditional genres.

Karl Kapp, assistant director of Bloomsburg University's Institute for Interactive Technologies, has overseen the building of many game-based toolkits. One appreciated feature is to, if the game is self-paced, provide an "I give up" button (Figure 4.2).

In other examples, students might get points for answering right questions or performing the right task. If they accumulate enough points, they win the round. The players might play against real people, or against avatars.

Pure Game Elements

There are some other more specific game elements that can also be used on their own:

- High scores lists or other competition between players
- Completing a task before a time expires
- Answering trivia for prizes

We will get into more game elements in the next section.

Figure 4.2. A Word Jumble with an "I Give Up" Button.

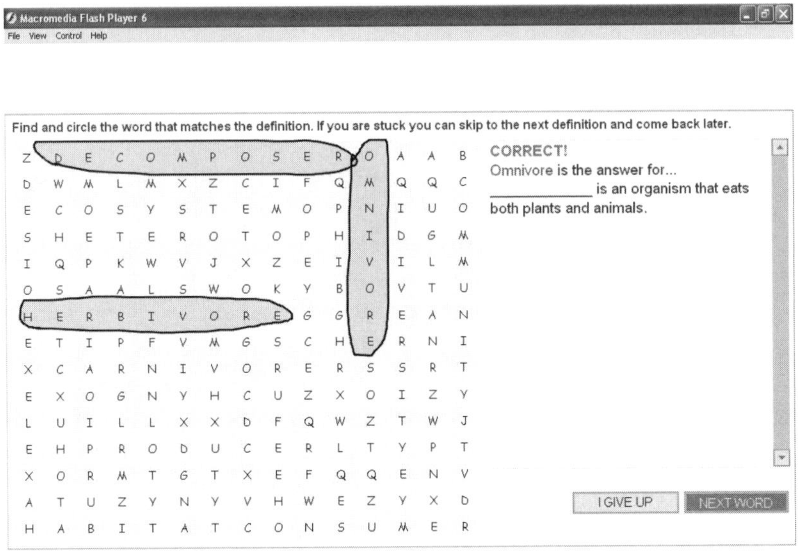

Source: Bill and Veronica Noone, Consultants, The Institute for Interactive Technologies at Bloomsburg University. Used with Permission.

Almost There

Jim Kirk, director of the master's degree program in human resources at Western Carolina University, has done research to suggest that this approach is becoming increasingly popular with trainers and professors. But the right combination of tools is not out yet. "Right now, instructors are going for the free tools, or they are making their own, rather than spending money to buy easier-to-use off-the-shelf programs. But in the long run, whatever the source of the program, teachers will have to be able to input their questions and answers into the system in less than ten minutes."

Pacing Jack

Harry Gottlieb, a designer of Jellyvision's popular computer game series, *You Don't Know Jack®*, wrote down the concepts that made the series so successful in the white paper, *The Jack Principles of the Interactive Conversation Interface.* Use as many as possible as often as possible when using game models.

JACK PRINCIPLES TO MAINTAIN PACING

- Give the user only one task to accomplish at a time
- Limit the number of choices the user has at any one time
- Give the user only meaningful choices
- Make sure the user knows what to do at every moment
- Focus the user's attention on the task at hand
- Use the most efficient manner of user input
- Make the user aware that the program is waiting
- Pause, quit, or move on without the user's response if it doesn't come soon enough

THE SIMPLE STUFF JUST MIGHT BE THE HARD STUFF At a vineyard outside of Redmond, Washington, I talked to Xbox® game designer Howard Phillips about the educational potential of console platforms. I was all excited about the complex systems that could be taught. "That's all true," he acknowledged. "But the biggest opportunity is to teach all of the introductory buzz words and rules of an area."

"Why?" I asked. "That seems like low value content."

"Don't look at it that way. People do great on their own learning the big concepts. Once someone gets into a discipline, then the real challenges and issues keep them engaged. But what keeps someone out of a discipline is the simple stuff. If we can get someone past that hurdle in a fun and engaging way, then he can learn the more complicated material."

APPLICATIONS

I have a quick question. Which of the following are true?

- I have used a game-based model in a course I have taken.
- I have used a game-based model in a course I created.

Now put the chart on the following page exactly five feet away from you on the floor. Take out six pennies. Use the first two as practice, then see how many of the last four you can get to land on your opinion.

Game-based models build buzz within training groups and good will among students. They tend to be easily accessible and a pleasant break from traditional linear content. They work very well when new names, jargon, acronyms, facts, and/or charts, boring but important, have to be rolled out across a large population, especially around a compliance situation.

I have a favorable impression of game-based models.

I have a mixed impression of game-based models.

I have a negative impression of game-based models.

Game-based models can also include both multi-player games, and/or high-score boards to instill competition. Games can be used live in a classroom or remotely over the Web.

"The game show draws on information or knowledge the user already has. So it is better at rewarding what someone knows than teaching them anything new," says Matthew Sakey. There is, however, an opportunity for question-based learning, if there is enough time to think about it.

Karl Kapp also suggests that this type of content should *not* be front-loaded in a class setting. It is better to teach some names, jargon, facts, and/or acronyms, then show how they apply, and then teach some more. Therefore it makes sense to have multiple game-based sessions at the appropriate intervals, not just one.

Simple Examples

David Forman, noted e-learning implementer, although better known as founder of e-learningjobs.com, likes putting little game elements into his material. In one course, he displayed a boat trying to get to an island. It take six right answers to propel the boat all the way across.

But if the student answers four questions wrong, the sky darkens, and the boat sinks.

Architecture

While classroom-based games can be done using just a laptop, PowerPoint®, and a projector, distributed game-based models tend to be delivered over the Web, launched by a learning management system (LMS). The role of the learning management system and the server becomes important to facilitate multi-player competitions. Games can also be delivered to wireless devices (Figure 4.3).

Development questions around game-based content include:

- What are the different game models that you use? When do you use which one?
- How do you quickly import questions and answers?
- How do you quickly export scores?
- What is the delivery method? If Web-based, what are minimum client-side requirements? What is the bandwidth required?

Figure 4.3. Game-Based Models Architecture Considerations.

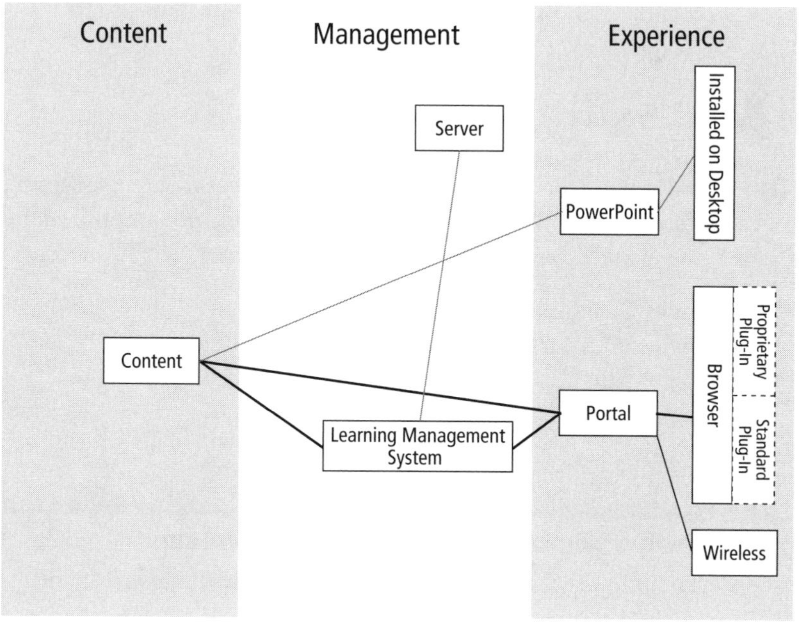

OTHER RESOURCES

- Dempsey, J. V., Haynes, L. L., Lucassen, B. A., & Casey, M. S. (2002). Forty simple computer games and what they could mean to educators. *Simulation & Gaming, 33*(2), 157–168.
- Dillon, N. (1998, September 28). Can games be training tools? *Computerworld, 32*(39), 39–40.
- Dunathan, A. T. (1978). What is a game? *Audiovisual Instruction, 25*(3), 14–15.
- Gilgeous, V., & D'Cruz, M. (1996). A study of business and management games. *Management Development Review, 9*(1), 32–41.
- Greenblat, C. S. (1988). *Designing Games and Simulations.* London: Sage.
- Phipps, J. L. (2003, April). Adding excitement to e-learning. *Industry Week, 252*(4), 51–53.
- Prensky, M. (2001). *Digital Game-Based Learning.* New York: McGraw-Hill.
- Rose, T. G. (1996). *The Future of Online Education and Training* (Report No. IRC.56641). Washington, DC: U.S. Department of Education. (ERIC Document Reproduction Service No. ED411814).
- Wehrenburg, S. B. (1985). Management training games: The play's the thing. *Personnel Journal, 64,* 88–91.

A Place to Practice

Try building a PowerPoint presentation that reproduces a game sequence.

Vendors and providers of game-based tools are not organized by industry. They include:

- EGames Generator (http://egames.carsonmedia.com/online/default.asp)
- Games2Train (www.games2train.com)
- Half-Baked Potatoes' Hot Potatoes (http://web.uvic.ca/hrd/halfbaked/)
- Interactive Games (www.oswego.org/staff/cchamber/techno/games.htm)
- LearningWare's Gameshow Pro Web (www.learningware.com/)

- QuizGame Master (http://cybil.tafe.tas.edu.au/~capsticm/quizman/qmhome.html)
- QuizStar (http://quizstar.4teachers.org/index.jsp)

A REVIEW

To review key words and phrases so far, see how many you can identify in this word search. Most middle managers find around five. Senior manager types tend to find ten, and those with CEO in their blood can find fifteen.

Z U G N I O D Y B G N I N R A E L B E L C H F P M
U N I V E R S A L T R U T H S C H E S T E R E O I
R L O E N U T R O F F O L E E H W W K V D H E W C
T E L L U B C I G A M R V I R T U A L L E A D E R
T E E H S D A E R P S E V I T C A R E T N I B R O
R W E I V E R N O I T C A R E T F A N V G C A P W
A S T C U D O R P L A U T R I V R E G O O B C O O
F B R A N C H I N G S T O R Y L O P O N O M K I R
D A E H G I B A S A H K R A L C M R O C S L K N L
L Q T H O L L Y W O O D S Q U A R E S C V L P T D
L E A R N I N G M A N A G E M E N T S Y S T E M S
E R I A N O I L L I M A E B O T S T N A W O H W X
C H O O S E Y O U R O W N A D V E N T U R E M K E
V I R T U A L C L A S S R O O M S Y D R A P O E J
X R O C K Y R O A D O F T E C H N O L O G Y S R Z

COMING UP NEXT

How do you simulate a car? Or a router? And is there a difference between marketing and training?

5

GETTING A GOOD FEEL FOR THINGS

Virtual Products and Virtual Labs

THE FOURTH TRADITIONAL SIMULATION GENRE includes *virtual products* and *virtual labs.* These are on-screen representations of objects and software that allow significant interaction, mimicking many of the physical characteristics of the real-life counterpart.

Virtual products and virtual labs combine many of the elements of the other three simulation types. They can have a strong context, like a story-based simulation. They are highly engaging and kinesthetic, appealing to a younger audience, such as a game-based model. And they can provide more open-ended exploration, such as with an interactive spreadsheet.

VIRTUAL PRODUCTS

Virtual products were popularized when they became part of a new product rollout (Figure 5.1), advertising campaign, or online sales program. When Palm Pilots were first rolled out, their site featured a Web applet that allowed perspective users to try out writing in graffiti (their character recognition language) to see how easy it was.

Not surprisingly, virtual products have often been the responsibility of marketing groups. Sometimes their origin starts even earlier in the value chain, as they are used to mock-up designs to test with users before the prototypes are even built.

Training organizations have been quick to see the immediate benefit of virtual products over real products. They can be "better than realistic."

Figure 5.1. Virtual Vault Storage.

Source: Kaon. Used with Permission.

DEPLOYABLE No matter how big, how heavy, or how expensive the product is, their virtual doppelganger can be cheaply deployed anywhere in the world. Potential customers, trainees, developers, and partners can all access the device using nothing but a browser and perhaps a plug-in.

ANNOTATED In real life, we are often not quite sure what happens when we press the wrong or even the right button. Virtual products can provide annotation as to their internal states and give users supervision (as well as super vision) as to what is going on and why.

COOPERATIVE Virtual products can allow physical exploration without regard to weight (so one could quickly look under a new BMW SUV, for example, which is trickier in real life). They never need to warm up or cool down, and they can be restarted instantly. And they do not break.

Don Schnell, who teaches automotive technicians, found that when he was traveling around the country, his equipment would not fare well. By creating a virtual edition, he always had exactly what he needed (Figure 5.2).

State-Based Architecture

Virtual products can be built in many ways. But the two most important elements are state-based architectures (Figure 5.3, Figure 5.4, and Figure 5.5), and some simple systems calculations.

Figure 5.2. Capturing the Essence of Reality.

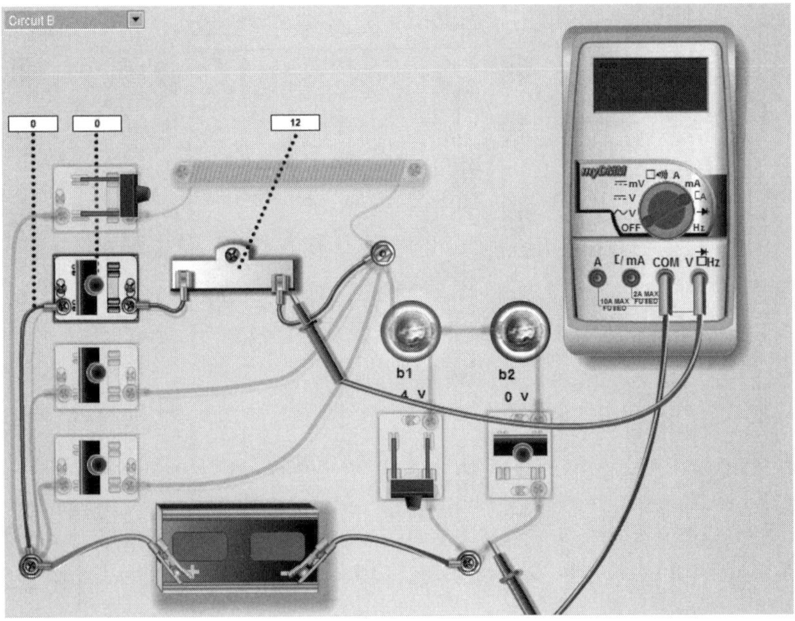

Source: Don Schnell, Tools For Education, Inc. Used with Permission.

Figure 5.3. A Simple State-Based Model.

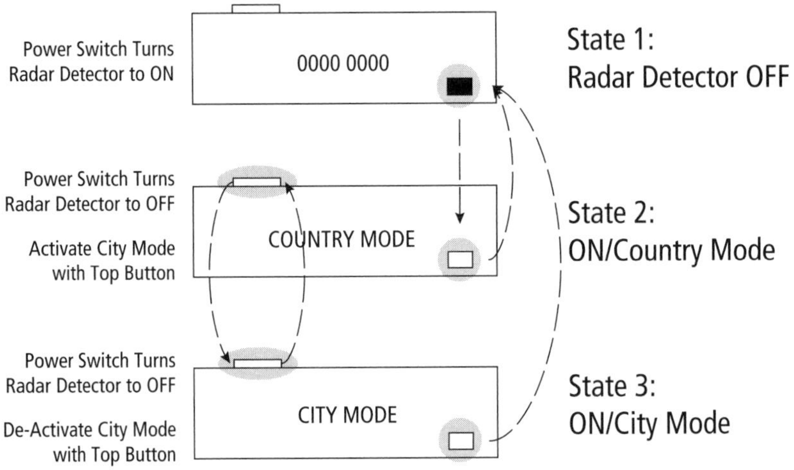

Source: I Made It up.

Figure 5.4. A More Abstract State-Based Model.

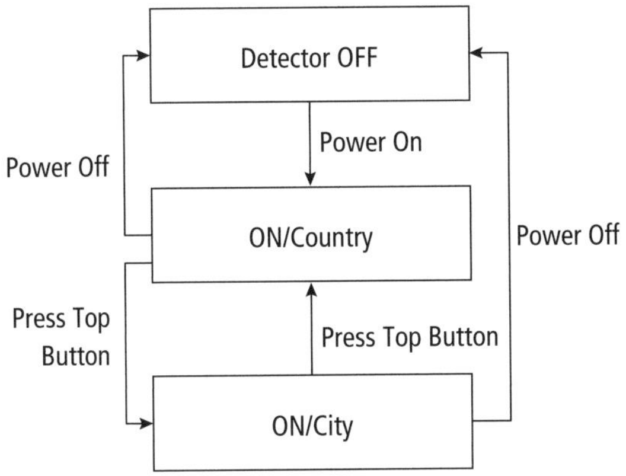

Figure 5.5. Virtual Watch with Statechart.

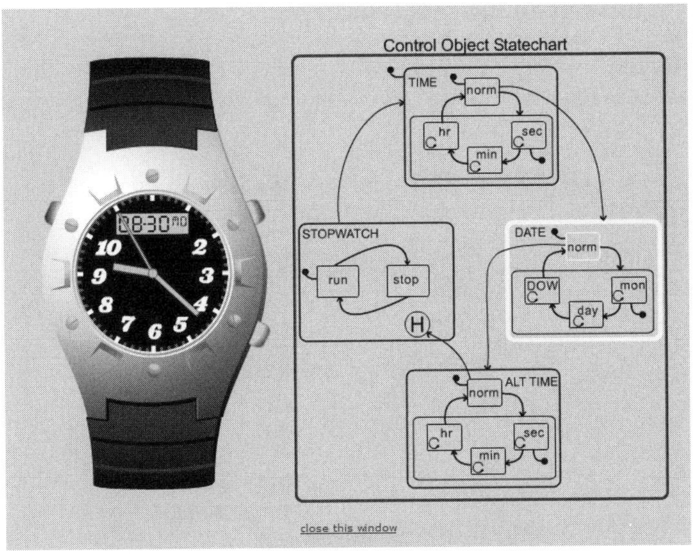

Source: Equipment Simulations LLC. Used with Permission.

Jonathan Kaye, president of Equipment Simulations LLC and author of *Flash MX for Interactive Simulation,* sums up the importance of good architecture: "We had a project that was going to be three or four months, that ended up being a year and a half.

"If we had gone ahead and just slapped stuff together, it would have been impossible to look back a year later and make improvements.

Because there is a standardized process, designed and built on a standardized and teachable process, I know exactly how changes will affect the rest of the system."

Newport Medical Instruments Example

One attribute of virtual products is their flexibility. Jonathan Kaye designed a virtual product/interactive product guide to be used with Newport Medical Instruments' training and operator proficiency certification processes. It began with a simulation of the ventilator (Figure 5.6).

To that core simulation, a series of training modules was added. Learners could walk through progressively more complex tasks and use of the various properties of the machine (Figure 5.7).

The virtual product was also to help users learn how to assemble the ventilator (Figure 5.8). The learner's performance in all of these activities could be documented, as a quality control means for healthcare managers.

Furthermore, the simulator and presentation are separable. For example, Newport Medical Instruments' staff can incorporate the

Figure 5.6. An Interactive HT50 Ventilator.

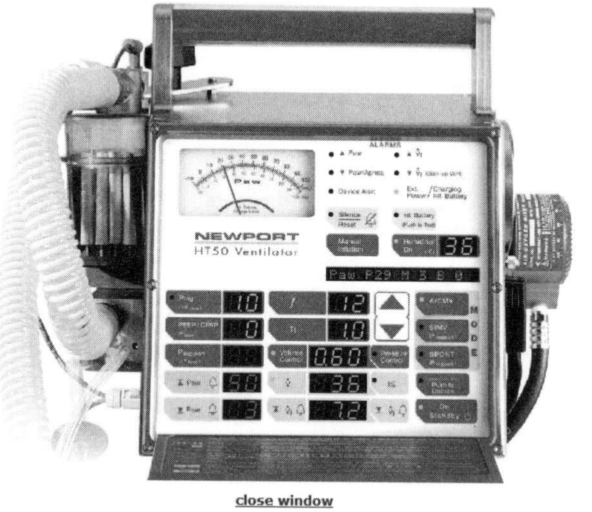

Source: Courtesy of Newport Medical Instruments, Inc., and Equipment Simulations LLC. Used with Permission.

Figure 5.7. Interactive Learning About Alarm Conditions on the HT50.

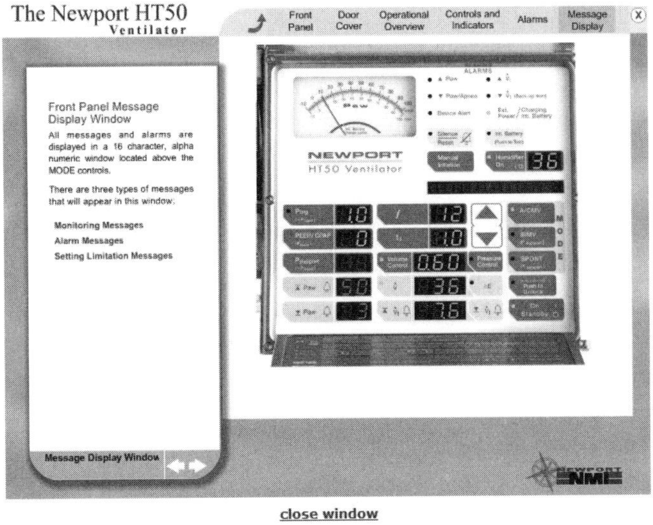

Source: Courtesy of Newport Medical Instruments, Inc., and Equipment Simulations LLC. Used with Permission.

Figure 5.8. Assembling the HT50 Ventilator Circuit.

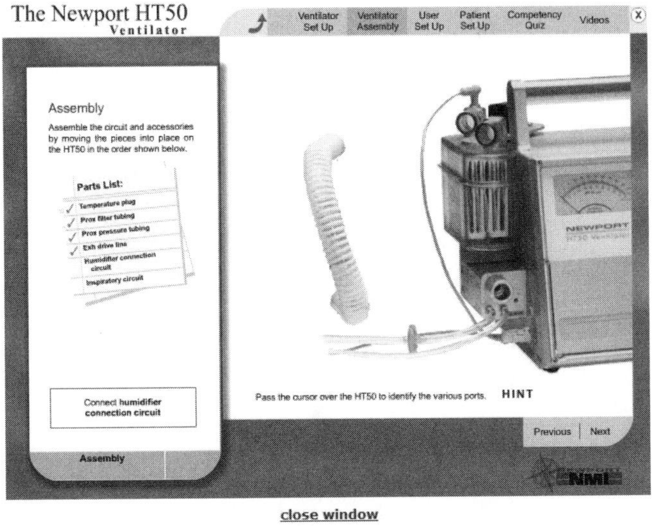

Source: Courtesy of Newport Medical Instruments, Inc., and Equipment Simulations LLC. Used with Permission.

simulator into PowerPoint® presentations, eliminating the need to take a real unit out of service and to carry it on training and sales calls.

Virtual Product Feedback

Virtual products can lack clear feedback cycles. It is one of their weak points. It is sometimes difficult for a user to know whether or not things are going as they are supposed to. There can be some absolute failure points, such as a patient dying. Beyond that, designers have to add visual clues to let the student know when things are going south.

VIRTUAL LABS

A bigger major weakness in virtual products is that all they are, well, is products (Figure 5.9). Most product training is that the experience is isolated from the experience of actually using the product in the real world. So no matter how realistic the modeling of the actual product, if it doesn't reflect the on-the-job experience, it is not as useful.

"I would want to know what people are having trouble with the traditional training, or no training. Having a simulation teaching people how to turn on a camera is not that relevant," said Jonathan Kaye.

Figure 5.9. Aspects of a Virtual Product with Analog Controls.

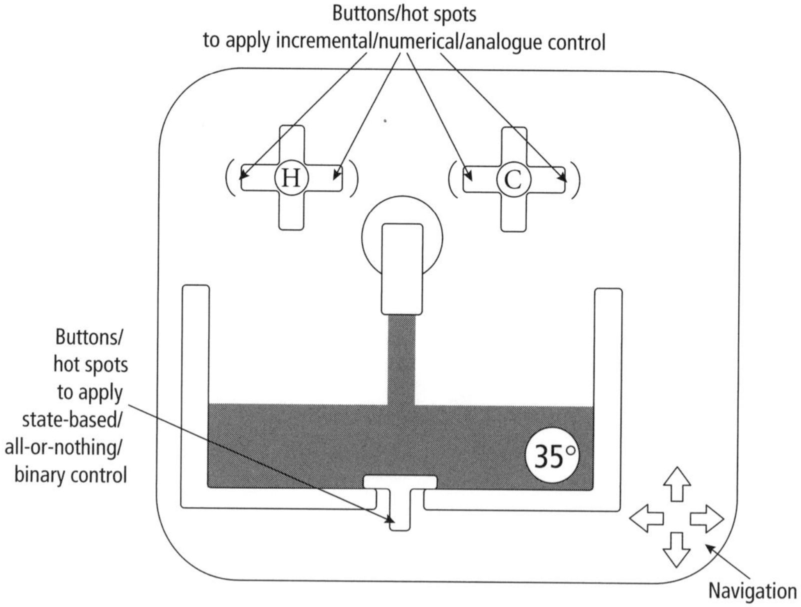

"When people approach the simulation of projects, I think a much better approach is to throw someone into the situation with the product he or she is using, challenge the person to do a task, and then if he or she can't perform the task, start providing layered feedback," said Jonathan.

Thus, virtual products are often better leveraged when packaged into scenario oriented virtual labs (Figure 5.10). Virtual labs trade some of the fidelity of a virtual product for a strong context and series of missions to accomplish.

Taking Labs to the Extreme

David Grant is the performance assessment manager for Raytheon Professional Services (RPS). He uses simulations to assess performances in lab settings rather than in the actual work environment.

One client is General Motors. General Motors Service Technical College trains eighty thousand service technicians working in over 7,200 General Motors dealerships. The service technicians have to complete a performance-based assessment as part of their program to become a GM Certified Master Technician.

David's simulations present typical vehicle problems. For example, a technician will receive work orders from the service manager, describing the customer's concern. The technician has to first verify the customer's concern, such as, "brake light always on." The technician will

Figure 5.10. Product + Scenario = Lab.

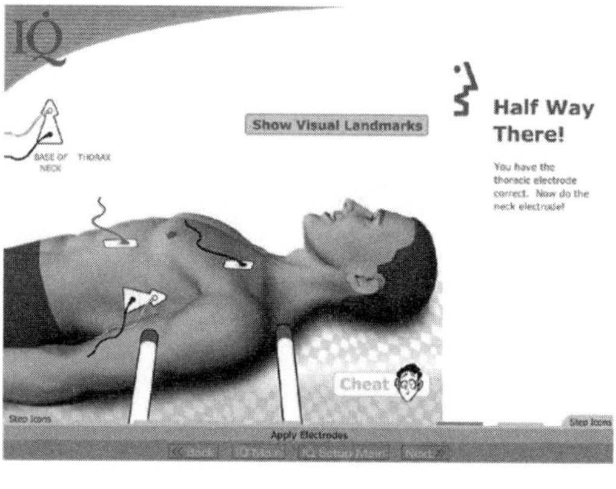

Source: Courtesy of Wantagh, Inc., and Equipment Simulations LLC. Used with Permission.

then have to use the tools available to him or her in the simulated lab to diagnose and solve the problem (Figure 5.11). The technicians are scored, with the highest values assigned given to those who follow the optimum path to solving the problem.

Raytheon Professional Services (RPS) has also developed simulations for the Manufacturing Skill Standards Council (MSSC) for a National Manufacturing Assessment System. The assessment is designed to evaluate the manufacturing skills of current workers, people just entering the workforce, and people returning to the manufacturing industry.

RPS' simulations are used to evaluate a technician's knowledge of manufacturing terms, procedures, basic skills, and other key competencies. During one type of virtual lab, a technician is provided job instruction and asked to perform job tasks at a workstation on the assembly line. Then problems are introduced into the workstation, by way of faulty equipment, safety problems, and/or product not produced to specification. If the technician recognizes the problem within a given time frame, he or she receives two points. If it times out, the simulation asks a question about the issue. If the technician answers the question correctly, he or she can still earn one point.

Figure 5.11. GM Virtual Lab.

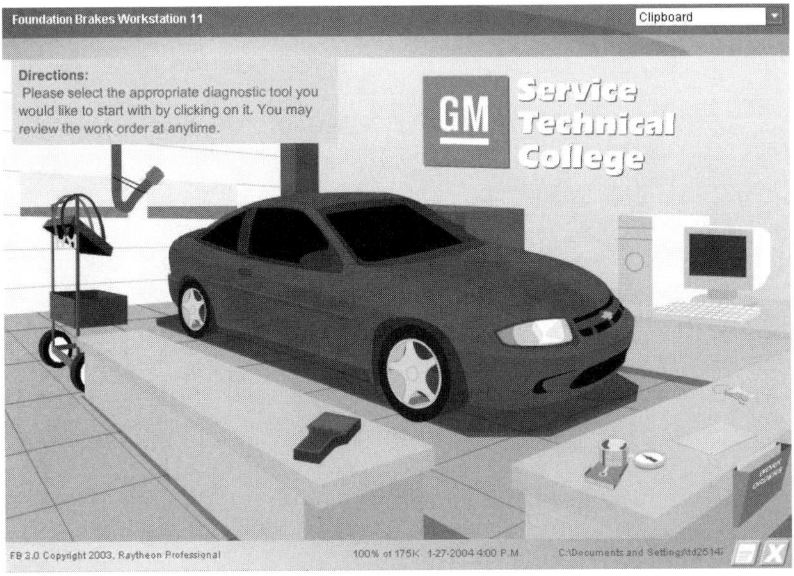

Source: General Motors.

Figure 5.12. Building Globes.

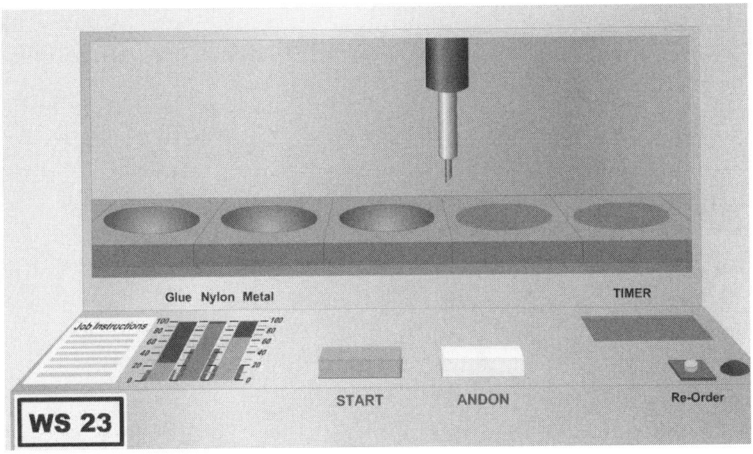

Source: © Manufacturing Skill Standards Council (MSSC). Used with Permission.

In the example in Figure 5.12 above, a technician is asked to produce globe halves. As the technician operates the machinery, he or she is required to maintain the proper quantities of parts by constantly monitoring the gages and re-ordering when necessary. If the technician does not realize the parts are low, the simulation will time the event and eventually stop the machine and prompt the production worker.

A Simple Drag-and-Drop Model

At times, a full virtual product or virtual lab may be overkill. In these cases, a simpler drag-and-drop model for some of the key features is effective (Figure 5.13).

Synthetic Microworlds

Some virtual labs more resemble synthetic microworlds. Rather than device simulations with discrete states and clear transitions between them, these simulations look similar, but use multiple equations to represent something more organic, dynamic, and fluid, such as chemical reactions or autonoma-style creatures. Found more in academic environments, rather than stand-alone, these tend to require teachers to help in the use and analysis.

Figure 5.13. A Simple Drag-and-Drop Model for a Nuclear Reactor (and Boy Do I Hope This Is Not the Extent of Their Training).

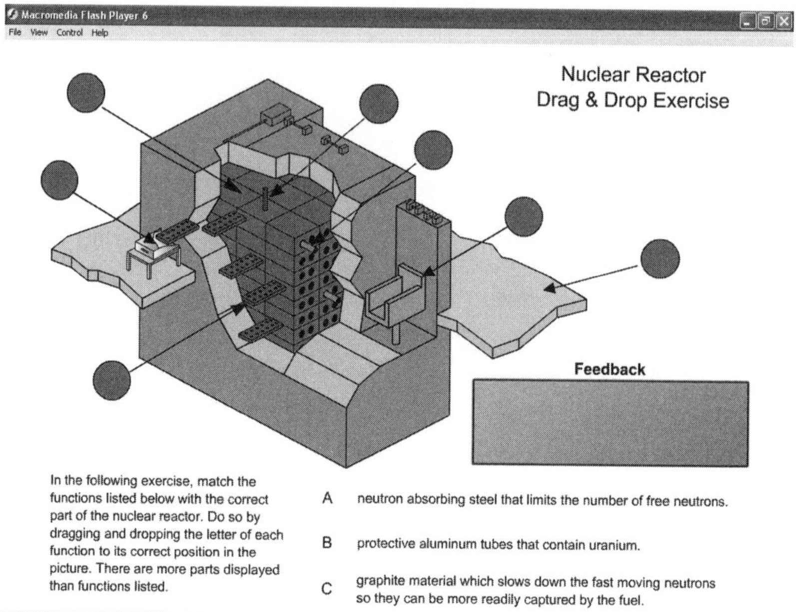

Source: Richard Peck, Multimedia Designer, The Institute for Interactive Technologies at Bloomsburg University. Used with Permission.

The users set variables, and then turn the "petri dish" on, watching the results of their decisions. They may or may not be able to tweak the variables on the fly. Daniel Roggenkamp asks a learner to establish hospital rules around the containment of SARS, challenging them to be neither too lax nor too draconian (Figure 5.14).

APPLICATIONS

I have a quick question. Which of the following are true?

- I have used a virtual product and/or a virtual lab in a course I have taken.
- I have used a virtual product and/or a virtual lab in a course I created.

Now put your finger on one box in Figure 5.15 and move it around according to the directions of the arrows to settle on the state that reflects your impressions of virtual products and virtual labs.

Figure 5.14. SARS Outbreak Synthetic Microworld.

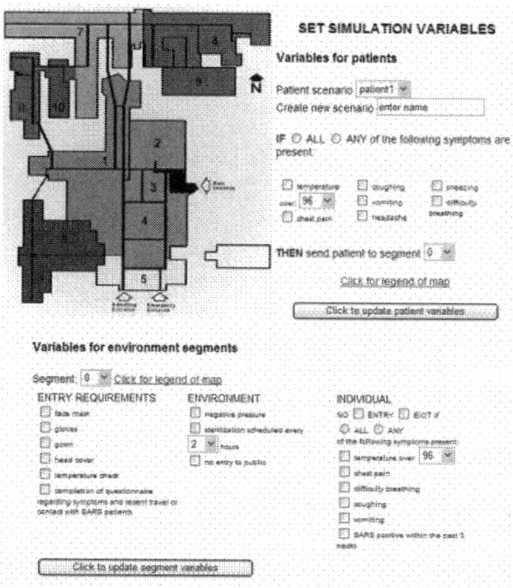

Source: Screen Shot Reprinted by Permission from Daniel Roggenkamp.

Figure 5.15. Possible Opinions of Virtual Products and Virtual Labs.

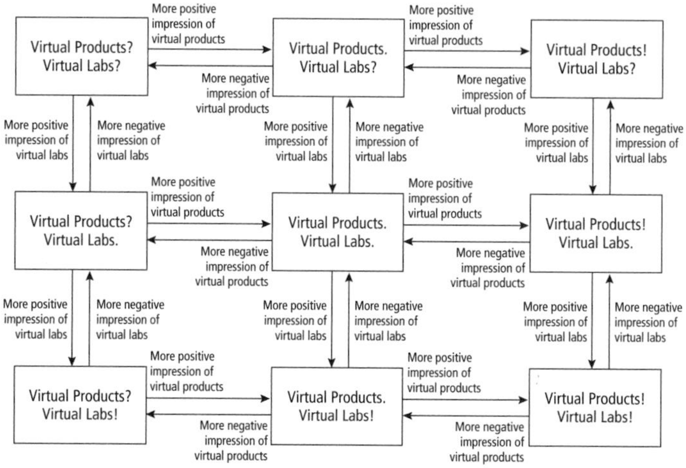

Again, appropriate use of virtual labs often determines the successful opinion of virtual labs. An organization should seriously consider virtual products and virtual labs if they produce or use high-cost and medium-to-complex devices (Figure 5.16), and they meet at least two

Figure 5.16. Traditional Virtual Product Vendors.

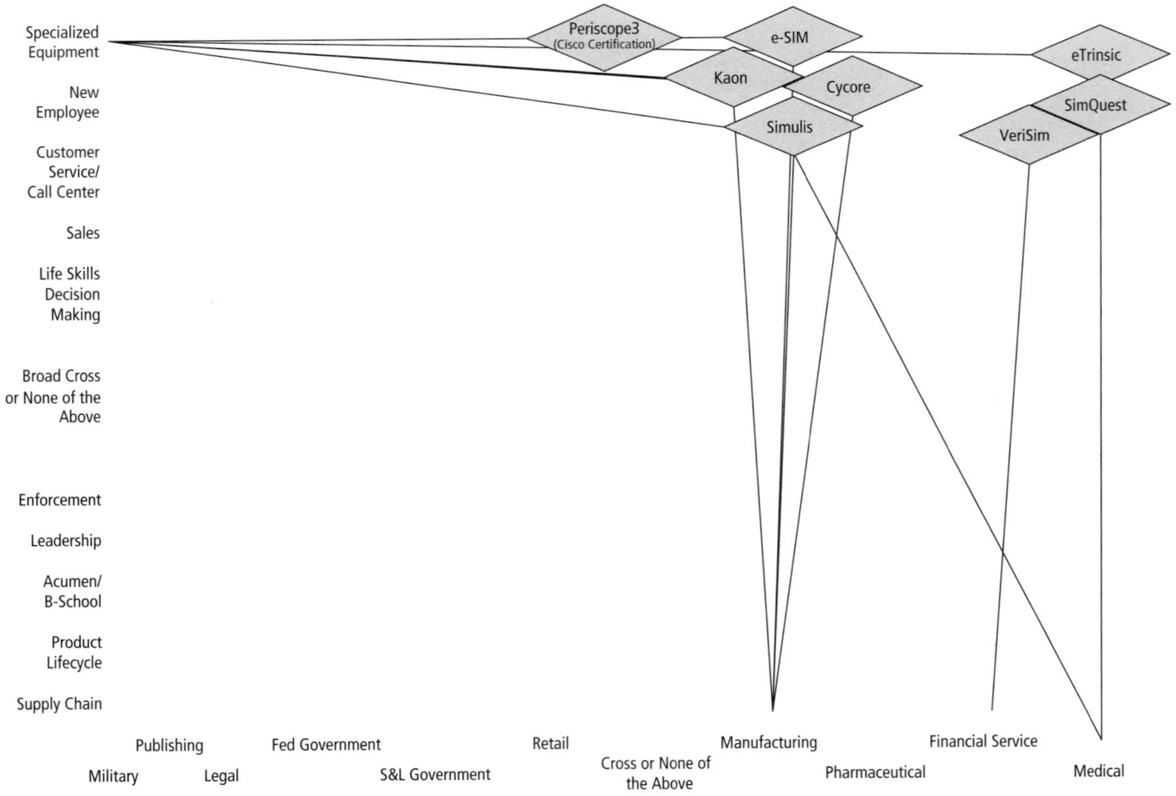

of the following three criteria:

- There is a high importance placed on people operating the devices correctly.
- Companies cannot send out practice devices to all users.
- Companies cannot send out an instructor to all users.

Architecture

Virtual products and virtual labs tend to be delivered over the Web, launched by a learning management system (LMS). The more sophisticated virtual products and virtual labs need either standard or proprietary browser plug-ins. In some cases, access to the virtual product or virtual labs is driven by customer relationship management (CRM) software (Figure 5.17).

Development questions around virtual products include:

- What is the download required for a user to engage a virtual product?

Figure 5.17. Virtual Products and Virtual Lab Architecture Considerations.

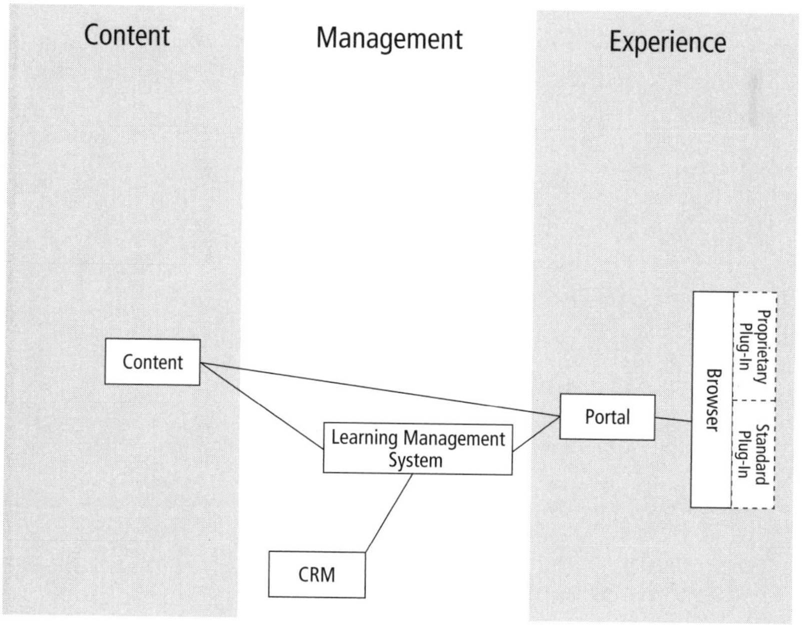

- What are comparable virtual products and labs that have been created? What were their budgets?
- How is evaluation performed (if the virtual product is used in an assessment capacity)?

OTHER RESOURCES

- Kaye, Jonathan, & Castillo, David. (2002). *Flash MX for Interactive Simulation.* Florence, KY: OnWord Press.

AS A SMALLER PIECE OF A LARGER WHOLE

Complex experiences, including computer games, use virtual lab type models to add realism. Players might pull up personal digital assistants (PDAs) or email (or telegrams) to get the next assignments or other critical information. Lights can be turned on and, often more importantly, turned off. Car dashboards have working speedometers. Vehicles can sustain damage, impacting different types of performance. Binoculars trade peripheral views for magnification. Flashlights slowly drain batteries. Players might take apart pieces of critical equipment, upgrade parts of it, or optimize it for a specific task.

COMING UP NEXT

We've just scratched the surface. Go a bit deeper, and do you know what you will find? A grand unifying theory of simulations! Actually, a few of them.

SECTION TWO

THE BROADER OPPORTUNITIES OF SIMULATIONS

6

A MORE COMPLETE PERSPECTIVE

Looking to the Broader World of Educational Simulations

A little simulation is a dangerous thing.

THESE FIRST FOUR GENRES, branching story, game-based, interactive spreadsheets, and virtual products/virtual labs, discussed in the previous section, are pretty powerful models of interactive content. From what I have seen, as I said before, any given teaching program should probably use one of them. Any training organization should use all four of them. And if you want to really advance your understanding, go to Appendix 6, Getting What You Want: The Black Art of Customizing the Four Traditional Simulation Genres.

But by themselves these first four are not sufficient. Not by a long shot.

For one reason, they are not sufficient in capturing others' current views of simulations. The more people you talk to about simulations, from engineers to our children to pilots to teachers, the more people refer to other simulation models. We have to understand them just to communicate effectively with stakeholders.

But more importantly, we are going to have to leave the comfort of well-understood models to draw inspiration and lessons learned from these alternative, highly evolved, and selectively effective simulations. Only through them can we create the transformational experiences that are within our grasp.

A MORE COMPLETE MAP

Because I was a research director at Gartner, an organization that analyzes the information technology markets, I have a compulsive need to map things out. (There may be deeper reasons than that, but I will let trained psychologists make that call. In all fairness, I haven't had to eat my food alphabetically in over four years, so I should get credit for that.)

I have found that putting everything on one page can include and organize everyone's perspective and can start to tease apart differences in areas that seem similar. It also helps clients, especially CEOs, get comfortable with first the big picture, then the details.

As I go through the mapping process, I not only find holes in my knowledge that I can tap others to fill, but I am surprised when seemingly disparate areas are closer on the market map than I would have thought, bringing forth a wave of new insights.

The biggest step in creating a useful map is to select the axis. Said technically, I have to figure out (read that, guess) what are the *two most relevant, non-correlating pairs of technology dichotomies*?

Teasing out the simulation pairs was probably my hardest topographical challenge to date (take a look at the Appendices for some other maps). But finally, I found two axes to be surprisingly useful: *Stand-Alone Versus Instructor* and *Linear Versus Dynamic Skills.*

Stand-Alone Versus Instructor

The first pair is stand-alone versus instructor-supported.

At first glance, the decision to make a simulation either stand-alone or instructor-supported seems almost last-minute, a mere technical detail. The appropriate analogy, one might forgivably think, is to sports fans that capriciously decide whether to support their team in the stadium or by watching on their big-screen television in the nicely appointed basement. The factors might include whether it was a home game, whether tickets were available, how cold it was outside, and previously how "lucky" each approach had been for the team.

But the more you understand about the role of an instructor, the more you realize how this tears through all simulation issues, including selection of genre, design, and use.

Just at a high level:

- *Stand-alone simulations* are easier to deploy, more consistent and scalable, although they require more time, expense, and iterations to trouble-shoot to get right up-front, and what is learned is often not as deep or transforming.

- *Instructor-supported simulations* are significantly more costly to deploy, are more flexible to evolve on the fly, can provide more handholding, and result in more transformational experiences.

The distinction between *stand-alone* and *instructor-supported* may be especially worth making today. The end of the 1990s and the first part of the 2000s brought with it a doctrine of non-supported, "fire-and-forget," e-learning-as-pre-reading content. Most of those supporters have been fired or have gone out of business, so we are now re-appreciating and even re-inventing the role of the instructor.

Linear Versus Dynamic Skills

The second pair to define the other axis is *linear* versus *dynamic skills.*

Most formal learning programs teach *stories* or *linear processes.* The expectation is that students are supposed to all walk away with the same content.

When students are tested, it tends to be on a single axis. For example, student A remembered 90 percent of the material, which is better than student B, who only remembered 85 percent. (Bad, student B, bad!) If student A is killed in a car accident, the obituary will say how extra sad it was because she was a great student. If student B is killed in a car accident, it will still be sad, but just not quite *as* sad, because he never really applied himself.

Linear content is *necessary* when the formal learning will

- Lead to some kind of certification, or
- Meet a legal requirement such as safety or sexual harassment training.

It is also appropriate for teaching any highly established process, such as:

- Using some new software, or
- Assembling equipment.

Traditional methods for teaching *linear* content include workbooks, videos, and lecture-based classrooms. Most of our formal schooling was around these convergent skills.

In contrast to formal learning, much of our informal learning, however, is *dynamic* or *divergent*. For example:

- Different people could all be apprentices of the same CEO, but learn very different content.
- A group could be involved in a "skunk works" research project, but each participant would likely take away different skills.
- No two attendees of a conference have the same observations, or even schedule.
- Researchers using the Internet to track down competitive information more often find different rather than overlapping information.

Bonus Question: One hundred students could listen to the same teaching assistant with really poor English skills and come away with one hundred different opinions of what he or she said. Is that *dynamic* or *convergent*?

The problem with *dynamic* content is, as we have mentioned, that it has traditionally been expensive and unpredictable for a training group to rigorously deploy. Simulations can, however, introduce a level of predictability and scalability.

(Having said that, *linear* training should always be used if it fully meets the learning requirement because of the lower cost involved, the relative speed of development, and the lower frustration on the part of the students.)

EDUCATIONAL SIMULATIONS AND TANGENTIAL AREAS

The new simulation space begins to take form. We can go from our original, back-of-the-napkin sketch (Figure 6.1). . .

. . . to a slightly more complete and organized version (Figure 6.2).

If you are interested, here are some definitions of the terms.

Quadrant I: Instructor-Supported Linear Learning

Traditional classrooms are the default models of instructor-supported experiences that teach simple processes and history. While shunned by early simulation purists, models of instructor-supported linear content will remain a critical part of successful educational experiences.

Figure 6.1. Facets of Educational Simulation, with the Four Traditional Corporate and Higher-Ed Genres in the Middle.

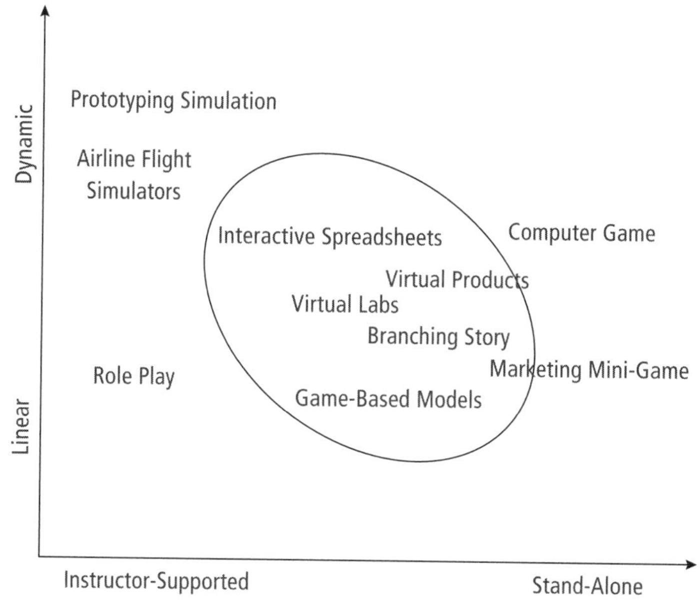

GAME-BASED (COVERED IN SECTION I) One of our traditional "simulation" genres falls into this category. As we discussed, with the goal of "making learning fun," students engage familiar and entertaining games such as *Wheel of Fortune*®, *Solitaire,* or *Memory,* with important pieces of linear or task-based content replacing trivia or icons. More diagnostic than instructional, game-based models nonetheless might be the technique of choice for traditional training groups looking to quickly goose their reputations, customer satisfaction, and even effectiveness. Instructors often host them. Confusingly, the game shells are sometimes dynamic, but the content, the questions and answers, are linear.

Quadrant II: Stand-Alone Linear Learning

Workbooks are familiar models of self-paced learning, so familiar that they dominated early e-learning. Quite a few early simulations fell into this category.

BRANCHING STORIES (COVERED IN SECTION I) As noted, in *branching stories,* students make multiple-choice decisions along an ongoing

Figure 6.2. Educational Simulations and Tangential Spaces.

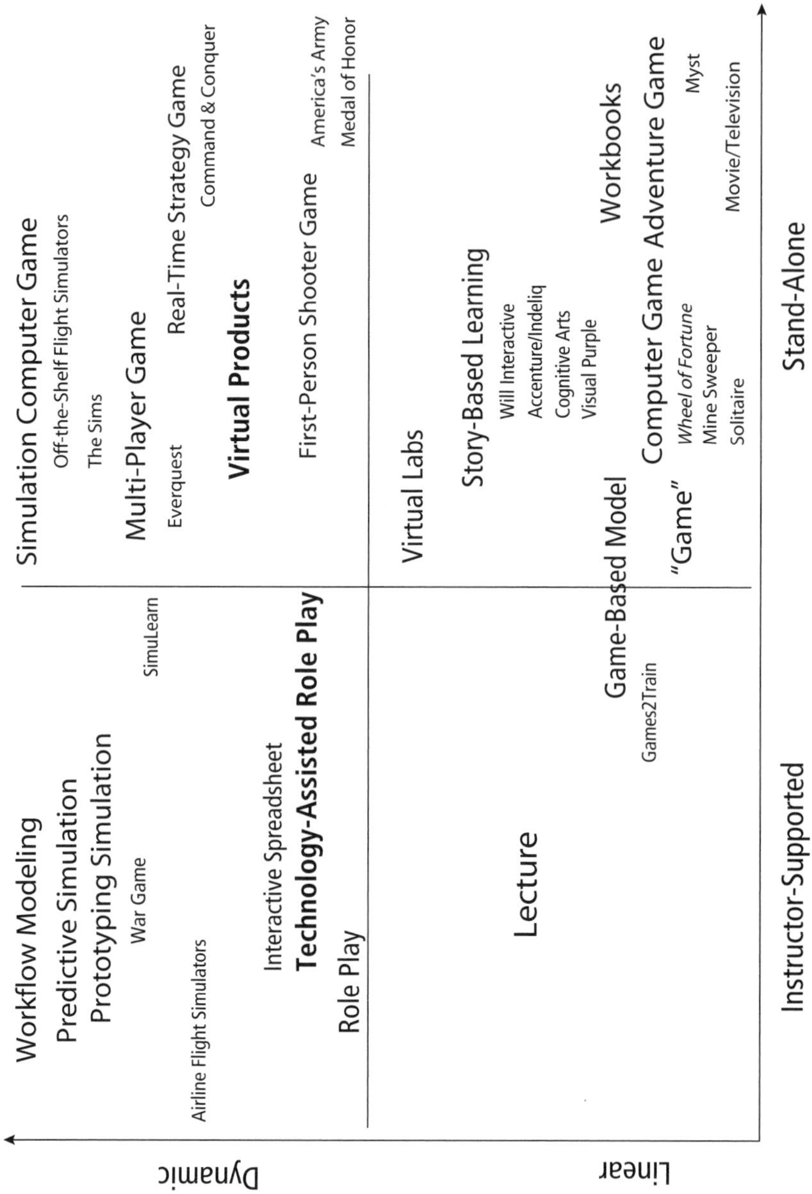
Dynamic
Linear
Instructor-Supported
Stand-Alone
Workflow Modeling
Predictive Simulation
Prototyping Simulation
War Game
Airline Flight Simulators
SimuLearn
Interactive Spreadsheet
Technology-Assisted Role Play
Role Play
Lecture
Game-Based Model
Games2Train
Simulation Computer Game
Off-the-Shelf Flight Simulators
The Sims
Multi-Player Game
Everquest
Real-Time Strategy Game
Command & Conquer
Virtual Products
First-Person Shooter Game
America's Army
Medal of Honor
Virtual Labs
Story-Based Learning
Will Interactive
Accenture/Indeliq
Cognitive Arts
Visual Purple
Workbooks
"Game"
Computer Game Adventure Game
Wheel of Fortune
Mine Sweeper
Solitaire
Myst
Movie/Television

sequence of events, often around what to say to another person in a given situation. The decisions impact the rest of the story, ultimately terminating in either successful or unsuccessful outcomes.

VIRTUAL LABS (COVERED IN SECTION ONE) Again, *virtual labs* forsake some of the fidelity of virtual products. They focus instead on the situation where, and context in which, the product is being used.

ADVENTURE GAMES GenXers and GenYers come at simulations as extensions of, or maybe just, computer games. They assume a *highly entertaining and relentlessly interactive* experience. Some computer games, such as adventure games, are story-driven and involve predictable and consistent paths and predictable and consistent (yet challenging and hopefully intriguing) puzzles to solve.

Quadrant III: Instructor-Supported Dynamic Learning

Incredibly common but under the radar of most e-learning-focused professionals, instructor-supported dynamic learning is highly effective and often a tad expensive.

TRADITIONAL ROLE PLAYS, INCLUDING MOCK CONGRESS, MOOT COURT (TO BE COVERED IN SECTION TWO) Traditional teachers and trainers look at simulations as extensions of role plays, even moot courts. They refer to simulations as environments that moderate aspects of *real-time multi-player* interactions, including enabling engagement between participants who are not co-located. They focus on the pedagogical and organizational role of the facilitator. This includes their actions before the role play, during the role play, and debriefing afterward.

WORKFLOW MODELING AND PREDICTIVE SIMULATIONS Engineers come at simulations from both a predictive and CAD/CAM angle. For them, the *accuracy of the simulation* is the single most important characteristic (Figure 6.3). As training becomes more rigorous, we will see a greater need for seamless relationships among the designers, trainers, service, and maintenance people (Figure 6.4).

For example, a 3D model of an airplane turbine might be built of thousands of smaller pieces that can be individually examined. One attribute of these smaller pieces could be at what temperature they fail. Thus a trainer could show students the sequence of parts failures as the temperature of the engine rose.

Figure 6.3. Very High Fidelity Models of Objects.

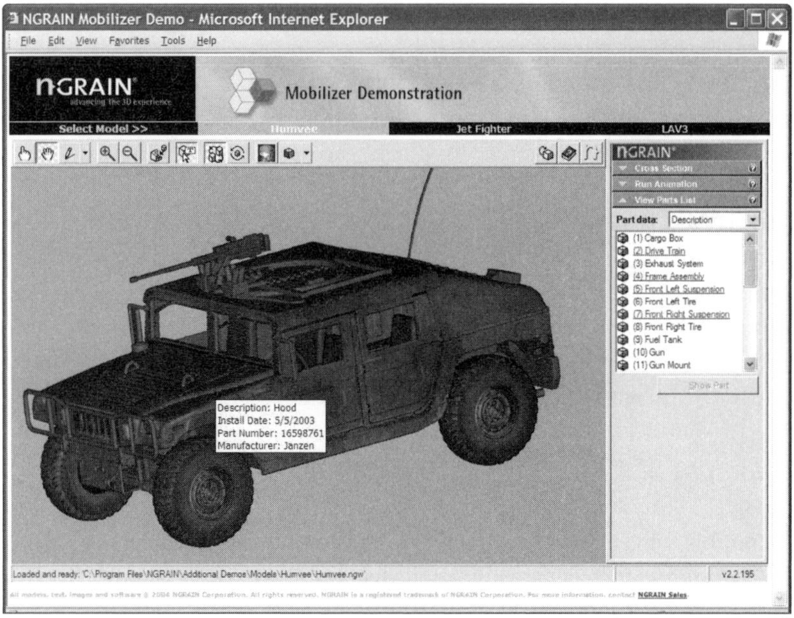

Source: NGRAIN. Used with Permission.

These annotated models also become the basis for knowledge management, as expert information is captured in annotations associated with specific parts or relationships. This greatly speeds up and enriches the process of creating a classroom or online training. Finally, when a crisis does occur, the models can be distributed via the Web to organize the problem-solving process.

AIRLINE FLIGHT SIMULATORS, WAR GAMES, AND TECHNOLOGY-ASSISTED ROLE PLAY (TO BE COVERED IN SECTION TWO) Military and airline people think in terms of war games and flight simulators. They invest hundreds of millions over many years, evolving simulations with a high *transferability* of actions from the artificial environment to the real one. They focus relentlessly on after-action reviews to examine what went right and what went wrong (Figure 6.5).

INTERACTIVE SPREADSHEETS (COVERED IN SECTION ONE) As noted, interactive spreadsheets focus on business school issues such as supply chain management, product lifecycle, accounting, and general cross-functional business acumen. Students allocate finite resources along

Figure 6.4. The Merging of Product Development, Training, and Maintenance.

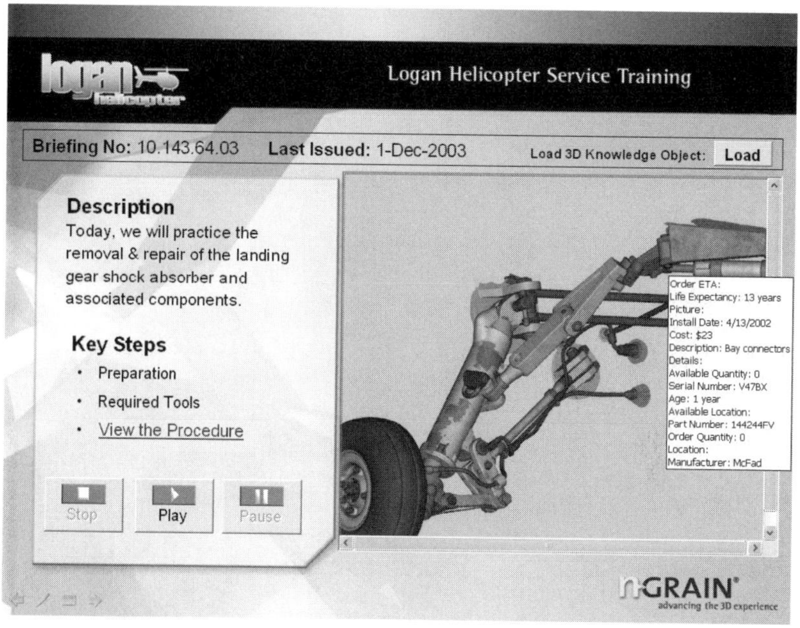

Source: NGRAIN. Used with Permission.

competing business categories at successive turn-based fixed intervals, and each time watch their results play out on dense graphs and charts. This is often done in a multi-player or team-based environment and often with facilitators.

The subtlety, unpredictability, and variability of interactive spreadsheets make them appropriate for high-potentials and supervisors through the direct reports to the CEO. They are often the cornerstones of multi-day programs to align a fractured department or organization by building shared knowledge and understanding.

Quadrant IV: Stand-Alone Dynamic Learning

Stand-alone dynamic learning is the holy grail (although not the sacred feminine) of early simulation designers. These models would be quickly accessible and result in deep, discovery-based learning. Models include the following.

VIRTUAL PRODUCTS (COVERED IN SECTION ONE) With *virtual products,* students interact with visual, selectively accurate representations

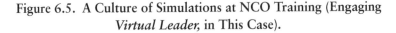

Figure 6.5. A Culture of Simulations at NCO Training (Engaging *Virtual Leader,* in This Case).

Source: Author.

of actual products without the physical restrictions of the reality. The interface aligns with the real function of the objects represented. Clicking the graphical "on" switch results in the lights turning on. The mechanics are predictable, although sometimes it is still easy to get confused and lost.

SIMULATION COMPUTER GAMES, REAL-TIME STRATEGY GAMES, MULTI-PLAYER GAMES, FIRST-PERSON SHOOTERS (TO BE COVERED IN SECTION TWO) As we said, GenXers and GenYers come at simulations as extensions of, or maybe just, computer games. They assume a *highly entertaining and relentlessly interactive* experience. Some computer games such as simulation-based games (for example, *SimCity*™, *The Sims*™, *Roller Coaster Tycoon*), real-time strategy games (for example, *Command and Conquer*™, *WarCraft*), and online multi-player games are unpredictable. Players cannot play the same way twice. Other games such as first-person shooters have a predictable pattern and flow, but involve highly attuned reflexes.

ALL ARE IMPORTANT

While many have their favorite type of simulations, all of these perspectives need to considered and respected. Politically, I have had to refer to all of these to facilitate agreement on definitions and expectations from the stakeholders, surfacing any hidden assumptions and inherent tradeoffs.

But also, each has inherent value. They all work, and each simulation model has attributes we will have to consider in the context of next generation simulations.

So for the sake of research, for the sake of politics, and even for the sake of inspiration, let's dig into these tangential simulation areas. There is a lot to learn if we are to build next generation learning experiences (next gen sims).

COMING UP NEXT

It has been said that the differences between education and training can be summarized by the differences between sex education and sex training. But there is a middle ground, a best of both worlds. There has to be.

7

RECOGNIZING NEW TYPES OF SCALABLE CONTENT

Systems, Cyclical, and Linear

WE ARE IMAGINING and beginning to create next generation educational simulations (next gen sims). To do this, we have to increasingly venture out of the tight-knit (inbred) community of academics and trainers and draw from a richer and deeper genetic pool.

One of the defining attributes of simulations (and computer games have explored this area in full force) is the concept of *dynamic skills.* So far dynamic skills have essentially been defined by the very unsatisfying "Well, they are not linear skills." Now, we will tease apart the concept of dynamic content into two groups; *systems-based,* and *cyclical-based.*

SYSTEMS-BASED CONTENT

Systems content exposes users to complex, intertwined relationships. This content includes the components, parts, pieces, attributes, relationships, rules, and principles that govern the operation of a system. It includes all of the variables of the system, from primary and secondary all of the way down and how those variables affect other variables (Figure 7.1).

Kym Buchanan, a doctoral student at Michigan State University, understands the importance of systems content. Kym is trained in chemistry and finds principles in that discipline that are critical to understanding just about anything. He explained, "You don't understand something until you understand the underlying *systems dynamics.*"

Figure 7.1. Manufacturing Systems Dynamics from STELLA Software.

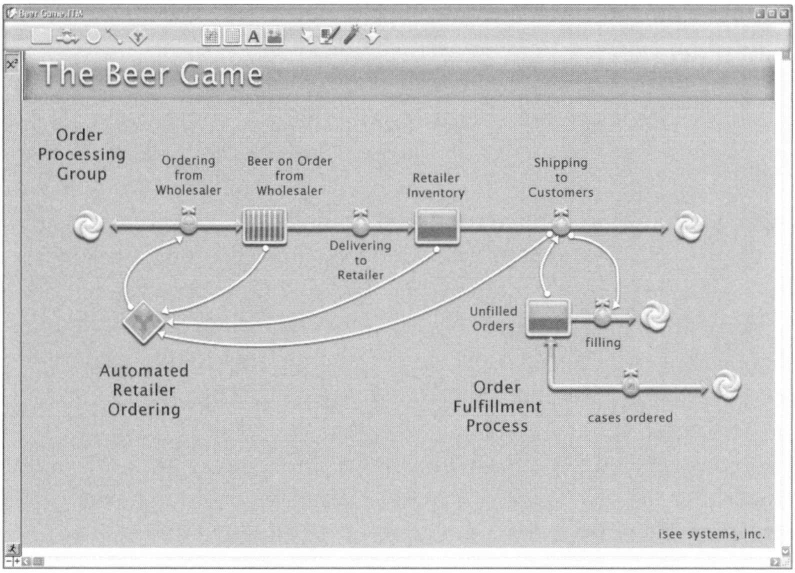

Source: Isee Systems, Inc. Used with Permission.

Recursion, balancing factors, and *feedback loops* are common systems constructs, seen both in models and in the real world. Kym adds other, less commonly identified examples.

There is a *systems* concept in chemistry, he explained, called *energy of activation.* Here a small amount of external energy releases a large amount of internal energy. A familiar example is a match, which does not just spontaneously combust, but has to be activated. This concept is critical to understanding seed grants and the world of venture capitalism, for examples.

Another systems concept from chemistry is a *rate-determining step.* An entire chemical reaction may be bottlenecked by a single step out of hundreds. Improvements to every other step are then irrelevant. But if you can accelerate that one critical step, you accelerate the entire process.

A principle that Kym sees misused all the time involves the need to *carefully calibrate your agents.* Imagine the following:

1 teaspoon of chemical A plus

1 teaspoon of chemical B combines and reacts to create

2 teaspoons of more valuable chemical C.

Adding more of, say, chemical B often doesn't help the reaction, either by speeding it up, making it better, or making more of it. *And* (this is the kicker) it could easily hurt it. More chemical B potentially dilutes or even contaminates the chemical C.

As a sobering example, people who make illegal drugs typically do not use the right ratios. The result? Street cocaine often has high contents of lead, causing yet more irreparable damage to the users.

You want to put exactly what you need into a system, with no leftovers or contaminants. Kym sees this failure playing out in universities and corporations. Supervisors often try to solve problems by throwing resources at them. As one little example, they put too many people on a committee. This creates waste and contamination that can hurt the end result.

There are simple examples of this every day. You might have a situation where you need a person for five minutes in a two-hour meeting, but the person feels obligated to stay for the entire two hours.

One of the simplest systems concepts is that of delay. *Cause A* may have *effect B,* but not for two months. Not appreciating the delay inherent in the system may cause an over-application of A, or even a cessation of A when B did not happen at the expected time.

More people are beginning to consider this *the apex* of instructional design. While it is not complete, I agree at least that most learning that does not involve a new or better-honed understanding of a system (or multiple systems) is of little real value in most real situations. Interactive spreadsheets represent a pure, if somewhat quaint, approach to systems thinking.

Tools

For many professors, STELLA software has provided an early and meaningful exposure to systems (Figure 7.1). STELLA software is a powerful, easy to use systems modeling software, sold by Isee Systems (formerly High Performance Systems, Inc.).

Systems Content Research Questions

Research questions around systems content might include:

- What are typical and/or successful strategies, when should they be used, and what are the impacts and tradeoffs of each?
- Are there broad factors that compete in the short term but support each other in the long term (used to organize the strategies)?

- What are the independent, interacting, and critical elements? What are the relevant characteristics of each element individually, and what impact do they have on each other?

CYCLICAL-BASED CONTENT

The second type of content, *cyclical,* addresses tiny activities that can be infinitely combined to impact an environment and create an outcome. These bundles of discrete action, timing, and magnitude are a natural concept to us when understanding how to operate a machine like a car, communicate by using a typewriter, or even perform with a piano. The opportunity, however, is to move beyond these kinesthetic examples to create cyclical content for all professional skills.

From a simulation perspective, cyclical content is dealt with at the interface level. More specifically, the interface for cyclical content is shaped more by capturing and mapping real actions that influence some part of the world, and less by standard Web, computer game, or book conventions.

Of the four traditional simulation genres, *virtual products/virtual labs* provide at least some use of muscle memory in simulations today, if only in the hard skills space. In Flashsim's watch example (Figure 7.2),

Figure 7.2. Virtual Watch with Statechart.

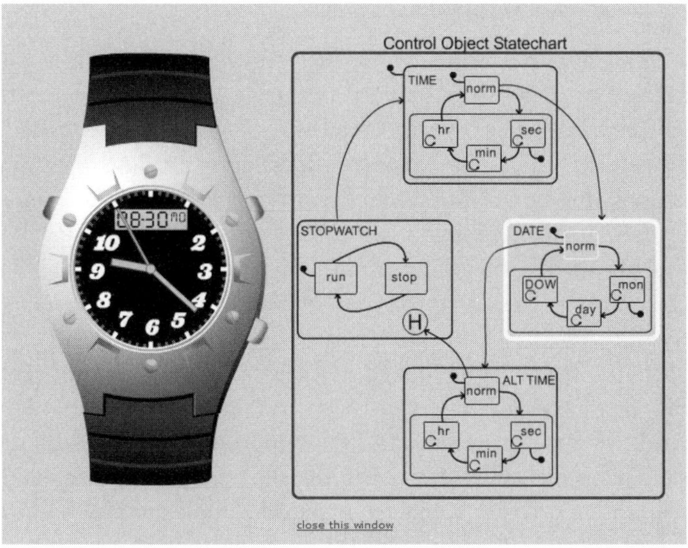

Source: Equipment Simulations LLC. Used with Permission.

there is a direct mapping between what you do with the simulation and what you do in real life:

- The reaction to pressing the button next to the *4* is dependent on the sequence that came before it.
- Working the stopwatch on the virtual watch or resetting the date requires *timing*. It is not enough to press the right buttons in the right order. You have to press the button at the *right moment* as well.
- And at different states, holding the button down longer has a different effect than pressing it quickly, such as resetting the stop watch all together.

One simulation, Allen Interactions' DialogCoach, aggressively uses cyclical content. To complete the lab, learners have to speak just as they would in their customer-focused job. Voice recognition software only gives the learner credit if it identifies very specific phrases, used at the right time and in the right order. The business impact of focusing on repeatedly practicing speaking, designer Jonathan Anderson has documented, are extraordinary.

Do we need to worry about the cyclical content? Only if we want our content to matter. If the interface does not line up with actual tasks in some real-time way, the learning will require many additional steps to apply in the world.

"This is just a vocational thing," the academics are sure to say. "You know, like cooking and woodworking. We don't have to worry about that, right?"

I couldn't disagree more. The most empowering and valued knowledge, including leadership, stewardship, negotiating, and project management, will all require great interfaces.

Having said that, for professional skills, distilling the discrete interactions (Figure 7.3), designing an interface (Figure 7.4), and then tuning the timing, requires a bit more finesse than working with a physical object. It requires an almost anthropological analysis of the discrete actions that a person has available when performing any activity.

Cyclical is the least appreciated of the three content types. Even people who "get" and advocate *systems-based content* in educational simulations have little appreciation of the importance of aligning interface to task. This is especially true when the skill is a professional skill and the task is a microcosm, such as in our leadership example. And yet the most powerful sims will use cyclical content relentlessly.

Figure 7.3. Some Tactical and Discrete Actions to Influence a Leadership Situation, Using a Meeting as a Real-Time Microcosm.

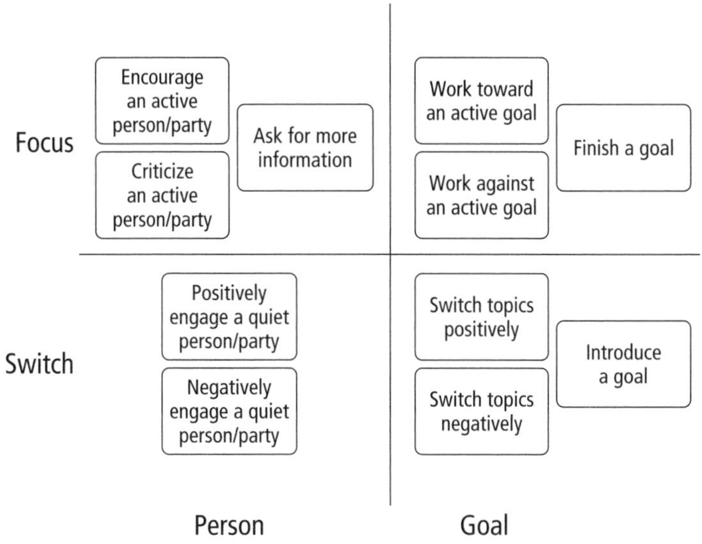

Source: SimuLearn Inc. Used with Permission.

Figure 7.4. Interface to a Real-Time Leadership Situation, Using a Meeting as a Real-Time Microcosm.

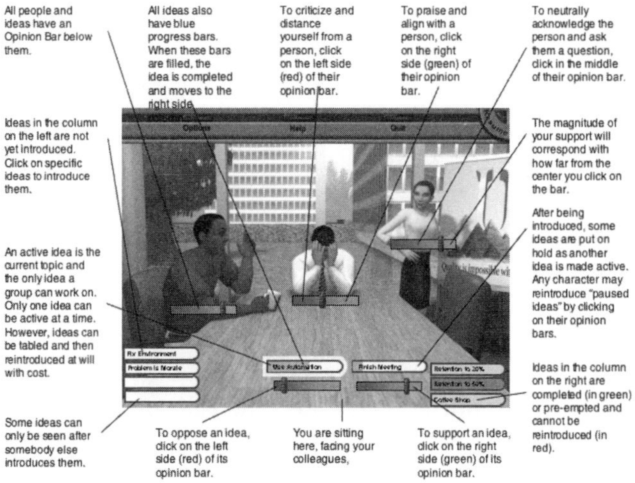

Source: SimuLearn Inc. Used with Permission.

From my work with different types of clients, this is an area where corporations have better intuition than academics, as corporations are more focused on the interface with the real world. This is also an area where all computer games with the exception of flight simulators provide remarkably poor role and deceiving models, because they too are not focused (nor do they want to be)(and nor, with so many violent games, do we want them to be) on transferability of skills.

Cyclical Content Research Questions

Research questions around cyclical content might include:

- What are all of the options that a person or organization has/discrete steps a person or organization can take?
- What are incremental signs that things are going well or going badly?
- Where is timing important/what are instances where doing the same thing a bit earlier or a bit later matter?
- Where is magnitude important/what are instances where doing the same thing a bit softer or a bit harder matter?
- Are there common situations that are representative of all situations, ideally that many people encounter at least once a week?

LINEAR CONTENT

The more we discuss other forms of content, the more we understand *linear content*. And we can better appreciate (read that, love) it for what it does so well.

Linear content remains critical in a simulation and in any educational experience. More like books or movies, this content type moves the user along a defined path from a beginning to an end.

Even computer games include a lot of linear content. Almost all dialogue, pre-rendered introductory sequences, and "triggers" (incidents that predictably and irrevocably alter the path of the game) are linear content. Many of the best-selling games of late are as characterized by their stories as by their interactions.

Linear Content Research Questions

Research questions around linear content might include:

- What are war stories?
- Are there general categories/archetypes?
- Have successful processes been established?
- What do success and failure look like?
- What are moments that, when they occur, are irrevocable, either in a good or bad sense?

THE CONVERGENCE

Some ask, with regard to next gen sims, why now? We have been educating for thousands of years, and computers have been around for decades.

There are many reasons, of course. But one of the biggest is that computing power has reached a point where it can cost-effectively cover systems, cyclical, and linear content *simultaneously* (Figure 7.5).

Figure 7.5. Linear Versus Dynamic Simulation Content.

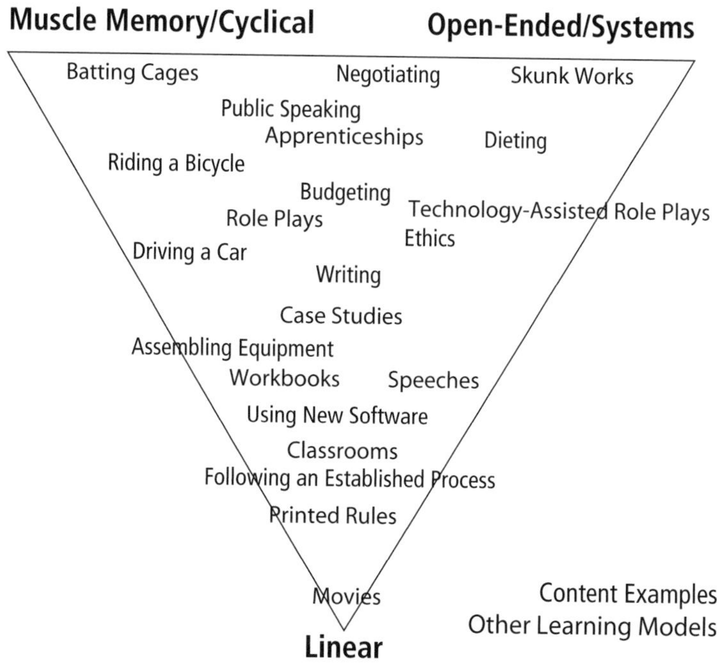

In the old days, you could have beautiful, pre-rendered pictures or animations, but with only limited, branching interaction (think of the PC game *Myst* or the arcade game *Dragon's Lair*). Or you could have fast, interactive animation that was of only very poor representational quality (think the arcade game *Asteroids*). Now, with 3D video cards and very fast processors, there is no longer a tradeoff of one for the other. You can have detailed *and* highly responsive environments.

SOME VENDOR FUN

Fidelity is simulation accuracy, loyalty to the original. To have some fun with vendors, watch how they loudly play up the fidelity in the content area where they have strengths, while desperately hoping you won't look at the other two areas. (They don't fully realize that a large number multiplied by zero still equals zero.) Only these three types of content types together, systems, cyclical, and linear, contribute to a simulation's true fidelity.

COMING UP NEXT

Is *SimCity*™ a game or a simulation? The answer has a profound impact on all educational experiences, from nursery school to med school.

8

THE THREE ESSENTIAL ELEMENTS TO SUCCESSFUL EDUCATIONAL EXPERIENCES

Simulations, Games, and Pedagogy

I made a perfect simulation about growing a company.
The only problem is that it takes twenty-five years to play.

—With apologies to Steven Wright

It's better to give than receive . . . advice.

IF THE THREE CONTENT TYPES ARE SYSTEMS, cyclical, and linear, what are the best ways of learning them? The answer is through (everyone together now) simulations, games, and (no looking at your notes) pedagogy.

GAMES AND SIMULATIONS

Games and *simulations* are almost always lumped together. Education and training conferences have special *games and simulations* tracks. Committees formed at universities and corporations are tasked to study the use of *games and simulations* for their students. People bring me in to build things that are *games and/or simulations.*

The two areas seem inextricably linked. And for good reasons. Computer games use abstracted but robust simulations. Simulations and their interfaces are getting more game-like.

Many educational philosophers have become tied up in the Gideon knot of what is a game versus what is a simulation, and how the two differ. I have been sucked into some of those conversations myself, and always hated myself in the morning for it.

Here's a better way. Rather than thinking about *games* and *simulation,* it is more productive to think about the distinct *elements,* namely:

- *Simulation* elements
- *Game* elements
- *Pedagogical* elements

Ultimately, the careful use of all three will result in the appropriate educational experience (Figure 8.1). It is getting the right use of each, and in the right proportions, that represents the challenge for all future instructional designers (and with computer game designers as well).

There is a practical benefit to this perspective. Take any educational program or experience about which you care. This works especially well with a program that you have revised at least once. As we go through the three elements, look at each of them as *places to evaluate and ultimately improve your existing program.*

Figure 8.1. Educational Simulations Happen at the Convergence of Three Elements.

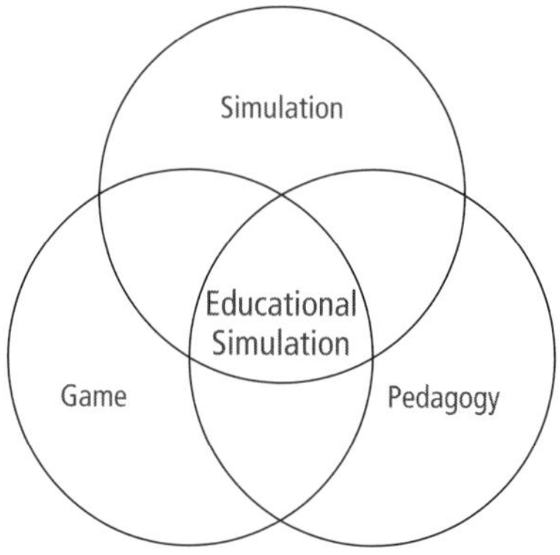

SIMULATION ELEMENTS

Simulation elements selectively represent objects or situations, and selectively represent user interaction. Simulation elements enable discovery, experimentation, role modeling, practice, and active construction of systems, cyclical, and linear content (Figure 8.2). Which means they enable a transferability to the real world.

To learn about *systems* in a simulation, users balance conflicting strategies and then discover diverse and often unscripted outcomes. Do we choose *A* or *B* or *C*?

To learn about *cyclical* content in a simulation, users practice their execution, including timing and magnitude. We know we are going to do *A*, but we are not sure if we should do it now, or wait a moment (or a day or a month). And we might not be sure how hard to do *A*. Soft A, or intense A?

Timing and magnitude are just as critical in executing professional skills such as negotiating, consultative sales, or relationship management as they are for hitting a tennis ball, dancing, driving, or having a romantic weekend in the city. Doing the same thing a bit too early or a bit too late, or a little too hard, or a tad too soft can have none of the positive effects, or even the opposite effect, of doing something the right way. (If you don't believe me, go on a date.) This type of content, also including *muscle memory* content, forces a user to adjust his or her timing almost imperceptibly in multiple, repetitious rounds (or cycles).

Figure 8.2. Simulation Elements Impact on Content Types.

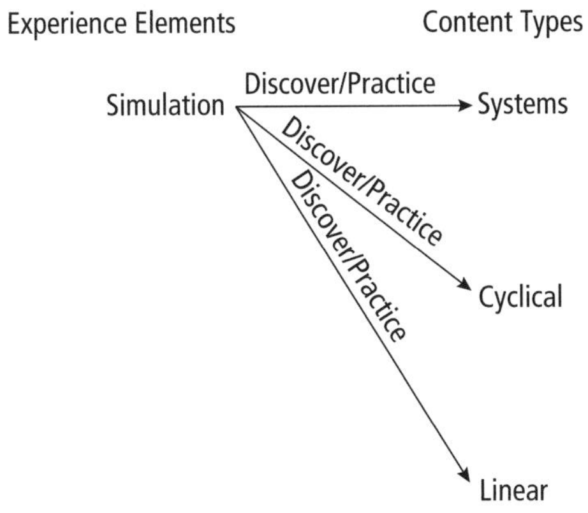

Both *systems and cyclical content* are subtle. Both can best be acquired through practice (or, if that doesn't work, practice).

Linear skills teach you *A* then *B* then *C*. Simulations also teach linear skills. Even when working with simulated systems, specific linear strategies might often enough work well:

- Car needs fuel; stop at the gas station.
- Fourth down and twenty-five yards to go; punt.
- Break a law; don't go on talk shows proclaiming your innocence.

There are also grander linear patterns that emerge from the interactive experience in general, just as from our own experiences:

- Birth; life; death
- Briefing; mission; debriefing
- Think your parents never have sex; know your parents have sex but still don't want to think about it
- Trust political commentators; don't trust political commentators

Good simulations also work because practice makes people better at what they do. In both World War II and the conflict in Korea, for example, the more experience a pilot had, the less chance he had of being shot down (Figure 8.3). (This, by the way, contradicts one philosophy of learning, *motivatism* (I may have made that term up) that suggests if a learner is sufficiently motivated, he or she will pick up everything needed on his or her own. I can only imagine that most pilots in combat conditions were highly motivated not to get shot down.

Specific Elements

Simulation elements include:

- The appropriate use of linear, cyclical, and systems content
- The appropriate use of simulation genres, including branching stories, virtual products/virtual labs, interactive spreadsheets, flight simulators, as well as new genres to be introduced
- The appropriate use of genre elements, including modeling, artificial intelligence, graphics, and interface
- Feedback from a decision (or series of decisions) that shows the natural consequences of the behavior

Figure 8.3. The Evolution of a Combat Ace.

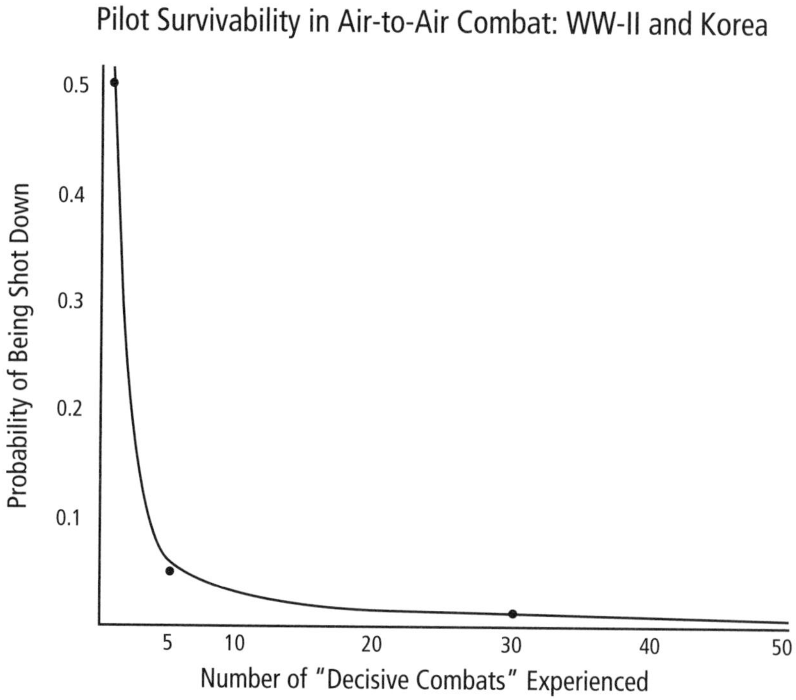

Simulations do not have to be interactive. Simulations elements can be

- A created atmosphere similar to the atmosphere in which the content will be used
- Written case studies, real or amalgam, without editorials, conclusions, or diagrams
- Videotaped case studies, real or amalgam, without editorials, voice-overs, text, conclusions, or diagrams
- A computational model "playing out" a situation

Context Alignment

What comes as a surprise to some is that accurate simulation elements are important, even when they do not directly apply to a specific learning objective. This could be any detail in the educational experience, no matter how small, that recalls the situation in which the skills will be applied.

Researcher Will Thalheimer explained to me one reason why: "The first thing that makes simulations work is *context alignment*. The performance situation is similar to the learning situation. Scuba divers can retrieve more information on land if they learned on land. The nugget there is that when you learn something, you are taking in everything—the learning method plus the entire environment. If you go into that context again, it allows you to search memory more effectively. When the learners enter a real situation, you want the environment to trigger the learning. That results in a 10 to 50 percent learning impact."

When I was a student (and every day I thank the stars I am not one now), I would, whenever possible, study for a test in the room where the test would be held. I would even reformat any electronic notes into the same font as the professor used for the test. It is scary how well that works.

Simulation elements will increasingly include reality as a prop for the simulation. With global positioning satellites (GPS) systems and cell phones/personal digital assistants (PDAs), simulations can use real locations as sets. Meanwhile next generation *virtual reality* systems can superimpose computer images onto real-time video goggles. Now soldiers, not just Alzheimer patients, can see snipers where there are none.

Reality can sometimes and selectively be substituted for any or all simulation elements. Obviously, safety, predictability, scalability, and cost-effectiveness have to be balanced against fidelity.

When to Use More

All of the three elements we will be discussing can be ramped up and ramped down. To create the first iteration of any educational simulation, we all guess as well as we can; but inevitably there needs to be some correction for subsequent versions. I ramp up the *simulation* elements if students are having a hard time transferring what they have learned, or if they need to better understand the systems and cyclical nature of the content.

When to Use Less

If students only need a high-level perspective or understanding, or if they are at the early part of a long learning curve, (or, and excuse me for being blunt, if a project is significantly under-funded [certain clients, you know who you are]), I lean toward including fewer *simulation* elements. And if there is no need to transfer a skill to real life, the use of simulation elements might be over-kill.

GAME ELEMENTS

Game elements provide familiar and entertaining interactions. Game elements increase the enjoyment derived from the educational experience. This can drive good will, but more importantly, drive more time spent with the experience, which increases learning, even taking time that had been "budgeted" for recreation by the learner.

Stuart Moulder was the former general manager for Microsoft's Game Studios. He is now in charge of Moulder Consulting, where he provides consulting services for game play, production, and strategic planning. According to Stuart, "Arbitrary (non-intrinsic) goals are often more motivating than real-world goals." The logic reads: Rather than make something take half as long to deliver, make it twice as long to deliver but a lot more fun.

Having said that, game elements are, from the perspective of both a student's learning time and your development resources, overhead. They do not support any learning objectives directly.

Getting a sponsor to pay for game elements is often difficult. Said University of Phoenix supplier Tata Interactive's Rupesh Goel, "Many colleges are apprehensive about any inclusion of game elements; they are worried that it might trivialize education." Corporations don't want to *waste* employees' time, nor pay for their vendors to *make games*.

Still, game elements are the spoonful of sugar that helps the medicine go down (the medicine go down, oh the medicine go down). Many simulation developers wisely and appropriately use game elements, but just as wisely and appropriately are reluctant to talk about them. In some cases developers may even pretend (read that, lie) to the sponsors that the contrivances weren't made.

There are many uses of game elements (Figure 8.4).

- Game elements can *surround* linear content that supports learning objectives.
- Game elements can *subvert* and *replace* simulation elements to make the experience more predictable and enjoyable—to keep, for example, engagement challenging, rather than fully accurate (where accuracy may be in fact harder, easier, or more dull). Games therefore encourage contrivances. Says Dr. Sivasailam "Thiagi" Thiagarajan, president of Workshops by Thiagi, a prolific writer, designer of hundreds of games and simulations, and perennial favorite at conferences, "There are built-in inefficiencies in a game. Obviously, there are more efficient methods for dropping a little white ball in eighteen holes than the rules of golf permit us to do."

Figure 8.4. Game Elements Impact on Content Types.

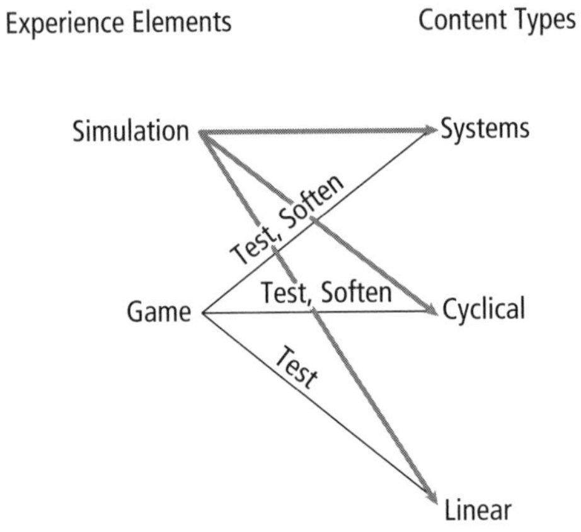

Specific Game Elements

One popular game contrivance that always intrigued me is *mixed scales.* This is most easily seen visually. The people in strategy games (such as *Rise of Nations*™) are smaller than cars, but only half as small. Cities are bigger than cars, but perhaps only five times as big. (This is not just a computer game thing. We also see this in almost all illustrations of the solar system, where a planet's *size* is scaled to other planets' *sizes,* their *distance* to the sun is scaled to the other planets' *distances* to the sun, but the *size* and *distance* to the sun are not scaled to each other.)

Mixed scales are even more prevalent "beneath the covers." In *Roller Coaster Tycoon,* a month lasts five minutes of real time. However, customers walk around the park in twice real time. So if you were focused on realism, any given customer spends about *five months* at a park. This drives subject-matter experts crazy. Rides cost a few dollars for a patron to engage, but only a few hundred to buy. And still, bigger rides cost several times more than smaller rides.

Other game elements can include (depending on the player [and yes, gender]):

- Simplified or abstract interfaces
- Use of established game genres, such as game shows, athletic competitions, computer games, card games, and kids games
- Clicking as quickly as possible
- Gambling models
- Putting the information into a clever song

- Certain exaggerations of responses to make play more fun
- Reliving the roles of heroes or role models
- Me, a name I call myself
- Fa, a long, long way to run
- Conflict
- Shopping
- Gratuitous, detailed, and entertaining graphics and sounds
- Creating order from chaos
- Choosing what your on-screen character looks like
- Mastering a simple cyclical skill (throwing a card into a hat, *Pac-Man*®)
- Competition between learners, including enabled by maintaining lists of high scores (this is especially effective with CEOs and salespeople)
- Any use of graphics of fireworks
- Accessible communities for competition, and/or sense of belonging
- Presenting a mystery or puzzle to solve
- Creating a huge and powerful force enabling you to not just defeat but humiliate and crush all of those who dare oppose you
- Making the player overly powerful or overly relevant in a resolution of a situation
- Immersiveness in a favorite or interesting atmosphere (SuperBowl, science fiction, graphic novel, film noir, 1973 Miami)
- Using new technology
- Having access to privileged information
- Choosing between multiple skill levels to better align difficulty with capability

When to Use More

I increase the use of game elements if people are bored, too taxed, and/or unmotivated to spend extra hours on the experiences.

When to Use Less

I wind down the game elements if people are feeling as if their time is wasted with trivial activities (especially if they are already fully motivated to learn the content as quickly and accurately as possible).

Simulations Punctuated by Game Elements

Ben Sawyer, a developer of one of the next generation simulations we will be talking about in the next section, suggests that game elements may be used to modify simulation elements after learners achieve certain levels of competency. For example, in a simulation designed to teach players to drive, there could be periodic "dream" or fantasy sequences. After players pass a module learning to parallel park in the real world, they might be treated to a driving sequence that asks players to get from point A to point B as fast as possible, ignoring all traffic laws and safety considerations. Or players might be allowed to drive in a low gravity environment, where if they hit a bump they would soar for a city block.

"We have to trust that learners can distinguish between reality and games, and take advantage of that to make the whole experience a lot more enjoyable," Ben suggests. That can easily motivate learners to spend more time learning the critical material. There is also a chance that during the game sequences, they actually learn more than first assumed, as they are given permission to forget the rules and try new approaches.

Von Trapp Reference

If you were reading through the above list of game elements, you found my Me and Fa references (a game element, in the list of game elements). The good part is that, hopefully, you smiled and it made you want to keep reading. The bad part is that it might have interrupted your focus and seemed like an unprofessional, distracting, and unwelcome intrusion, and well, pretty lame.

That is the balancing act that all game elements must walk. (This moment of self-reflection was brought to you by Thiagi. More on him later.)

PEDAGOGICAL ELEMENTS

At the highest level, an educational simulation's pedagogical elements are learning objectives, the reasons for building the simulation, and deciding what to simulate. Below that are wide ranges of more subtle choices.

It was the naïve hope of early educational simulation designers that the interactive experience would be sufficiently engrossing. They hoped that students would voluntarily spend hours exploring on their own, discovering and learning in a purely natural way. They thought their simulations would compete with the leading entertainment titles and other leisure activity for people's free time.

Sadly, they were wrong. Spending one session with a group of real students watching them interact with your simulation dashes those hopes quickly and decisively. Seeing the furrowed brows of dozens of participants is sobering. Seeing tears is downright discouraging.

Pedagogical or didactic elements surround the game and simulation elements, better ensuring that the students' time is spent productively (Figure 8.5). Pedagogical elements in real life include nametags, caller ID, and the warning on certain cars that a "Student Driver" is operating them.

In educational experiences, pedagogical elements also help the learners avoid developing superstitious behavior, such as believing they are influencing something by a particular action when they are really not.

Specific Elements

Pedagogical elements include:

- Background material, including case studies, visual or text representations of systems models, and descriptions of interfaces to be encountered
- Scaffolding, such as letting the learner know what is going on and giving suggestions, either through voice or graphics

Figure 8.5. Pedagogical Elements Impact on Content Types.

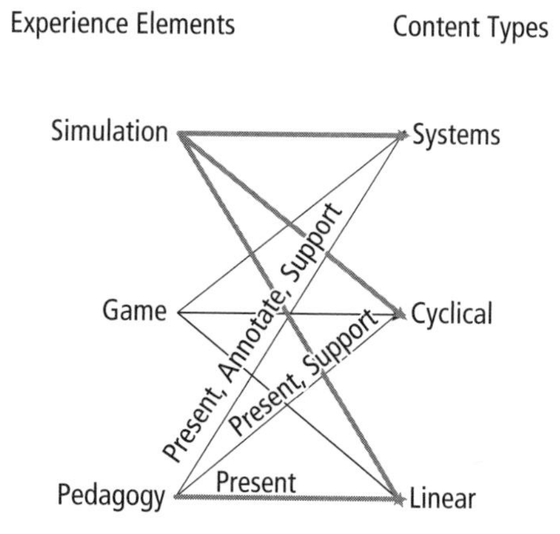

- Diagnostic capabilities, including scoring
- Introductions giving tips
- Visualization of relationships
- Debriefing, including linking the simulation to the real world, either extending from narrow to broad, or broad to narrow
- Forced moments of reflection
- A pause button
- A speed-up/slow down switch
- A replay option
- Libraries of successful and unsuccessful plays
- Links to chat rooms where people can brag about how they achieved a high score
- Tests and quizzes
- Acronyms or other mnemonic devices to trigger memory of processes
- Coaching
- Pop-up prompting and help, either text or a voice, giving specific tips

When to Use More

I have ratcheted up pedagogical elements if people are lost and confused or don't see the relevancy of the experience to the real world (Figure 8.6).

When to Use Less

I tone down pedagogical elements if people are feeling manipulated or not owning the material, not engaged by any simulation elements, or they feel that they are following directions instead of discovering.

Beyond the Sim

In some cases, the pedagogical elements to support a simulation are identical to the pedagogical elements to support a real-world engagement. In other cases, the pedagogical aspects such as background material are done so well that they become more used than the simulation. In both cases they become integrated into real life as a support system.

Figure 8.6. A Pedagogical Moment.

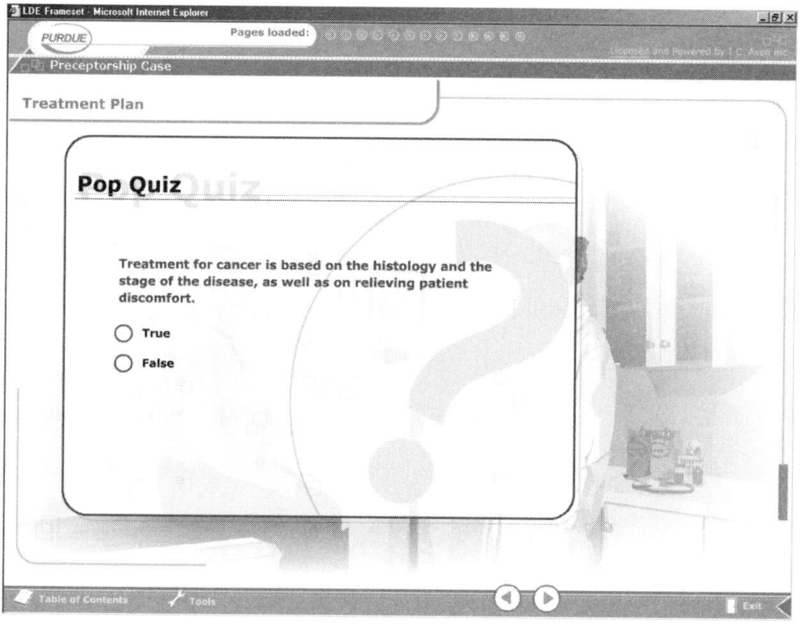

Source: © 2004 Purdue Pharma L.P. Used with Permission.

UNIVERSAL TRUTHS

One property is necessary to understand the other three elements of simulation, games, and education, *universal truths.*

There are two ways of looking at universal truths (Figure 8.7). One is that these are simulation elements that are highly abstracted. The other is that these are refined game elements. Believe it or not, there are actually quite heated and prolonged debates in academic circles arguing one side or another (and that makes me want to be an academic less, not more). Summed up, universal truths either reflect our cultural wisdom or our cultural clichés.

Both are right, depending on the situation. When designers use universal truths as the core of a learning objective, they are simulation elements. When designers use them to get or keep a learner's attention, they are game elements.

There are some very high universal truths like creative problem solving and communicating. Here are some slightly lower-level universal truths.

Figure 8.7. At the Intersection of Game and Simulation Elements.

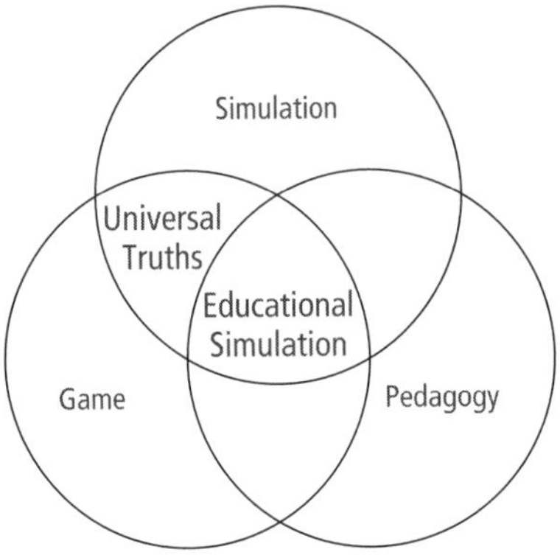

RACES AND CHASES *The game element:* Tag, you're it. First person through the culvert wins.

The high-level simulation element: Many tasks are competitive. Speed is an advantage. Roles can reverse.

ROCKS-PAPER-SCISSORS *The game element:* Rocks beat scissors. Scissors beat paper. Paper beats rocks.

The high-level simulation element: Nothing is invincible. Strengths and weaknesses are relative. Shifting strategies is important.

WHACK-A-MOLE *The game element:* Every time a mechanical mole pops up, smash it with a hammer.

The high-level simulation element: There is no universal defense. Problems shift quickly, so recognizing and reacting quickly is necessary.

I include Whack-a-Mole not only because I have used it a few times in learning experiences, not only because Whack-a-Mole is a good example of a universal truth, but also because I just like writing "Whack-a-Mole."

POWER-UP PILLS *The game element:* The Pac-Man eats the power pill and can now turn on its enemies. Getting the laser supercharger makes you a much more formidable space ship.

The high-level simulation element: Power shifts. There are accomplishments that change everything. Many of these advantages are short-lived.

EXPLORE, THEN BUILD, THEN EXPAND *The game element:* In strategy games, players generally follow a pattern of exploring, building up a base, and then planning and executing massive attacks on the enemy.

The high-level simulation element: Reap, then sow. But then reap again.

START EASY, GET HARDER *The game element:* In everything from jacks and hopscotch, to Doom, to courses, start easy and get harder as competence is displayed.

The simulation element: The better you get, the more challenges you will be faced with to continually test you, and the higher the rewards. (Yes, this is also a pedagogical element.)

DIFFERENT LENSES *The game element:* In computer games ranging from *Splinter Cell®* to *Deus Ex* to *Aliens vs. Predator™* to *SimCity™*, you can change the way you see the world, from infrared to light enhancing to seeing through walls to layering crime rates to normal. Depending on where you are, each has its advantages and disadvantages.

The simulation element: Everyone comes with ways of looking at the world that are incomplete. Some of us develop the invaluable ability to switch lenses. Few of us still know when to use which lens or have the ability to switch rapidly between them.

Reminded and Invoked, Not Taught

Universal truths provide substantiation to pioneers who believe games are inherently educational. There are some who believe that:

- All game elements are universal truths, and thus
- All games are simulations, and thus
- All games are educational, and thus
- Everything that isn't a game isn't educational (phew!)

However, there is a risk at being over-enamored with universal truths. The tremendous amount of pedagogical elements required to make universal truths relevant makes them tricky to use effectively, and often results in their misuse. "Some experiences are so abstract, no one knows what they are for," commented Saul Carliner, assistant professor at Montreal's Concordia University, of some past programs with which he had been involved. "We would do group challenges like rope courses and trust falls, and we never tied it back to anything. It was enjoyable, but not concrete."

Further, many students already have a gut feeling for the material, and so will feel as if their time is wasted. At the same time, like clichés, the accessibility and profoundness of universal truths cannot be denied.

THE INTERSECTION OF GAME AND PEDAGOGY

There is also an intersection between game elements and pedagogical elements. We discussed some examples, like hangman and word jumbles, in the chapter on game-based models. Two other categories worth highlighting are *stories* and *salience* (Figure 8.8).

Stories

A story puts the users in a position where they know what is going on and why they have to do what they are going to do. Gaming the story means making the players very powerful, pivotal, and/or desirable characters, unlike what they are in real life. It is not always necessary: *SimCity*™ and *The Sims*™ are great example of entertaining simulations without any story.

Cartoon strips can also fit here. A good comic can add both clarity and humor.

Figure 8.8. At the Intersection of Game and Pedagogical Elements.

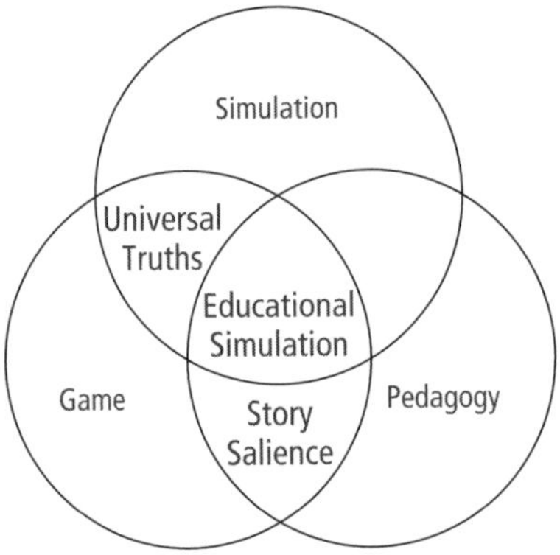

Source: A Dream I Had Once When I Was Eight.

Salience

Exaggerating effects, both making results bigger and making results happen sooner, have both game and pedagogical impact. Contrast is at the heart of pattern recognition. And in both cases, they come at a cost of simulation accuracy.

A 1950s SITCOM

Dr. Freud suggested that we have three forces controlling our actions, the *ego, superego,* and *id.*

Anyone who thinks about educational experience elements might do well to think of even more powerful forces influencing their design—members of the 1950s sitcom family.

Dad, somber and straightforward, argues for the *simulation elements.* "Keep it honest, keep it real," he tells us from his dark, paneled office when he gets home from his mystery job at 5:05 p.m. "You are not there to do anything but capture the truth. Real interactions, and real consequences." Then he smokes his pipe.

Mom, perky but caring, argues for the *pedagogical elements.* She tells us from the kitchen, "Help out. Keep your sister from getting lost. Do unto others. Eat your vegetables. What are you doing to the cat?" Then she offers us some cookies out of the oven, and excuses herself to get her hair done.

And of course there is the older brother, who takes out the car without asking, never does his homework, and breaks the window while sneaking back in past curfew. He is always game. He tells us, "Don't tell Dad where I was or I'll kill you." Then he hits us in the shoulder.

OTHER RESOURCES

- Game Elements: Thiagarajan, Sivasailam, & Thiagarajan, R. (2003). *Design Your Own Games and Activities: Thiagi's Templates for Performance Improvement.* San Francisco: Pfeiffer.
- Universal Truths in Storytelling: McKee, Robert. (1997). *Story: Substance, Structure, Style and the Principles of Screenwriting.* New York: Regan Books.

COMING UP NEXT

Why are so many teachers and trainers obsessed with multi-player computer games, especially since most have never played them?

9

LEARNING FROM LIVE ROLE PLAYS

AGAIN, THE MORE PEOPLE YOU talk to about simulations, the more people refer to all sorts of different simulation models. We have to understand these alternative views to communicate effectively with stakeholders, and also to draw inspiration and lessons learned.

I work with a lot of traditional instructors, who often look at simulations as extensions of *role plays*. They think in terms of *real-time, multi-player interactions*. Therefore in the view of many instructors, *computer-based simulations* primarily keep track of the rules of the role play, as well as enable engagement between participants who are not co-located. There is a lot to like about these approaches.

SALES APPLICATIONS OF SIMPLE ROLE PLAYS

It is hard to imagine a sales program that focuses on face-to-face techniques that does not involve role playing. Salespeople break off into twos or threes. One takes a turn as the practice person, another as the practice partner who plays the foil, and if a third person is there, he or she takes the role of observer (hopefully adding pedagogical comments to the players). Then the participants switch roles. Sometimes serious, sometimes lighthearted, these simple role plays help students take any theory and come close to making it real in what are typically hour-long breakouts.

EXTENDED, MULTI-DAY ROLE PLAYS

David Forman, a noted e-learning implementer and founder of e-learningjobs.com, tells of his most memorable role-play-based simulation. It didn't involve technology at all.

He designed it back in the late 1980s when he worked for Spectrum Interactive. (And this being the training market, I should note that this happened back when there *was* a Spectrum Interactive.)

The program would be called *Strategic Account Management* (SAM). David had the goal of getting the highest level of salespeople, the kind who were making hundreds of thousands per year, to think more about strategic sales.

What he designed was a four-day, classroom-based immersive role play.

Day One: The Company

On day one, the salespeople learned that they were employees of the fictitious company United Glass Corporation. The instructor played the CEO.

The participants were given coffee cups with the United Glass logo and other contextual material to reinforce the simulation. The CEO/facilitator handed out his UG business cards.

The CEO wanted to use information technology to make a channel system to extend the market for their products. It was a task similar to what American Airlines did with the SABRE reservation system.

The first job was to come up with recommendations, as well as to identify risks. The CEO broke the large group into smaller groups to work.

The participants learned about the company through realistic work artifacts, such as letters, memos, spreadsheets, and company financial statements, all with the appropriate clues as well as formatting and logos.

To analyze the material, they used two frameworks. The first was the McKinsey "Seven-S" Model for organizations that includes the components *Strategy, Staff, Style, Skills, Systems, Structure,* and *Shared Values*. The second was Michael Porter's external factors model.

The first half-day was always the most stiff, David remembers. There had to be some handholding as people made the transition. And with any newly formed group of people, to use a framework pioneered by dogs everywhere, they had to pass the initial "sniffing" stage.

The CEO then brought everyone together as a large group to present their recommendations on execution and uncovering of weak spots. The CEO even sent groups back in a highly public and embarrassing way to do some more work if a group did not perform sufficiently.

There were several cycles of coming together and breaking apart during the course of the day. By the end of the day, everyone was pretty much exhausted.

Day Two: The Department

"Every day began the same way," David explained. "We had a video segment interviewing executives from top companies on how they liked to deal with vendors. That was to constantly ground the simulation, to make it real."

On day two, participants were assigned functional positions. Each had individual, and sometimes conflicting, goals.

A lot of the instructors/CEOs gave awards to the best team. David concluded: "This ratcheted up the competition between teams and created a very intense atmosphere. The participants were salespeople, don't forget, who are naturally very competitive anyway."

Day Three: The Vendors

By the third day, the participants understood the company, their roles in it, the politics, their strategies, and their tactics. They even had built a network of allies and enemies.

Then they were introduced to vendors who were trying to sell them systems to help them accomplish *their* goals. They needed the right vendor; but the wrong vendor would sink them.

"The beauty of it," recounted David, "was that they were looking at mirrors of themselves, coming into the company to make the sale. The salespeople had all become customers. They had to make a recommendation to a demanding CEO. And these salespeople became very, very critical of the sales presentations."

Day Four: The Disruptions

The morning of the last day was spent dealing with a dramatic change to the business process. The disruption might involve new regulations, a breakthrough technology, or new threats from competition. Sometimes each small group worked on the same issue; sometimes they worked on different issues to increase exposure of the whole group to the kinds of issues that could happen.

These provided a final context to view the vendor selection and vendor role in the organization. Some decisions and relationships that had made sense in a perfect world came apart at the seams.

Finally, the last part of the last day was spent tying the whole experience back to real world. "It couldn't just end," said David. "It had to end with purpose and meanings. We had to make it tangible."

Iterative Improvements

The Strategic Account Management program was sold to companies, including IBM, Xerox, and Honeywell. It generated millions in revenue and became the single most successful program at Spectrum Interactive (a measurement that beats the stuffing out of ROI or other Kirkpatrick metrics.

I asked David what changes he made to the program as it evolved over its five years.

"We made it easier to find the problems in the source material. In the first versions, for example, we had clues to the organization's problems buried in the middle of the financial statements, a situation where someone was overstating the value of their assets," David said. "We had to make this easier to uncover, as participants both didn't have the skill set to read financials, and also were skimming the materials."

The quality of the instructor was also paramount. This became more important, as the program needed up to six qualified instructors at the same time. The instructor had to make a *credible* CEO. David could not just hire trainers. He had to find people who had actually run divisions.

Issues

Across the years, the program did not always go seamlessly. Sometimes the chemistry of the class did not work. And it seemed that across the groups, there were always 10 to 15 percent of the participants who never quite got it.

The experience never went global, David noted, by design of Spectrum Interactive. And at the time he did not have the experience and awareness.

But looking back now, with his new perspectives of two decades of international implementations, David concluded, "We would have had to be very aware of the receptivity issues if we wanted this to be a global product. We would have had to spend a lot of time making sure that a sense of comfort and trust had been built. Especially in the Asian cultures, where the instructor is almost revered, where the lecture was the preferred method of getting content, you would need a very supportive culture to accept this kind of participative, facilitated model."

Selling was always an issue. The program did not fit the traditional definition of "a course." There were not models per se that were being taught, but experiences delivered. This flummoxed a lot of traditional trainers who were asked by their organization to evaluate it.

Some organizations also had to get over the broad banding of training categories. A decision maker would say, "We already use vendor X for our sales training." Only over time would they realize that this program augmented, not displaced, their original tactical training.

Results

The training was successful from the traditional metrics. It taught about using frameworks for strategy and looking at external factors.

But the single most important thing it accomplished, more than any cognitive learning objective, was that the *salespeople began to think like customers.* They understand why CEOs lose sleep.

"I don't think that could have happened under any circumstances," David suggested. "Most people who went through it felt it was a unique program. Most people wouldn't even call it training. I doubt this could have happened electronically. In areas involving attitude changes, you need the personal touch." David concluded, "I loved being part of its creation."

ROLE PLAYS AS INPUTS, NOT OUTPUTS

For some people, simulations and role playing case studies are also viewed as an *input,* not just an *output.* This has a lot of advantages. Here are two examples.

Dietrich Dörner put professionals in complex simulations to detect and categorize common places where they went wrong. This methodology was the core input into his book, *The Logic of Failure: Recognizing and Avoiding Error in Complex Situations.*

Robert Rosell is president of Quality Media Resources. And he had a different use of simulations, embracing the resulting heightened emotions.

He was to produce a new training series on dialogue skills. This course had to deal with the challenges of talking about difficult topics, such as sexism, racism, age discrimination, unfair politics, and ethical issues in the corporate environment.

Robert wanted to show, on videotape, painful and challenging conversations. But his two traditional options were inadequate.

On one hand, he could not record real conversations from real corporations. No enterprise would allow that kind of uncontrolled access to negative, emotional situations.

On the other hand, Robert did not want to script the situation using case studies and then hire actors to play it out. No matter how good they were, they would not be convincing enough. Robert had seen too many painfully unauthentic scenes fail on video.

This might be a good place to note that Robert has a theater background, where he coached a lot of actors in improvisational techniques. He understood both the potential and even the emotional risks of unconstrained role play.

Robert recruited a group of people who did not know each other. He asked each to play a constant role for a few hours a week, for two months, in a dedicated Internet chat room. Robert worked with each person individually beforehand to create a history, attitude, and goal for his or her character. "I gave each person a secret—something that only he or she and I knew. It might have been around an unfair promotion, an impending change in business conditions, or something more personal," remembered Robert.

Through the two months, in the chat rooms, they got to form a real relationship with the other characters. Robert was the not-so-invisible hand that guided the conversations.

Then Robert brought the group together, live, for the first time. With two video cameras running to capture speaker and reactions, he facilitated a several-hour dialogue around one of the difficult topics (Figure 9.1).

"From a director's or facilitator's point of view, I didn't know what we were going to get," he recounted. But he got what he hoped and thought he would. "The participants completely lost their real selves in the new selves they had been developing. They jumped into these characters. We talked about a lot of very tough themes. Many of them were shaking and crying by the end."

Robert then edited the several hours down to a twenty-minute dialogue. It looked and felt real. He did the same process three times,

Figure 9.1. Role Plays Can Create Real Conversations.

Source: From *Dialogue: Now You're Talking!* © Quality Media Resources, Inc. Used with Permission.

around three different topics. This became the core of his course, *Dialogue: Now You're Talking!*

The prestigious *Training Media Review* would write about it: "You will find no better video-based program to help you than *Dialogue: Now You're Talking!* It is extraordinary."

CONCLUSION

For many instructors, role plays are simulations. They represent easy-to-implement, zero-technology activities that students enjoy.

Real Time

Role plays happen in real time. While back-story time can be compressed, interaction happens at the same pace as the real situation. This adds a visceral excitement that just can't be matched in turn-based experiences. Real-time simulations make sense for any activity that is real-time in real life.

Multi-Player

The single most defining aspect of educational role plays is that they involve multiple live students interacting together. In simple role plays, the students are often set up in conflict with one another, the resolution of which becomes the success criterion of the experience.

Open-Ended/Limited Scalability

There is a degree of open-endedness and systems content with role plays. As in real life, students' decisions and reactions can never be fully anticipated.

Players can take it seriously, or lightly (that is, high simulation/low game, or the other way around). Instructors can add a lot of pedagogy, or none. The same group might handle a situation differently before lunch and after. This mutation is great for evolving programs but less beneficial for getting a large organization on the same page.

All Cyclical Content All the Time

Role plays involve using the full range of the human voice as input. They have to say the right thing at the right time in the right way. The cyclical content also includes sniffs, scratches, leaning forward, leaning backward, coughs, and shrugs.

Fully Engaged (When You Are in the Hot Seat)

Role plays fully engage the participants. However, one challenge is that often only one role play happens with a group at one time. The good news is that other students can learn at a pedagogical level from watching. The bad news is that a lot of students are just watching.

Ease of Implementation

There are also no technical interface issues in role plays that don't involve technology. Participants mostly just have to talk.

Having said that, even this lack of interface can sometimes be an issue. Says James Hadley, an instructional designer at JHT Incorporated, "Because there are no established interfaces for role plays, the players are constantly looking at the instructor and audience for when to start, when to stop, how they are doing, how they did, what is too much, and what is too little. The audience and instructor become an interface with inconsistent rules, and this can lead the players to do things they normally would not in a real situation."

One Shot

From my perspective, one of the greatest weaknesses of any role play that involves people who play other roles is their "one shot" nature. Role plays don't allow replaying a scenario easily. A student can't think of a new strategy and try it. People get used up quickly, or soon fall into their own ruts.

The Balance of Rules

There are role plays without boundaries, Kym Buchanan (our doctoral student at Michigan State University) recounts, but they tend to hit walls. Imagine two kids playing cops and robbers. One says, "I shot you," the other says, "No you didn't," and that ends that.

More sustainable role plays need some rules. It might be a facilitator, or even a rulebook and a pair of dice.

But while the concept of a simulation is highly structured, scientific, highly rule-governed, the important thing in a role play is not to have too many rules, either stated or implied. The concept could come closer to a consensual hallucination.

10 to 15 Percent Not Getting It

Especially in extended role play, there is a contingency of people who just don't make the transition into the simulation. While steps can be taken to reduce the percentage, there may be a floor of between one and two people out of every fifteen participants who will never buy into the experience.

They get hung up on the little contrivances or inaccuracies. A trained facilitator can best identify these people by their subtle yet pointed moments of discord, such as their editorializing, "This is stooopid."

Fidelity

The Achilles heel of role plays is their often dependence on the players simulating the conflict. That is problematic because participants in role plays tend to be on their best behavior, and they need to resolve the conflict to conclude the experience.

As a result, I have never been in a role play where everyone did not agree at the end. Any activity that assumes people will both behave well and have a similar perspective on the world might have some insurmountable authenticity problems. People might act like Ken Blanchard's or Stephen Covey's ubermensch when in a room with peers, but back at the office they are pure Dilbert.

Direct Map/Cyclical Content

Most role plays are directed around the specific behavior and activity. Salespeople practice selling. Managers practice managing. They still tap the abstract, but through the concrete.

COMING UP NEXT

Technologies can't change role plays that much, can they?

10

ROLE PLAYS REDUX

The Revolutionary Role of New Technologies

TECHNOLOGY IS PLAYING A LARGER ROLE in role plays. But the types of impact are more significant and more transformational than I originally thought. Here are three takes, ranging from a simple and tactical use of communication technology, to creating a multi-player extended role-play of a session of Congress, to building scalable "virtual experience spaces."

SIMPLE ROLE PLAYS EXTENDED THROUGH VIRTUAL CLASSROOMS

Virtual classroom technology uses the Internet to facilitate live experiences with participants who are not co-located. Jennifer Hofmann, author of *The Synchronous Trainer's Survival Guide* (Pfeiffer, 2003), explained to me how to use virtual classrooms for role plays, and how it differs from physical classrooms. As with many of the very practical examples described in this book, her advice works for all of the subsequent "bigger" examples as well.

"Critically," she began, "you need virtual classroom technology that can separate the participants into *breakout rooms*. Then, use the same numbers per breakout as traditional classrooms—one player, one partner, and one observer."

As Jennifer was showing me a few virtual classroom-based role plays run their course, I was struck by how bad so many teachers are at giving instructions, and how bad so many participants are at listening.

We have all grown used to a traditional classroom, where a failing role player can catch the eye of the instructor if things are going south, or an instructor can scan the room to see who looks confused.

As a result, a lot of groups enter their breakout rooms and just freeze. They forget what they are supposed to be doing.

Jennifer warns, "Directions need to be very specific. You need to put a student in charge in each breakout room, presumably someone who gets it. You don't have as much time in a virtual classroom before people zone out, so you have to strip away the 'nice-to-have's,' and just focus on things people really need to know."

You should spend ten minutes per role play. You don't want to leave people alone in a breakout room for more than half an hour.

The numbers are also important. The tendency is to want to push fifty people into a large class, simply because the technology now enables it.

"I would be hesitant to do more than four or five breakout rooms," Jennifer said. "And even then, you probably want more than one facilitator. I would leave one instructor in the main classroom, and have the other person moving from breakout room to breakout room. They don't need to be intrusive, if things are going well. They might just want to write on the whiteboard and move on."

Using virtual classrooms for role plays seems non-intuitive. At least it did to me, at first. After all, one reason to do role plays at all is to train someone to use the 70 percent of communication that is body language, right?

But, and this is pretty important, with more and more supervisors and salespeople communicating remotely, using a virtual classroom is closer to their real mode of communication. Learning not to rely on body cues is becoming increasingly more useful in this distributed world than learning to read body cues.

Architecture

Virtual classrooms are delivered over the Web, in some cases launched by a learning management system (LMS). They often require proprietary plug-ins or downloads (Figure 10.1).

MULTI-PLAYER EXTENDED ROLE PLAYS

Technology is also changing the more extensive role plays. It is bringing new models to market.

Figure 10.1. Virtual Classroom Architecture Considerations.

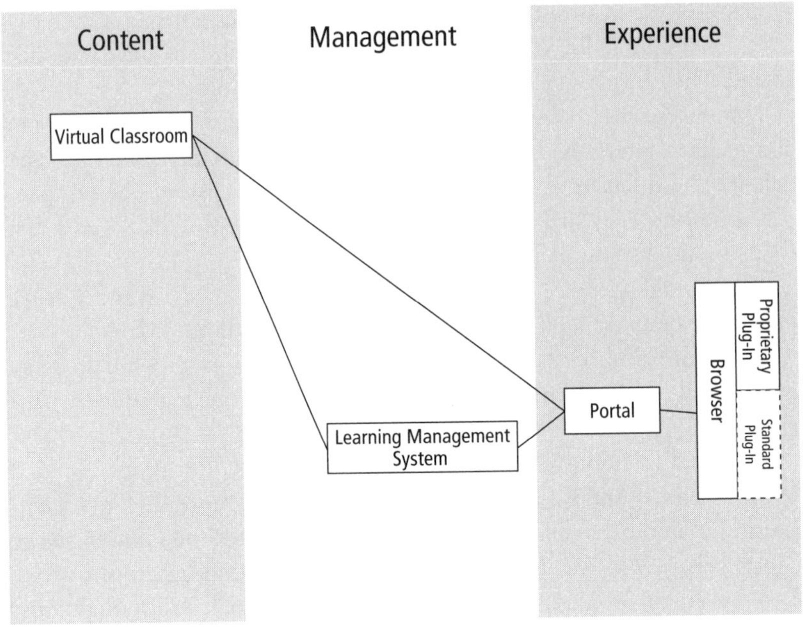

John Wilkerson is an associate professor of political science at the University of Washington (a place, I hasten to add, that just seems buzzing with simulation innovators). He teaches a class on the U.S. Senate.

Version One: Classroom-Based Role Play

Originally, he led the class in a role play at the end of the semester about the senate in action. He would give them an issue, say universal health care, form committees, and let them see what happened.

In the original iteration, the role play took four classes: set-up, committee, general debate, and then debrief. John was frustrated because there was never enough time to learn anything. There was no trial and error. There was no opportunity for students to start with an assumption, for example how power works, and have that assumption challenged.

Version Two: Online Multi-Player Role Play

"We wanted to extend it over a period of time," he told me. So he hired some undergraduates to set up a website called *Legsim*. First, it was just straight Web pages using HTML, and later database-driven SQL was added.

Now the role play takes all semester, facilitated by an online site. "We don't provide any scenarios. The students pick a district and represent that district. There is an ownership to it. It is a simulation, but when it goes on for six or eight weeks, students become highly vested in their ideas," said John.

This is the fourth year, and the program is still evolving. John explained: "I started originally by making everything completely wide open. Since then I have made it more pedagogical. I have been making the experience connect with the reading and the lecture. Students now write in their journals every week. This all is making a stronger connection between the educational components."

One problem is that students just want to do the simulation. It is hard to get them to pay attention to the formal pedagogical material that makes it relevant. For example, there are procedures, which are the rules of the game. Knowing the rules is key to success. Students have to know how to manipulate the rules to get a policy outcome. But the students just did not focus on the rules on their own, or only too late. So John added a test (a good pedagogical element), which introduced that dynamic much more quickly.

Unlike many evolving simulations, content has become increasingly detailed and accurate over the iterations. He has added an authorization and appropriations process, and also a process to introduce disruptive events, such as 9/11. There have also been technological improvements, such as real-time chat to committee meetings to make it more engaging.

This continued rigor impacts the students' "buy-in" level. A third of the students never get engaged, slightly higher than in other simulations. A third are more engaged then an average class, and certainly more than the 5 percent of their grade would justify. But a whole third become addicted.

We talk about metrics when talking about simulations, and we should. But a letter that John Wilkerson received from a student sums up more than most numbers:

> "I'm pretty sure it's too late to do anything and I'm not sure if you can do anything to help, but it's just that I feel so passionate about my bill (PB 109) and it's killing me inside that it has been tabled in the Rules Committee and there's nothing more that I can do. I know that I'm not a real representative, but I have gotten myself so into this class that I feel like I have become one! You compared

> Congress to a game in the beginning of the quarter, and I guess I just didn't realize how much of a game it really is until these past couple of days.
>
> "I feel like I have done as much as I could have to pass this bill, but I guess it just wasn't enough. I have contacted all representatives who have submitted amendments and suggestions and created new text to satisfy their concerns and asked each if the new text satisfied them. I have contacted Rules numerous times about the status of my bill and was told last Wednesday that there were only two bills before mine. Friday after lecture, I talked to Rules again and was told that it had been tabled until this past Sunday.
>
> "Last night I was notified that due to the lack of time on the floor, my bill would not make it out of Rules. I have contacted the Speaker (who has cosponsored my bill) and the President for help, which neither could give.
>
> "It's really frustrating to put your heart into something you feel so passionate about and have no ability to help it, but I guess it's all part of the game. Thanks for reading all about my frustration. If there is any way that I can get my bill to the floor, I would love to know!"

This buy-in, and even frustration, is the hallmark of any good simulation. It is no surprise that *Legsim* was the winner of the 2002 Information Technology and Politics Award of the American Political Science Association.

Architecture

Multi-player simulations are delivered over the Web, in some cases launched by a learning management system (LMS). Community tools and records must be maintained over time (Figure 10.2).

EXPLORING A VIRTUAL EXPERIENCE SPACE

Here is another example of technology increasingly automating, augmenting, and expanding role plays. And this might just be a dominant model for the near future.

Students in traditional role plays often explore some created *experience space* as input to their work. As we described last chapter, this space is defined though prop documents handed out over the course of the role play, and interactions with people, including the instructor, playing assigned roles.

Figure 10.2. Multi-Player Simulation Architecture Considerations.

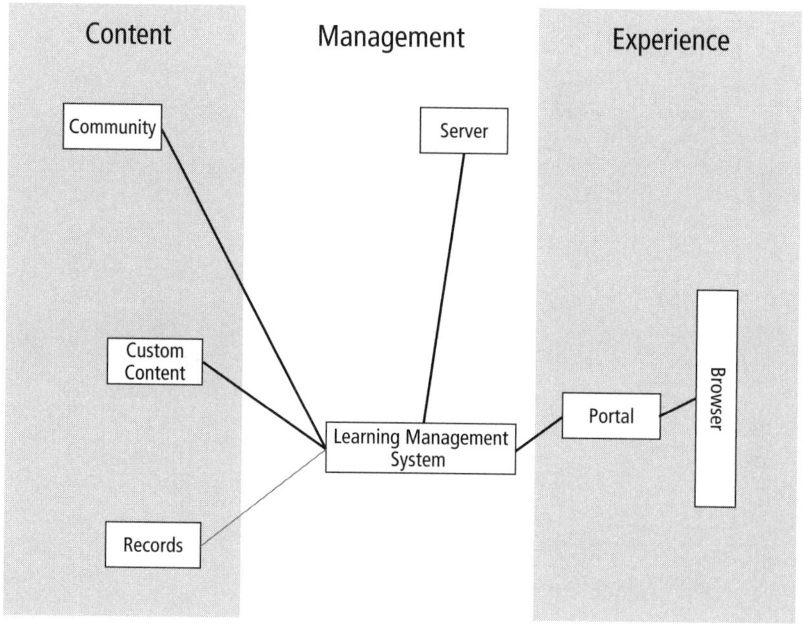

Now, using relatively commonplace web technology, instructors can create large, hyper-texted, multi-media repositories for students to explore. The media can include emails, video interviews with the CEO or other clips (Figure 10.3), and PowerPoint® presentations, all accessed through a common portal (or portals if there are multiple teams).

Furthermore, only certain links in the repository can be open at the start of the role play. Then new links could open up based on different types of triggers.

For example, at certain time intervals, the instructor (or the simulation on its own) opens up some links that create the effect, for the students, of time passing. This could simply represent the start of a new week or, more dramatically, of an external event happening, such as a hostile takeover or the death of a senior executive. Again, video clips and emails would become available to the role players that were not there before. Of course, time can also cut off certain links, making them no longer accessible.

There could be different types of triggers as well. For example, if a player in the role play was reading an email, he or she might want to ask a follow-up question of the fictional character. He or she would

Figure 10.3. Players Explore Multimedia Repositories.

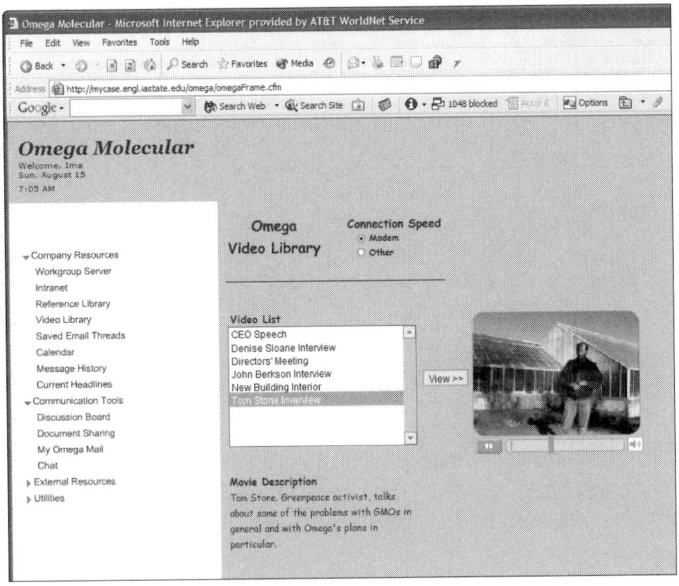

Source: David Fisher. Used with Permission.

"email" the character. Then either an automated system or the instructor would "reply" to that email, opening up a link that would result in a new email appearing in the person's inbox (Figure 10.4). During the beta roll-outs of virtual experience spaces, the instructor has to be "live," carefully monitoring the queries of the students, creating new information that will then be refined and added to the canned experience in the next iteration.

Critically, players and teams explore the same space differently. As a result, each person has different access to information and experiences (Figure 10.5). David Fisher is a Ph.D. student of rhetoric and professional communication at Iowa State University and works with the Department of Agriculture and Biosystems Engineering. He is a pioneer in the area of virtual experience spaces.

In his classes, students play the role of consultants building content (ranging from a website to an ethics policy) for a client, with whom they interact through this virtual experience space. They talk to others via a discussion board (Figure 10.6).

David Fisher explained to me, "The different experiences that each player has during the game—after the players *discover* that they are having different experiences—gives them a reason to communicate

Figure 10.4. Examples of How a Player Grows His or Her Virtual Experience Space.

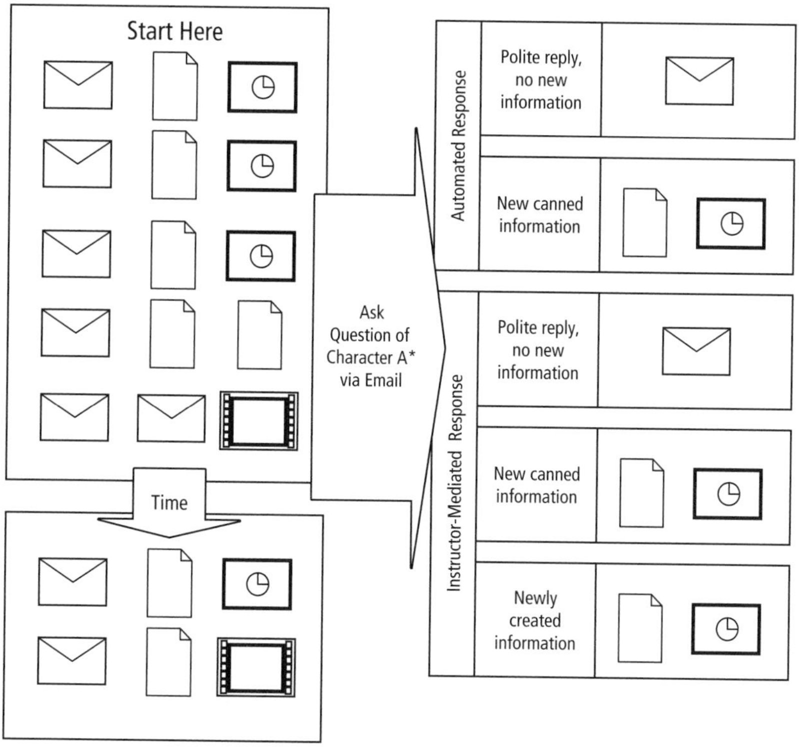

with each other, to share or hide information, *and* to think about why they are sharing or hiding information. Stimulating this type of communication and reflection is one of the chief goals of our project."

This type of virtual space can greatly increase the scope, fidelity, and predictability of a role play. Commented a student about David Fisher's class:

> "It was a lot more like the real world. It's not like every other class where you ask the teacher how to do it, and then they tell you. In the first weeks we came in and the instructor, Dave, basically told us we had to do this. But that's it; that's all he was going to tell us. We had to figure it out all by ourselves.
>
> "And it wasn't really even until toward the end of the semester that we actually saw where we were going with this or understood exactly what we were supposed to be doing. It all kind of came together, though, at the end."

Figure 10.5. Different Players Evolve Different Virtual Experience Spaces.

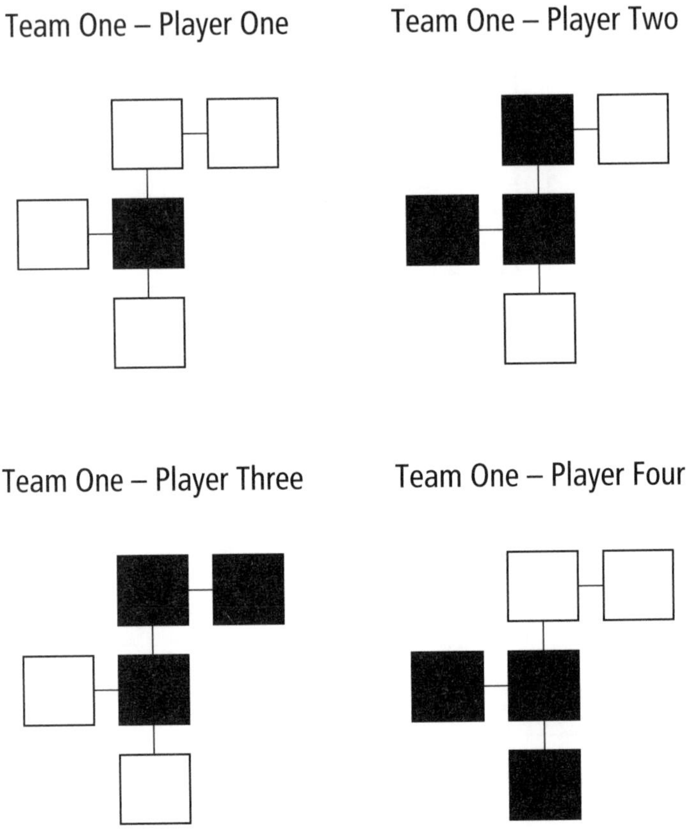

David told me, "In one running of the case, several students, despite having been told about the environment, believed the simulated organization was real. Students broke out cell phones and tried to call the company. We attribute this, in part, to the Web interface and the 'in-box' genre (Figure 10.7), a look and feel that mimics interfaces encountered by increasing numbers of workers."

He agreed that perhaps 20 percent of the students never really bought into the role play. He shared with me a quote from an evaluation of the course:

> "The vagueness of the assignments led to a lot of the confusion in this class . . . but the most amount of confusion was caused by the students themselves not wanting to buy into the fact that we were

Figure 10.6. Players Can Share Thoughts with Each Other on a Community Board.

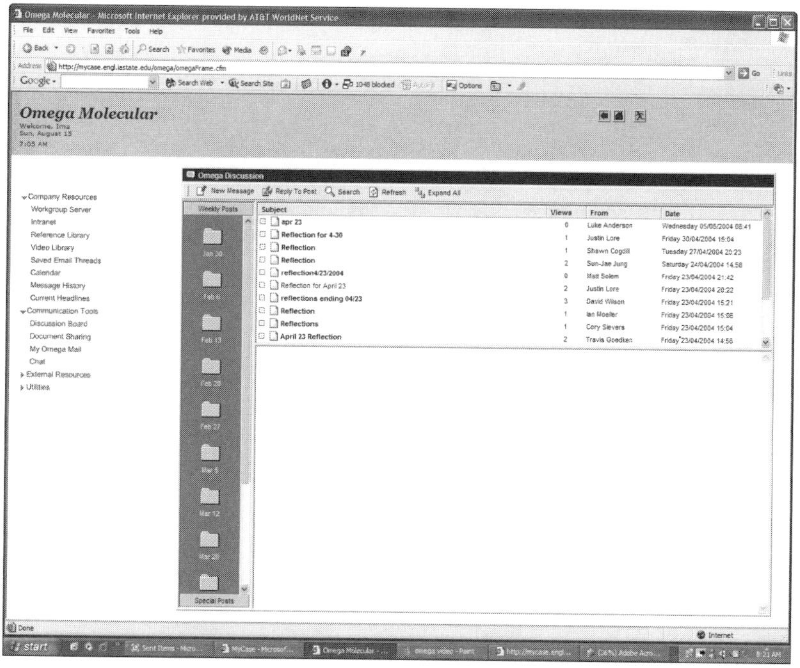

Source: David Fisher. Used with Permission.

> 'playing consultant.' Many of the students I talked to were still in the frame of mind that they were working to please the teacher and not working as a consultant for the fictional organization."

David concluded, "The experience has caused our students to think across traditional disciplinary boundaries as they work to complete tasks, which is what they'll have to do when they leave school (and should be what they're doing in school). It is not uncommon for teams to contact professors from a number of departments for help with their analysis of the simulated organization and its technology."

Carnegie Mellon's Suzanne Garcia, another pioneer in this area, has worked on role plays using variations of virtual experience spaces around complex negotiations with multiple stakeholders. She says, "There were a lot of courses in this area that went broad. We needed to go narrow and deep."

Figure 10.7. Players Receive Emails from Role-Play Characters.

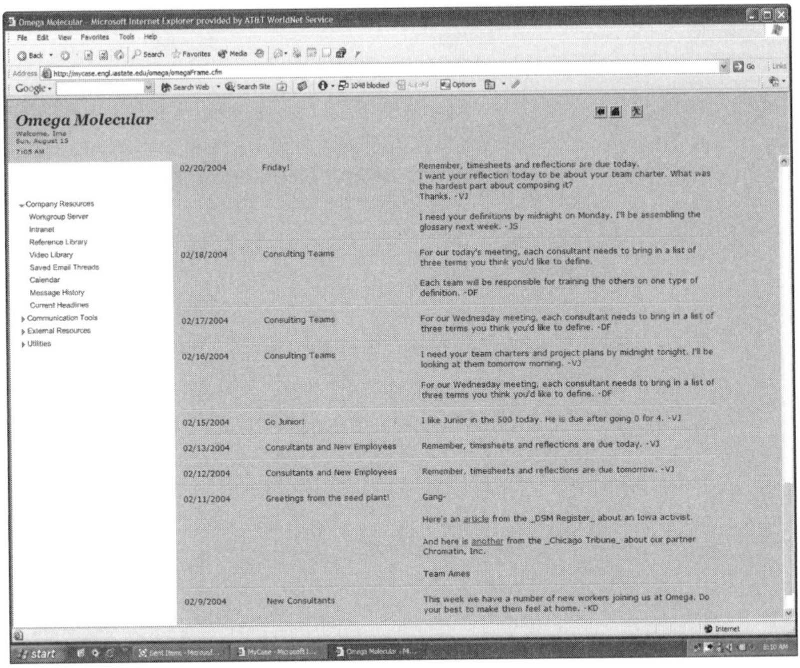

Source: David Fisher. Used with Permission.

In her role play, teams of government employees and vendors had to figure how to create a joint technology platform where there was no single solution and a lot of ambiguity. At many times, there was much more motivation for the team players to quit then push on.

To give you a feeling for scale, Suzanne built thirty-five non-playing characters (NPCs) with whom the players had to interact. And in addition to the virtual experience space, she also designed, built, and circulated physical artifacts. Finally, her team installed real computers and a real email server around the role play.

Unlike longer, sprawling classes, these were focused, full-time sessions. The meetings would go one hour, then a half-hour break, then a second hour. But the catch was that during the half-hour break, the participants had to stay in character.

She also took advantage of a key lesson from traditional role plays. While the teams consisted of two people, Suzanne added *actor observers*. For every two people playing the role play, two were watching. "They are given lists of things to watch," she explained. "At the end of each turn, the debrief starts with the observers, then the facilitators, and finally the players."

She summed up several key lessons about all simulations. "There were inevitably authenticity discrepancies. For some people, these discrepancies got in the way. The people who stretched into roles found it easier to act in the spirit of the role, as opposed to people who really knew the space and had real roles in it." She added, "We had to evolve the program, based on real experiences. We started off with too much information processing, and the explicit decision making wasn't until the end. Through several versions, we got the timing much more aligned."

I look forward to seeing more permutations of virtual experience spaces. They use familiar experiences, role plays, and familiar Web-based content. The content is meaningful, requiring interesting and creative roles for students. These environments can grow organically as instructors grow and prune them. They can even be first-person and stand-alone, using something like a branching story format to move the player along to open up or close down links. Finally, they can be purchased as textbooks and rolled out to thousands or hundreds of thousands of students. What's not to love?

COMING UP NEXT

Can the most profound simulations also be the most simple?

11

USING SIMPLE, PEOPLE-BASED GAME AND SIMULATION ELEMENTS FOR DEVASTATING EFFECTIVENESS

YOU CAN GO THROUGH ASPECTS of our civilization and feel good about some and not so good about others. I feel good about the areas where there seem to be mechanisms in place for renewal and improvement.

In my humble opinion (IMHO), I am encouraged about the mechanisms around government, medicine, law, capitalism, and food production and distribution. Especially as you look across history, you have to take some genuine pride in how well these things work. In contrast, I feel much less good about the environment and education. There is a constant sense that we are winging it, and coming up with local one-shot solutions.

PACKAGED BRAINPOWER

One of the reasons I feel good about medicine is the pharmaceutical industry. Before there was a mature pharmaceutical component, doctors were pretty useless (and yet their numbers still increased, which is more than a little unnerving).

Over the last century, the pharmaceutical industry has evolved their business model to be able to put tremendous intellectual resources on specific medical problems.

- They can spend hundreds of man-years on a single pill.
- Solutions range from very broad to narrow.
- They have multiple paths to the end-user, directly through pharmacies, indirectly through doctors and HMOs.

- They have multiple price points.
- Their value proposition is clear, in many cases dramatically improving the lives of large numbers of people.
- Generics keep pressure on prices after the patents expire.

It is my hope that education content providers will one day be structured similarly to pharmaceutical companies. Only then can we improve the world.

And yet . . .

And yet sometimes when you have a headache (after, say, a day of tough business negotiations, golf, or both), the water you drink with the aspirin is more beneficial than the aspirin itself.

Complicated is not necessarily better.

I talk with Thiagi to get ideas for client projects, and in this case to look at some of the simplest simulations that also happened to be some of the most powerful.

"LET THE INMATES RUN THE ASYLUM"

Thiagi sucks content out of the audience the way an otter sucks yolk out of an egg. One of his simplest techniques is by asking open-ended questions (he eschews the closed questions of branching stories) (although he would never actually use the word "eschews").

If he were here right now, he might ask *you* the following questions:

- How would you bring simulations into your organization?
- In what subject areas?
- Whose support would you need?
- What worries you the most about simulations?
- What excites you the most?
- How did I get here?

Stories

Or he might give you a piece of a story or scenario, and then ask what comes before it and what comes after. For example, consider this:

> Then e-learning took off. It changed the world. Attracting all of the best and brightest talent, it became the fastest growing industry of the 21st century.

Thiagi might ask you:

- What came before this to make it happen?
- What came after it as a result that made it matter?

As an alternative, he might start with a paragraph, and have every person (you and the readers next to you) add the subsequent paragraph. For example:

> It was the best learning experience any of them had ever been involved in. It gave them all newfound perspective and excitement and power. And to think it had all begun just three days ago, when they first met Chester. . . .

Debates

Another technique is setting up a jiffy-debate. Take a controversial statement, and break the audience into three groups: one to argue for the statement, one to argue against, and the third to vote on who is more convincing. For us:

> Simulations are the only way to efficiently teach linear, systems, and cyclical content to thousands of people.

The Game Game

This one requires consumable props, so I know it must bug Thiagi. Pass around some homemade board games. Base it on something like *Chutes and Ladders*®, but involve elements like *Chance* cards. Let people play for about ten minutes. Then hand out blank boards with blank cards. Let people make their own game-based simulation on the topic about which they are "supposed to be" learning.

UNIVERSAL TRUTHS

Thiagi's work also deals head-on with the area of universal truths. The mechanisms he uses are characteristically both familiar and profound.

Zero-Sum?

The set-up: Teach everybody in the room how to thumb wrestle. Pair them up. Give them a reward for the number of times they "pin" their partner during a forty-five-second time period. At the bell, most people will struggle, battle, and score a few pins. One or two pairs, however, will realize that they are not in competition with each other, and take turns quickly pinning each other. They rack up scores of dozens of pins each.

The universal truth: Assume cooperation first, competition second. The world is not zero-sum.

Tragedy of the Commons

The set-up: A pot in the middle of the room has $50 in play money. Three players surround the pot.

There are the certain rules:

- The point is for each to get as much money as he or she individually can.
- The three players cannot communicate with each other.
- At the beginning of each turn they privately write down how much they are going to take out of the pot, either $0, $5, $10, or $20.
- When everyone is done writing, they reveal their numbers and take that amount from the pot.
- Between turns, the amount of money left in the pot doubles.
- The game lasts twelve turns.

The universal truths: There are finite resources, on which many depend. One greedy person can make more in the short term but ruin everything for everybody in the long term.

The Cash Game

The set-up: The instructor holds up a dollar. He or she is going to have an auction for the dollar. The bidding starts at 50 cents, and can only be raised in 5-cent increments. The only catch is that the instructor can collect both the winning bid and the second-highest winning bid, while only paying out the one dollar. A few people start the bidding . . . 75 cents . . . 80 cents . . . 85 cents. . . . It should be over when someone reaches one dollar. But no, because the 95-cent bidder realizes that he or she will be out 95 cents if the other person wins. It is worth it to bid $1.05, and only lose 5 cents, rather than lose 95 cents. And on it goes. Thiagi has seen it go as high as $25.

The universal truths: Don't put good money after bad; sometimes not playing is better than winning; short-term optimization strategies do not always work.

Karma

The set-up: There is the karma stack that starts with ten red cards, each with one number ranging from 1 to 10. There is also a second stack of ten black cards, again ranging from 1 to 10.

- Every turn, the player is given a random card from the karma stack.
- If it is a red card, as it always is at the beginning of the game, with a value of 5 or less, the player gets those points, and the card is returned to the karma stack.
- If the card is red and higher than 5, the player has a choice. The player can take the points on the card, but if the player does, he or she also has to add one random black card into the karma deck. Or the player can pass on the points. In either case, the red card is also put back into the deck.
- Finally, if the player's random card from the karma deck is black, he or she loses the face value of the card.

This can work on its own. But Thiagi also has the learners playing against each other, or sometimes against a computer-driven character. People, he found, tend to make more risky decisions when they are competing and losing.

The universal truth: Shortcuts can come back later to hurt you.

Architecture

People-based simulations require nothing from a technology perspective, but everything from a trained instructor perspective (Figure 11.1). It is up to the perspective of the reader to decide whether this infrastructure burden is trivial or overwhelming. I have heard more than a few people, when watching Thiagi, say to me, "I could never get away with that."

Figure 11.1. People-Based Simulation Architecture Concerns.

RORSCRATIC?

Thiagi uses the term "Rorschach" a lot when talking about these examples. The premise is that end-learners bring with them all they need to know, and the exercises are just ways of bringing it out. There is also a characteristically self-deprecating aspect of the comment—anybody more full of themself would call his or her own processes "Socratic."

Plus, when you work with a group, you automatically get credit for being more than Socratic. You are now tapping the group's knowledge, and the content the group produces is more than any one of the members. Brainstorming creates value.

But I think it goes one big step further. The *content* that the group is producing is really just linear. It is lists and charts. That is all well enough.

The real value delivered is the *framework,* the mechanism. Thiagi is teaching ways of looking at the world. He gives his audience models that they can store away, and hopefully pull out at a point of need. He is teaching *systems* content that is much more powerful and flexible than any list of facts.

OTHER RESOURCES

- Thiagarajan, Sivasailam. (2003). *Design Your Own Games and Activities: Thiagi's Templates for Performance Improvement.* San Francisco: Pfeiffer.

COMING UP NEXT

The oldest technology-based educational simulation is also the most effective. And expensive. But is it the right model for anything else? Everything else?

12

LEARNING FROM FLIGHT SIMULATORS

"A Flight Simulator for Business Skills!"

—Words that appear somewhere on seemingly every corporate simulation vendor's sales and/or fundraising slides (including mine)

IF YOU MENTION SIMULATIONS TO many military and airline people, they think in terms of *flight simulators.* And when you consider how many of the older (and by older, I mean older than I am) corporate leaders came out of the military, this prejudice is quite significant.

Quick question. With which one statement do you most agree?

- Flight simulators are entertaining.
- Flight simulators are rigorous.
- Flight simulators are neither rigorous nor entertaining.

I will bet you chose one of the first two: perhaps the first if you are a student and the second if you administrate training. Regardless, you probably did not pick the third. Flight simulators have pulled off quite a trick. They have an image of being rigorous or fun, *in theory* appealing to a wide audience.

As a result, flight simulators have enjoyed a great PR buzz in the e-learning world. More than a few first generation simulation companies have plastered images that resemble flight simulators on their Web pages and investor and customer presentations. (And, as a historical point, flight simulators are the first true next gen sim.)

Flight simulators seem to effortlessly make the case for simulations. Learn by doing. It is better to crash a hundred times in simulation than once in real life (Figure 12.1). A simulator is very cost-effective. The organizations that care the most about training use simulators.

TWO QUESTIONS ABOUT FLIGHT SIMULATORS

Pilot training is highly successful. So two sets of questions require answers.

The first set of questions is about the training program itself. What does the training program look like? How does it use flight simulators? What else does the program entail?

My second set of questions focuses on how completely this model could be used in a broader context. Is it a real model for business and academic learning, or just slick and potentially misleading advertising?

Figure 12.1. A Flight Simulator.

Source: Lockheed Martin. Used with Permission.

Training Air Force Pilots

FlightSafety Services Corporation is the world's leading private producer of flight simulation equipment. They not only train pilots, but all of the crew involved in civilian and military flights. Their outputs are simulators, simulator experiences, documentation support, and traditional e-learning.

I talked to Chuck Nichols, the courseware manager at FlightSafety Services Corporation, to learn more about how Air Force pilots are trained.

"The whole process takes about three years," he explained to me. "We start by giving an Air Force kid basic flight training. We cover the 101 curricula, like, 'this is a wing and this is a door.'

"Then we start them down in Colorado Springs. We give them flight training in a small, two- or four-person plane to learn basic flying skills. They then move on to larger and faster planes, often down in Texas. We have special side-by-side jets built by Cessna.

"Then there are two different tracks. Some people go toward the big stuff, the heavies. Others become fighter pilots and learn high-performance maneuvers. About three years from the time they start flying, they move into the right seat of the plane."

"During that time," I asked, "how much time do they spend in the simulators?"

"Most pilots will go through eight to ten simulator experiences," he said nonchalantly. A "simulator experience," I later learned, did not begin to capture the magnitude of the program.

A Sample Run

Seeing a full flight simulator in action is a daunting experience, no less impressive the tenth time as the first. If the sheer magnitude of the facilities and commitment doesn't shock you, the organization and precision will.

In a C-5 mission, just one example, there is a pilot in training in the left seat, a co-pilot in training in the right seat. Behind those two students is a pilot instructor. There is a flight engineer in training who sits behind them, and also a flight engineer instructor.

"If we were training boom operators," Chuck told me, "we would also have a boom operator and a boom operator instructor."

There is a crowd outside this $25 million simulator (they range from $2.5M to $15M in the commercial sector). A maintenance technician is monitoring all of the computers and hydraulic pumps. There is a maintenance supervisor overseeing the technician, and even an instructor back-up keeping tabs and, well, drinking coffee.

As you watch from the outside, you can see this large white box jerking about on all six axes. It is impressive, but more in a "I hope that thing doesn't fall on me" kind of way.

Once you step inside, however, the magic begins. The clearness and depth of the pilot's view is startling. FlightSafety Services Corporation has what they call their VITAL 9 visual system, which produces visuals of unnerving smoothness and clarity (Figure 12.2). You can see the stars. You can see familiar city landmarks. You can see emergency vehicles coming to put out the inferno that is your plane when you crash.

"How real is this?" I asked.

Chuck is proud. "At this point, the simulator provides about 98 to 99 percent fidelity."

Of course, one advantage of a flight simulator is also how unreal they can be. During the session, instructors can back up, rewinding the

Figure 12.2. A Flight Simulator Cockpit.

Source: Lockheed Martin. Used with Permission.

scenario the way an Elway fan rewinds and fast-forwards a SuperBowl XXXII DVD. With a few clicks they can drop the plane down hundreds of feet, get some wind shear going, knock out a few engines and maybe the left landing gear wheels, or teleport it to a different location altogether.

At the end of the day, everybody is exhausted. The pilots are drenched with sweat. Their hands are shaking from focusing on such minute, subtle manipulations. Between the pre-briefings, the simulated flight, and post-briefings, the whole experience has takes seven intense hours.

Commercial pilot programs are similarly rigorous. American Airlines has nine thousand active pilots using thirty-three full-motion simulators that are operational 365.25 days a year. Pilots have to train intensively initially, but also every nine months, *and* when they switch aircraft types.

THE ULTIMATE?

Is this the ultimate in simulation-based training? Is this the state of the art?

Not according to TRADOC's William Melton. "In the military, we are going to the digital battlefield. Today, we have all of the command center staff working in a simulation using the same computer-generated imagery that they would see in real life. There is another whole area of simulations called *embedded training*. The simulations are attached to actual, real, no-kidding field equipment.

"With all of our *recent* and *going forward* acquisitions, whatever optical and audio devices exist in our hardware, they can be run in simulation mode. Now our troops can do training with the actual equipment."

I ask eagerly, "So would that be like the movie *The Matrix*? Could you learn how to use equipment on the way to the battle?"

William is polite, but he now realizes that I am a little dim. "You would never want simulated output potentially interfering with real output."

"Oh, yeah," I mumble.

He continues, but I couldn't help but notice he was speaking a bit more slowly to me now, "We are also working on high-level architectures (HLAs), so that the embedded training modules can talk to each other. This pushes us to higher numbers of coordinated users. We will eventually get to the point of being able to do a *distributed integrated simulation.* Mind you, this is not ready yet. But we could soon have *actual* equipment in a big warehouse, in some cases on hydraulic lifts, able to engage in coordinated simulations.

"So, for example," he continued, "you can have an entire tank platoon, each one in simulation mode. During the course of the computer battle, they could call in an air strike. That would signal real pilots to do a simulated launch off a simulated aircraft carrier. On their screens, they could see where the tanks were supposed to be, and the tanks could see the airplanes flying in and hitting their targets.

"And" William concluded, "with distributed networks, we could have multiple players at completely different locations playing different roles, of course."

"Of course."

Architecture

Flight simulations are delivered via specialized hardware and software (Figure 12.3). In some cases, network connectivity will be added.

Figure 12.3. Flight Simulator Architecture Considerations.

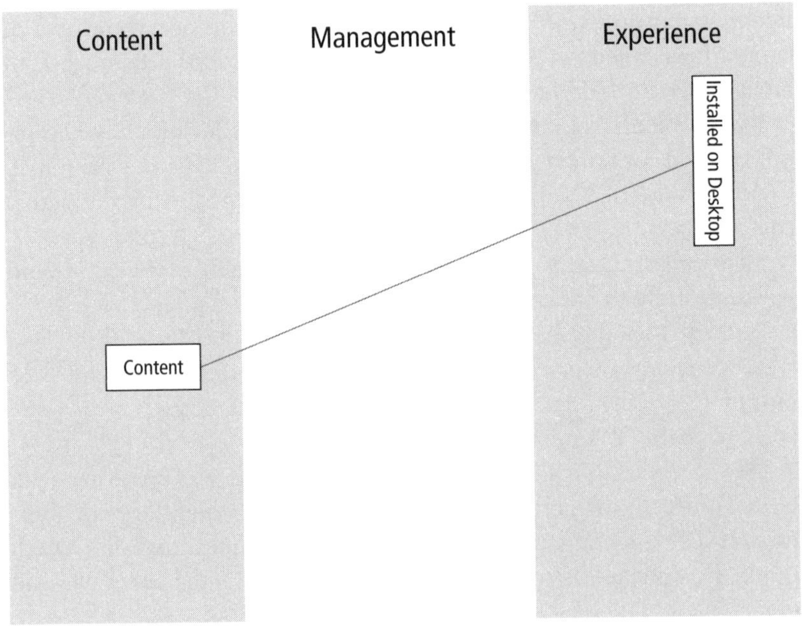

THE RIGHT MODEL BEYOND PILOTS?

Flight simulators are the right model for training pilots. I would not want my plane to have a pilot who did not have simulator training.

But what are the implications for formal education everywhere else? Is this the model for all training?

Role of Instructors and Students

Real flight simulators require more than one support person for every student. While this works for senior managers, it cannot work for larger pools of students, including corporate trainees and students of higher education.

Having said that, some role for humans in the equation seems critical. Many training groups lost influence at the top of organizations to *corporate coaches,* who were more than happy to teach one-on-one.

Professional instructors have a role with simulations. And it is a higher-value role of *coaching* and *diagnosing,* rather than the lower-value role of *lecturing* and *grading.*

Highest Fidelity Simulation

There is no talk here about eye-candy with these flight simulators. No one refers to the realistic graphics as "bells and whistles" (the favorite derogative term of vendors of last-generation e-learning technology). No traditional training instructor is in the corner muttering that all of this is unnecessary; all you need is a whiteboard and a deck of cards.

This simulator does everything it can to mimic the reality. Period. Flight simulators teach *cyclical content* through muscle memory. Pilots learn to nudge a bit to the left, or a bit to the right. They learn the difference between putting down the wheels a few seconds too early (not so bad) and a few seconds too late (bad). They are fully kinesthetically engaged in the environment. They also learn the *systems* of flying inside and out. Compare that to a multiple-choice interface, and understand more clearly the absurdity of some e-learning simulator's claims of being a "flight simulator for business skills."

Simulation and Pedagogical Elements (No Games)

The hardware takes over the job of the simulation elements, and the instructors handle the pedagogy. But there are very few game elements here. Unique in all of the simulation experiences, game elements (with the possible exception of competition, ranking, and high scores) just have no place here.

It Matters

Imagine a modern classroom, say at a university in oh, Providence, Rhode Island. Say a professor is lecturing to a classroom on existentialism, or Russian pre-revolution history, or computer programming. Let's put this oh, around 1988, and it could be me sitting in the classroom.

What were the consequences of me not learning that material, to the college and to the professors? Nothing. (It turns out that I never even had a situation where my school records impacted an acceptance to a job or advanced program, so, it didn't matter to me either, other than the cumulative meeting of the degree criterion, which mattered immensely.)

Don't get me wrong. There were processes that were followed. There were office hours, and teaching assistants, and extra reading available. The professors were well-rated, animated, entertaining, passionate about their subject areas, and knowledgeable. But it just did not matter, and we all knew it.

One of the most amazing parts about seeing pilots trained is that it matters that the material is learned. Everyone cares. When there are accidents, thousands of professionals pray that they were not part of the process that led to it.

Without this caring, even the best program in the world will suffer ennui. And, with this caring, even the worst program will get much better.

CONCLUSION

Improving training at the Air Force is constant. But one area receiving increased focus is crew resource management or cockpit resource management. This means not only how did pilots react to a fire on an engine, but also did they listen to their crew's comments. As technical skills become so refined, the interpersonal skills become the rate-determining step.

Today, the interpersonal training still looks closer to the plywood flight simulators of the 1930s and 1940s. How they will pull this training off might finally role model "a flight simulator for business skills."

But Wait. There's More

Do you want to hear about more military simulations? Go to Chapter 19, Military + Computer Game = Full Spectrum Experiences.

COMING UP NEXT

Computer games as models for educational content? Sure, but only if you can avoid a trap that has caught most pioneers so far.

13

THE MOST POPULAR SIMULATIONS

Computer Games as Expectation Setters and Places to Start

Teach someone a computer game; and you have engaged him for today. Teach someone a computer game genre and you have engaged him for a lifetime.

—With apologies to the old Chinese proverb

I WAS BORN IN 1967. I was probably part of the first generation to grow up on computer games. I would go over to my friends' houses and play on their Apple II+ or Atari game consoles. I was too cheap to actually invest a quarter into a coin-operated machine (I don't mean to sound puritanical; I was saving up for comic books), but I would spend hours watching those who did.

And so, like many GenXers and GenYers, my native expectation of educational simulations is that they be an extension of computer games. We assume a *highly entertaining and relentlessly interactive* experience. I was naïve (read: stupid) enough in 1999 to be quite surprised that my first e-learning experiences were not more interactive.

Research is on our side, kind of. There is a growing sense that computer games are in fact educational. They do teach something. I was discussing this with Gonzalo Frasca, a game designer in his own right and Ph.D. candidate at Copenhagen's Center for Computer Game Research.

"Well," he started, apologetically, "computer games are not very good for learning facts, like names and dates. But they are good for teachings systems."

This was not the first time I had heard that, but I was still amazed. Not at the fact that computer games taught systems. But I was amazed that he was apologetic about it.

Soon, I hope people will say. "Of course computer games teach. And they do real teaching—systems, not that useless facts crap."

Some quick questions. With what computer games have you played?

- I have played a game in an arcade.
- I have played a game that came with my computer (such as Solitaire).
- I have played a console (PlayStation®2, Xbox®, GameCube™) single-player game.
- I have played a multi-player game with at least three other people.
- I have played a game on a portable player (cell phone, Game Boy® Advance).
- I have played a massively multi-player online role-playing game (such as EverQuest®, World of WarCraft™).
- I have spent over three hours at one time on one game.
- I have gone to an online community to get help with a game.
- I have downloaded a "mod" for a computer game.

If you chose more than four from the list, you can skip right to the heading "Topics." If you chose two or fewer from the list, you may want to play a few more games (just as research—do not have fun).

WHAT WE LEARN FROM COMPUTER GAMES

We do learn a lot of universal truths from most computer games. "Experts" will spend years debating over what one actually learns from computer games. (And starting with *a computer game* and then figuring out *what one learns* is very different from starting with *critical things to teach* and then figuring out how to *use computer game methodology* to aid in the instruction.) But here are some that Gonzalo and I thought were most important.

1. You Are the Key to Success

Computer games have to be the most empowering activities around. Few players lean back in their chairs while engaging a computer game.

Contrast this to so many activities, from movies to classroom lectures to reading books to being a stockholder, that are inherently passive. There are clever ways of goosing them up: sudden loud music, shower scenes, pop quizzes, shareholder votes. But most participants are like a passenger on an airplane. They worry about little things—getting peanuts and drinks, reading, staying comfortable—all the while confident that they will arrive at the end of the day.

Playing a computer game is different. Playing a computer game is more like being late for an important meeting and your car won't start. Either you make things happen, or they do not happen.

2. Mistakes Are Necessary on the Path to Success

I was watching people play a project management simulation I designed at a major British company. And I was amazed at how much a room full of adults was loath to try new strategies.

One of my pieces of advice is always, "Don't do anything and see what happens."

"But then I won't do well," they protest.

"It is just practice. Watch and learn. Then the next time you will do it much better."

My nephew doesn't have that problem with a computer game. He will crash into things, playing at the boundaries all day long.

And give any gamer a virtual rifle range with a drill sergeant issuing orders, and at some point during the first hour, the gamer will spin around and shoot the drill sergeant. Guaranteed. (Having said that, I might worry a bit if it is the first thing the player does.)

3. Things Are Connected

A lot of things are connected in a computer game. There are very complex and intertwined systems at play. If you over-use or over-depend on something, it tends to push back in unexpected ways.

As a corollary, there are rules. And while the rules can't be broken, they *can, should,* and sometimes *must* be surprisingly and creatively exploited.

4. How to Learn

The scariest thing for all educators is not that people learn from computer games, but that they *learn how to learn.* They expect for the environment to get harder gradually as they get better. They expect to go at their own pace. They expect to be fully engaged. They expect to be involved at a tactile level and at a high-level intellectual level at the same time.

5. Computer Literacy

This point is so obvious that I almost forgot it. People who spend time playing with computers become very comfortable with computers. Computer games present an increasingly complete exposure to computers, including installation, learning new interfaces, networks, even file structures for the advanced users.

There is a lot more specific learning than the five listed above, of course. But now you have to look at computer games, not as a whole, but by genres.

Genres

It is probably worth a moment here to discuss the concept of genres, because it might be one of the most important concepts for understanding the future of educational simulations.

If you are an art major, you might think of a genre as a combination of subject, style, and time period. For you, familiar art genres include *surrealism, expressionism, impressionism, nakedism, scribblism, whywouldanyonelikethisism, sternpeopleism, post-impressionism,* and *really-post-impressionism.*

The rest of us can identify with genres with regard to television shows or movies. Our knowledge of genres sets our expectations. How powerful is the influence of genres? Try this quick test.

Imagine yourself turning to a favorite fictional show. Play out the introduction and opening credits. Fast forward past the commercials. See the first establishing shot and hear the familiar background music.

Now a new character is introduced. From the moment he walks in the door, he is witty, polite, and well dressed, but clearly worried about something. He jokes suggestively with the show's female lead. This rubs you-know-who the wrong way.

Suddenly, that new character is shot down in a hail of bullets that came from the window. He is dead before he hits the ground. Blood is everywhere.

If your favorite show were a situation comedy, this scene would be quite shocking and disturbing. It would stick with you, unpleasantly resurfacing throughout the next days and weeks. If your favorite show was a police medical drama, it might warrant a shrug.

That is the nature of genres.

In computer or video games, genres are even less about topics and even more about structures. Here are some examples.

And yes, genres can be crossed and mixed.

REAL-TIME STRATEGY (RTS) In real-time strategy game genres such as *The Rise of Nations*® (Figure 13.1), *Command and Conquer*™, *StarCraft*®, and *WarCraft*® the player is a disembodied, undisputed commander of some type of military operation.

Figure 13.1. Microsoft's *Rise of Nations*®.

Source: Screen Shot Reprinted by Permission from Microsoft Corporation.

Some RTS games have evolved the experience by including:

- Hero units that have stronger abilities than other units
- Branching points, to radically improve one part of your operation over another
- Multiple victory options, including military or cultural dominance

Real-time strategy games might be the most intense learning experiences. You manage the concepts of exploration, building, defending, logistics, and conquering:

- You have to juggle a lot of things at the same time, and coordinate several tasks.
- You have to prioritize.
- Perhaps most difficult, you need to switch strategies at the right time.
- You need long-term philosophies, not just minute-to-minute reactions.
- You balance short-term and long-term goals.
- You learn the use of time.
- You have to move between the small and big picture, juggling a few key troops and moving armies.
- You make tradeoffs—I will lose some soldiers to accomplish a bigger task of distraction or destruction of a key facility.

FIRST-PERSON SHOOTERS (FPS) If you are a male, *first-person shooters* are the Manolo Blahniks of the computer game world. The player sees the world through the eyes of his or her onscreen counterpart, or avatar, if you are an academic, usually down the barrel of a weapon (Figure 13.2 and Figure 13.3).

Some FPS have pushed the envelope by including:

- Having to decide which weapons to bring, rather than bringing all
- Selectively improving certain aspects of your character, such as speed, strength, or good looks (that last one has not yet been a real option, but I would select it)

Figure 13.2. A First-Person Shooter, *Delta Force®—Black Hawk Down®*.

Source: By Permission of NovaLogic, Inc. ©, All Rights Reserved.

Figure 13.3. A First-Person Shooter, *Halo®: Combat Evolved.*

Source: Screen Shot Reprinted by Permission from Microsoft Corporation.

- Trying to sneak past guards, instead of killing them
- Integrating vehicles as an alternative to walking
- Using a third-person perspective (where you can see your character/avatar), rather than see the world through the avatar's perspective

There is certainly some high-level learning going on, beyond the general learning mentioned above. There is hand-eye coordination, how to read and use maps, problem solving, and how to build complicated internal representations of environments.

All right, we may be scraping the barrel a little bit here. But no more, frankly, than when the kindergarten teacher tells us that the children are developing spatial relationship skills, building fine motor coordination, and engaging in interpersonal parallel play, when they are in the corner stacking blocks.

If you squint hard enough, you can see a slight similarity, perhaps a common ancestor, between first-person shooters and interactive stories. There are at least some common philosophies.

MANAGEMENT SIMS/GOD GAMES Management simulations, such as *Roller Coaster Tycoon®*, *Railroad Tycoon®*, or *Sid Meier's Civilization®* series, present examples of combining b-school with computer games (and perhaps a dash of interactive spreadsheets). Similar to real-time strategy games, players control enterprises or nations over decades (Figure 13.4).

Like a good God/manager, you are the undisputed ruler and look down on the little people and decide their fates. And similar to b-schools, there is only a small relationship between mastering the high-level intellectual models and the day-to-day activities of really working in an enterprise.

ROLE-PLAYING GAMES (RPGs) There are role-playing games, such as *Star Wars®: Knights of the Old Republic™*. In these games you manage a person or team through increasingly challenging scenarios, deliberately building your character's skill sets and inventories to meet the increasing and evolving conflicts. You also find treasures of high value, such as a powerful weapon or impenetrable armor, but sadly not a nice bottle of Leoville Barton, 1871.

Role-playing games started off with having the "God/manager" perspective of management sims, but have evolved to look more like first- (or third-) person shooters.

Figure 13.4. Microsoft's *Zoo Tycoon*®.

Source: Screen Shot Reprinted by Permission from Microsoft Corporation.

Some have said this game is most like life, reflecting the long-term career and life decisions most of us make. At the very least, it teaches the scarcity of development opportunities and the absolute need to align development with strategy.

MASSIVELY MULTI-PLAYER ONLINE ROLE-PLAYING GAMES (MMORPGs) In massively multi-player online role-playing games, a persistent online world hosts an essentially unlimited number of players taking on first-person shooters and role-playing missions and activities. MMORPGs teach how to meet strangers and either form deep relationships with which to perform heroic quests carefully balancing each other's strengths and weaknesses, or alternatively cheat, rob, and kill them.

SIMULATION, GAMES, AND PEDAGOGY

What makes computer games so murky to separate from educational simulations is that computer games also represent a convergence of simulation, games, and pedagogical elements. Most new games start with a high-level simulation at their core. There is a situation being modeled.

- For example, management sims involve the representation of business issues, as subtle as the price of capital to borrow, or the logistics of trains versus trucks to transport goods.
- Real-time strategy games involve modeling some aspect of warfare, such as the advantage gained from the high ground, or the importance of supply lines.
- Even the critters that you battle in a first-person shooter (FPS) are given simulations of "intelligence" to wait for you to show up, then to run to a place where they have a clear shot, and aim and shoot at you until either they or you are killed. In more advanced games, critters can chase you, track you, mob you, call in reinforcements, swim in your pool when you are not home, and borrow your car without refilling the gas tank.

Then the situations are tweaked considerably to make them fun to play. In our first-person shooter example, the designers might add more critters if the experience is too easy, or take away some if it is too hard. They might change the number of first aid kits or the power of accessible weapons.

Finally, there are some instructions and tutorials, both before and during play. Console games are very good at flashing instructions as you are playing (PRESS A TO OPEN DOOR, PRESS R TO RELOAD, or PRESS R-MOUSE BUTTON TO HEDGE AGAINST INFLATION). Of course, for computer games, the game elements trump the simulation aspects in any internal debate.

TOPICS

We have a curriculum in this country built around teaching history. For a lot of academics considering games and simulations then, the natural question is, "How do we use simulations in our curriculum," which means, "How do we simulate history," or at least, "How do we simulate participation in history?"

A first instinct is to simulate the great conflicts. War games provide broad genre templates, as do some of the civilization games.

Hearts of Iron, a WWII simulator, includes not just the military aspects of the conflict, but also the diplomatic, economic, and scientific. The game allows you to play virtually any country in existence at the time and try your hand at resolving the conflict.

Noah Falstein has served in programmer, project leader, and executive producer roles for organizations including LucasArts Entertainment, The 3DO Company, and Dreamworks Interactive. He now heads The Inspiracy, a consulting firm specializing in game design and production. Noah noted that "*Sid Meier's Civilization® III* along with the book *Guns, Germs, and Steel* would be a great mini-course. The game would give students a gut feeling for the importance of resources, technology, and geography, and the book would help sort out the real-world facts from the game simplifications."

Chris Schuller, formerly with Microsoft and now a simulation consultant, remarked, "The campaigns in *Age of Empires* have taught my nephews more about history than school has. They talk about time periods as if they are talking about levels of *Halo*."

Here are some games by topic.

BUSINESS, GENERAL

Capitalism series, Enlight Software**
Gazillionaire®, LavaMind**
Giant series, JoWooD Productions**
Profitania®, LavaMind**
Roller Coaster Tycoon® series, Atari***
Tropico™ series, Gathering of Developers**
Zapitalism®, LavaMind**
Zoo Tycoon® series, Microsoft****

CAREERS, MEDICAL

Emergency Room series, Sierra***
Vet Emergency series, Encore Software***

CONFLICTS, HISTORICAL

1503 A.D. The New World, Electronic Arts**
Hearts of Iron™, Strategy First*
Medieval Total War™ series, Activision**
Sid Meier's Gettysburg!® series, Electronic Arts**

*Developed for education markets, not computer game markets
**Broadly interesting across older age groups
***Aimed at teenagers
****Aimed at children

Stronghold: Crusader™, Gathering of Developers**

The Rise of Nations®: *Thrones and Patriots*, Microsoft**

EDUCATION

School Tycoon, Global Star Software****

Virtual University, Digital Mill*

ENVIRONMENT AND ECOSYSTEM

Civilization: Call to Power series, Microsoft**

Sid Meier's Civilization® series, Activision**

Sid Meier's Alpha Centauri, Electronic Arts**

The Living Sea, Montparnasse Multimedia****

Star Wars®: *The Gungan Frontier*™, Lucas Learning, 1999****

SimCity™ series, Electronic Arts**

Zoo Tycoon® series, Microsoft****

ECONOMICS, HISTORICAL

Railroad Tycoon® series, Gathering of Developers**

HEALTH

Hungry Red Planet, Health Media Lab*

LEADERSHIP

Virtual Leader, SimuLearn*

NATIONS, HISTORICAL

The Age of Empires®, Microsoft**

The Age of Kings®, Microsoft**

Caesar III™, Sierra**

Europa Universalis® series, Strategy First**

Patrician series, Strategy First **

Pharaoh, Sierra**

The Rise of Nations®: *Thrones and Patriots*, Microsoft**

Sid Meier's Civilization® series, Activision**

PHYSICS

Physicus, Viva Media****

POLITICS

Power Politics, CinePlay Interactive**
The Doonesbury Election Game, Mindscape**
Power Politics III, Kellogg Creek Software**

TIME MANAGEMENT

The Sims™ series, Electronic Arts***

URBAN PLANNING

The *SimCity*™ series, Electronic Arts***

Architecture

Computer games are easy to deploy over the Internet, except for the Internet part. For PCs, they are delivered via CD-ROM or DVD and

Figure 13.5. Computer Game Architecture Considerations.

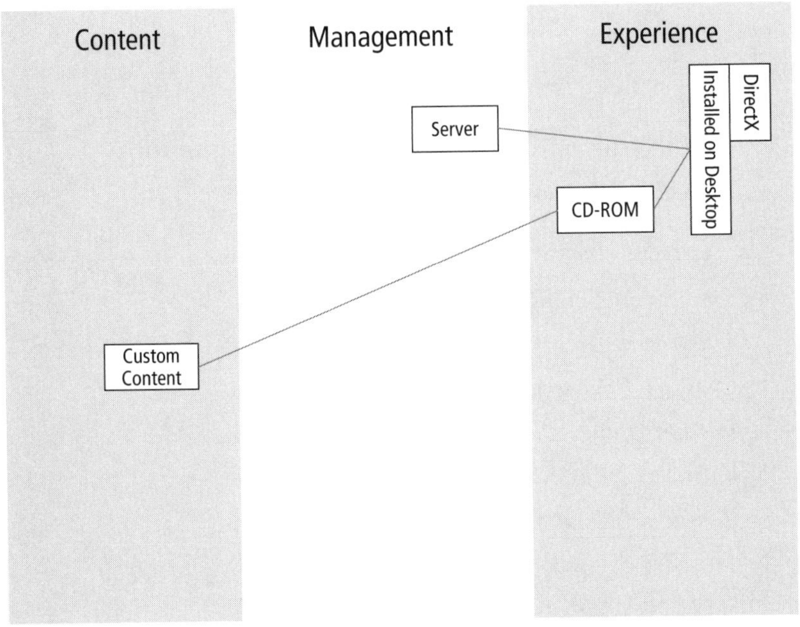

installed on the hard disk of the computer using Microsoft's DirectX as an API. They can be connected to servers, either local or via the Internet, for multi-player capabilities (Figure 13.5).

SMALL GAMES

Over the last two or three years, an alternative business model for Web games has emerged. Small games (two to five megs) are downloadable. Consumers play them for free for an hour, or play a few levels. Then, to continue, the users pay $10 to $30. The most successful of these tend to be abstract, *Tetris*-like games. This has been facilitated by comfort with commerce on the Web, and faster networks to facilitate the download.

COMING UP NEXT

Yeah, but are computer games the right model for education? Well, they are very, very close.

14

COMPUTER GAMES REDUX

The Right Model? How Right?

A QUESTION, AND FOR SOME *THE* QUESTION, is to what degree are computer games a model for the future of education. The answer is, of course, complicated.

CHEAP

You can buy a movie that costs eighty million dollars to develop for about $15 to $30 on DVD that can be watched in about four hours, assuming you go through it twice. That's pretty amazing, when you stop and think about it.

You can buy a computer game that costs ten million dollars to build for between $20 and $50 that can provide at least thirty hours of play, and sometimes much, much more. Finally, you can gorge yourself on television content for free, and even more if you subscribe to cable services.

These are the results of successful business models, including a ready audience and distribution channels. Educational simulation producers drool at such numbers.

Instead, the pressure on commercial educational titles today, the so-called *edutainment* programs even though most are neither, is to sell for around $20 in lackluster quantities. It's no wonder that most aren't very good.

This market reality traps certain vendors in a low cost/low production value spiral. This loop is so intractable that some people believe the only hope for educational simulations will be massive intellectual infusions from the corporate or government markets. Anything to break the cycle.

FUN

Another issue is fun. Fun gives me a lot of unhappiness. Fun is a very difficult concept for educational simulation designers.

First, and this goes without saying, is that computer games are meant to be fun. They are designed to be fun. Computer games' *raison d'etre* is fun.

So naturally, those people who play computer games expect educational simulations to be fun. Many of the teachers and professors who want to bring computer-game-like educational experiences into the classrooms expect them to be fun, although not too fun. And some believe that all learning all of the time should be fun, or it's not really working.

There are a few issues, however.

Targeted Audiences

No single game, just as no single movie, appeals to everybody. Browse through the selection of computer games and it becomes clear that any given game is only fun for some people. There probably isn't too much crossover between the "pink doll takes her pony to the shopping mall" crowd and the "World War I trench warfare with accurate weapon clip sizes and recoil" fans. Gamers have learned to up their chances of getting something they like by sticking to familiar *themes* and *genres.*

If you think an educational simulation should, but of course, be fun, imagine this scenario. Imagine a computer game is named "best of the year" by several publications. The gameplay is refined, the graphics are great, and the multi-player component is seamless.

Now, find all of the people who spend more than two hours a week playing computer games. Then make them play this award-winning product for five hours. Tell them that their teacher or boss cares about how well they do.

How many of those people do you think would call the experience "fun"? I am betting less than 20 percent.

By the way, five hours is not that much time in the world of computer games. Kurt Squire, a former elementary and Montessori teacher, is now an assistant professor at the University of Wisconsin-Madison in the Educational Communications and Technology Division of curriculum and instruction. (He is also a visiting Research Fellow at MIT and co-director of The Education Arcade. So there!)

Kurt's dissertation focused on how playing *Sid Meier's Civilization III* changed students' understandings of world history. He found "it took two to three hours for kids to learn the interface, and ten to twelve to really understand the gameplay. Any sort of 'mastery' (can you reliably survive for a few hours) took closer to twenty." No doubt about it—games, especially simulation-heavy games, are a major investment.

Computer game advocates talk about how much fun educational simulations will be. This reminds me a bit of the teacher who fell in love with a novel she discovered during her junior year abroad as an intern at, say, the Institut National des Sciences Appliquées de Lyon, where by the way she also met the man she would later marry while hang gliding over the Vivarais Mountains, and decades later is confused when her high school students, assigned the same novel as summer reading, don't develop a similar passion. It is a great idea, but for now, immature.

Perhaps someday we will get better at swarming on students' interests. This would require a broad portfolio of curricula that would also have to be constantly updated to leverage the hype generated by popular culture (a la the Discovery Channel, the History Channel, and the television program "Biography"), including movies, books, comic books, and computer games, as an entry point into a deeper world of multi-disciplinary knowledge. Until we are there, we shouldn't assume educational simulations to be fun. (Rewarding, yes; relevant, yes; intense, yes; eye-opening, yes; inspiring, yes; high production values; yes; transforming, yes; fun, maybe.)

Not So Much Fun by Design

Sivasailam "Thiagi" Thiagarajan tells of a funeral home simulation that is deeply moving and emotional, effective, but not fun. Some simulations, by design and subject matter, should not be fun.

Precision

Finally, Douglas Whatley, who has built both military flight simulators and entertainment flight simulators with Breakaway Ltd., explains just one of the differences between the two.

"In games, people want to do the fun stuff as quickly as possible. They want to get into the flight simulator and shoot down an enemy.

"In the military, pilots will spend a lot more time doing things like practice re-fueling. The military simulations are more mundane, less fun, as it should be. The public isn't going to be interested in after-action reviews (AARs)."

Kym Buchanan (our doctoral student at Michigan State University) adds, "First-person shooters have made up physics. Take being a sniper, for example. Sniping is a lot of fun in an FPS. The programs don't worry about wind and they don't worry about gravity. The distance from your target is irrelevant. In contrast, sniping in real life is very scientific. Some people say that these games train people to be snipers. If people are learning from FPS, they will be pretty bad snipers."

And while I agree with those thoughts, I recently watched a friend play the program *Construction/Destruction*™. You run a construction yard and perform meticulous tasks with your equipment. Watching him spend an hour cleaning up debris from a job site, I can't figure out if it is a really bad game or a really great simulation.

Fun is good. But from a design perspective, it is a complicated topic.

- There is the fun that is a natural part of learning. Fun is the result of a well-designed learning and interest curve.
- There is *also* fun that surrounds and props up learning.
- *And then,* most controversially, there is fun that comes by selectively subverting an accurate simulation.

Learning is often not fun, although at the end of the day it should be very satisfying. The concept, and necessity, and worst of all the expectation, of fun may get in the way of simulation development and deployment, not support them.

DYNAMIC

As with flight simulators, leading computer games use dynamically rendered animation, not video or Flash®. With the exception of simple Web games, across all of the other variations of computer games, and despite the cost, this real-time rendered technology seems to be a necessary aspect of the interactive experience, and over time a necessary aspect of most educational simulations as well.

GENRE-DRIVEN, COMFORTABLE, LIGHTWEIGHT PEDAGOGICAL ELEMENTS

Computer games come in *genres*. This provides a quick way for players to buy a new game and use it within minutes of installing it. There are some built-in pedagogical elements, but they are relatively lightweight, just enough to teach people how to engage this variation of a genre.

To fully use systems, cyclical, and linear content, however, educational simulations will be more about introducing new genres than about absorbing old ones. There has been a lot of praise of Will Wright's best-selling computer game, *The Sims*™. But all of the conversations that I have seen missed one of the most important points: how the world learned to accept and play *The Sims*™. It was a completely new genre that, because it was based on real life, conflicted with one's own sense of the world. You could only eat one or two meals in a day. Cleaning took hours.

It seems that the solution to new genre acceptance includes marketing, word of mouth, game reviews, peer goals and influences, and a whole lot of luck. Creating and teaching new simulation genres will be a defining characteristic of next gen sims. So we had better figure out how to build a comfort level.

COTS/INSTALLED TO BE RUN

Computer games use commercial off-the-shelf equipment (COTS). Compared to the multi-million-dollar custom flight simulators, that's the good news.

But even so, computer games are very large programs. They are compressed onto 670 Meg CD-ROMS (sometimes two, three, or four CD-ROMS), and can take up twice that amount on a PC's hard disk. (In contrast, my last book fit in a file of about 3 Megs, and had plenty of elbowroom at that.) They are either installed via a CD-ROM that has to be distributed through trucks and warehouses, or downloaded for a very long time. DVDs can also be used, with much greater storage capacity.

Computer games are applications that need to be installed to run. And that presents a problem. IT departments have layers of tools to keep people from doing just that. They can "lock down the desktops," making unauthorized installations impossible. Even installing the Microsoft code called DirectX that enables high-end graphics and sound, and not standard on operating systems until Windows XP, is forbidden. Further, any corporate application, and certainly an application such as an educational simulation with the footprint of a computer game, has to be tested rigorously to make sure it is compatible and stable with other mission-critical applications.

There is also a power issue. Less than half of the corporate PCs meet that very conservative criteria for adequately running a current computer game today, and many won't get refreshed for more than two more years. This is an area where I have seen chief learning officers and chief information officers go into screaming fights. Computers in academic labs are often no better. In other words, at best, these programs will not be evenly distributed across an enterprise. At worse, they won't even get a chance.

Keep in mind as you read this that the computing *power* exists, just not always in the right places. *The Sims*™ and related expansion packs alone have sold about twenty-eight *million* copies. Home machines are often more powerful than their corporate counterparts, and they certainly have easier access rights. But training groups worry that giving a CD-ROM for the home machine sends a mixed signal about working on the weekends. (One Swiss client insisted on using high-bandwidth video to keep employees from taking it home.)

Some suggest a short-term answer is computer game consoles. "Using PCs for simulations gets expensive. When you use an Xbox® as a platform, they can get the unit for $150," notes former Microsoft employee Chris Schuller. But there are licensing issues that emerge with using consoles for education, as we will take a look at later with *Full Spectrum Warrior*™.

And if you can get past all of that, with either a PC or a game console, there is a "launch" issue. e-Learning standards such as AICC and SCORM are only set up to launch web-based content, not installed applications.

HIT-DRIVEN, CONSUMER-FOCUSED, RETAIL-FOCUSED

Computer games fight hard for shelf space in the CompUSAs and Circuit Cities of the world. Like movies, they appear, and they either take off or disappear into the discount bins in a matter of weeks. Only one in four computer games makes a profit. It is hard to imagine educational simulations surviving in that environment. LeapFrog, thankfully, provides a great counterpoint to my argument.

Lots of Them

Computer games are very popular. Very, very popular. According to one study, everyone plays them all of the time (although that particular study used a very small sample set).

Does that mean that games are the right models? Not necessarily.

Early dot-com companies used the rapid increase in Internet access as the first slide in their investment pitch and, by extension, an indicator of their inevitable success. There is a connection, but looser than a lot of enthusiasts would like us to believe.

Built Using the Same Tools?

To what degree can the educational simulation industry piggyback off of the computer game industry today? I don't just mean culturally, but technically. Many people think this is the answer to a lot of problems.

Keep in mind a premise. Computer games have evolved into *genres* that are focused on being *entertaining*. Their interfaces, while highly refined, are not designed to teach transferable skills. Their underlying systems are very abstracted guesstimates (at best) of real phenomena.

Educational simulations need to evolve new *genres,* as similar and different from computer games as computer game genres are from each other. The flight simulator is the first educational genre example (if and only if it is used by a pilot as part of the learning process).

Building an educational simulation using an existing game genre risks "genre resurgence." This is a phenomenon where the resulting product is much more game-like and much less educational than the designers had intended.

If this is a critical topic for you, start by reading Appendix 6, Getting What You Want: The Black Art of Customizing the Four Traditional Simulation Genres. For everyone else, I can summarize it by saying there are no real short cuts today; there is a direct link between work required and results gained (Figure 14.1).

Languages

Computer *languages* give us the ability to interoperate directly with the lower-level computer architecture. It is very time-consuming, but with it we can get a program to do pretty much what we want. Many computer game designers work at this level.

Figure 14.1. From Mods to Programming Languages.

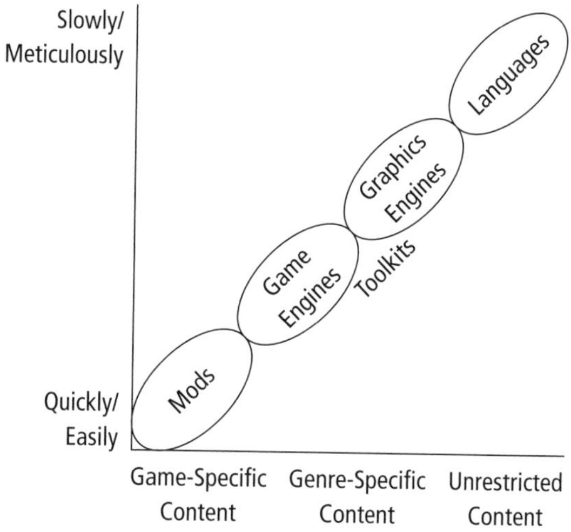

Engines

Increasingly, however, the computer game industry is building middleware/toolkits (*game* engines and *graphics* engines) to speed up, lower the cost, and increase the quality of computer games. Can these two be used for educational simulations? Absolutely and with caution, respectively.

Graphic engines effectively transform the computer code we write to good-looking images on the screen. They shave time off the development cycle, in exchange for costing some money.

Game engines, in contrast, complete a lot more of the computer game experience. They cost much more than a graphic engine, but provide a lot more functionality. As with a graphics engine, buying a game engine includes the right to distribute the resulting experience.

Game engines are typically genre-specific. A game engine locks a developer into a specific game genre, be it first-person shooter or real-time strategy. For *game designers,* that frees them to worry about the story and the look and feel of their product.

We have seen a few dozen educational simulations built on narrow game engines. The experiments have showed some potential, but the engines have trapped them into a set of conventions that has ultimately prevented them from doing what they wanted to do and has led to genre resurgence.

Popular game and graphic engines, which range in price from hundreds to hundreds of thousands of dollars, include:

- Unreal Engine 3 and Unreal Engine 2 from Epic Games
- OGRE (Object-Oriented Graphics Rendering Engine) from Steve Streeting
- Jupiter from Touchdown Entertainment, Inc.
- The Valve Source engine from Valve
- DarkBASIC from The Game Creators Ltd.
- V3X from Realtech VR
- The Torque Game Engine from GarageGames*
- TrueVision3D*
- Virtools*
- Quest3D*
- Anark Studios*

I put an asterisk by those most accessible at a low cost. For an updated list, see www.devmaster.net/engines/.

Mods

In contrast to the game and graphic engines, mods are new content that can overwrite or augment specific aspects of a commercial computer game. Recall our chart looking at linear versus dynamic skills, focusing on cyclical versus systems content (Figure 14.2).

With that as a model, here are what mods can do (Figure 14.3).

Here's what I mean by the various terms (and skim it if you don't care):

- *New Models or Objects:* Computer objects populate computer worlds. You can change the look of any or all of them. For example, instead of having your trolls and orcs spend time gathering jewels, you can have your lawyers and paralegals gathering facts. Going one step deeper (and more specifically, one step deeper than you probably care about), these objects tend to have a mesh (model) and a skin. The mesh is the 3D object itself, and the skin goes over it. Skins can be made by any traditional drawing program, but models need to be built using dedicated 3D tools that include such commands as *extrude, bevel, slice,* and *tessellate* (I swear, I am not making that last command up).

Figure 14.2. Linear vs. Dynamic Simulation Content.

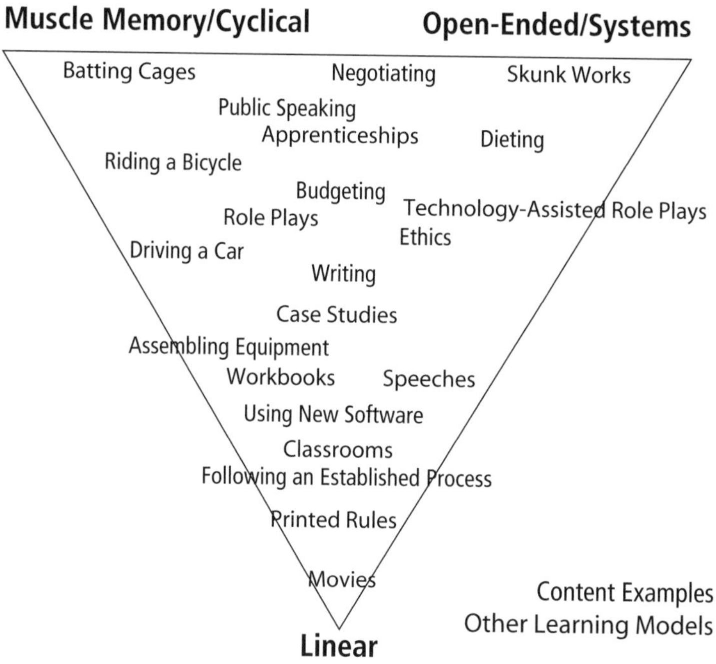

Figure 14.3. Customization Options Through Mods.

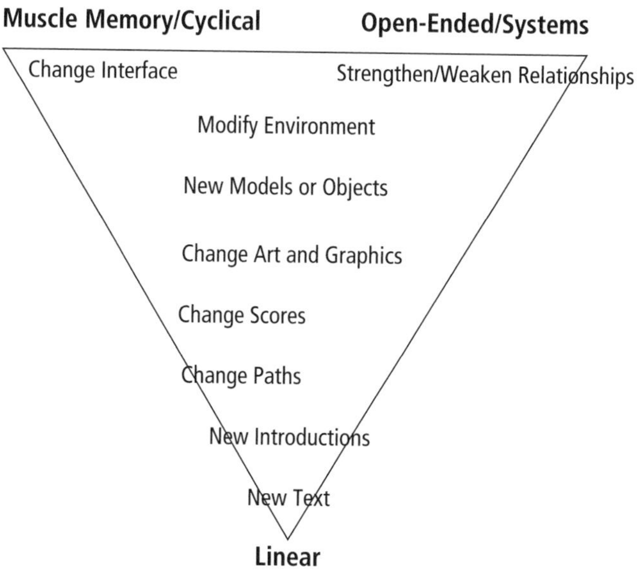

- *Change Interface:* Add or subtract buttons. Change how the user can interact with the simulation.
- *Change Weights:* Change cost of something (such as making lawyers much more expensive than paralegals) or their properties (making a lawyer faster than a paralegal).
- *Modify Environment and Create New Maps:* Create or change the shape of the virtual world (from caves to a map of the city or the State Hermitage Museum).
- *Change Art and Graphics:* Change any flat graphics, including open scenes, logos, and backgrounds.
- *Change Scores:* Alter the way the scores are tabulated. Change the value associated with discrete and/or analogue events.
- *Change Paths:* Alter the sequence of events and/or the connection between events.
- *New Text:* Add or subtract words from any text fields. Change languages (even to non-Roman languages if Unicode-compatible).
- *New Scenes:* Add a new scene, with the same engine and same graphics, but new starting parameters and victory conditions.

Today, volunteers build most mods. "One of the biggest challenges I have discussing concepts of games with non-gamers is that of the mod community," said Bart Pursel, from the Office of Learning Solutions at Penn State's School of Information Sciences and Technology. "It's so difficult to explain the huge community of gamers out there who devote endless hours to modifying existing games, then sharing them with the rest of the community to enjoy. People I talk to just don't understand why or how the gaming community does this. People understand the concept of modifying games, but they don't understand the breadth and depth of the mod community."

And modding is addictive. Getting things "just right" involves hours of tweaking.

A Faustian Bargain

These lists of changes are extensive. But keep in mind that even if you made all of these changes to an experience, the core gameplay remains the same.

On top of that, one challenge to the modding model for next gen sims is the licensing model. To access the mods, one has to buy the original game, and then download and apply the mod. MIT's Games to Teach program built an impressive *Revolution* role-playing game to teach about the social dynamics that led up to the American Revolution. The team built it to be used in classrooms, even going as far as chunking assignments and projects into forty-five-minute segments. But because it was built by modifying the game *Neverwinter Nights*™, every student who wants to access it has to buy the retail game *Neverwinter Nights*™, as well as procure the intellectual property that represents the *Revolution* game.

As Educational Genres Arrive

As educational genres arrive, game engines and mods will become very powerful approaches. Buying an existing educational genre engine and adding all new content to it, or modding an existing educational genre to more tightly meet requirements, will both transform education and be quite profitable. Consulting and academic institutions will have teams to do both.

COUNTERCULTURAL?

There is a weird logic that goes something like, "I am a science teacher. Kids are bored to death in my classroom. Then they go home and play games for hours and have a great time. How can I make my science lessons more like a computer game?"

One question that Kurt Squire brings up is this: Are computer games necessarily and inherently countercultural and escapist? Is what makes them engaging, like rock and roll (and frankly like poetry), their protest, desperation, and defiance? Or, like comic books and movies, their ability to transport one to a different and irrelevant place?

While Kurt is more rigorous than I am, I tested this notion casually with a random walk through aisles of computer games at a local mall. Most of the games focused on cars crashing and guns blazing. Meanwhile, the volume of cheaters in multi-player games is legendary.

More subtly, even more realistic business *Tycoon* programs focus on exercising complete control of a company, army, city, or country. Even in purely management sims, the games aren't about negotiating with employees or a board of directors—they are about re-carving the world in the players' image.

Pushing the Envelope

Here's another take. A lot of people like to listen to or watch the news every day. And yet very few people are interested in engaging recorded news from a week ago. We invest a huge amount of time engaging content today that will be of almost no value in just a few days.

New technology is very expensive when it first comes out, even though it is often buggy. It gets much cheaper and better even six months after it is first released.

When new computer games first appear, they are quite expensive, in the $40 to $60 range. Six months later, the same game is often half the price. Two years later, the title is half the price again.

Is a *sine que non* appeal of computer games (like news and technology) that sense of pushing of the envelope, the promise of doing something never before done? Are experiences that "push the envelope" inherently incompatible with the education system. Or are they necessary for it?

GAME COMPONENTS

Computer games represent models for next generation educational simulations (next gen sims) in so many ways. They have pioneered the combination of game elements, simulation elements, and pedagogical elements. They have pioneered the combination of systems, interfaces, and linear. The have provided placeholders for different categories of components (Figure 14.4).

Figure 14.4. Game Components.

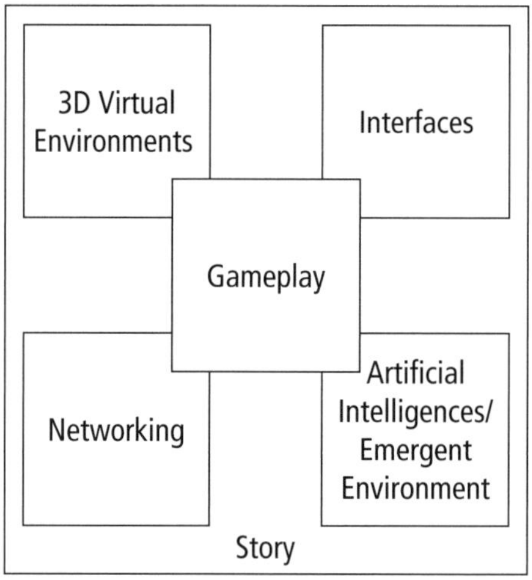

Perhaps the most enthusiastic (and honest) (and scary) thing I can say about computer games is that they are such a compelling model that *the interesting questions now are not how next gen sims are similar to computer games, but how they are dissimilar* (did I mention scary?). That is the real challenge.

But Wait. There's More

If you want to look at a timeline of computer games (and e-learning), go to Appendix 7, e-Learning and Computer Game Milestones.

If you would like to read more about what some computer game gurus think are important to educational simulations, go to Appendix 8, Full Interviews with Jane Boston, Warren Spector, and Will Wright.

OTHER RESOURCES

- Gee, James Paul. (2003). *What Video Games Have to Teach Us About Learning and Literacy.* New York: Palgrave Macmillan.
- Grossman, Austin. (2003). *Postmortems from Game Developers: Insights from the Developers of* Unreal Tournament, Black and White, Age of Empires, *and Other Top-Selling Games.* Gilroy, CA: CMP Books.
- Salen, Katie, & Zimmerman, Eric. (2003). *Rules of Play: Game Design Fundamentals.* Cambridge, MA: MIT Press.

COMING UP NEXT

Is that the end-all on computer games? Nope! There is one more type of computer game that is becoming more common than all of the others put together.

15

THE MOSQUITOES OF THE EDUCATIONAL SIMULATIONS ECOSYSTEM

Marketing Mini-Games

Computer games aren't addictive. And I ought to know—I play them every day.

BIG-BUDGET COMPUTER GAMES GET a lot of attention. They are loud, cutting-edge, and often use stars that you actually have seen. But greater numbers of GenXers and GenYers (and beyond) are also playing *marketing mini-games*. Sponsored by corporations, causes (including political and religious), and even social commentators, these downloadable games are easy to play, shallow, accessible, free, unabashedly biased (think *Fox News*), and Web-deployed. And, did I mention, they may just be the key to the future of education.

One person behind many of these experiences is Tom Jacobson, chief gaming officer of Superdudes.net, an online gaming community. He has built marketing mini-games for such mom-and-pop companies as Sony, Procter and Gamble, and Microsoft.

In creating a marketing mini-game, his goal is to increase exposure to a brand (Figure 15.1). And he faces many of the challenges that an HR manager faces with deploying e-learning simulations.

"My job is to build games as cheaply as possible, today often between $2,500 and $4,500," said Jacobson. "The budgets for complicated Web

Figure 15.1. A Marketing Mini-Game.

Source: TSK 2 Game from www.superdudes.net. Used with Permission.

games are going down. With a few exceptions, such as movies that use games for exposure and background, there is a race to the bottom in our industry."

There are Technical Issues . . .

Pure HTML is dull, so the right plug-ins for the web browser are necessary. Flash® and Shockwave® work, but other special plug-ins decrease usage dramatically. Few people want to install anything beyond that.

The size of the game is also important. If it takes too long to download, people will abandon it. How big is too big? Well, that changes every month. Broadband is changing the rules. (And those who think people don't download at work are quaintly and amusingly misguided. According to Jacobson, traffic for the United States during the week is twice that of the weekend.)

. . . And Design Issues

Any successful marketing game should not require the use of instructions. Teenage game players may try to master the subtleties of a hot video game, but most others will not spend that kind of time on a free download.

You have to get the message right, or at least not wrong. And it has to be right the first time.

Advertisers, like corporate leaders, want control of their programs. Television has allowed them to put out a new marketing campaign with supporting commercials, and then retract it at a moment's notice. But games on the Internet, especially small, free ones, are mirrored (that's copied, if you are over forty) on sites, potentially all over the world. Once it is out there, it could be out there for years.

Jacobson also has another rule: "The first level can never be easy enough, the last level can never be hard enough. You can lose people in the first level if they are frustrated for five seconds. But once people learn it, they want a challenge and a payoff."

The total time for playing a marketing mini-game? Between three and five minutes. "That is a long time for intensely engaging something, compared to thirty seconds of passive exposure during a commercial." But not that long compared to a five-day workshop at Stanford.

WHEN POLITICS ARE INVOLVED

Some marketing mini-games have a higher goal than just building a positive brand. Some actually try to teach players a new perspective. To accomplish this, marketing mini-games tend to present new and simple interfaces and gameplay (Figure 15.2).

Way back in late 2003, there was a Democratic candidate named Howard Dean. His campaign commissioned a "Dean for America" marketing game that, while it did not help Howard Dean in Iowa, was a very clever example of a marketing mini-game with a real, quasi-instructional goal. Gonzalo Frasca, who also designs mini-marketing games for the Cartoon Network, co-designed it along with Ian Bogost.

"There were a lot of interesting factors in creating the Dean for America game," Gonzalo recounted. "The first is that it had to be

Figure 15.2. A Marketing Mini-Game from DeanforAmericaGame.com.

Source: Dean for America.

completed in two weeks, and for less than twenty thousand dollars. Second, thematically, Howard Dean's team did not want to convince new voters, but influence supporters."

The game therefore involved performing activities that Dean supporters might actually do, such as showing the Dean sign to people passing by and handing out pamphlets. There was no winning or losing, although there were scores that people could try to optimize. People had to feel good at the end.

"You have to be extra careful in building a political game, because everything is meaningful. People can potentially read in a lot to any animation or gameplay element, so you are playing with fire. You have to do testing for interpretation, not just bugs," noted Gonzalo (Figure 15.3).

"The style of graphics has to be appropriate for the targeted audience. In Dean for America, we wanted something that could have come out of *The New Yorker.*"

Figure 15.3. No Losing.

Source: Dean for America.

One tracked metric was exposure. Seventy thousand players engaged the game in the first week, despite the hurdle that it was launched on Christmas week, a traditionally very bad time to launch a marketing game. In terms of number of hits, anyway, the game was very successful.

THE NEW GAMES?

It is amazing, the more you look, just how accepted these mini-games have become. We are no longer "in the know" for understanding them; we are hopelessly outdated if we do not.

Barry Joseph works with high school students in the New York City boroughs. He worked as a for-profit Web designer and then was trained at the Ford Foundation funded Academy for Educational Development, where he made the switch to the nonprofit organization Global Kids Inc.

"Global Kids had always used playing and making paper-based and role-playing games as a way of exploring issues. The question was how do we bring this technique online?" he explained. "The idea hit me when I read the game issue of *Wired* magazine in 2001. The issue discussed what I was seeing myself with my own nieces and nephews: that games had gone from geeky, when I was in high school, to mainstream for high school students today. And in so many ways, young people are moving ahead of us in their use of technology.

"We wanted to make online games for a lot of reasons. One was to broaden our reach, to add scalability to Global Kids. With technology, we have a chance to reach thousands, even hundreds of thousands of people at a time.

"Second, computer is the medium that speaks to these kids. They spend their free time playing computer games. This way, we are empowering them to be media creators. We want them to build, not just consume. We wanted to explore what happens when online games are treated as just another form of youth media."

"We got together some interested students, with the goal of making something socially relevant. The topic we chose was *airport profiling*. The students wanted to explore the boundary between protecting security and threatening civil liberties."

Barry continued, "In the game, the players are the profilers [Figure 14.4]. They see people running around the airport. The profilers are asked to stop and interview all of the people who meet certain criteria, such as shoe size, within a given time frame. The catch is that there isn't enough time to stop everybody. Therefore the players have to introduce their own, additional criteria to decide which people to stop. Here we get to bias.

"Each level takes about two to three minutes, at the end of which we would record how well they did. Then, after a few levels, we would

Figure 15.4. An Early Prototype of *Airport Profiler,* Featuring Passengers with Exaggerated Identifiable Characteristics.

Source: Global Kids Inc. Used with Permission.

also tell them what bias they brought to the simulation, whether it was skin color, religion, destination, or gender."

Barry explained, "To evolve the project, we hired independent game designers gameLab. They taught us about the concept of core mechanics and made us look at alternative possibilities. One of the biggest things that all of the students learned was how iterative the development process was, and how much time and money it takes to build a game."

There is also potential financial upside, described at the end of last chapter. "Game portals are proving the market for quick, consumable, Web-delivered content. We have an opportunity to combine this emerging market and business model with socially impactful content and children as designers. How can we not make it a priority?" Barry asked.

Architecture

Marketing mini-games are delivered over the Web. They use a browser and primarily Macromedia's Flash® plug-in (Figure 15.5). In some cases, other plug-ins are necessary. Designers should not assume a computer has sound capability.

Figure 15.5. Marketing Mini-Games Architecture Considerations.

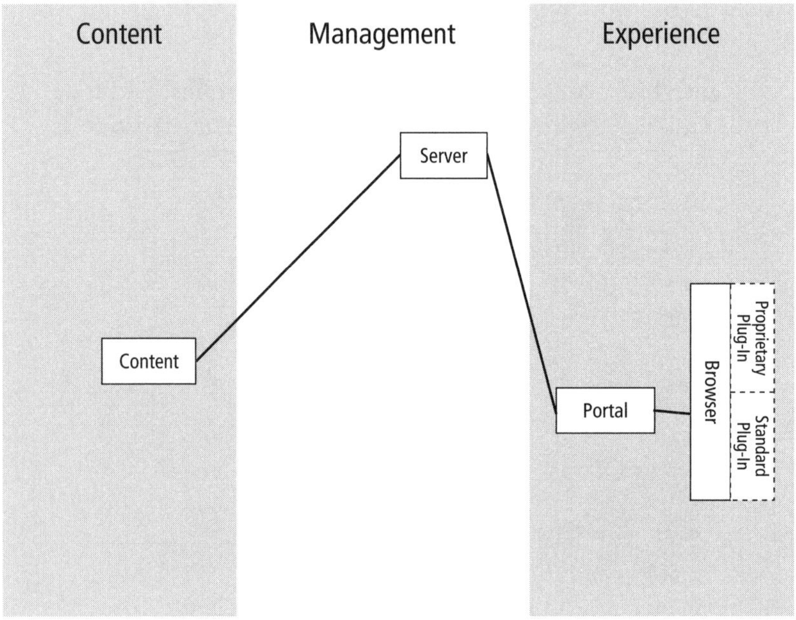

THE RIGHT MODEL?

Marketing mini-games might be the insects of the educational simulations ecosystem. Ubiquitous, inventive, quick to mutate, quickly replicating success, this unassuming vehicle might be the vector that most quickly spreads the simulation message. And, ah, the Pepsi® message.

Quick to Produce

Who wouldn't like a program that can be pushed out the door in two weeks? Most corporations spend longer than that trying to decide where to hold the meeting to decide to pick the group who will then have to hire the vendor.

Explore New Genres

If the greatest challenge of educational simulations is creating new genres, mini-games might be a way to test out new models. Genres involve new interfaces and new interactive models, all possible through Flash.

Easy to Deploy

Most computers in corporations have an Internet connection and a browser. Mini-games are small enough not to impact business-critical applications if downloaded en masse during the weekday, or they can be downloaded easily on the weekend over a 56K dial-up connection at home. But if content is easy to deploy, that also makes it . . .

. . . Hard to Control

The lack of control over the campaign will make some executives shiver. The better the game is, the more likely thousands of unintended users will see and play it, including competitors (don't make it too helpful), board members (don't make it too fun), and even rogue lawyers (don't make it too aggressive).

Simplicity of Message

Marketing mini-games can make one point and, sometimes, exposure to just one image. Is that enough for a training group? Probably not.

Notes Ben Sawyer, a developer of one of the next generation simulations we will be talking about in the next section, "If we are not creating complex things with computer game complexity, we are not going to provide much real value. And we are also not going to make any money. That is critical, because if there is no economic benefit to the producers, they will not show up."

For now, marketing mini-games might remain the province of marketers, and next perhaps, corporate communications groups.

COMING UP NEXT

Has anyone made a next generation simulation? A few. And what they have to teach us is volumes.

SECTION THREE

NEXT GEN SIMS

16

THE ADVENT OF NEXT GENERATION SIMULATIONS

"I understand this simulation. But most people who work with me will not."

—Common response to next generation educational simulations

THE TRADITIONAL SIMULATION TYPES and tangents are growing in sophistication and effectiveness. They are models that will be around for the foreseeable planning horizon.

Having said that, *next gen sims* are also emerging. They use *systems, cyclical,* and *linear* content aggressively, in parallel, for their *simulation,* not just *game,* value. They present new ways of visualizing and compartmentalizing activities; they also represent new types of interactions between students and computers.

Collectively, next gen sims are defining new educational genres. By 2010, at least ten or fifteen next gen sim genres will be created, and each will be a milestone in education history.

To accomplish this, the creation of next gen sims uses competencies from across the current simulations and tangents, and beyond. Design teams need to be able to:

- Create new models of action
- Create 3D virtual environments that can be sensed in multiple ways (visual, auditory, tactile, etc.), and selectively dynamic

- Create interfaces to enable participants to interact with the system
- Implement networking technologies to enable large numbers of participants to join in a simulation regardless of their physical locations
- Create artificial intelligences to be convincing adversaries and allies, even mentors
- Create compelling stories and modify gameplay

A FULL PRODUCTION

From a production perspective, the development cycle of any full simulation most closely resembles the development of a computer game (Figure 16.1). It requires at least ten person-years of resources to create, often twice or three times that.

And yet, many people from the traditional training and education industries balk at that level of investment. I have been balked at personally hundreds of times. I am still trying to get some of the balk out of a few of my jackets. They say, "How can the education industries move forward if it takes that magnitude of resources and specialization of skill sets?"

Underneath is the educators' supposition: "We need free tools so that existing teachers can create educational content in their spare

Figure 16.1. Next Gen Sims Components.

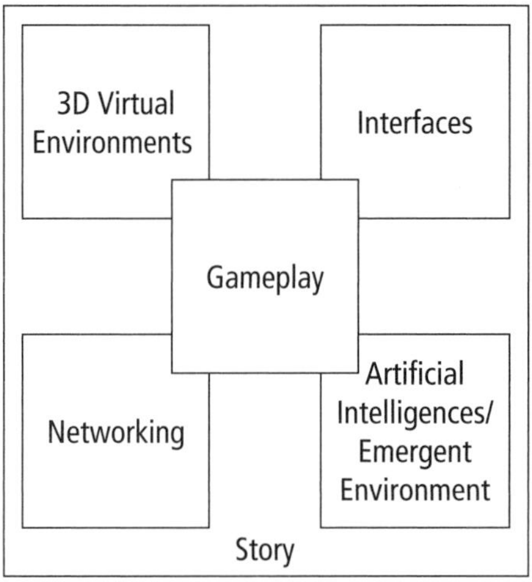

time. Or we need vendors that will accept boxes of chalk or gold stars instead of money. Anything else won't work in this industry."

I think the opposite.

- On one hand, education consumes hundreds of billions of dollars in the United States alone. K-12, higher ed, government training, and corporate training spend a big wad o' dough. The money is there.
- On the other hand, everything we touch, everything we count on, from the automobiles to telephones to computers to roads and buildings, represents deep, specialized skills and long development efforts. We would not tolerate anything less. As well, all of these industries have been restructured using technology to free up under-performing assets. Why would we expect the education industries to evolve without the same?

Nevertheless, the magnitude of time and investment, and the specialty of skills involved, is why *third parties* will create most next gen sims. Implementing institutions and enterprises should *procure* next gen sims as they would hardware or even vehicles: by finding an 80 percent modifiable solution and tailoring it the last 20 percent. The vestigial, ego-driven desire of a corporate training group to fully control all aspects of a program's look and feel will finally fall away, enabling speed, 100x quality, cost-effectiveness, and predictability of results.

The only exception to external development is when an organization realizes that they will need to train either their employees or customers on a similar skill set over four or more years. IBM may realize that it will need to help its customers understand how new products fit into legacy architectures for the foreseeable future, for example. Foundations might commit to a critical soft skill, such as awareness of sexually transmitted diseases. The World Bank could build programs on capitalism 101 (although consistent with their philosophy, I suppose, they would probably wait for the market to create it, and then they could just license it). CitiGroup, as a random example, could commit to leadership, the way Xerox had committed to Quality. All of these are candidates for internal long-term next gen sim programs.

MORE PARALLELS TO COMPUTER GAMES

There are at least two more parallels between next gen sims and computer games, on top of the skills sets and development resources required.

First, the IT footprint of a next gen sim is closer to a computer game than a Web page (Figure 16.2). It will require modern computers with 3D graphics cards and powerful processors to run.

Second, like any interactive content, *you have to engage it to understand it.* This is a subtle point, with significant implications for anyone in this area over forty.

I was visiting Microsoft when Xbox'® Howard Phillips was showing some of their technology to a military and academic audience. What was interesting is that Howard did not show actual gameplay. He instead showed the introductory sequences to several hot new games.

He knew something that the rest of us are only just learning. Watching someone else play an unfamiliar computer game is bewildering. The spectator invariably asks, "Why did you do that?" or "How can you tell what is going on?"

Unaware of the subtle cues being generated by the game, or the subtle strategies and tactics being used by the player, spectators leave far more confused than when they started. The experience appears to be pure chaos. Some even leave judging the experience as disjointed by linear standards. Even most screen shots of computer games, say on the back of boxes, show some dramatic angle or moment not actually usable from a gameplay perspective.

Figure 16.2. Computer Game Architecture Considerations.

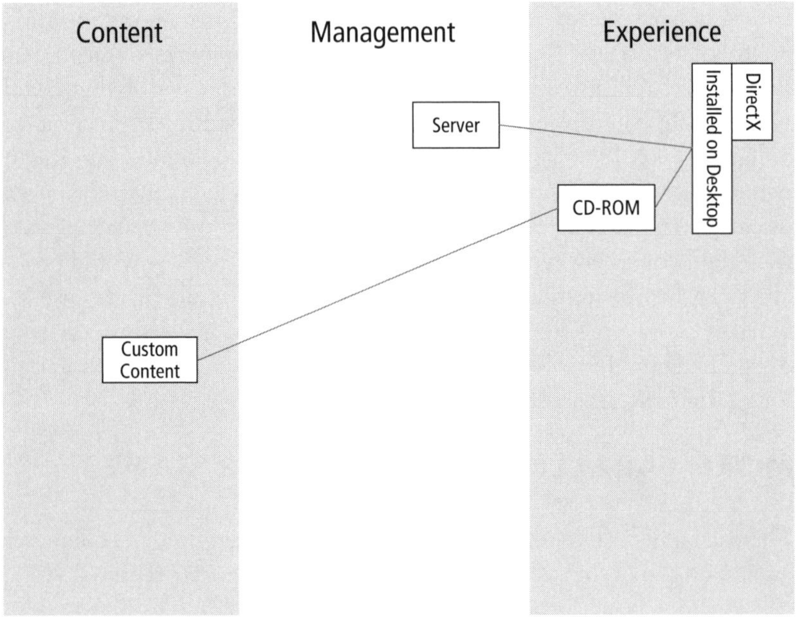

Simulations, especially unfamiliar genres, cannot be skimmed. They cannot be browsed. They cannot be shown. *They can only be truly understood through active trial-and-error engagement.*

By the way, this significantly challenges the sales process. Given that sim vendors only have about an hour total time in front of a potential customer, the time to actually show the sim is less than twenty minutes. That leaves the vendor with a choice—demonstrate a simple situation that the potential customer will say is too simple, or demonstrate a complex situation that will lose the potential customer all together. Or, if the potential customer does get it, she or he will almost always say, "I got it, but I don't think anyone who works for me will."

I have found the best way to get around this is to show prospective clients videotaped interviews with students who have gone through about two or three hours of the simulation. These real testimonials, filled with subtlety, precision, and even passion, always makes an accurate and positive impact.

THE BEGINNING OF THE ROAD

When I was a Gartner e-learning analyst, I enjoyed my conversations with various reporters covering the industry.

"How's it going," I asked one.

"Same old thing. Look for three data points and call it a trend," she replied.

"Really?" I asked, surprised. "You wait for a third?"

Next gen sims on a good day represent maybe one and a half data points. They straddle the line between theory and innovation.

We do not know nearly as much about them as the earlier models discussed. We do not have hundreds of examples to generalize. Many are new enough not to have detailed results.

We can get excited; we can make some early guesses; we can observe some faint patterns. But we have to accept our own ignorance as much as our excitement.

COMING UP NEXT

Everybody, it seems, wants to simulate history. Or do they?

17

WHAT IF WE REALLY REALLY SIMULATED HISTORY?

First Flight—The Wright Experience Flight Simulator

High production values that restrict interactivity I wouldn't give a fig for. High production values that open up interactivity I would give my career for.

—With apologies to Oliver Wendell Holmes

I HAVE A FASCINATION with the process of going from a book to a movie. Some movies are better than the books (*Jaws, Gone with the Wind*). Most books are better than the movie (*Wuthering Heights, Gone with the Wind*).

But what to leave out, and what to add? Where do you get the new material you suddenly realize you need. How accurate should you be versus how to best tell the story for the given medium? That issue is magnified when going from any linear content to an educational simulation.

CULTURAL LITERACY AS SIMULATION

We mentioned some history-themed computer games. Microsoft's *Age of Empires*™ is most often quoted, and is even a fun game. Actually, strike that. Microsoft's *Age of Empires*™ is most often quoted *because* it is a fun game.

But the most authentic example, the deepest case, of real history-to-simulation is *First Flight—The Wright Experience Flight Simulator*™. I have never seen this rigor before.

In the history books, we learn that Orville and Wilbur Wright were inventors who also repaired bicycles. They built the first airplane, which they proceeded to fly down a hill in Kitty Hawk, North Carolina, in 1903.

First Flight—The Wright Experience Flight Simulator™ was to go just a bit deeper. It set out to accurately simulate three airplanes:

- The 1902 glider that the Wrights used to investigate unpowered flights down the Kitty Hawk sand dunes
- The 1903 Wright Flyer that made history
- The more powerful and maneuverable 1911 Model B that was the culmination of the Wright Brothers' research, and the country's first military airplane

MULTIPLE COMPETENCIES

First Flight—The Wright Experience Flight Simulator had two audiences. One audience was computer-game flight enthusiasts who used it on their PCs, with joystick and keyboard controls. The second audience, and this is really cool, was the *actual pilot* who was to fly the accurate replica of the 1903 Wright Flyer at Kitty Hawk for the 2003 centennial celebration.

Pulling this off was not easy. It requires a unique gathering of talents and competencies.

Physics Engine

Bihrle Applied Research Inc. provided the *physics engine*. This software describes what happens during the flight in the computer-generated world.

It's worth noting that any physics engine provided by Bihrle is the real deal. Birhle's pedigree could not be more impressive or rigorous. They are a world-class aerospace technology company specializing in the testing and simulation of military and commercial aircraft, including F-16s.

Most "for-entertainment" flight simulators (to be said with a bit of a condescending scowl) use scripted responses to the range of flight conditions and pilot inputs. *First Flight—The Wright Experience Flight*

Simulator would use non-linear equations of motion, with a complete set of non-linear table-based coefficient data representing the appropriate aerodynamic characteristics (if you are taking notes, please do not highlight that sentence; it's not that important in the scheme of things, and I don't really know what it means either. It won't be on the test.).

Accurate Data

This level of precision and computational rigor would be useless without very accurate modeling of the flight characteristics of the airplanes to be flown. Even the best algorithms with "garbage in" give you "garbage out."

So Old Dominion University was responsible for collecting real data. They used *actual* wind tunnel data, which they would collect in the Old Dominion University full-scale wind tunnel (Figure 17.1) located at Langley Air Force Base in Hampton, Virginia.

The Airplane

Of course, if you have a wind tunnel, then you need actual, real, no-guesstimates-allowed airplanes. This would have been a bigger problem,

Figure 17.1. Wright 1902 Glider Reproduction Underwent Wind Tunnel Tests at Langley Full-Scale Tunnel.

Source: Chuck Thomas, Old Dominion University. Used with Permission.

but that a plane-restoration facility in Warrenton, Virginia, had been commissioned by the Wisconsin-based Experimental Aircraft Association (EAA) to duplicate the plane to re-create the flight for the then-upcoming Centennial celebration.

Graphics Engine

Bihrle had several graphics engines they used with their military and commercial-grade flight sims. But they were not designed for personal computers, which had been decided as the platform for the off-the-shelf product. So *First Flight—The Wright Experience Flight Simulator* licensed a graphics engine (Figure 17.2) from Third Wire Productions, creators of flight simulation games for hobbyists, including *Strike Fighters: Project 1*, featuring combat jet aircraft from the 1960s.

Project Management

Bihrle's Jack Ralston served as the project manager: "The project took us about two plus years altogether. We probably spent one and a half man-years specifically invested in building the three simulators."

Figure 17.2. Simulating Flight.

Source: Bihrle Applied Research Inc. Used with Permission.

Jack explained the different experiences *First Flight—The Wright Experience Flight Simulator* would encompass: "The most modern of the three planes, the 1911 model B sim was the first one we did. And it is actually enjoyable to fly, once you get the hang of it. It was their first practical airplane, designed for the military, and it handles relatively nicely. The 1902 glider is interesting. You can see why the Wright Brothers used it for practice. It is forgiving. It is unstable, but not as demanding as far as pilot attention.

"The 1903 plane was the hardest. It was hard for us because we had to wait on the wind tunnel data. It is also just a hard airplane to fly. The 1903 requires a lot of assistance to fly, even in the first few attempts. The faster you go, the more rapidly you have to respond."

MEASURING THE REAL LEARNING

For the Centennial celebration at Kitty Hawk, only one pilot would get to fly the historic 1903 replica in front of the crowds and cameras. Two pilots were selected to be prepped.

One was Dr. Kevin Kochersberger (pronounced KEV-IN) an associate professor of mechanical engineering at the Rochester Institute of Technology. The other was Terry Queijo, an American Airlines pilot.

"Kevin spent a lot of time on the simulator," Jack told me. "The program was hooked directly into a hip cradle and pitch stick, modeling the controls for the airplane. He also had a second copy of the simulation that he kept on a laptop, which he used a joystick to operate."

Kevin grew to understand the engine performance and takeoff speed. While at Kitty Hawk, for example, he put markers where he knew he needed to pull back. Meanwhile, the other candidate and a real pilot, Terry, according to Jack, "never used the simulation."

Those who like simulation metrics will be happy. Learning on the simulation correlated directly with success in flying the 1903 replica.

According to the *Baltimore Sun,* "Kochersberger had two successful test flights with the Flyer reproduction, and Queijo's one flight had ended in a crash" (Jonathon E. Briggs, *Baltimore Sun,* December 17, 2003).

As a result of his two successful test flights, Kochersberger was chosen to fly on the Kitty Hawk anniversary. This was a unique honor in the world of pilots.

The story ended a bit anti-climactically, as the weather prevented a successful flight. "Humidity crippled the performance of the replica's primitive twelve-horsepower engine, causing it to produce less power than needed. A driving rain and blustery conditions forced re-enactors to skip the attempt at 10:35 a.m." Briggs would further write, "During later tries at 12:30 p.m. and 3:45 p.m., the lack of a stiff wind dashed efforts to get it airborne."

But those in the audience were still thrilled to see a live replica of one of the most defining moments in the 20th century. Realizing the difficulty of something now thought of as inevitable must have put the original flight in the proper context.

THE SIMULATOR EXPERIENCE

It is one thing for a dedicated pilot to practice on a realistic flight simulator. It is another for one to be released to the general public.

Project manager Jack Ralston said, "A lot of people have emailed us and told us how difficult it has been. Should we have done the Microsoft route of making it fly the way people thought it should fly? It would have been easier to make it easier. After a lot of discussion, we thought it would diminish the experience.

"I got to hear a lot of feedback live at the Centennial celebration. One person got very frustrated; I heard him turn to friends and say, 'There is no way that was right.' I intercepted him, gave him the backstory, and coached him. He finally got the hang of it, and ended up buying a copy of the program. He was a lot more appreciative."

I asked Jack about how the program has impacted people learning about the historical Wright flight in schools. "We have received letters from schools whose shop classes have built models and put students in cockpits," Jack said. "One girl flew over 1,500 feet, longer than the Wright brothers. We heard about one college running the simulator off a big projection screen for a whole audience.

"Our next use of the technology is to build a couple of pilot stations and market it to museums. We have to simplify the interface, so that all you need are three buttons to run it. Obviously, we can't require a coach or operator to help out."

I asked what surprised him most about the process.

"The Wright brothers had to jump through a lot of hoops, beyond just the technical. There were a lot of issues, like politics and who was in charge.

"We had to deal with a lot of our own political issues. Ford and Microsoft were key contributors to Experiment Aircraft Association (EAA), which funded some of it, and had some control. There were constant battles between The Wright Experience, EAA, even Microsoft, who was trying to imply that their software was used to train the pilots.

"Around us, NOVA and Discovery Channel were threatening lawsuits over the video rights. There were quite a few times that we felt like the Wright brothers. We were all relieved when we finally got it out."

One has to be a bit amused at the potential irony. There is a chance that simulations become a major industry, a defining force, and driver of world change. I personally believe it could be the case. What if in 2103 they have a centennial celebration of one of the first great working simulators, that itself was created for a centennial of one of the last generation's great inventions?

THE CHALLENGE OF HISTORY-BASED SIMULATIONS

First Flight—The Wright Experience Flight Simulator™ was never intended to be a, er, pilot for teaching history. And yet it is a perfect example.

Accuracy? Difficulty

The Wright brothers' flight happened slightly more than one hundred years ago. The important records of the event were preserved, including the exact location and the plans for the planes.

What happens when the level of exactness is not available? How will mechanisms be devised? Will committees guess at all of the specifics? How much generalization will be acceptable? How will instructors deal with the difficulty of managing troops, or economies?

First Flight—The Wright Experience Flight Simulator also makes a very appropriate point. It is quite a bit easier to take over the world playing *Risk* than to take it over in real life.

Being a President of the United States during a crisis is very difficult. You would not want a random person at that helm. Commanding Napoleon's army is very hard—most of us could not do it. Running a civilization takes more than most of us have.

We are used to the trivializations of computer games. Or we are used to the passivity of history texts. What happens to our concept of history the more real we get, and the richer the content types we use?

If we make simulations too accurate, they will be too hard. If we make simulations too easy, they will be irrelevant. Good luck.

Pushing History Over the Edge

There is a bigger issue. History, as we currently know it, is always on shaky ground.

It is not that simulations are not good for teaching history, although many will increasingly say that. It is that simulations might derail the contrivances of convenience between:

- Historians, who have only a remarkably thin knowledge of the past against the higher standard of simulations (consider how useful history books were for creating *First Flight—The Wright Experience*)
- Students, who want to know as little as possible simply to pass and/or get a good grade (How many buy history books on their own as a percentage of how many who have taken two or more history classes?)
- Businesses who don't care at all about history for their employees (quick proof: How many organizations have internal programs to remedially teach history?)

Now that I have thoroughly offended all history teachers, buffs, and majors, let me complete the thought. History as we will rethink it will be the key to so much understanding. More on that thought in the Conclusion.

How Possible?

In many ways, *First Flight—The Wright Experience Flight Simulator* was conservative. The designers took an established game genre, the flight simulator, and adapted it to a historical model. While very appropriate for this, many other historical simulations will not fit so neatly into an established genre. Then things will really get hard.

COMING UP NEXT

Simulations for, about, and in the classrooms? The future is now.

18

VIRTUAL UNIVERSITY AND UNDERSTANDING THE VALUE OF A CLASSROOM

The release of the second version of any next gen sim is cause for a bigger celebration than the first version.

VIRTUAL UNIVERSITY

The Alfred P. Sloan Foundation did something very clever. The foundation has the broader goal of improving education. Part of that means sharing best practices about managing universities. In their words:

> "Overemphasizing higher education's importance in America is hard. It is a huge and influential enterprise. Roughly half of all young people enter a higher education institution. About fifteen million students currently enroll. Faculty numbers are about 900,000. In 1995, spending totaled close to $180 billion. (http://phe.rockefeller.edu/CyberCampus/index.html)

To accomplish a nice double play, they sponsored a product called *Virtual University* (VU). VU was to be a piece of *game software* in the spirit of *SimEarth*™ or *SimCity*™ that improves a player's understanding of the intricacies of university management. Players learn this by being put in charge of a university, making the kinds of strategic decisions that people make when they actually are in charge of a university. Then they see the results.

On one hand, VU teaches *something* that can probably only be taught via an educational simulation. On the other hand, VU teaches someone *how something can be taught* via an educational simulation.

The primary developers of *Virtual University* were Dr. William Massy of the Jackson Hole Higher Education Group (formerly of Stanford, which I add because I never heard of the Jackson Hole Higher Education Group) and Enlight Software of Hong Kong. Ben Sawyer from Digital Mill joined the development team for the last nine months of the two-year development process and has been responsible for many of the continued updates and implementations ever since.

Virtual University does have the feel of *SimEarth* (Figure 18.1). Think of it as an interactive spreadsheet brought to the next level of interactive graphics and complexity.

There is a *scenario mode,* where you have a *single goal.* You can just focus on that goal to meet victory conditions in a certain number of turns. Some of these goals include:

- Increase the faculty pay
- Improve the quality of the teaching of the classes
- Improve research performance
- Win athletic games
- Reduce tuition
- Balance the budget

Then there is the more open-ended (in the parlance of many tycoon games) "sandbox" mode. You are given a fully, if sub-optimally, functioning university, and your job is to manage it well. There is no specific goal, no specific victory condition (although you can drive the school into bankruptcy or turn the board against you, either of which results in you being fired), and no specific time frame. In other words, it has more simulation elements than game elements and is a lot more realistic—but also overwhelming.

Players go into this part of the game and start looking for things they want to tweak, primarily to match up the organization against their principles. They then get a sense for how everything is connected.

TRACKED RELATIONSHIPS

Virtual University tracks many primary, secondary, and tertiary variables, including those related to (and this would be a good list to skim):

Figure 18.1. For Those Who Want to Lead.

Source: Virtual University. Used with Permission.

FACULTY

- Faculty distribution by gender and ethnicity (Figure 18.2)
- Activities, including teaching load, course preparation, out-of-class student contact, educational development, research, and scholarships
- Salary

STUDENTS (KEEP SKIMMING)

- By level: Undergraduate traditional (number and percentage), undergraduate nontraditional (number and percentage), master's students (number and percentage), doctoral students (number and percentage)
- Distribution by gender and ethnicity group
- Satisfaction in academics, student life, and athletics
- Gross tuition income, student life, change in tuition rate

COURSES (SKIM AWAY)

- Class type, number of sections, enrollment, average class size
- Students denied entrance to course
- Percentage of students failing courses

ATHLETICS DEPARTMENT (SKIM HO, JEEVES)

- Current intercollegiate level of competition
- Special admissions treatment for top athletes, special financial aid treatment for top athletes

PERFORMANCE (SKIM, SKIM, SKIM)

- Faculty teaching performance rating
- Faculty educational development time, technology utilization in teaching
- Faculty research performance, sponsored research
- Quality rating for doctoral students
- Number of doctoral students per regular faculty members

SCORE ELEMENTS (SKIM MILK IS MORE HEALTHFUL THAN WHOLE, AND I THINK TASTIER)

- Degrees granted
- Prestige, educational quality
- Scholarship, broadly defined
- Student diversity, faculty diversity
- Faculty morale, student morale, staff morale
- Current surplus (deficit) as a percent of expenditure
- Deferred maintenance backlog

SIMULATION ELEMENTS (AWWWHH, THAT'S THE END OF THE SKIMMING)

Many have found that *Virtual University* has a very steep learning curve. It is very complex, and dominated by simulation elements (Figure 18.3).

"For example," says Ben Sawyer, "When you start out, faculty morale is 40 percent. Most players' first thought is that things are

Figure 18.2. Some of Your Faculty.

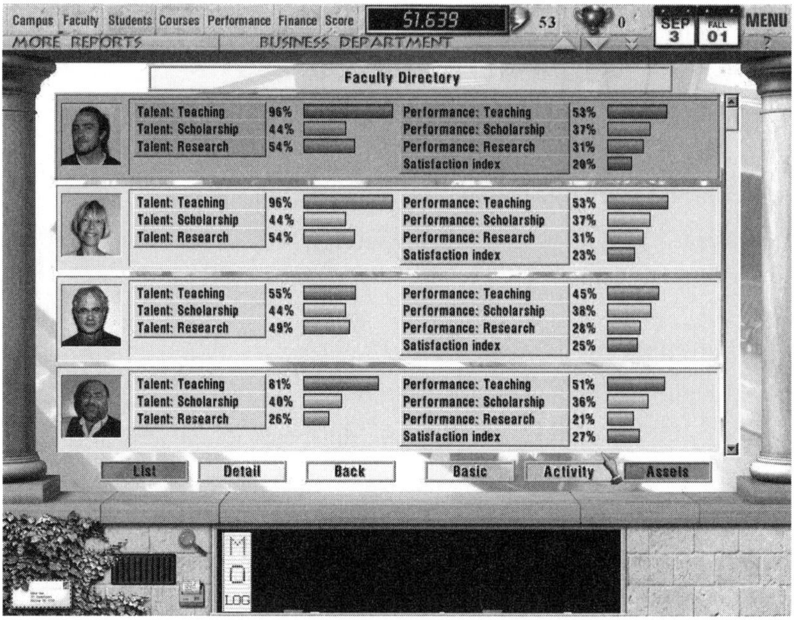

Source: Virtual University. Used with Permission.

really bad. Forty percent is a failing grade, after all. Most first-time players want to take drastic steps. But in *Virtual University,* as in real life, most faculty morale bounces between 35 and 45 percent. I tell players not to focus on the absolute morale; I say focus on the shifting. As with real managers, they should make it better. Don't focus on making it perfect."

Over time, players get a better feel for how it all works. They go from worrying about tactics to gaining a sense of strategy. For example, if the challenge was to *improve research performance,* advanced players would know that they would need to employ a "faculty-based" strategy. They know that only good faculty researchers could improve research. They would recruit "new blood" with a high priority on research performance. They would place a priority on research activity of their faculty, and they would over time retire "old" faculty, to be replaced by "new blood."

Ben continued, "As players continue to engage *Virtual University,* they begin acting more and more like real heads of universities. I have seen people get very excited about upping a key variable by 3 percent,

Figure 18.3. Virtual U Feedback.

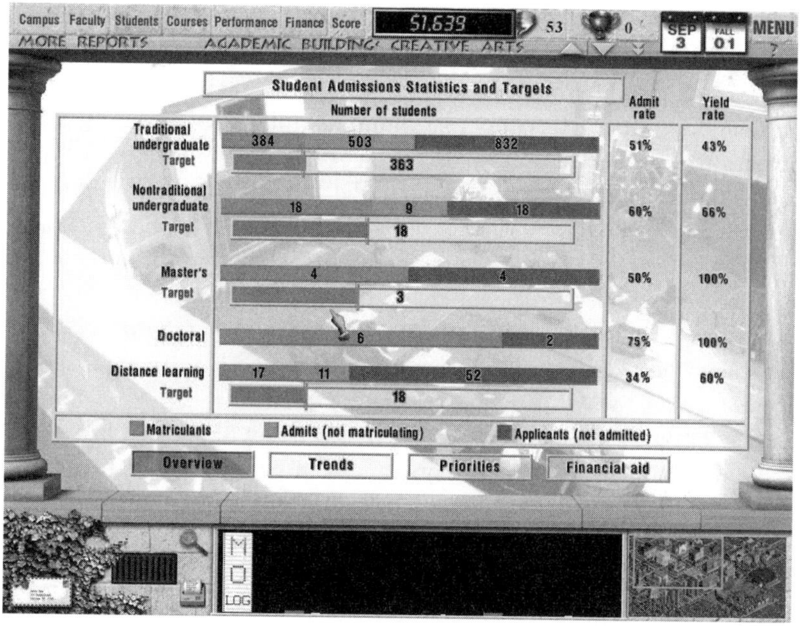

Source: Virtual University. Used with Permission.

which is constant with real life, but not something you would see in a traditional, more exaggerated game.

"The most advanced players also begin to realize something that professionals managers call *equilibrium,*" Ben explained. "If you are fluctuating between –5 percent and 5 percent budget movement, you are doing a better job than if you are fluctuating between, say –12 percent and 12 percent."

DATA

For *Virtual University* to work, the data had to be very good (simulation quality, not just game quality). Dr. Massy developed the initial data for Virtual U with assistance from the Institute for Research in Higher Education at the University of Pennsylvania. Much of the data was from the Integrated Postsecondary Education Data System, collected by the National Center for Education Statistics and then organized by the developers (any simulation developer should be, at this point, muttering, "show off").

AUDIENCES

While the intended audience was always meant to be broad, one original core audience of *Virtual University* was the actual university managers, including presidents and provosts. (Provosts tend to be second in command of the business of running a college or university. They traditionally spend about 25 percent of their time explaining to outsiders that they haven't just made the title of provost up, but that it is a real job.)

"The people for whom *Virtual University* could have been the most directly influential turned out to be the most busy people, and they were less willing to put the time in to take advantage of it," Ben recalled. "We were more successful in positioning it as an exploration tool, but also a way for them to train their staff."

One of the best applications of Virtual U was with faculty. It became the cornerstone of a several-day training program, and it became a way to uncover the management nerds. Those who really dug into the program became the best candidates for promotion along a management path.

The second big audience, and in fact the biggest single audience for Virtual U, was students in a classroom environment. And in retrospect, it was amazing how the Virtual U team (and almost every next gen sim designer) originally neglected this most critical audience.

VERSION 2.0

The first major revision of *Virtual University* was recently released. And trust me when I say that the release of the *second* version of any next gen sim is cause for a bigger celebration than the *first* version.

"We had feedback from users," Ben said. "A lot of feedback. And aside from the bug fixes, most of the new features went into making Virtual U more accessible, and more suitable for classroom deployment."

In short, they had built a rich simulation. Then needed to add game and pedagogical elements.

Version 2.0 filled a lot of these gaps.

New Additions

Now a player can tick a box to literally overemphasize certain results and relationships. Things happen sooner and more dramatically in response to new tactics.

A player can also turn off certain random and external variables. A player can make it so unlike life, he or she is the only reason things happen.

Version 2.0 has other little upgrades, like having purple numbers that show the player where values started next to where values currently are. This allows them to see, even twenty years into the simulation, how far they have come.

Instructor Support

Version 2.0 also came with a lot more instructor support. Ben is emphatic here. Building an educational simulation "without teacher and classroom support is like swinging on a trapeze without a safety net. You can do it, but why? This thought is counter to a lot of gamers, but it is crucial. We were not giving people the tools to use the game."

Talking to all developers, he emphasized, "You are going to spend hundreds of thousands to millions on a product. There is no way you can provide a product that will be used even close to its potential without documentation and support. One of the biggest truisms is that teachers can't support what they don't understand."

Output Engine

Another feature that is obvious when you think about a simulation's use in a classroom but foreign in the context of a computer game is the ability to print. "The game developers behind Virtual U never had to do printing," Ben stated. "So in the classrooms, we had to do some screen dumps, which was clumsy. More often, students had to copy down scores, which they rightfully complained about. And even then, just having a few scores from each student was not that useful for a teacher or professor.

"So we did two things. First, we built a printing engine from scratch that produced a great-looking document that students could hand in as homework. In addition, we added the ability to output every value to a spreadsheet. This allows students to do their own analysis.

"As a result of the changes, classroom experiences could be much more valuable. Professors began caring less about the final scores that the students achieved and began caring more how well the students were able to defend their strategy in front of a class. This created yet more realistic situations for all involved."

Business Model

"Oh yeah, there is one more thing about version 2.0," Ben told me. "Sloan decided to give it away instead of sell it."

Now to me, that is a pretty big "oh yeah." That is like "oh yeah, I am married," or "oh yeah, my handicap is plus 8.3."

"That helped tremendously with meeting the program goals," Ben said. "It expanded the impact, which also leads us to the people who become our most innovative users.

"Counter-intuitively, it also helped our business model. What we do now is to give away the game, and sell the training. It used to be that we would charge, oh, 5K for software, and 5K for training.

"We were told that the accountants had no problem with the dollars spent for training, but that a separate review process had to happen to buy the software. It derailed many accounts and potential users. Now we just charge the full 10K for training, and they get the software for free. I believe what money that VU had coming still came to us. But we gave up a lot of headaches. It allowed us to focus on a value proposition, which was B2B, not retail."

CLOSING THOUGHTS

When all was said and done, I asked, realizing that neither statement was true, what had he learned?

"Don't use calculus when you can get away with algebra. By trying so hard in getting the sim right, we originally lost track of both the game elements and also the appropriate use of the experience.

"There is a story that you probably heard. A person needs to have a ball move from one side of a room to the other almost instantly. He brings in two friends to get their ideas. The first plan is very expensive and time-consuming, and, looking over all of the complexity, the person wondered even if it would work at all. A trained engineer submitted that plan. The second plan was only five pages, one-tenth the cost, and it looked like it couldn't fail. That second plan was handed in by a trained magician.

"Looking back," Ben said, "We could probably have used a few less engineers and a few more magicians."

COMING UP NEXT

If there were a contest for best educational simulation, here's what would win.

19

MILITARY + COMPUTER GAME = FULL-SPECTRUM EXPERIENCES

THERE IS DIRECTNESS TO THIS STORY that belies the complexity and organization involved. The high-level sequence is straightforward enough.

- New technology enables a new approach to learning.
- New global events require new long-range content to learn.
- The old organization, realizing that its current structure is insufficient, creates a new organization, drawing on new skills to bring these together and make it happen.

This should be playing out in colleges. Or K-12. Or business schools. Or training organizations. This should be describing IBM, or Brown University, or the California community college system.

But no. At least for now, it is a success of the greatest training organization in the world: the U.S. military.

BACKGROUND

To allow you to appreciate some of the nuances, I would like to give you just a bit of a starting point.

"Traditionally, there is more money put into hard skills than soft skills. You can justify the simulations, because the equipment costs big bucks. A mistake in flying a bomber could cost hundreds of millions of dollars," explained TRADOC's William Melton.

"With systems training, we have been able to purchase them with procurements dollars. Congress allows for us to do that. Non-system training, which deals with interpersonal or even multiple systems, we have to eke out of our training budget. And the total budget for all non-systems training doesn't equal the budget for one system component."

A CHANGE IN TECHNOLOGY, AND THEREFORE APPROACH

James Korris, creative director and project manager of the Institute for Creative Technology's *Full Spectrum Warrior*™, explains how that process was changed.

In 1997, National Academy of Science released a report called *Modeling and Simulation: Linking Entertainment and Defense*. It contained the following assertion: the private sector had surged ahead of the military in computation simulations, a place that the military had created and dominated. The emerged computer game industry was productively driving three critical areas:

- Game craft
- Game technology, including graphic engines, AI, and rendering
- Game hardware, including game consoles and graphics cards

The concept of *game craft* had special interest. A lot of military simulation work has been quite comprehensive, but the goals have been pretty straightforward, for example, to replicate the specific experience of driving a tank.

Computer games differ from a simulation, in part by their attitude. (That would be 'tude, if you are under twenty-seven but over twenty.)

Simulations aim for the greatest fidelity possible. Games aim for a specific result. All of the entertainment industry focuses on what they call *an end-space*. They want people to laugh, or cry, or be exhilarated, and will do what it takes, slay the villain, save the puppy, play the music, blow things up, and show the perfect bodies to get there.

The military believed it was important to tap these technologies and development skills. And so the question was, "Is there a way to leverage that capability?"

There were some initial efforts to reach out to larger media producers, including Disney, Paramount, and Viacom. But it was difficult. The entertainment industry does not run to the same rhythm of *low-cost bidder.* Plus, once you become a government supplier (and this might be worth passing on to your loved ones), you are open to endless audits and scrutiny. This would have imposed a significant burden on these organizations. And so, frankly, they were not interested in working hard for the business.

This is not uncommon in the history of the military. This problem is most acute, according to James, around tapping some of the unique intellectual capability at academic institutions.

Consider a robotics research project. The best robotics researchers are at Carnegie Mellon or MIT. But the military could not even bid it out, because the organization that would win the contract would almost certainly be a university that was not of the desired caliber.

To get around this, the military arrived at a novel conclusion. They created University Affiliated Research Centers (UARCs, from the same linguistic tradition as hoo-ah). These would be partnerships with strategic universities to fast-track innovations.

The military, to explore the space between games and simulation, wanted UARCs around the motion pictures, televisions, and computer games. They partnered with USC and formed University of Southern California's Institute for Creative Technologies.

A CHANGE IN THE WORLD, AND THEREFORE CONTENT

A lot of the hardware, training, and even organizational design of the military had evolved based on the cold war. During that prolonged time, the United States had a known enemy. There was also a mindset that, if the country stayed focused almost chess-like, it could counter moves of the Soviets.

For example, if the Soviet Union developed a new submarine, the United States could develop a new type of satellite. The Soviets increased their number of tanks, the U.S. military fortified the access bridges and roads into Germany from the west, so the NATO army could drive in tanks quickly.

And it worked. The United States won the cold war.

But when the Soviet system unraveled, the level of *community violence* accelerated. There was no longer a barrier from either superpower to regional aggression. This surprised a lot of people.

Now, throughout the forty-year cold war, the prevailing wisdom for soldiers had been "don't dismount." More specifically, urban warfare was to be avoided at all costs. U.S. soldiers didn't go into cities.

The kinds of enemies that the United States began facing understood if they met the American military on rolling terrain, they would lose. They had better odds in urban environments. These enemies also fought asymmetrically. They accepted the tactical advantages (at the cost of increased risks to local civilians) that came with not wearing uniforms. They used every home-field advantage.

U.S. troops increasingly had situations where they did not know whether the person they are looking at was trying to kill them. Was that person over there an enemy, or a police officer, or a civilian who was angry but harmless, or just someone trying to survive?

As one general put it, quite quickly, the last four hundred meters became where everything had to be done. Conflicts were becoming engagements between individuals and groups of individuals.

Project manager James Korris said, "In 1999, we knew we would be stuck in a lot of tough, urban situations, so that is what we focused on. The military did not have methodologies for close urban fighting."

This was not about using a new piece of equipment. There was a challenge of pushing decision making as low as possible. And that had never been done before in a simulation.

FULL SPECTRUM WARRIOR

"We wanted to do two projects—one to take advantage of state-of-the-art PCs and one to take advantage of state-of-the-art consoles," James told me. The issues we had to work with included processor speed, graphics, and memory.

With consoles, the Xbox™ was the only viable choice at the time. It was the only unit with a hard drive. This was critical because it enabled a post-game review session (that the military calls *After Action Reviews* (AARs)). In the military, these are very big deals, the same way that air is a very big deal. AARs are where your actions are dissected to see where you went right or wrong. Some in the military believe that AARs are the primary (read that, only) thing that has value in a simulation.

"We were attracted to first-person shooters as a genre. They are easy to use, very accessible, and very entertaining. This is what became *Full Spectrum Warrior*™" (Figure 19.1 and Figure 19.2).

"We spend a great deal of time looking at the current work in the artificial intelligence (AI) of the virtual humans. If you have a simulation where the AI doesn't work, it isn't very satisfying. In commercial projects, the artificial intelligence (AI) wasn't good enough.

Figure 19.1. ***Full Spectrum Warrior*™ Interface.**

Source: Full Spectrum Warrior™. Used with Permission.

Figure 19.2. ***Full Spectrum Warrior*™ Interface.**

Source: Full Spectrum Warrior™. Used with Permission.

"We developed a robust AI. But it was processor-heavy. This meant that the most virtual humans we could model was thirty entities. This allowed a sergeant, two teams of four, with the rest being civilians and enemies."

The next question is: What kind of interface could you have with no keyboard and no mouse. How could you interact with the system? "We did not want to do target practice, or a first-person shooter. We needed to put the player in the position of making decisions," James explained.

Full Spectrum Warrior™ therefore put someone in the position of controlling two fire teams (alpha and bravo). At an interface/cyclical level (Figure 19.3), the player can order each team to:

- Move
- Hit the dirt
- Attack a person
- Take cover
- Breach a building
- Guard a location

This enables strategies such as using the player's two teams effectively to cover and support each other, moving safely from one location to another, and pinning down and flanking enemies where appropriate.

The player can also give instructions to individual soldiers, to tell them to:

- Move a bit
- Supply suppression fire
- Examine an area in more detail

The soldier avatars ("bots" to people under thirty) even had some variations. They could be more or less trained, for example. The less trained, the harder they are to control. Their attention will wander, or they might continue to aim a weapon as an allied soldier walked in front of it; you might tell them to move to a new location and they will walk casually past an alley.

"We had a General from West Point," James said. "It took under three minutes to train him. It was fascinating watching him maneuver. He was very focused and nearly completed the mission. I was stunned. I had never seen anyone get that far on the first try. That real experience made a difference was exciting."

Figure 19.3. *Full Spectrum Warrior*™ Controls.

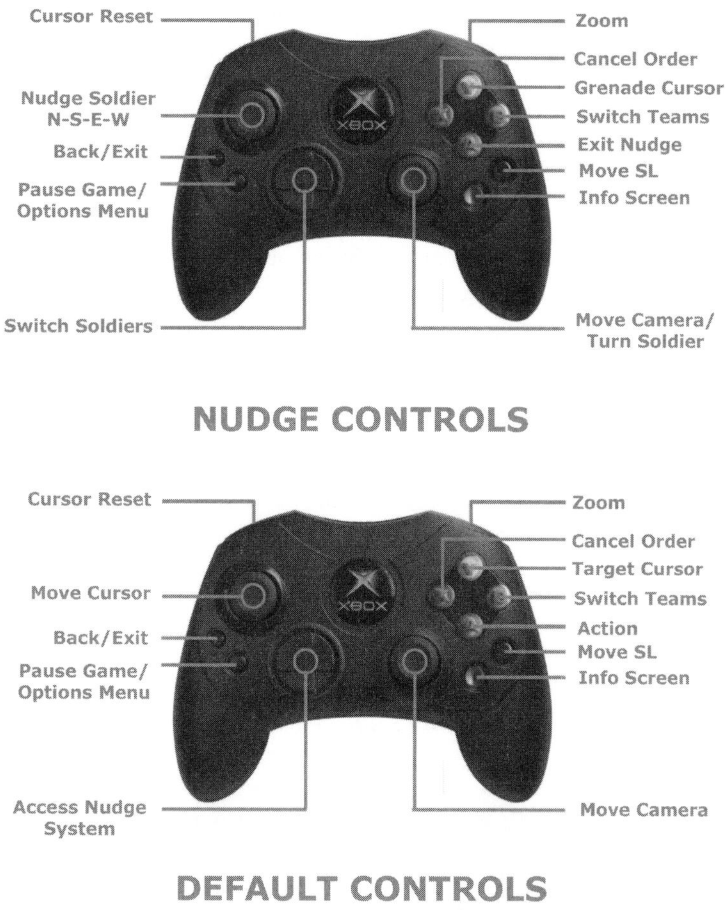

Source: Full Spectrum Warrior™. Used with Permission.

Off-the-Shelf Computer Game as Well

James continued: "To ensure that we got a platform license from Microsoft, we needed a commercial version on the same disk. Because Microsoft loses money on every Xbox® console they sell (they make it up on the platform licenses they grant to software companies), they are nervous about having one Xbox® per product. The army version is only available with an unlock key."

FULL SPECTRUM COMMAND™

Full Spectrum Command™ is the PC initiative. Because a top-of-the-line personal computer has more capability than an Xbox® console, there was more that could be done. Recall that the biggest resource drain was the artificial intelligence (AI). With the increased capability, The Institute for Creative Technologies could model about two hundred entities (Figure 19.4 and Figure 19.5). "That gave us the headroom to do a light infantry company—over one hundred people versus an opponent of forty small units, each between one to four," adds James.

The game that emerged is closer to a real-time strategy (RTS) game, but with real locations and deeper play. Much deeper play.

Explainable AI

Because of the importance of AARs (after-action reviews), *Full Spectrum Command*™ captures a lot of information, such as numbers of casualties on both sides, the status of the soldiers and enmities, and milestones reached. It also has what they call an *explainable AI.*

Full Spectrum Command™ records the state of all of the AI entities at certain key points, beginning of task, end of task, first contact with

Figure 19.4. *Full Spectrum Command*™ Interface.

Source: Full Spectrum Command™. Used with Permission.

Figure 19.5. *Full Spectrum Command*™ Interface.

Source: Full Spectrum Command™. Used with Permission.

the enemy, and so on. Then, after the simulation, the player can move in on any given entity and query; for example, "Why weren't you shooting at the enemy?" The answer might be he was out of ammunition or did not have a clear shot.

Deployment

"We are still figuring out the right ways of deployment," said James. They are integrating *Full Spectrum Command*™ into the program at Fort Benning. It will be part of the sixteen-week course to train a captain. "My initial hope was that we would open it up and have people wander in and have people just play. We are still working that out."

James continued, "But right now, we are experimenting. We even bought a laptop and sent it to Afghanistan. There are a lot of models that are working. We just have to isolate what makes each work."

CONCLUSION

There are a lot of points that one can draw to conclude this example. But I am going to pick two issues, an input and an output, that to me are both habitually under-appreciated.

First, James and team looked at off-the-shelf games to modify, as well as graphics engines, but ended up building their own.

Second, the design of both the user interface and the AAR graphics have inspired people in the military to use them outside of the context of the educational simulation.

Well-designed simulations will change our view of our actions. It will ultimately change not just our awareness of the world and our options in it, but even the interface and function of our productivity software, and ultimately, our vocabulary itself. Here, with *Full Spectrum Warrior* and *Full Spectrum Command* we are just scraping the surface.

COMING UP NEXT

Have we left anything out of the conversation on educational simulations? Just building and using them.

The opinions in this book are solely those of the author and do not constitute an endorsement by the United States Army or the Department of Defense.

SECTION FOUR

MANAGING THE SIMULATION PROCESS

20

WHEN ARE SIMULATIONS A SOLUTION?

For the most important skills, we are moving from hunter/gatherers to developers.

SIMULATIONS MAKE SENSE in a growing range of situations. We have discussed quite a few. Take a look at Appendix 1, Aligning the Right Instructional Solution for the Right Problem, for a detailed look at where simulations are in accord with your results, and where other options might be better.

THE LOWEST HANGING AND RATHER TASTY FRUIT

But some opportunities are just too compelling not to use simulations, especially the traditional models. Here is my top list.

New Employees and High Turnover/Branching Stories

Any organization that has a high turnover in some area would be well served using branching stories to ground the new employees.

Branching stories can expose employees to first-person detailed scenarios, preparing them for common situations that they might face in the course of their new jobs. They provide highly specific advice and templates, build confidence, and let students make common mistakes in a safe environment, minimizing the chance that they will make the same mistake in a "real," high-pressure situation.

Complicated Equipment/Virtual Products and Virtual Labs

As more industries produce more complicated devices, virtual products and labs are increasingly appropriate solutions. These can greatly increase effective use while decreasing costs of error and traditional training.

And sometimes, what is being supported and modeled with virtual products and virtual labs is another training simulator. Let me explain. One airline had put pilots in four-hour blocks of flight simulator time. By shaving off just fifteen minutes per four-hour session with a simpler simulation, the airline saved over a million dollars a year.

New Consultant Team Building/Role Plays with Virtual Experience Spaces

When a group of new consultants is formed, or the old groups have to assemble, present, sell, and deliver new value propositions or solutions, role plays with virtual experience spaces can give them practice before the big show of interacting with real clients.

Shared Understanding of Complex Systems, Especially Cross-Functionally/Interactive Spreadsheets

Whenever there is a need for a group to understand a similar set of connected interactions, consider interactive spreadsheets. As we discussed, interactive spreadsheets compress time, allowing students to see quickly the results of their actions. They present a complex system, allowing individuals to better understand how their actions affect others. They also surface hidden assumptions, allowing significantly richer and more aligned conversations between decision makers.

Sales/Branching Stories

Elaborate and sophisticated branching stories can be deployed to all salespeople at the same time. These are effective, especially around new products, new processes, and new competitors.

Exposure to a New Perspectives/Branching Stories, Interactive Spreadsheets

Role plays put users in new shoes. Whenever there is a need to truly transform people's perspectives, to change attitudes, emotional crucibles need to be utilized. Either branching stories or interactive spreadsheets do this reasonably well. More intense experiences do it better.

A Big New Idea/Marketing Mini-Games

Sometimes, a group (potentially infinitely large) needs to consider and digest a single, focused new idea. Flash-based marketing mini-games are great techniques for engaging a population, sparking a more intimate and robust knowledge as well as a broader conversation and dialogue.

THE NOT SO LOW HANGING BUT REALLY TASTY FRUIT

The higher potential use of simulations is both harder to achieve and more relevant. In terms of the rocky road framework from the introduction, it is a role for *innovators*. CEOs either care, or they will be replaced by someone who does care (unless they have a lot of friends on the board, in which case they don't have to worry about it). These are skills that are real, actionable, can be applied immediately across a range of situations, help students in the workplace, and yet are in no way *vocational*.

These areas include:

Communication	Creating and using boards and advisors
Decision making	Innovation/adaptation
Negotiation	Nurturing/stewardship
Project management	Relationship management
Researching	Risk management
Turning around a bad situation	Security
Solutions sales	Sourcing/contracts
Teamwork	Creating new tools

Any skill or philosophy truly valued by an organization, including those above, has traditionally had to be hired, found, or developed slowly and/or expensively. The only chance to develop the organization's people quickly, rigorously, but cost-effectively will increasingly be through next gen sims.

Within academics, the high-potential uses of simulations are a bit different but just as important. These areas include:

- How to think like an historian
- How to think like an archeologist
- How to think like a physicist
- How to think like a writer

APPROPRIATE RESOURCES

Clearly, pragmatically, one of the most important aspects in selecting a simulation (and one reason for testing for accord in Appendix 1) is making sure enough resources are available to do a complete job. The amount of resources each simulation genre requires varies tremendously (Table 20.1).

Another issue is stand-alone versus instructor-supported. In some environments, despite the value, one or the other is required.

And don't forget, increasingly, simulations will be hybrids of combinations of genres. Innovative designers will merge two or three distinct genres to meet their learning objectives.

Table 20.1. Different Total Development Resources Per Genre.

Genre	*First*	*Second/with Toolkit*
Branching story (simple)	5 person-months	1 person-month
Branching story (complex)	10 person-months	5 person-month
Interactive spreadsheet	5 person-months	1 person-month
Game-based	5 person-months	2 person-days
Virtual product	8 person-months	4 person-months
Virtual lab	10 person-months	5 person-months
Marketing game	2 person-months	1 person-months
Microworld	5 person-months	4 person-months
Virtual experience space	10 person-months	5 person-months
Next gen sim (simple)	15 person-years	1 person-year
Next gen sim (complex)	30 person-years	2 person-years

TECHNOLOGY INFRASTRUCTURE OF TARGET AUDIENCE

Finally, each simulation type has different deployment characteristics. Survey the hardware, software, bandwidth, bandwidth accessible, and IT policies (Do the governing computer people allow installed programs or even Internet plug-ins? If not, can they be overridden or replaced?) of your potential audience (Table 20.2). Plan a solution to meet the technology infrastructure of the second-lowest fifth of your audience and above (the lowest fifth will either be upgraded, or find some other channel). Also remember that the local IT department will fight most things you want to do. You have to work with them, of course, but you also can push back if the benefit to the enterprise is compelling enough.

Table 20.2. Examples of Technology Profiles and Corresponding Media.

Thin Pipe

Infrastructure
- Low bandwidth
- Standard browser

Media Option
- A few small pictures
- Mostly text
- Light Macromedia Flash®
(if plug-in is available)

Corporate Standard

Infrastructure
- Medium bandwidth
- Standard browser
- Standard plug-ins (Macromedia Flash, Apple QuickTime®)

Media Option
- Many larger pictures
- Medium Macromedia Flash
- Apple QuickTime Virtual Reality (potentially optimized by Sorenson filtering in Flash)
- Compressed sound (if sound card is available)

Fat Pipe
- High bandwidth
- Current browser, possibly with custom plug-ins

Media Option
- Full-screen streaming video
- Dense Macromedia Flash

Full Interactivity
- DirectX® installed (standard with Windows XP® and beyond)
- 3D graphics card
- Speakers

Media Option
- 3D-rendered graphics
- Full video
- High-quality sound

(It is important to note briefly that the IT departments fought against every major advance in computing technology, including: PCs, graphic user interfaces, color printers, Internet access, PDAs, cell phones, and even enterprise resource planning (ERP) systems and customer relationship management (CRM) systems.)

More technology specifics are included in Appendix 2, e-Learning Architecture Considerations Today.

COMING UP NEXT

How do you research a simulation? It's easy. Figure out how you would research a traditional class, and just do the opposite.

21

RESEARCHING A SIMULATION

A New Competency

Games can teach some things well, but not everything at once—choose your battles.

—Stuart Moulder, former general manager for Microsoft's Game Studios

ONCE YOU HAVE DECIDED TO DO A SIMULATION, and have identified the right problem, and have considered a few possible simulation genres, the next steps are needs analysis and research. This can take *many months* for even a simple, custom simulation.

According to Forio's co-founder Will Glass-Husain: "One of the biggest issues is of scope. Many people get so excited that they want to model everything. Or worse, they want to model what they know well. But the point is to help customers address their issues, and it is expensive and unproductive to model anything but the learning objectives."

"For example, we could have built a simulator to help people learn how to use their phones better," virtual lab designer Jonathon Kaye agreed. "But salespeople all said that knowing how to use the phones was not their problem with selling. A better simulation, one we ended up building, turned out to be how to upsell a client to pay for more features."

RESEARCHING SYSTEMS

Will Glass-Husain explains his process for finding relevant primary, secondary, and tertiary elements for the *systems* of his interactive spreadsheets: "We try to start with the people who are responsible for the business area, as high up as possible. They tend to know how the material is going to be used and have the broadest cross-functional perspective.

"We use a facilitated process to define both issues and scope. We brainstorm, using big, six-inch hexagon shaped Post-it® Notes. We gather key components, and then we organize them by broad category.

"We look at how success is measured. Is it cost? Capacity utilization? Customer satisfaction? We then drill down to the key variables that impact these. Salaries? On-time performance? We tease out strategies people might use, for example, the differences between preventative maintenance versus unscheduled maintenance.

"We look at both the routine variables, but also the big surprises—a strike for a manufacturer, a power outage for an electrical company. We look at them in some cases as outputs, results of decisions, and in other cases as inputs, things that pop up that impact the business.

"These meetings are four- to eight-hour meetings. By the end, we are pretty comfortable that we have defined the scope and subject area. Then we will engage people closer to the individual issues to get more specific relationships."

For creating virtual labs, Jonathan told me, "I also like the troubleshooting sections of manuals or bulletin boards as a key source of material. Those become the basis of what you are going to teach. Those sections are when you have to use composite knowledge (you really have to think about the whole system) to solve a real problem. You have to bring together your knowledge of several skills."

Research questions around *systems* content might include:

- What are typical and/or successful operations strategies, when should they be used, and what are the impacts and tradeoffs of each?
- Are there broad factors that compete in the short term but support each other in the long term (used to organize the strategies)?
- What are the independent, interacting, and critical (primary) components?
- What are the relevant characteristics of each element individually, and what impact do they have on each other? What are the secondary and tertiary components?

RESEARCHING LINEAR

It is easy to find "success stories." But it takes a careful interviewer to find the warts in the process, the places where things either almost or completely derailed. One technique is to interview multiple people around a single case. While individuals will paint themselves in the best possible light, some people, especially salespeople, are more than willing to trash their colleagues.

Research questions around linear content might include:

- What are war stories?
- Are there general categories/archetypes/patterns?
- What are the successful processes that have been established?
- What do success and failure look like?
- What are moments that, when they occur, are irrevocable?

RESEARCHING CYCLICAL

Researching cyclical content requires an anthropological approach. Watch and organize what people really do during the course of the activity. Note especially where timing is critical—doing the same thing a bit too early or a bit too late (or a bit too soft or a bit too hard) has the opposite effect of doing it at the right time (in real time, not over many weeks or months). Remember that, while linear content is *a* then *b* then *c*, and systems content is often *a* or *b* or c, cyclical content is often *wait, wait, wait, soft a, wait, hard a, wait, wait, wait, wait, wait, wait, wait, hard a.*

Research questions around cyclical content might include:

- What are all of the real-time options that a person or organization has/discrete steps a person or organization can take in a given situation?
- Are there exact spoken phrases that are used that correspond to success?
- What are incremental signs that things are going well or going badly?
- Where is timing important? What are instances where doing the same thing a bit earlier or a bit later matter?
- Where is magnitude important? What are instances where doing the same thing a bit softer or a bit harder matter?

- Are there frequently occurring situation that are analogous to all situations, ideally one that many people encounter at least once a week?

FINALIZING THE GENRE

During the research process, you probably have further eliminated certain simulation genres and maybe even added some that you had initially ruled out. James Hadley remembers, "I've worked on three projects where we selected a genre up-front to help us visualize the product, only to change it later because the content demanded something else."

Now, entering the production stage is the time to nail down the exact form.

COMING UP NEXT

There are four optional stages to rolling out a successful simulation experience. Except for the optional part.

22

DESIGNING A SIMULATION

Keys to Success

The goal of instructional simulations is to stimulate the creation of mental models within the learner by having them discover rules and principles through experimentation. Designers should constantly be asking themselves, "How do I help the learner discover this principle and then verify that they know it?"

—James Hadley, instructional designer at JHT Incorporated

WE LOOKED AT TATA INTERACTIVE'S DESIGN and development process for interactive spreadsheets (Figure 22.1), at least at a high level. And we know, each genre is different to design: obviously computer-game-based models require a different path than video-based branching stories.

But I would like to generalize and flesh out places of common ground across designing different types of simulations. Here are some rules and philosophies that can augment a more traditional process around each medium and genre.

Let me step back just a bit. Successful simulation deployments today, in corporations or academics, live, remote, or mixed, use up to four stages, or *slates*. Each slate has different, unique requirements of the simulation that must be built into a program.

Figure 22.1. An Interactive Spreadsheet Development Process.

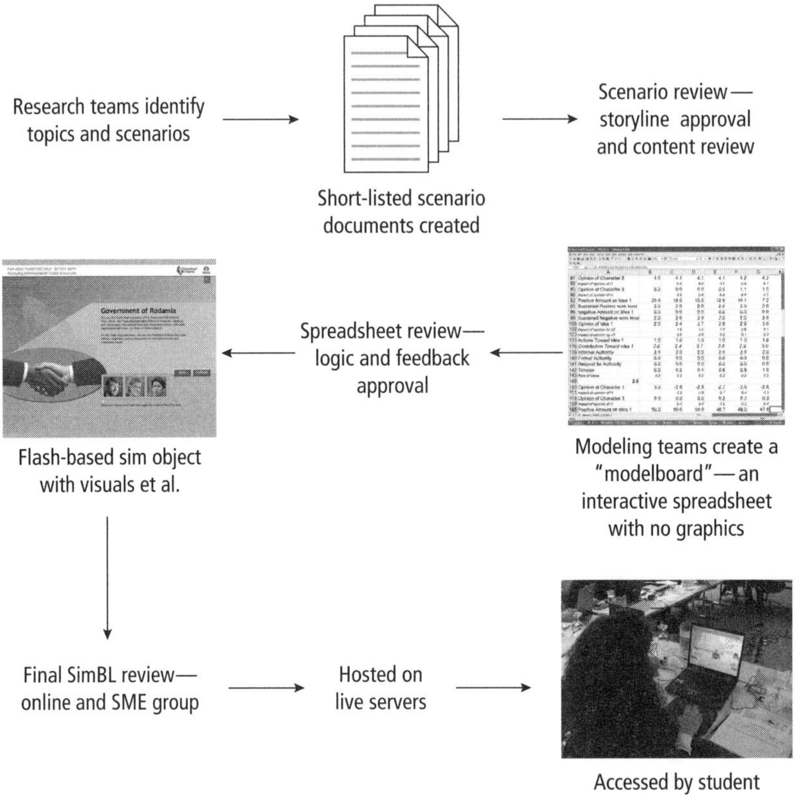

Source: Tata Interactive Systems. Used with Permission.

- In *slate one,* students hear about the goals of the program, the models used, the time frame involved, and some background. This part of the process is probably most akin to the time in a *locker room,* when the coach gives strategies and a pep talk.
- In *slate two,* learners experiment hands-on with the interface and interact with isolated and comparatively simple systems, a "dumbed-down" version of the full simulation. This is our *shallow end of the pool.* You can still drown, but it takes hard work.
- In *slate three,* students engage the full simulation for the first time. There is no one way for the student to do anything. There is not "the answer," just out of reach. Here they have to improvise in unfamiliar, challenging, and open-ended situations. This is our *deep end of the pool,* a little dark, and a little cold.

- The *fourth,* final slate is unchaperoned engagement. The students spend their time practicing their skills, pushing the envelope of the experience. This is our *free swim,* where some people will even invent new games with new restrictions just to test themselves.

The different slates have different durations, depending on the genre (Table 22.1), and of course, your mileage may vary. Just scan the chart now, and we will go into more detail over the course of this chapter.

THE CONCEPTUALIZATION

A Different Order

The components of an educational simulation are not designed in the same sequence in which they will be deployed. The order, once you

Table 22.1. Different Slate Deployment Times Per Genre.

Genre	*Background*	*Introduction*	*Engagement*	*Practice*
Branching story (simple)	5 minutes	1 minute	30 to 90 minutes	—
Branching story (complex)	10 minutes	10 minutes	1 to 3 hours	—
Interactive spreadsheet	30 minutes	15 minutes	30 minutes to 4 days	1 hour
Game-based	1 hour	5 minutes	30 to 60 minutes	—
Virtual product	1 minute	1 minute	—	10 minutes
Virtual lab	1 hour	5 minutes	1 to 3 hours	—
Marketing game	1 minute	1 minute	—	5 to 10 minutes
Microworld	5 minutes	5 minutes	—	30 minutes
Virtual experience space	1 hour	5 minutes	1 to 12 hours	—
Next gen sim (simple)	5 to 60 minutes	15 minutes	1 to 3 hours	1 to 3 hours
Next gen sim (complex)	5 to 60 minutes	30 to 120 minutes	1 to 12 hours	1 to 60 hours

have the learning objectives and research, is (Figure 22.2):

1. First design the simulation.
2. Add feedback.
3. Game it up.
4. Finalize the story.
5. Add the relevant introduction (the shallow end).
6. And then last, create the background content the students will see first (the locker room).

Most simulation developers will make many iterations of the design process, going through these stages first at a very high level, and then each time adding more and more detail.

First, Slate Three: Engagement

Slate three, the deep end of the pool, involves the core simulation, often preceded by a set-up story and followed by some feedback. Again, in the design process, conceiving the full simulation (engine and data) is done first. It takes the longest; it requires the most focus in isolation.

Figure 22.2. The Iterative Order of Design.

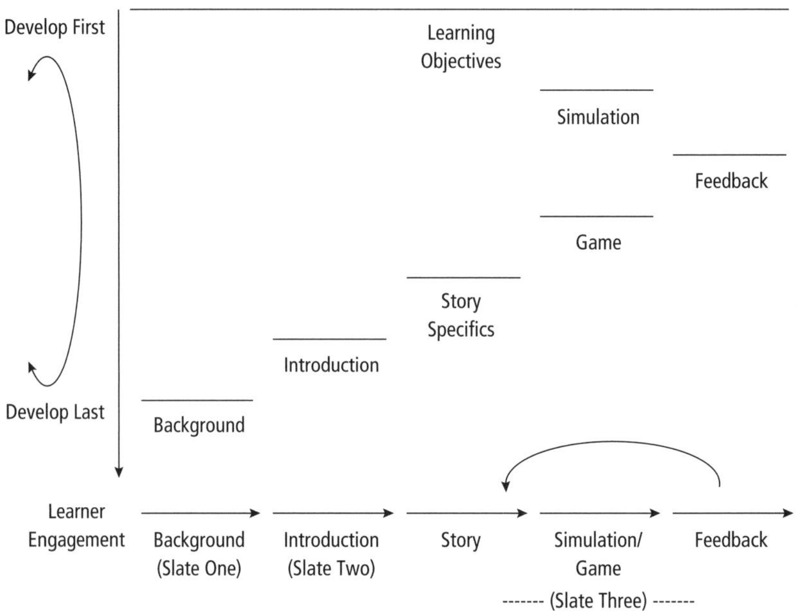

We have discussed many of the elements of an educational simulation:

- We have looked at the systems, cyclical, and linear content (Chapter 7, Recognizing New Types of Scalable Content: Systems, Cyclical, and Linear).
- We have compared the different uses of the four traditional simulation types as complete simulation mechanisms, but also as frameworks for defining support mechanisms (Section One, Building and Buying the Right Simulation in Corporations and Higher Education Today).
- We have talked about different computer game pieces (Figure 22.3) and genres that at least provide a starting point (Chapter 13, The Most Popular Simulations: Computer Games as Expectation Setters and Places to Start, and Chapter 14, Computer Games Redux: The Right Model? How Right?).

Each perspective may be more or less important, depending on your project. Now here's one way of looking at the whole experience:

- Consider your learning objectives.
- Think of a free and open environment, without a defined beginning and end, where a motivated user could just experiment, build, play, and see what happens. These interactions would be based on your earlier needs analysis. Where there are resources

Figure 22.3. Computer Game/Next Gen Sims Components.

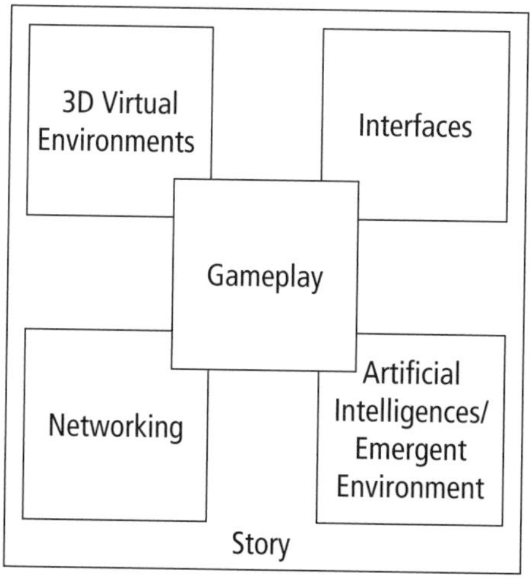

(money, time, supplies), imagine that a player has unlimited amounts, but still figures out ways of gaining and losing resources. These interactions are the vowels of your simulation.

- Then around that, think of the triggers, the discontinues moments that first set up the experience and goals, then advance the goals, and then wrap up the experience in either victory or defeat. These moments are the consonants of your simulation.
- Finally, begin pulling back on the amount of resources the player has.

Let's dig into those pieces.

ALL KEY SIMULATION VARIABLES AND RELATIONSHIPS, WITH FORMULAS If you are using equations, try them out on spreadsheets (Figure 22.4). Get a feel for multiple iterations of interacting formulas. (It can be frustrating to map out a simulation on paper. So resolve your frustration by bringing in non-linear visualization and experimentation tools, such as Excel®, the better.) This is also where you will start defining the properties of any *units* in your simulation.

Figure 22.4. Create a Spreadsheet to Map Out Variables and Relationships (Your Results Will Look Like This).

	A	B	C	D	E	F	G
81	Opinion of Character 2	4.0	4.1	4.1	4.1	4.2	4.2
82	*Impact of opinion of i1*		*0.8*	*0.8*	*0.7*	*0.4*	*0.1*
85	Opinion of Character 3	0.0	0.0	0.0	0.5	1.1	1.5
86	*Impact of opinion of i1*		*0.0*	*0.0*	*0.4*	*0.6*	*0.7*
92	Positive Amount on Idea 1	20.0	18.0	15.6	12.9	10.1	7.2
95	Sustained Positive work level	2.0	2.0	2.0	2.0	2.0	2.0
96	Negative Amount on Idea 1	0.0	0.0	0.0	0.0	0.0	0.0
99	Sustained Negative work level	2.0	2.0	2.0	2.0	2.0	2.0
100	Opinion of Idea 1	2.0	2.4	2.7	2.8	2.9	3.0
102	*Impact of opinion by c2*		*1.6*	*1.4*	*1.0*	*0.6*	*0.1*
103	*Impact of opinion by c3*		*0.0*	*0.0*	*0.0*	*0.1*	*0.3*
133	Actions Toward Idea 1	1.0	1.0	1.0	1.0	1.0	1.0
136	*Contribution Toward Idea 1*	*2.0*	*2.4*	2.7	2.8	2.9	*3.0*
139	Informal Authority	2.0	2.0	2.0	2.0	2.0	2.0
140	Formal Authority	0.0	0.0	0.0	0.0	0.0	0.0
141	Respect for Authority	0.0	0.0	0.0	0.0	0.0	0.0
142	Tension	0.0	0.2	0.4	0.6	0.8	1.0
143	*Role of ideas*	*0.2*	*0.2*	*0.2*	*0.2*	*0.2*	*0.2*
149	**2.0**						
150	Opinion of Character 1	-3.0	-2.9	-2.8	-2.7	-2.6	-2.6
151	*Impact of opinion of i1*		*0.8*	*0.8*	*0.7*	*0.4*	*0.1*
158	Opinion of Character 3	0.0	0.0	0.0	0.2	0.3	0.3
159	*Impact of opinion of i1*		*0.0*	*0.0*	*0.2*	*0.2*	*0.0*
165	Positive Amount on Idea 1	50.0	50.0	50.0	48.7	48.0	47.8

SIMULATION TRIGGERS Triggers are mechanisms that can advance the action when certain conditions are met during the educational experience. Triggers might end the simulation if things get too good or too bad. They might introduce new elements when certain conditions are met. Pedagogical triggers can launch information that ranges from how to use the interface to how to think about strategy. They might interrupt the play with a video, or seamlessly superimpose text on the screen. Map out as many triggers as you can think of.

ALL SIMULATION USER INTERFACES AND CONTROL CONVENTIONS Look to your work in researching cyclical content to shape the design of your interface. This is more critical than it might first appear.

While an interface for an application such as a Web-based tool should be seamless, inviting the plea from the user, "Don't make me think," a simulation presents a new way of looking at a potentially familiar situation. This "new way of looking" requires new thought and is a critical part of the learning. The successful adoption of cyclical/muscle memory skills, and the learning of timing, depend on the interface.

Diagram all interfaces and examples of use (Figure 22.5). Lay out the screens.

REPLAYING A SIMULATED SEQUENCE I believe another critical design element for any simulation in replayability. People should play a simulated sequence several times, trying different approaches (Figure 22.5). For a quasi-volunteer audience, such as corporate audiences, that restricts the total time of each simulated scenario to about ten to twenty-five minutes. For a military audience, their tolerance is much higher—a simulation will be replayed up through forty-five minutes.

DRAWINGS OF ANY SIMULATION SETS AND CHARACTERS To the degree that you will be using characters and sets in any of the slates, background, introduction, or engagement, visually define them. Draw every set.

When describing characters for production artists, don't write:

> Oli hates his job. The only reason he works in the call center is to earn enough money to pay the plane fare to visit his girlfriend, who is a merchant banker in Hong Kong. But the distance and different levels of career ambition are straining the relationship, and every time Oli leaves her he thinks it is for the last time.
>
> Oli feels distrust for the corporation and feels used by upper management, whom he resents for their salaries and perks and

Figure 22.5. Diagram the Complete Interface Under Different Conditions; Storyboard Models of Potential Play.

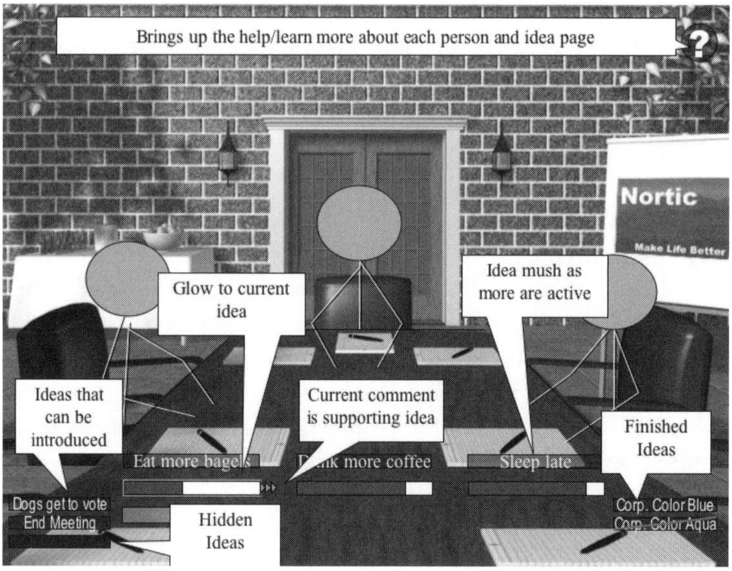

Source: SimuLearn Inc. Used with Permission.

> self-centered behavior. This distrust is an extension of the mistrust Oli has for his parents, whom he feels never prioritized him over their own hobbies. He smiles all of the time at work, taking on the role of class clown, because he wants other people to like him. But he knows other people think he is a slacker. During the day, he views himself as someone who just has not found the right mixture of opportunity and reward, but at night he worries they are right. He sometimes thinks he will never be happy.

Such text descriptions of visual elements guarantees frustration. You will be amazed at how much graphic artists are determined to misconstrue what you described.

Get a stack of magazines and hack them up. Think kindergarteners on steroids. Cut out examples of architecture and people. Create composites from several sources (Figure 22.6). This will greatly help in the development (Figure 22.7). If you are making a simulation for a business audience, use only business magazines, such as *Forbes* or *Business 2.0*.

As much as possible, avoid trendy outfits and styles. Simulations have a long development cycle and, unlike, say, a chief learning officer, a long life.

Figure 22.6. Create a Composite to Be Visually Specific.

Source: SimuLearn Inc. Used with Permission.

ALL WRITTEN TEXT THAT THE USER WILL ENCOUNTER DURING THE SIMULATION, INCLUDING SETS-UPS, DESCRIPTIONS, AND HELP SCREENS. ALL DIALOGUE THE USERS WILL ENCOUNTER You will be amazed at how many pages this will consume. Simulations suck up content the way building stone walls sucks up stones, or old dark wood sucks up white paint.

When writing dialogue, also jot down generic dialogue for both any narrators and characters. Create quotes as general as you can, that you can later augment with different pictures and specific text.

FEEDBACK Most likely, part of your simulation will let the users know how they did. Some pedagogical considerations:

- Visualize the flow of the event that can be reviewed after the gameplay is over (Figure 22.8).

Figure 22.7. In Case You Are Curious, Here's How That Character Ended Up.

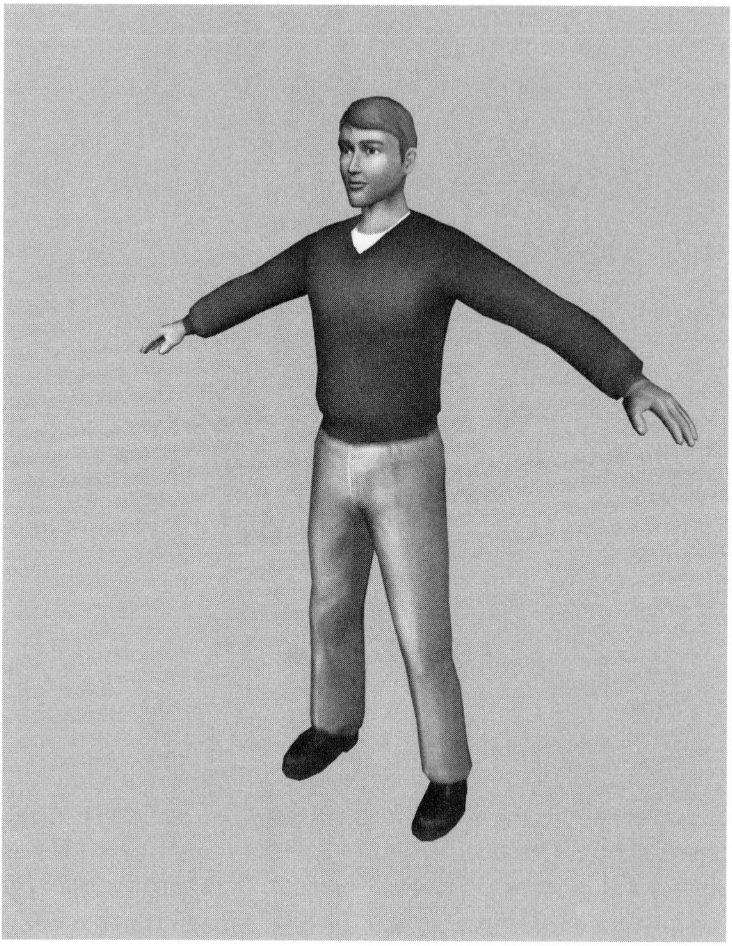

Source: SimuLearn Inc. Used with Permission.

- Track the key variables, and any other helper numbers.
- Display the appropriate text, pictures, sounds, and/or video.

People in Simulation Feedback

As you are designing your simulation, don't forget that some of the best educational experiences to date involve instructors, not just the simulation program, for feedback (and other pedagogical elements). Obviously the deployment might restrict this.

Figure 22.8. A Twenty-Minute Play at a Glance.

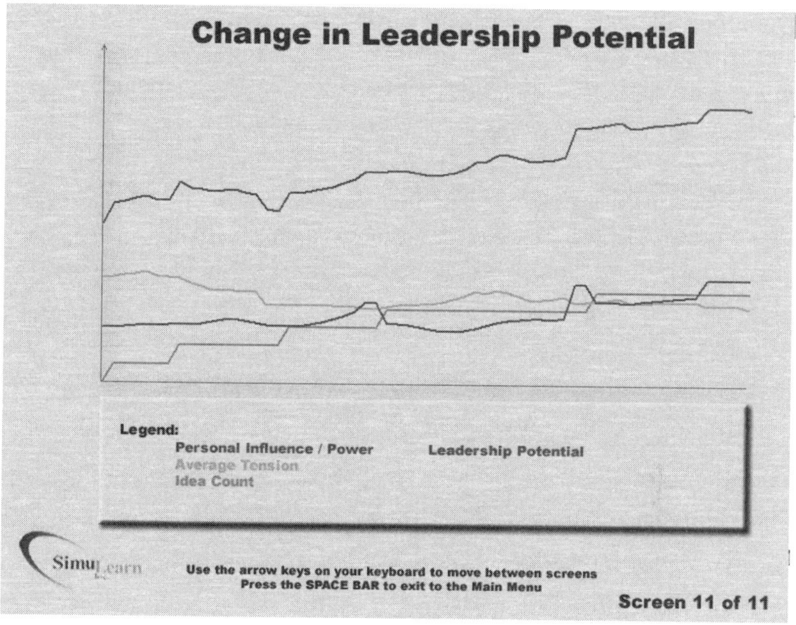

Source: SimuLearn Inc. Used with Permission.

The students might, for example, go through the simulation and then create a document (such as a proposal or plan) and/or a presentation that is evaluated by a real live person.

Learners' work to be evaluated by a person can include:

- A suggestion or proposal for either a real or fictional situation
- A defense of strategies used during the simulation (a favorite approach of instructors who currently use off-the-shelf computer games)
- A tying of the experience to real-life
- Observations of discrepancies between the simulation and real experience, perhaps with suggestions on how to improve the experience

Involving humans to judge or even participate obviously restricts repeatability, while sometimes increasing fidelity, and certainly increasing flexibility. Again, hopefully all simulations will eliminate the low-value repeatable role of humans, such as lecturing or administrating, in favor of the higher-value, more customized coach role.

ADD GAME ELEMENTS As the simulation firms up, start considering game elements for your *deep end of the pool.* The game elements are there to support the simulation elements. Ben Sawyer describes, "It is easier to tune the game elements once you have certain things that are unmovable." Start to sketch out what types of game elements to include.

Recall that some popular game elements include:

- Simplified or abstract interfaces
- Use of established game genres (game shows, athletic competitions, computer games, card games, and kids' games)
- Clicking as quickly as possible
- Gambling models
- Certain exaggerations of responses to make play more fun
- Reliving the roles of heroes or role models
- Conflict
- Shopping
- Gratuitous, detailed, and entertaining graphics and sounds
- Creating order from chaos
- Choosing what your on-screen character looks like
- Mastering a simple cyclical skill (throwing a card into a hat, Pac-Man)
- Competition between learners, including facilitated by maintaining lists of high scores (this is especially effective with CEOs and salespeople)
- Any use of graphics of fireworks
- Accessible communities for competition, and/or sense of belonging
- Presenting a mystery or puzzle to solve
- Creating a huge and powerful force enabling you to not just defeat but humiliate and crush all of those who dare oppose you
- Making the player overly powerful or overly relevant in a resolution of a situation
- Immersiveness in a favorite or interesting atmosphere (SuperBowl, science fiction, the Oscars, film noir, 1973 Miami)
- Using new technology
- Having access to privileged information
- Choosing between multiple skill levels to better align difficulty with capability

ADD MORE PEDAGOGICAL ELEMENTS I hear a lot of people talking about the idea of a simulation that knows the end-user intimately. This goal is increasingly becoming possible.

But when people talk a lot about sophisticated AI systems to handle this, I get a bit more nervous. It is a bit like flying a new helicopter before the insurance policy is finalized. It is tempting, but boy are mistakes expensive.

The goal is to have as simple of an "intimate system" as possible that still works reasonably well. Again, to quote Ben Sawyer, "Don't use calculus when algebra will do."

Jack Principles to Create the Illusion of Awareness

Recall the game *You Don't Know Jack®* had nothing but a sophisticated branching scheme as its driving mechanism. Harry Gottlieb, in *The Jack Principles of the Interactive Conversation Interface,* wrote that the game series was so effective at creating an illusion of awareness because it specifically responded to:

- The user's actions
- The user's inactions
- The user's past actions
- A series of the user's actions
- The actual time and space that the user is in
- The comparison of different users' situations and actions

Role-Playing Strategy

A slightly more complex approach is to track some number of variables about the user. Each action can impact any or all of these variables slightly. These variables then influence which of multiple dialogue messages or even simulation experiences the user encounters.

Examples include:

- Level of mastery
- Level of mastery desired
- Speed of uptake
- Level of game elements desired
- Level of pedagogical elements desired
- Level of simulation elements desired

Manuals for Pedagogy

Another place where educational simulations have to escape the influence of computer games is manuals. Most computer games have poor manuals that players cursorily scan and discard. Educational simulations might evolve to have manuals play a greater part in the process (Figure 22.9). If students are required to take notes or record opinions and scores, these documents can also be turned in as homework.

SIMULATION STORY SPECIFICS Prepare the story to set up the immediate experience. Even in the story, balance simulation (be realistic), game (put people in an interesting and powerful situation), and pedagogical (telling them what to do and what to look for) elements here.

Slate Two: Introduction/Play with Concepts

In the second slate of the user experience, our so-called *shallow end of the pool,* the learner will engage in a practice simulation. Slate two will vary, depending on genre (Table 22.2).

Table 22.2. Different Slate Two Deployment Times Per Genre.

Genre	*Background*	*Introduction*	*Engagement*	*Practice*
Branching story (simple)	5 minutes	1 minute	30 to 90 minutes	—
Branching story (complex)	10 minutes	10 minutes	1 to 3 hours	—
Interactive spreadsheet	30 minutes	15 minutes	30 minutes to 4 days	1 hour
Game-based	1 hour	5 minutes	30 to 60 minutes	—
Virtual product	1 minute	1 minute	—	10 minutes
Virtual lab	1 hour	5 minutes	1 to 3 hours	—
Marketing game	1 minute	1 minute	—	5 to 10 minutes
Microworld	5 minutes	5 minutes	—	30 minutes
Virtual experience space	1 hour	5 minutes	1 to 12 hours	—
Next gen sim (simple)	5 to 60 minutes	15 minutes	1 to 3 hours	1 to 3 hours
Next gen sim (complex)	5 to 60 minutes	30 to 120 minutes	1 to 12 hours	1 to 60 hours

Figure 22.9. Manuals Are an Easy Place to Add in Pedagogy.

Scenario One Scoring

- ❑ When you have completed Scenario One for the first time, copy the results in the boxes below from the 1st of the 11 feedback screens
  - Leadership ___%
    - Power ___%
    - Tension ___%
    - Ideas ___%
  - Business Results ___%
    - Financial Performance ___%
    - Customer Satisfaction ___%
    - Employee Morale ___%
- ❑ Do not hit the space bar. Click the → arrow twice on your keyboard to change the screen to number 3 of 11 — Leadership Style. Enter your results below

	You	All Players
• Number of Dialog Turns		____
• % of Dialog Turns	___%	

Given the Number of Dialog Turns, was it a short or long meeting?
Check your length below

❑ Short Meeting (15 to 30 turns)
❑ Medium Meeting (31 to 60 turns)
❑ Long Meeting (61 to 80+ turns)

Given the % of your dialog turns for Scenario One, were you passive, active, or dominating?
Check your style below.

❑ Passive/Delegating (0% - 30%)
❑ Active/Participative (31% - 80%)
❑ Dominating/Directive (81%+)

What do you think these two scores convey about your leadership style during this play?
What could you do to more closely represent your natural style?
Review all eleven samples of the feedback screens

- Use the following pages to help self-diagnose your performance after completing each scenario

C

Page 1

Source: SimuLearn Inc. Used with Permission.

You will need to design these practice simulations. This is like the full simulation (it should use the same engine), but greatly simplified. Each practice simulation should focus on one set of variables, demonstrating how both the interface and the relationships work.

Ideally, the second slate experiences are highly annotated. It is easy to see why things work, and why things don't work. Onscreen characters, if they exist, can give instructions and advice. The experiences should also be highly modular, allowing students to practice at their convenience, often in small chunks. This also provides less opportunity for users to get lost and more opportunity for them to be rewarded for doing something right. Finally, they should show some simplified feedback during and after the session. If designed and built well, the simulation should not require an instructor at all during slate two.

WALKTHROUGH TO PLAY WITH CONCEPTS The practice simulations should include very specific introductions, even annotated walkthroughs (Figure 22.10). It is critical to lower the tension of the player.

Slate One: A Pure Pedagogical Background

The first thing the learners will see is a presentation. Students hear about the goals of the program, the models used, the time frame involved, some motivation, and some background. An actual *locker room* is optional.

There is a range of options for this, from traditional classroom, to virtual classrooms, to pre-canned, pre-recorded sessions. Much of the traditional instructional design applies here, and just here (Figure 22.11).

Figure 22.10. An Annotated Walkthrough.

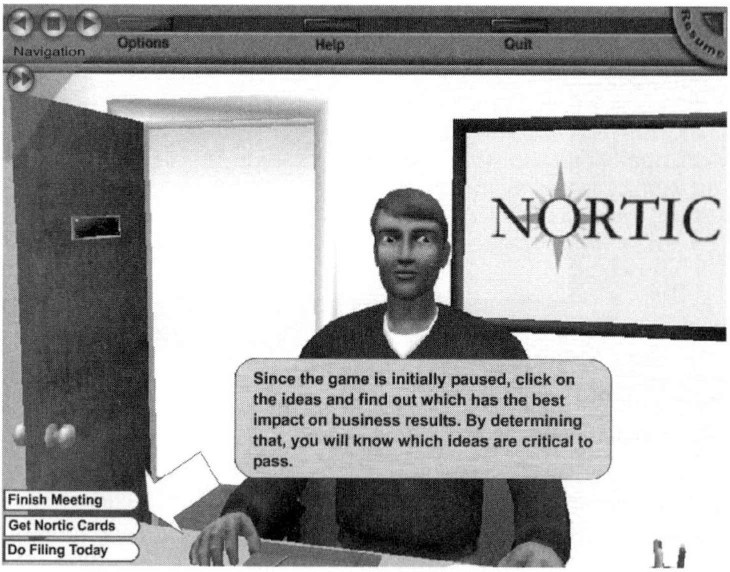

Source: SimuLearn Inc. Used with Permission.

Figure 22.11. Background Information Can Be Interactive.

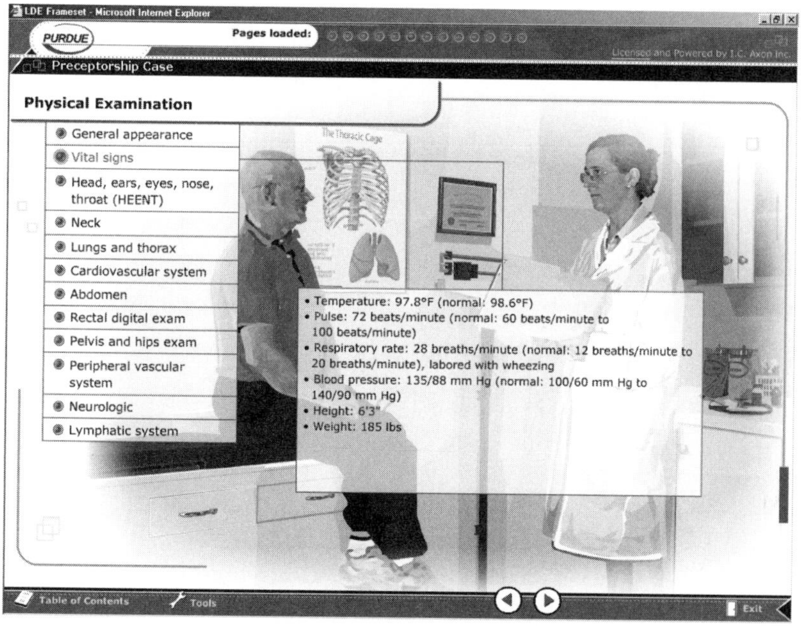

Source: © 2004 Purdue Pharma L.P. Used with Permission.

Where possible, storyboard all linear sequences (Figure 22.12). Where not possible, make it possible.

The Workflow

At some point you are going to have to worry about every event in the entire simulation, such as the start/home/navigation page (Figure 22.13).

And you will have to map out the entire sequence. It might look a bit like Figure 22.14.

Creating a Demo

Some simulations, especially the more complicated next gen sims, require a significant investment in time in order to learn from them. In most cases, the "real learning moments" don't come until an hour or two into the experience.

This time commitment (Table 22.3) can greatly interfere with the sales cycle, or even the "buy-in cycle" from people who will need to

Figure 22.12. Storyboard Everything.

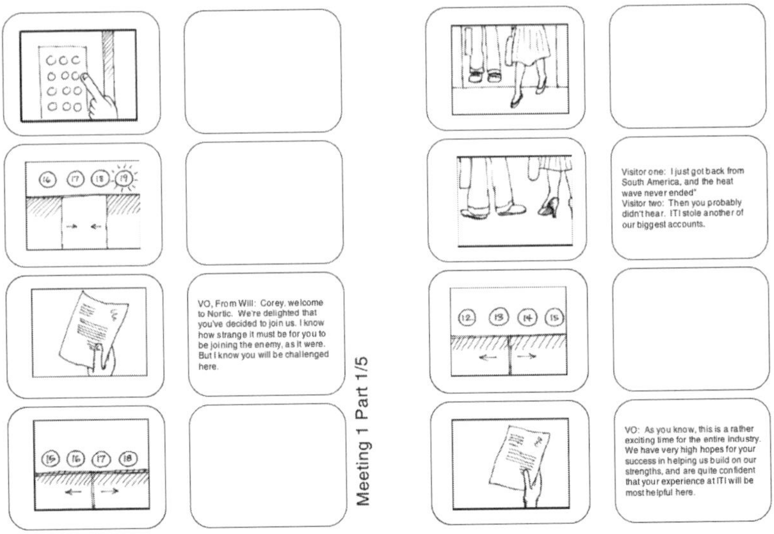

Source: Author.

Figure 22.13. A Start/Home Navigation Page.

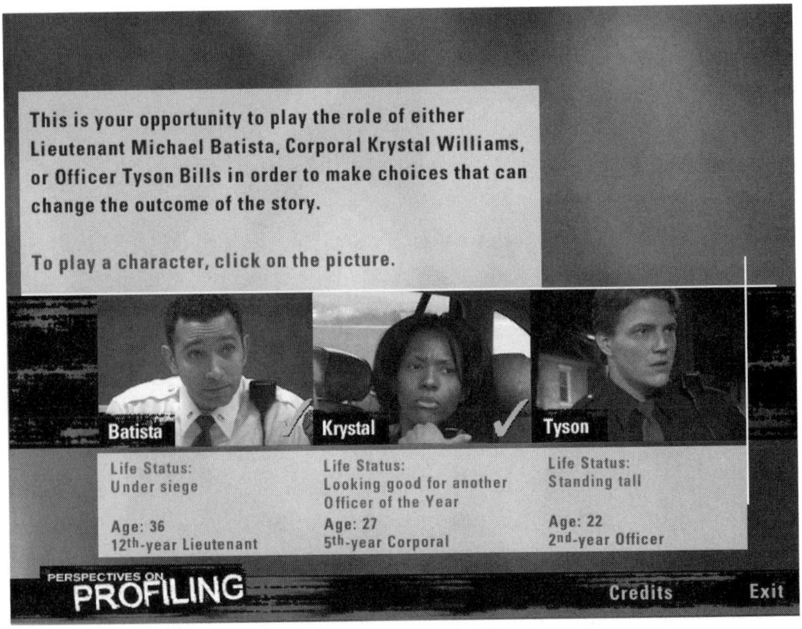

Source: WILL Interactive. Used with Permission.

Figure 22.14. A Generic Workflow of the User Experience.

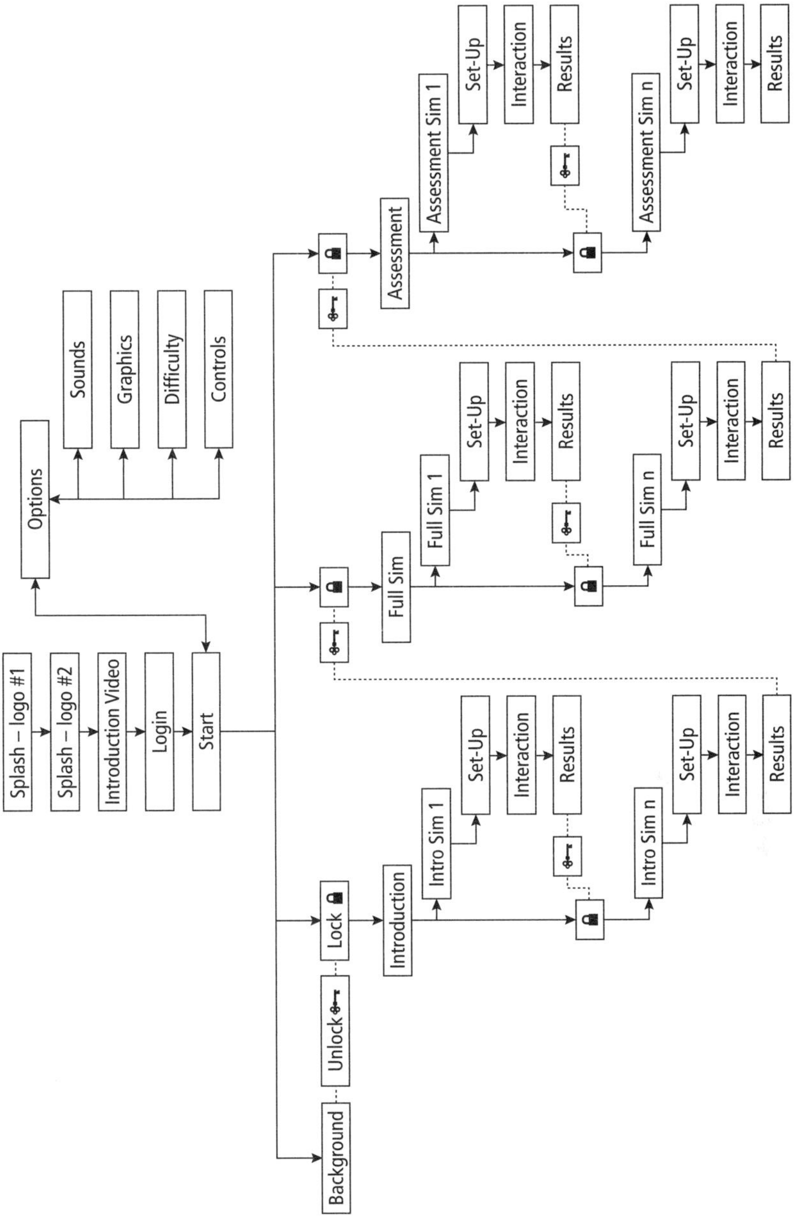

Table 22.3. Time Commitment for a Next Gen Sim.

Genre	*Background*	*Introduction*	*Engagement*	*Practice*
Next gen sim (complex)	5 to 60 minutes	30 to 120 minutes	1 to 12 hours	1 to 60 hours

be advocates. Said Pierre Henri Thiault, the project manager for *Virtual Leader,* "Decision makers will most likely spend less than thirty minutes reviewing your simulation to make an evaluation and see if it is worthwhile to pass it on to someone else or do a pilot. You want to answer their short-term satisfactions." So while you are building the full simulation, and your team is intact, build a demo as well that compresses the best of the full experience.

It is worth noting here that the creation of demos comes at the end, not the beginning of the development process. I say this because many clients ask for a sample of the full product just 10 percent into the development to make any course corrections. "But I only want the first scene, not everything," they defend themselves by saying, "just like a publisher would ask for the first chapter of a book."

That is closer to asking a car designer for a test drive of the new car 10 percent into the process, with the justification that you are only going to drive it for ten minutes. I show storyboards, equations, and past projects. Simulations don't come together until the last 10 percent of the development process.

THE DESIGN DOCUMENT

After the first design iteration of the simulation (out of probably six), start putting all of the content in the form of a comprehensive design document. There are two important rules here. The first rule is that *everything* needs to be planned out in advance, and I forget the second one. Every last character, every last equation, every last room or environment has to be mapped out. *Everything.*

This document is where you want to experiment. Changes are at least fifteen times cheaper here than once the simulation is being put together. The design document does not have to be pretty. Don't waste time on formatting or on making the disparate pieces look the same. It is not a class project. But it does have to be complete.

Here is a datum point for grounding us. The design document for an Xbox® game runs three or four hundred pages.

After you are done with the design document, go through and *check everything again.* Go down one more layer of detail. And then one more. A design document is not like a business plan for venture capitalists—*write it to follow it* (did I say that out loud?).

THE EXECUTION

As we said, there are many books on software project management, including shooting video and building games at one extreme and creating websites at the other. Many are listed in this book. But there are a few other notes worth passing on.

A Different Order Than Learner Engagement

The order of the *development* of a simulation will also be closer to the order of *creating* the design document than to the order that the simulation will be engaged from the student (Figure 22.15).

With the design document created, first build the simulation, add feedback, game it up, add story specifics, then add the introduction and background.

Figure 22.15. A Simulation Creation Milestone Model.

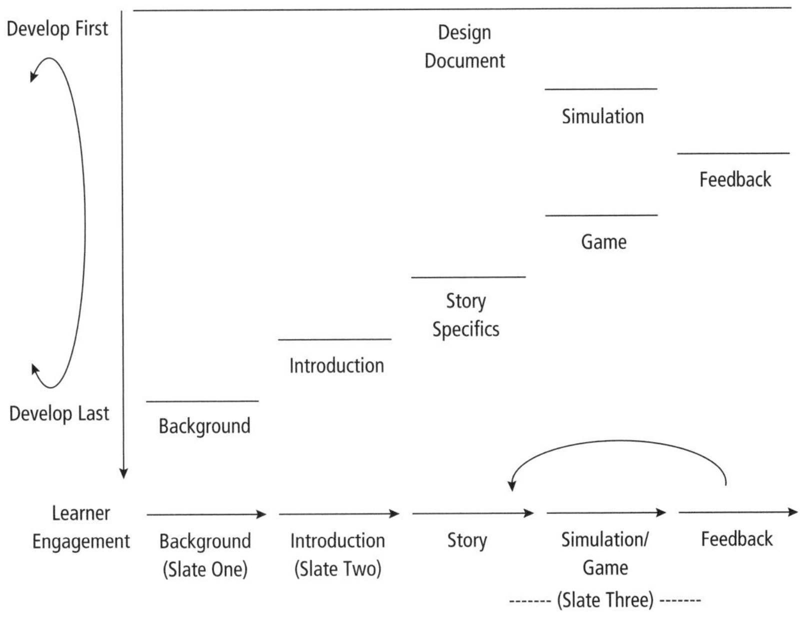

Keep Options Open

Every effort should be made to make a simulation easy to modify and customize. If you cannot make the simulation easy to modify, save yourself time and jump out of the penthouse window now.

Keep as many of the numbers as accessible variables as possible. In *Virtual Leader*, we had a four-hundred-page XML that drove the precise value of many variables and relationships per simulated situation. This allowed us to make changes on the fly using nothing but a text editor, never having to touch the compiled code. By keeping all of the text in the XMLs, for example, we made it easy to translate the program into different languages.

In some cases, the variables will need to be fluid in the final simulation. The variables will be able to be changed by either the player, say in setting difficulty level, or by the instructor, in advance or even live.

"Some of the simulations we make," said Pjotr van Schothorst, technical director, VSTEP BV, "our clients will use in a classroom, as a way to discuss the best way of attacking the incident, which the instructor projects on a large screen. Before showing the incident, the instructor can set some parameters with a built-in GUI, like size of the fire, wind direction, wind speed, day or night, and level of fog. That way, he can present a different incident every time, so people can learn how to act different, dependent on such environmental conditions" (Figure 22.16).

While you are at it, create plenty of "blank triggers" that can be invoked later in the tuning process if needed. You will need many more of these than you think.

Feedback

Get the feedback system up and running as soon as possible, as that will be a critical debugging tool as well.

The People and the Process

Pierre-Henri suggests, "Be open to different means of communication and especially ICQ or Messenger. We were able to get a decision made by communicating via ICQ to a computer connected via a cellular phone on the French bullet train going at 200 mph, while on the phone between Atlanta and New York."

He continued, "Start with the end first and work back to see if the timeline is feasible. Have measurable results. Have weekly assessments

Figure 22.16. Instructors Set the Parameters for Replayability.

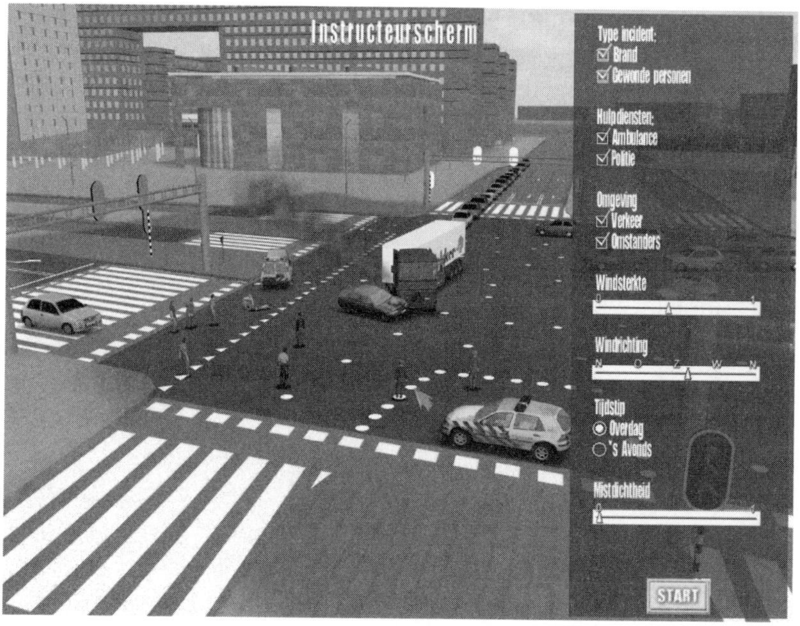

Source: VSTEP Virtual Training (www.vstep.nl). Used with Permission.

and break your weekly goals into tasks. Plan your work and work your plan. Be rigorous with your team leaders. Empower them to communicate as soon as an issue arises. This will show as soon as your project starts to be off track and can correct it before it becomes a major issue."

The Pilot Process

According to Forio's Will Glass-Husain, performing usability tests might be the single most important step. "When we are three quarters through the development, we have people play it. All of the developers can watch, but not intervene. We see what they do. We take notes as to where they get stuck. Always, the first time through with any new simulation is terrible. The brilliant insights that you put in there, a price war for example, the users are just not getting. We invariably go through and have to better highlight certain pieces of information."

Pierre-Henri noted, "Detach yourself from project. Ask people to review it for the first time and listen to what they have to say. Do not defend your point of view. Just listen and learn."

And Will added that you don't even have to wait until you are even that far along before you can test your material: "As soon as we have them, we tend to prototype the individual elements, such as the interface, the story, and the variables at the same time, just to different people, and with more hand-holding."

Pierre-Henri concluded, "Don't start selling too soon. Make sure you have a product at least in beta before hiring your sales force and going to trade shows."

FOR MORE INFORMATION

- Aldrich, C. (2004). *Simulations and the Future of Learning.* San Francisco: Pfeiffer.
- Bates, B. (2001). *Game Design: The Art and Business of Creating Games.* Roseville, CA: Prima Tech.
- Crawford, C. (1982). *The Art of Computer Game Design.* www.vancouver.wsu.edu/fac/peabody/game-book/Coverpage.html
- Salen, Katie, & Zimmerman, Eric. (2003). *Rules of Play: Game Design Fundamentals.* Cambridge, MA: MIT Press.

COMING UP NEXT

Fear, uncertainty, doubt, pain. Why would you want them in your education? But a better question is, why do you think your education can work without them?

23

DEPLOYING AN EDUCATIONAL SIMULATION

It's Not What You Think

An inexperienced learner is thrown by frustration,
but a good learner uses it.

—With apologies to the late actor Carroll O'Conner

IN CASE YOU WEREN'T PAYING ATTENTION in the last chapter, let me try again. Really good educational simulation experiences, the ones you write home about, cover four different stages, or slates. They are: *Background; Introduction; Engagement;* and *Practice*. Each slate is different from the last, but they carefully build on one another.

By the way, this four-slate process also works with using computer games, such as those listed earlier, in classrooms. The instructor will simply have to work a bit harder to introduce the game in the front end (slates one and two) and then make relevant the game at the end (slate three).

(And in case this looks a bit familiar, many of these ideas were first surfaced in my article "The four slates of educational experiences" in *On the Horizon. Special Issue. Second Generation e-Learning: Serious Games, 12*(1), 14–17, 2004.)

SLATE ONE: BACKGROUND (THE LOCKER ROOM)

Most students have never learned via simulations.

Meanwhile, most of us have spent far too long in formal educational experiences that were lecture- or book-based. Most of us are used to taking a seat and waiting for the class to be over. Or turning the pages until we are at the end of our assignment.

And so, no matter their work experience or extracurricular activities, few are prepared for the shift in education models that simulations represent. Even if they think they are.

In slate one, students hear about the goals of the program, the models used, the time frame involved, and some background. There is a range of options for this, from traditional classroom, to virtual classrooms, to pre-canned, pre-recorded sessions. Slate one also has to build motivation and establish expectations. (Virtual lab creator Jonathan Kaye suggests that, more than any technical feature, *motivation* is the most important element of a simulation.)

Students are often anxious. They almost always consider themselves quick learners and people of action. This background material might be appropriate for the others, the less gifted, they think, but not for themselves.

They want to skip the pedagogical elements and dive in as quickly as possible to the full simulation (slate three, the deep end of the pool, the whole enchilada, the "Full Monty"). They recount their disdain for manuals when playing computer games. But that is often a mistake for educational experiences. If this slate is skipped, students will be confused about, frustrated with, and then disinterested in the simulation. Still, some will skip it (I never require it), but hopefully are mature enough to come back to it later.

SLATE TWO: INTRODUCTION (THE SHALLOW END OF THE POOL)

In *slate two,* learners must understand the interface and interact with isolated and comparatively simple systems.

Some students will think the experience is too easy. They will soon enough get their wish for a harder experience in *slate three.*

Some students balk at the game elements, the contrivances that are part of a smooth ramp-up to the full simulation. The experts in the subject-matter area may start trying to establish their own credibility by loudly disparaging relatively trivial elements.

Most learners' experience will be that of frustration. This is good. But most users fight their own frustration. They resent it. That is bad.

Learning the Interface

As we discussed last chapter, for many educational simulations, the interface is a crucial part of the learning. It presents a new way of looking at work, which should be different from how the participants natively see work. Learning the interface of a well-designed educational simulation is usually about a third of the educational value of the entire experience.

The First Frustration-Resolution Moment

This first encounter with frustration, whether around the early interactions and/or the interface, is a key learning opportunity. It is also a meta-learning opportunity, a chance to learn about learning.

If you left a gym after two hours without having broken a sweat, without aching muscles, you would suspect that you had wasted your time. (Some people have different success criteria for a trip to the gym, of course, but that is a different story.) Any good trainer knows his or her role is not to eliminate or even reduce the burning in the muscles, but to encourage it (with safety parameters), and to reframe it. Without pain, there is no gain. The ache is the feel of progress.

So too do we all need to rethink frustration in the context of learning. If you leave a learning program without having felt waves of frustration, you probably wasted your time.

Computers can distract from this message. So sometimes it is easier to think of a non-computer-simulation example: If you were a manager learning to listen more, it would be painful to not talk during a staff meeting. If you were a division head learning to source staff internationally instead of using local people, you would also be frustrated.

Having said all of that, students should expect to resolve their frustration in the learning experience. Just as our athlete should soon feel good about his or her new muscles, our manager learns to appreciate the comments of others and the division head builds a capability abroad, so students should have every right to expect that after they work at understanding a new way of interacting with this new, simulated world, they will become comfortable. And they should also expect to have learned something useful and practical, even if they go no further.

Frustration during the learning program and then the feeling of resolution afterward is the most reliable sign that learning is going on. This first frustration-resolution moment should be celebrated. It will play out repeatedly in slate three.

Many branching stories and virtual labs rip through this slate pretty quickly.

SLATE THREE: ENGAGEMENT (THE DEEP END OF THE POOL)

In slate three, students engage the full simulation for the first time. Here they have to improvise in unfamiliar, challenging, and open-ended situations.

Group Learning

Borrowing a page from role playing, slate three is often more successful if people learn in groups.

For more personal scenarios, putting two or three people per simulation, allowing one to observe, exposes each to alternative approaches and decreases learning time (Figure 23.1). (Headphone splitters are very helpful when working with a large group of paired-off students.)

Figure 23.1. Engaging a Simulation with a Buddy.

Source: SimuLearn Inc. Used with Permission.

For simulations that replicate more group situations, the teams can be larger. Surprisingly, creating the right team is important. Will Thalheimer recounted a leadership simulation he created and helped facilitate. "The teams didn't do as well when there was just one perspective, such as when the teams were made up of just accountants, lawyers, or marketing people. They got through it quickly, but they did not realize the alternatives. The groups that had a diverse background were more thoughtful and introspective. They tended to learn more."

Chat rooms can be used if the students are not co-located. This can also increase the effective "workgroup" to hundreds.

Role of Instructor

Unlike, say, with computer games, instructors can also add significant value at this point. This difference comes from at least two reasons.

The first is that simulations are not necessarily fun and entertaining like their game counterparts, although fun is often a good thing, depending on the topic area.

Second, what is learned has to be applied in a real-world situation. Most of us would be content if armchair pilots learned how to use a flight simulator on their own. But with real pilots, not so much. And we want those executives who are learning supply chain management to really know it.

Most of instructors' value in this slate comes from one-on-one contact with the students. They go from being presenters to being coaches. This is more effective live, but with distance learning technologies, the coaching can also be done remotely, even asynchronously.

FRAMING THE SIMULATION Members of the audience will challenge any simulation at some point. And again, the more technically familiar a participant is with the subject area, the more he or she will find (often irrelevant) issues to challenge.

Researcher Will Thalheimer remembers, "We scored everyone. And of course people were pissed off if they didn't get certain points. When we first did it, I defended the simulation. But that didn't work. You can't fight the audience. They either leave, or mentally drop out. Then we changed. We would say, 'The simulation has a point of view. You can unplug it and it goes away. But why do you think it has that point of view?' Later, I played devil's advocate. I would ask, 'This is what the simulation said. What do you think would have happened?'"

Enspire's Bjorn Billhardt handled the same issue slightly differently: "We always attach personalities to the feedback avatars. One reason for doing that is to tell the students that the board members are not always right. You don't have to always agree with them."

CUSTOMIZED HELP Coaches will spend some time handholding, helping on the technical or interface issues. Hopefully, most of these have been resolved in the second slate.

They will spend a lot of time dispensing customized, pedagogical elements, relying on their own instincts about how much help to give a participant. Their job is to let people get frustrated, but not too frustrated. They will leave some people alone and walk others through step-by-step (Figure 23.2).

Figure 23.2. Coaches Can Be Critical.

Source: SimuLearn Inc. Used with Permission.

For students who are blazing ahead, the instructor might want to challenge them with new approaches or conditions. "Try maximizing customer satisfaction," or "See if you can get to the same results, but more quickly." Or they could pair them off with students who are not doing so well.

PLAY COMMENTARY After each play, there should be some form of after-action review to reflect on what happened. If simulations are well designed for slate three, the program contains a visualization of the flow of a simulation play at a glance. That way, if a student is engaged for twenty minutes, the teacher can, in a few moments, get a feel for how the experience progressed, in order to provide meaningful diagnostic feedback (Figure 23.3).

If the instructor is involved asynchronously, then he or she could review the charts as convenient and email back some observations and advice. In any case, experienced instructors will become very good at finding patterns of behavior.

DEBRIEFING Slate three is also more effective if it includes established debriefings, outside of the immediate review session of the simulation.

Figure 23.3. A Twenty-Minute Play at a Glance.

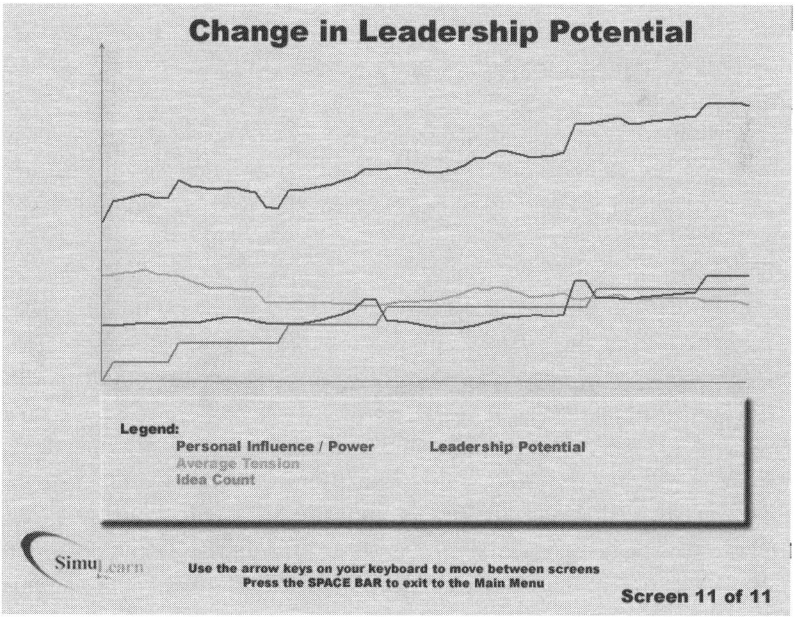

Source: SimuLearn Inc. Used with Permission.

Participants stop playing and formally reflect on their experiences. They may discuss specific situations, voice their approval, or vent their objections with the characters or conditions in the simulation (for example, "If that person were in my organization, I would fire her immediately").

Debriefing must let people connect their learning to the real world. This might be done individually, in small groups, or with the entire group, depending on the class topology.

PRESENTATION AND JUDGING In some cases, the simulation does not evaluate the learner's performance—humans do. In these cases, learners present and/or submit to one or more judges and/or classmates during slate three. Then, either in real time or within a week, they would receive their scores and feedback.

Shuffled in with the Real World

Consider the research of Will Thalheimer: "Most forgetting happens quickly. Repetition is the most powerful of learning factors. And by spacing that repetition over time, you can significantly minimize that forgetting."

The United States military has tracked this phenomenon carefully. Reports one study: "Within at least forty-five days after leaving Fallon detachment, a pilot's bombing accuracy returns to the accuracy he had just before reporting to Fallon."

Skills that are not used are lost (Figure 23.4). Think about how much you remember from your calculus classes. Therefore the nature of the spacing of simulation experiences changes depending on the types of skills being taught.

FREQUENTLY USED SKILL/INITIAL TRAINING Some simulation programs teach frequently used skills. These skills include call center client engagement, public speaking, and leadership. There are two different models for rolling these out (Table 23.1).

Simulation can be mixed in with real experiences over multiple days. Ideally a student first engages the simulation (slate one through three), then engages real situations for a few days to test and hone the skills, and then re-engages the simulation at slate three. In these situations, you can often get away with lower fidelity simulations. I always push for a lower-end simulation here because its role is often just to add some frameworks to augment the real situation.

Figure 23.4. A Forgetting Curve.

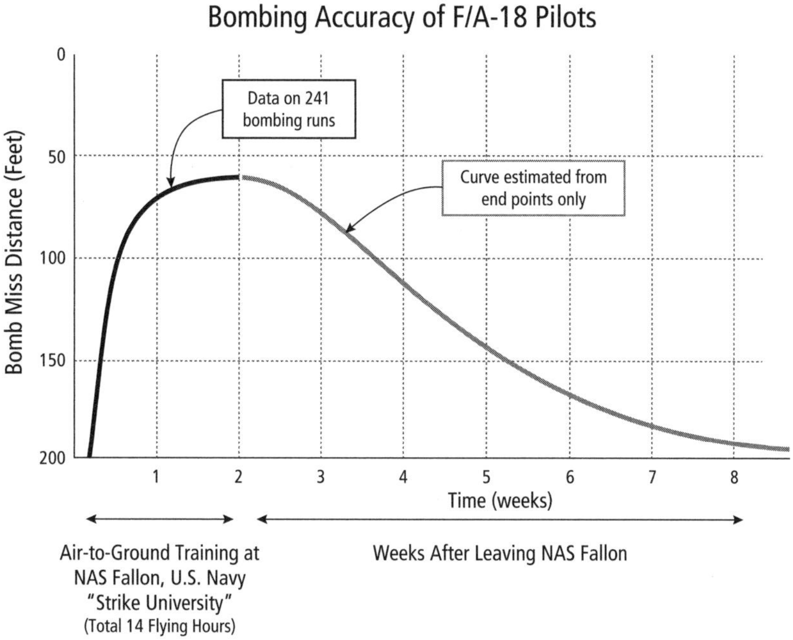

Table 23.1. Frequently Used Skills vs. Infrequently Used Skills.

	Initial Training	***Follow-Up Training (at least every 9 months)***
Frequently used skill (data entry, call center, public speaking)	Low fidelity mixed w/real experience over multiple days Or High fidelity in isolation single day	Refresher
Infrequently used skill (disaster recovery, violence in the workplace)	Very high fidelity, in isolation	Robust

When multi-day programs are impractical (and the higher ed people are now laughing at the corporate trainers), simulations can also be delivered as an isolated, "one shot" program to prepare students for frequently used skills. In these cases, a very high-fidelity simulation is needed.

INFREQUENTLY USED SKILL/INITIAL TRAINING Some simulation programs teach infrequently used skills. These include disaster recovery, fire, and violence in the workplace.

In these cases, the simulations can still be spaced out over several days, but much more tightly. There is no reinforcing with real-world experience (hopefully).

The fidelity of these simulations always has to be very, very high. The training has to be completely sufficient to prepare participants to handle the situation successfully.

FREQUENTLY USED SKILL/FOLLOW-UP TRAINING Follow-up training for frequently used skills such as public speaking should still happen. But the programs can be short, relatively infrequent, and casual. The point is to update people on new techniques and to remind them to use their old ones.

INFREQUENTLY USED SKILL/FOLLOW-UP TRAINING Follow-up training for infrequently used skills such as disaster recovery has to be robust. Because there is no other opportunity to prepare for the event, full immersion is required. The follow-ups may not be quite as extensive as the initial training in terms of slate one (background) and two (introduction), but they are just as intense in slate three (engagement).

Wrap-Up

In slate three, the learning is emotional and becomes, with practice, intuitive. If this slate is skipped, if students go directly to unchaperoned experimentation, students will get some of the value from a simulation. But it will take longer and require more discipline, and the learning might be incomplete. Any rigorous formal assessments using the simulation will most likely happen here.

SLATE FOUR: PRACTICE (FREE SWIM)

The fourth, final slate is unchaperoned engagement. The students spend their time practicing their skills, pushing the envelope of the experience. Spending at least three or four hours on the interactive spreadsheet is necessary for a student to work the skills to an intuitive level.

Slate four requires ongoing access to the simulation, either via the Internet for lower-fidelity simulations or through a centralized lab or distributed through a medium including CD-ROMs and DVDs for robust simulations.

Some organizations may use extensive game elements here, such as have ongoing contests for high scores. And some students will modify the simulations directly, potentially building entirely new scenarios, adding another intellectual layer of knowledge on top of the developed intuition.

CONCLUSION

These four slates are critical to successful skilling and up-skilling. The feel of the process is probably best summed up from Dr. Jana Roberta Minifie, professor at Texas State University—San Marcos. "For me," she said, "the best part of the simulation *Virtual Leader* was watching the students go through the change process. At first, students resist this new technique. They drag their feet, complain it's too hard, not real enough. As a teacher you can't give in. As the students go through the various modules, there is a wonderful change that occurs. Students go from resistance to acceptance. When the 'light bulb' goes off, there is such a satisfaction that learning has really occurred. Students then talk about how they are using the concepts at work, in student group projects, and in other areas. It truly makes a change in how they approach people."

The four slates are also critical to successful benchmarking. As more groups get better at deploying simulations, the ability to compare strategies by slates becomes critical to continuous improvement.

Here is a curious observation. Consider again our educational simulations chart (Figure 23.5).

As you understand the four slates, and overlap each slate across our simulation chart, you can find an interesting pattern emerging (Figure 23.6).

As the human fetus develops in the womb, it retraces the evolutionary path of all humans. It evolves gills, for example, and then replaces them with lungs.

The slates of background and introduction may shrink as engagement and practice evolve. But they will always be there, not vestigial, but critical elements of the learning process.

Figure 23.5. Educational Simulations and Tangential Spaces.

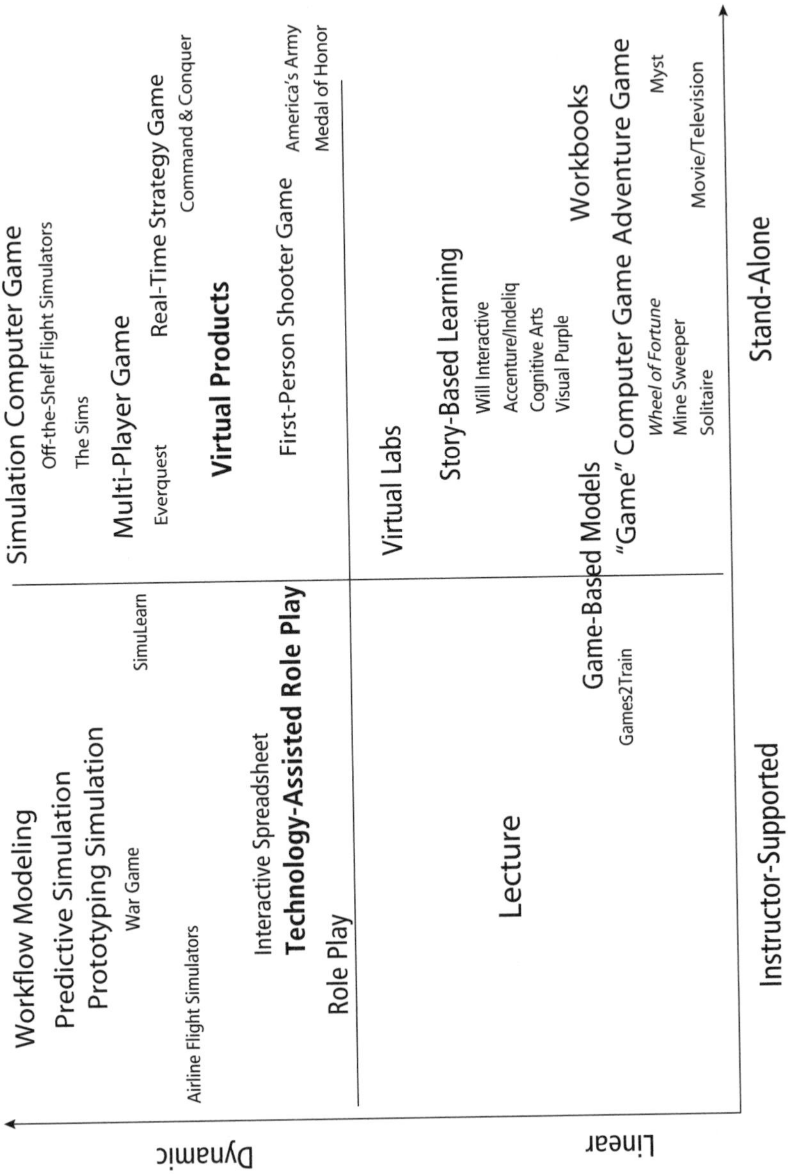

Figure 23.6. Steps in the Process.

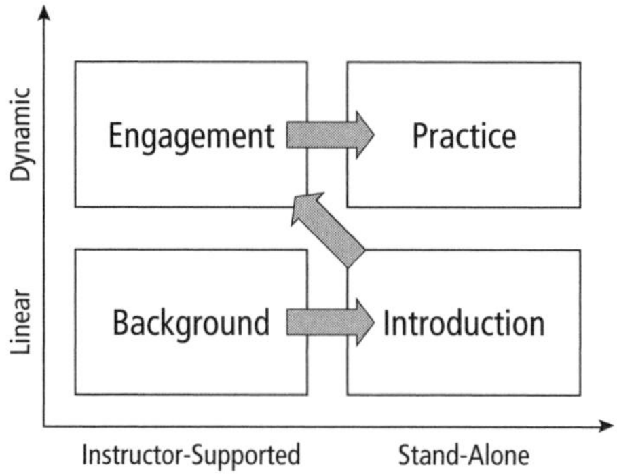

COMING UP NEXT

If you don't build this single step into simulation design, you will fail.

24

ITERATIONS

Because You Won't Get It Right the First Time

Asking most training managers to evaluate educational simulations is a bit like asking George Lucas to evaluate the first Pac-Man arcade game in 1980.

I CANNOT IMAGINE A SITUATION in which a designer will get the perfect combination of all of the content types (systems, cyclical, and linear) and elements (simulations, games, and pedagogy) the first time around (Figure 24.1). Or the second time. Or the fifth time around.

Again, flight simulator designer Douglas Whatley: "One of the things about working with the military is that it is not that you are successful and done with it. Every year is further improvement. You don't end a contract with 'It's done.' You end each cycle with a 'There is still so much to do, and how are we going to do it?' Our metric is that people feel they are getting benefit, and they want to further invest in."

It has to be planned, therefore, that successful programs will be launched with enough runway and flexibility to slowly evolve to better meet the variety of requirements. The wonderful thing about all of these simulations (even video-based branching stories) is that they are changeable, one way or another.

Figure 24.1. Elements and Content.

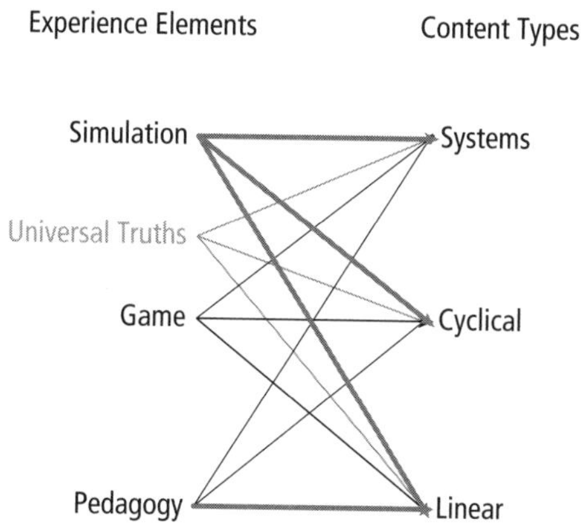

PEDAGOGICAL ELEMENTS

The easiest aspects to change in an educational simulation are *some* of the pedagogical elements—the set-ups, the wrap-ups, the onscreen words. Paper-based manuals that can be accessed during the simulation became the most convenient place to make quick changes.

When to Change Pedagogical Elements, Part I

We have said that if people are lost and confused, or don't see the relevancy of the experience, designers might need to ramp up the education elements. And if people are feeling manipulated or they do not "own" the material, designers might need to ramp down the educational elements.

When to Change Pedagogical Elements, Part II

That is all true. However, the experiences of some of the simulation designers started me thinking.

It is hard to be on the innovative edge of anything, especially educational programs. You spend months preparing, researching, identifying teaching objectives, and then putting all of the material together. Frankly, you are buoyed by the fact that everyone seems to share your contempt for traditional lectures. You prepare this great feast of learning, and you put it out in front of your students as a master chef might put out a banquet.

The students pour in for the pilot program. They are excited about their involvement in this new kind of learning experience. They have imagined in full detail what the perfect learning experience looks and feels like.

After the introduction, the students are asked to do some work. This involves some kind of analysis, some kind of decision making, some kind of "learning by doing."

They get stumped. They don't find the key piece of data. They don't read enough of the background material. Or they try and fail. And they become frustrated.

A few people actually complain. Then a few more. Is this experiment really what they should be doing with their valuable time? Is this new way of learning still too young, too unrefined? The training sponsor shifts uncomfortably. The two of you exchange nervous glances. As the creator and champion of the program, you feel every bit of pain in the room.

The program goes along, bumpier than you had hoped. Frustration levels skyrocket on several occasions, and ultimately the students leave, drained.

IMPROVEMENTS . . . Luckily, this is going to be a repeatable program. And so you take the opportunity, before the next one, to make things more direct. You unhide content. You make the directions more explicit. You allow less opportunity for failure.

Over the course of multiple iterations, the frustration goes down. Layers are introduced to ramp up more carefully to the hard content. Everyone agrees the program is more accessible.

. . . **OR NOT?** But here is the rub. Is the frustration a result of bad design, or is it a sign of real learning occurring? Is reducing the frustration making the program better or, gasp, worse?

There are many stakeholders in education: teachers, students, parents/managers, training directors/deans, and politicians/CxOs. Any one of them can derail a program by complaining loudly enough.

My point, and I do have one, is that only by balancing the *long-term learning objectives* with the *short-term satisfaction of students* do we get a complete picture of when to ramp up pedagogical elements. Eliminating bad design is critical. But too quickly pulling the trigger and adding more help to relieve frustration may be doing more harm than good. Jack Nicklaus or Donald Ross would never flatten one of their courses just because of a few swears.

James Hadley said it better than I: "Designers should try to place learners in a situation where they can learn on their own. Does it hurt, through cognitive dissonance, frustration, and confusion? Yes. Is there a recovery time, through after-action reviews, translation, reflection? Yes."

Are there alternatives to meaningful learning? No.

From People to Technology

Pedagogical elements have a relevant design component. Do they reside in the technology or in the people deploying the educational simulation?

If live instructors are involved, everything they say to everyone more than a few times should eventually be encapsulated in the technology. The goal is not to replace instructors, but to keep them adding customized, user-specific coaching.

GAME ELEMENTS

Through the successive iterations, designers have the ability to change some of the game elements. The most accessible opportunity to improve the game elements is to tweak simulation relationships to make them more dramatic or obvious or to make it generally easier or harder to accomplish a given goal. Keep in mind that every change made for game reasons (not simulation reasons) risks accuracy, creates a brittleness that might be exploitable by future students, and complained about by purists.

When to Change the Game Elements Redux

As discussed, if people are bored and/or unmotivated to spend extra hours on the experience, the designers need to ramp up the gaming elements. If people are feeling as if their time is wasted with trivial activities (for example, if they are already fully motivated to learn the content as quickly and accurately as possible), the designers might need to ramp down the game elements.

SIMULATION ELEMENTS

It is very hard to add simulation elements at this point. About the best you can do is leverage every editable variable that you gave yourself early on ("little gifts," as you will come to refer to them). You can, as you could for game elements, tweak up or tweak down relationships and perhaps replace an under-performing element, be it graphical, voice, or logical. The sum of all of those types of changes could be packaged into a single *mod*.

When to Change Simulation Elements Redux

Again, if students are having a hard time transferring what they have learned, or they need to better understand the systems and cyclical nature of the content, the designers of an educational experience might need to include more simulation elements. If students are having a hard time seeing the patterns over the minutia of minute-to-minute activity, the designers of an educational experience might need to include fewer simulation elements.

NOT GETTING IT

When I first rolled out *Virtual Leader,* I was surprised and frustrated to realize that between 10 and 20 percent of the people were not getting it. And, unlike in traditional classes, where people who don't get things sit quietly, people who don't get simulations are *very* loud.

I cursed my own design and format. When I first started talking to other people, I realized that, across almost all of the computer simulations, from very high-end on down, that number held constant. Around 20 percent were not making the leap. This later dovetailed with some of my other simulation rollouts.

Upon further digging, I learned that it was not a computer thing. Other simulations, people-based role plays, hit the same wall.

Then, finally, I understood. In any formal learning situation, (simulation or not, e-learning or not) about 20 percent weren't getting it. The problem was not that simulations were leaving people behind. The problem was that because simulations require active participation, those who were not getting it could no longer hide. (People sometimes call the results *bi-modal,* characteristic of most real *learning events,* versus results that look like a bell curve, which are more characteristic of a *diagnostic event.*)

"Is there a way to make it so that the last 20 percent get it," I was asked by a student where I was guest lecturing. "Yes," I had to agree, "but it meant gutting the simulation to a point where it was no longer a simulation. And for that, you lose a lot more than 20 percent."

COMING UP NEXT

Want an example of how this whole simulation thing can look when it works? Alrighty, coming up next.

25

ONE BRANCHING STORY BUSINESS MODEL

A business model, a business model! My kingdom for a business model!

—With apologies to William Shakespeare.

ULYSSES LEARNING is a tight example of a simulation model. They use simulations as the core of their solution to help call centers, although it is a solution that also brings in facilitation and coaching. Their approach contains many elements that are worth understanding and emulating in other industries and across other simulation types.

Ulysses Learning makes their sales by focusing on improving call centers with their internal processes, such as decreasing the average handle time, and external processes, such as improving the customer experience and resolving their issues in the first call.

Rather than focusing on the hard skills of reps working the equipment, they focus on the broader soft issues of reps and managers. This includes issues like empowerment (in certain defined parameters, the rep needs to be able to make decisions, such as giving the customer a discount, or sending information via overnight mail) and judgment.

RESEARCH

Once a sale is made, the research begins. Ulysses will spend a few days on the client site, interviewing and conducting focus groups with reps, coaches, and managers, listening in on calls, and looking for behaviors that are either working well or failing consistently.

"What is the leverage point?" Mark Brodsky, president and CEO of Ulysses Learning is fond of asking. "Where can we make the biggest impact?"

It is worth noting here that Ulysses has built a modular off-the-shelf library of over a hundred educational simulations of customer calls, in the form of branching stories. These are roughly organized both by verticals (for financial institutions, insurance companies, and telecoms), and horizontals (in-bound sales, in-bound customer service, and coaching).

They do not build simulations for specific clients. Based on their research they will select the right modules from their library and customize certain aspects, for example, putting in the company name, greeting, and selected offerings in the text of their branching stories answers.

It is also worth noting that customers ask them to customize more, something they resist. "It is often unnecessary, especially when justifying the potential incremental benefit versus the additional expense," Mark said. The discipline of pushing back on customers is one that all simulation vendors need to practice.

Once the right simulation elements are chosen, there are at least two other areas that are impacted by client-side research.

The first is the modifications to the experience delivered through people. These can all be relatively easily customized per client and so are tightly mapped to client processes, policies, and procedures.

For slate one (background), the facilitators introduce the program and link the call center's issues to the simulations the people will encounter. For slate three, the facilitators design people-based exercises to augment the computer-based branching stories. They also prepare coaches to monitor calls and provide one-on-one feedback to the individual call center reps.

The other research-based decision relates to whom to include for participation in the initial program pilots. For some call centers it might be new hires, or veterans, or the under-performing, or a combination.

ROLLOUT

Then comes the rollout. Participants start with a simulation based pretest that tailors how easy or hard the subsequent simulations will be. Mark estimates that about 65 percent fall into a basic path, 30 percent qualify for an advanced path, and, if the organization permits it, about 5 percent test out altogether.

After the slate one background, the participants spend time in parallel engaging a series of simulated calls.

In the simulation, the reps put on headsets. The phone would ring, and their script would come up. After the reps read their script and hit a button, a tape of the customer would play. "You would hear, say, a pissed off customer, and it sounded real," said Ed Arnold, a former implementation consultant with Ulysses. The reps then had a multiple-choice response (Figure 25.1). They then heard the customer reaction and had a meter (a pedagogical element) that would say how well they did with that response, with another meter that reported how well they were doing overall to that point in the call.

"It seemed kind of real, even though you knew it was fake. If reps screwed up, the customer got really mad at them. They would start to

Figure 25.1. Call Center Interface.

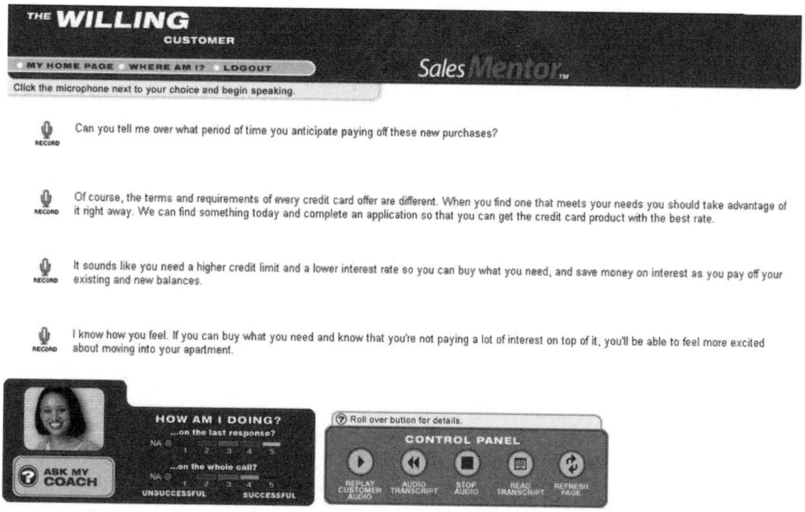

Source: Screen Shot Reprinted by Permission from Ulysses Learning.

sweat," said Ed. "I would find myself having to say to the students not to take it so personally—that when they hit 'end,' the customer forgets. The simulation does not hold a grudge."

The shorter calls lasted around four minutes. The longest took about fifteen minutes.

One challenge for all classroom-based simulation deployments is that people go through the experience at different rates. To keep people generally on track, the facilitators ask the quicker students to redo simulations, first trying to stabilize their scores (get predictable results), and then to practice extreme behavior to get out of their own comfort zones, even if it means receiving a bad score. This benefits the students by letting them further learn how their decisions impact the customer and how to recover if their calls ever go off path.

Then the facilitators stop the class and engage everybody in group discussion and exercises. "They bring in an emotional component, and it also lets people vent and discuss best practices for overcoming call obstacles," Mark added.

The total time in class is about two or three hours a day over three days, bringing the total to six to nine hours. Most often, the class is spread out over a Monday, Wednesday, and Friday.

Ulysses uses one-on-one coaching in the off days. The coach sits side-by-side, listening to the calls. The coach is trained to listen for the skills. He or she picks the one skill used (or not used) that was the make-or-break of the call, then provides immediate feedback.

At the end of the last class session, students take a final assessment. This is another set of branching stories, but this time without coaching and other pedagogical elements. "Even though we do not encourage the use of the simulations as the primary form of assessment, based on their results in the final simulation," Mark noted, "we can tell with near-100 percent certainty who are going to be the star reps and who is going to drop out for failure to perform. Once the reps learned the model, and once they finished the program, they literally had dozens of examples under their belt. And they knew it. They acted more confidently on the phones."

TRAIN THE TRAINERS

Ulysses' employees always begin with the role of facilitators and coaches, but they wean themselves off that role during the course of the initial deployment. They have a rigorous train-the-trainer program, where the host company's training staff start by participating as reps;

then they coach, then shadow, then co-facilitate; then they do it with Ulysses staff observing; and finally they become certified. "We then certify a master coach to coach the coaches. And we certify master facilitators to coach the facilitators," Mark said.

"We improve the simulations," Mark concluded, "over the course of many client contacts. That keeps them cost-effective for clients, with predictable results."

TRAINERS AS TECHNOLOGY CUSTOMERS

I believe this model is mature, and many other simulation approaches would do well to emulate many aspects of it. But to make this case study complete, I do have to add one more thought from Ed: "The training managers can be the most challenging clients. Typically, they do not take risks. Their biggest motivation is not to get in trouble and not to spend money."

Ed continued, "For the training person, getting them to use technology required, not just hand-holding, but a full intervention. If anything went wrong, like the screen saver came on if they hadn't typed anything in a few minutes, they would call panicked. I would get phone messages like, 'Your program crashed. It is showing all of these weird graphics. What should we do?' My response was, of course, 'Try wiggling the mouse.'"

COMING UP NEXT

Want some proof positive that simulations work? So did I. And here it is.

26

THE BUSINESS IMPACT OF NEXT GENERATION SIMULATIONS

Simulations may work in practice, but they certainly do not work in theory.

WHEN WE WERE FIRST ROLLING OUT *Virtual Leader,* we knew there would be a lot of skepticism. People might be willing to believe that a soup can be eaten like a meal, or that it takes a tough man to make a tender chicken, but they sure weren't going to believe that you can learn leadership from what looked like a game.

We knew we needed to study the hell out of a few implementations. Here's one.

THE NEED FOR INFLUENTIAL LEADERS

The challenges at a division of a Fortune 100 company were typical. The groups needed to relate better across departments, achieve desired meeting outcomes, use time better, and build healthy relationships.

To create "influential leaders," the division heads brought in three elements:

- *Virtual Leader,* the off-the-shelf version of the leadership simulator from SimuLearn
- Corpath, a firm focused on executive coaching
- GEMA™-Lead360, one of the most rigorous 360-degree assessment tools on the market today

PROCESS

A 360-degree pre-assessment was conducted around the participants. The managers themselves, their peers, their subordinates, and their supervisors were given an extensive questionnaire about the managers' performances.

The managers were then introduced to *Virtual Leader* and were required to spend eight two-hour lab sessions on the simulator, broken up over four weeks. The labs were available twice a week, allowing flexibility for the managers, and were staffed with a Corpath facilitator to answer questions. Half-way through the lab sessions, the Corpath facilitator spent one-on-one time with each participant, reviewing the results of his or her original 360-degree assessment and putting it in context of his or her behavior in the simulator (Figure 26.1).

The participants "graduated" five weeks after they began the program. Then, six months after the program began (five months after the last contact), the managers again were assessed, both on business performance changes (something the organization rigorously tested) and on a second 360-degree evaluation.

Figure 26.1. The Calendar for the GEMA™-Lead360/ Corpath/SimuLearn Rollout.

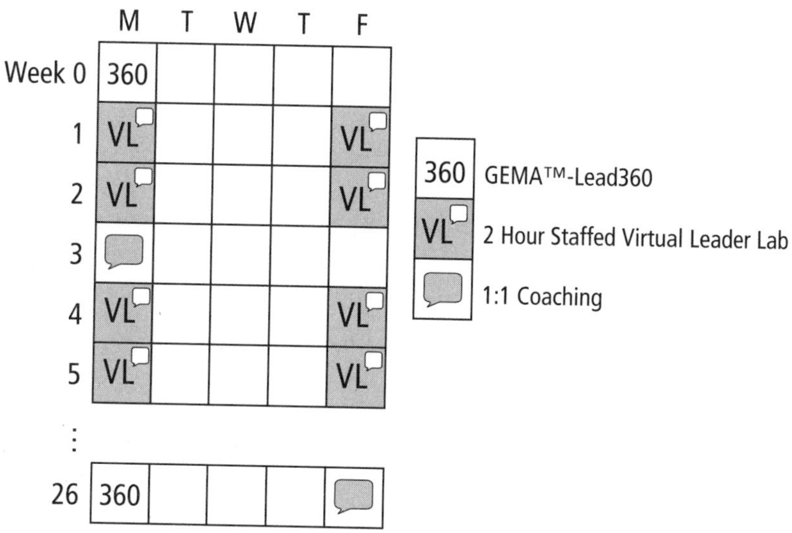

This process was designed for the group, not just to optimize learning, but also to meet their schedule and even to maximize the use of the physical environment. Many other approaches were possible.

AREAS COVERED BY GEMA™-LEAD360

GEMA™-Lead360 is well-known, not only for the rigor by which it analyzes results, but also for the predictive areas it covers.

GEMA™-Lead360 looks at dozens of *positive* behaviors, including:

- Achievement Seeking—Actually creates useful contributions
- Affirming—Seeks out ways to affirm others
- Encouraging—Actually helps others do better
- Enthusiastic—Has a positive attitude toward ordinary work activities
- Equality Seeking—Promotes the attitude for treating others as equals
- Leading—Masterfully creates organizational visions
- Nurturing—Makes earnest efforts to nurture others
- Persuasive—Is respectfully persuasive
- Responsive—Makes efforts to respond to others
- Task Centered—Creates activity that promotes meaningful work
- Thought Expressed—Tends to express thoughts and ideas

GEMA™-Lead360 also looks at dozens of *negative* behaviors, including:

- Action Suppressed—Appears to have little energy for ordinary work activities
- Action Suppressed—Avoids using energy for ordinary work activities
- Critical—Tries to control others with the use of criticism
- Detached—Avoids interacting with others
- Egotistical—Brags about own achievements as being superior to others
- Indifferent—Seems indifferent to ordinary work activities
- Intimidating—Tries to intimidate others with excessive self-importance

- Manipulative—Manipulates others for own self-serving advantage
- Revenge Seeking—Gets even; is quick to retaliate
- Ruling—Tries to be a ruler over others
- Self-Centered—Expects favors from others but does not return favors
- Thought Suppressed—Avoids expression of thoughts and ideas

RESULTS THAT ENDURED

The business results were significant. The participants who went through the coaching/simulation program improved their teams' relative performance rankings, on average, 22 percent. The measurement was a non-subjective metric on volume of successful client jobs completed.

Just as relevant was the way these managers got these results (Figure 26.2). Six months after the program, the increases in positive

Figure 26.2. 360-Degree Assessment, Pre- and Post-Simulation/Coaching.

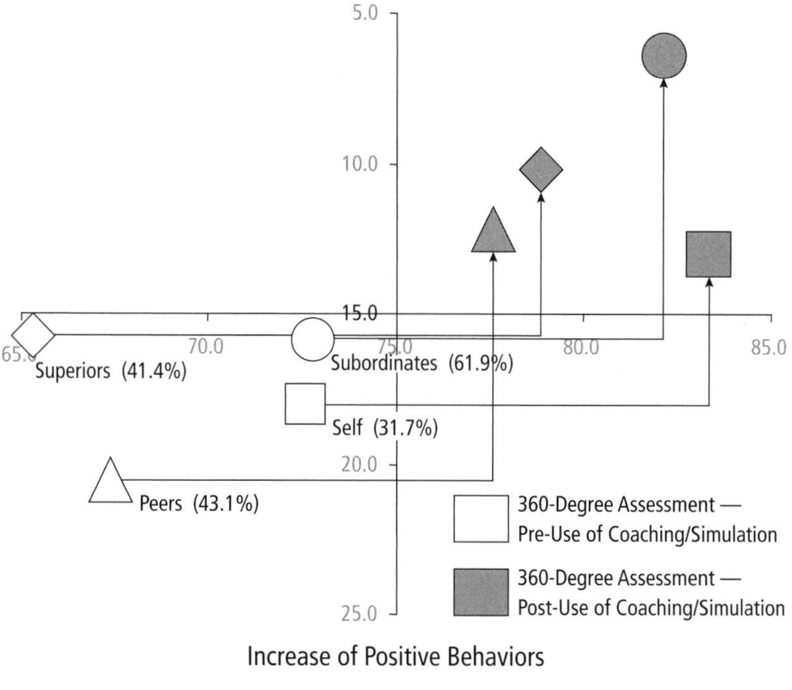

Source: SimuLearn Inc. Used with Permission.

Table 26.1. Analysis of Increase of Positive Behaviors.

POSITIVE BEHAVIORS—SERVICE BEYOND SELF				DIFFERENCE	%
		Pre	*Post*	*Scores*	*Increase*
Contribution	Self	69.2	81.1	11.9	17.2%
	Superiors	61.3	72.5	11.2	18.3%
	Peers	63.9	75.5	11.6	18.2%
	Subordinates	69.4	77.6	8.2	11.8%
Cooperation	Self	75.8	86.3	10.5	13.9%
	Superiors	65.2	86.2	21.0	32.2%
	Peers	68.3	77.0	8.7	12.7%
	Subordinates	71.8	82.8	11.0	15.3%
Connection	Self	72.6	82.4	9.8	13.5%
	Superiors	69.2	77.6	8.4	12.1%
	Peers	69.7	80.0	10.3	14.8%
	Subordinates	76.8	85.8	9.0	11.7%
	Average Increase				16.0%

behaviors (Table 26.1 above) and the cessations of negative behavior (Table 26.2) across peers, subordinates, and superiors were unprecedented in GEMA™-Lead360s fifteen-year history, including previous Corpath/GEMA™-Lead360 joint engagements.

PEERS, SUPERVISORS, SUBORDINATES, SELVES

To sum it up, the managers who went through the assessment/coaching/simulation program significantly improved their value to the organization, while strengthening their relationships with their peers, supervisors, and subordinates.

Simulations are hard. They force us to innovate. They are a challenge to create, and not the easiest things to deploy.

But the good news is that they work. And as we learn more and do more, they will work better than we can imagine.

Table 26.2. Analysis of Reduction of Negative Behaviors.

NEGATIVE BEHAVIORS—SELF BEYOND SERVICE				DIFFERENCE	%
		Pre	***Post***	***Score %***	***Decrease***
Superiority	Self	15.8	9.4	−6.4	−40.5%
	Superiors	12.8	7.8	−5.0	−39.1%
	Peers	21.6	10.4	−11.2	−51.9%
	Subordinates	13.2	4.6	−8.6	−65.2%
Domination	Self	16.1	13.6	−2.5	−15.5%
	Superiors	15.4	10.0	−5.4	−35.1%
	Peers	20.1	10.4	−9.7	−48.3%
	Subordinates	17.3	6.6	−10.7	−61.8%
Withdrawal	Self	22.1	15.9	−6.2	−28.1%
	Superiors	18.7	12.5	−6.2	−33.2%
	Peers	19.6	15.5	−4.1	−20.9%
	Subordinates	16.7	7.6	−9.1	−54.5%
	Average Decrease				−41.2%

COMING UP NEXT

Are *Life's Little Instruction Book* and *The Rise and Fall of the Roman Empire* more related than we thought? And what is the implication for, well, everything?

27

CONCLUSION

Scalable Skills (a.k.a. a Heapen' Helpin' o' Hype)

Globalization depends on an informed and educated citizenry.

—With apologies to Thomas Jefferson

THE DEFINITION OF EDUCATIONAL SIMULATIONS

So educational simulations are a variety of *selectively interactive, selectively representational environments* that can provide highly effective learning experiences. They do this in part by teaching cyclical and systems as well as linear content.

At the same time they include not only the pure modeling elements of simulations but two other elements:

- *Game elements,* to make the experience more enjoyable (or at least less tedious or frustrating)
- *Pedagogical elements,* to *set up* the experience by explaining the critical elements, to help *during* the simulation, and then *at the end* to explain what happened and how it ties back to real life

TEACHING IN NEW WAYS

But that is a definition only an analyst could love. In keeping with the spirit of futurists and visionaries everywhere, let us define simulations as well as tools for doing no less than completely transforming learning. What if students everywhere, in addition to just reading books, listening to lectures, and writing homework papers, truly engaged (and ultimately created) wondrous new environments?

HISTORY A student could play with history (Figure 27.1). He or she could have conversations with people across the ages. Different people would have different opinions about the same event, of course. But even the same person could have different opinions years later. And the student could share his or her own observations about the future, even lie about the politics and technology of our century to befuddle or incite various figures.

Or students could spend, for example, a day on an early New England farm, fixing the mill and delivering goods to town. They might make decisions: invest in growing the farm; maybe design the new barn

Figure 27.1. *Revolution.*

Source: A Role-Playing Game of the American Revolution from MIT's Game to Teach Program.

given the purpose and weather conditions; bring food scraps out to the three pigs, Pork, Chop, and Bacon.

Or students could "change" history. Teams could face off; one team could be officers in the Roman army and the other in the Carthaginian army. The winners could mix salt into the fields of the loser.

Of course, if history is changed, is it still history? And if history does not change, is it still a simulation?

Regardless, modding communities would be everywhere, building new models of tools, towns, and characters. Debates would rage about the exact shape of a tool or color of a garb. How easy to grow was the first wheat crop? And exactly what was its impact on quality of life or birth rate compared to the food before it? 6.25 or 6.37?

SCIENCE A learner could be a bat, seeing the world as blurs of radar images, trying to catch enough mosquitoes to stay alive. What happens when a neighbor sprays pesticides in the air?

We could see the heavens, switching perspectives between Newtonian and superstring. We could take a virtual walk in the woods, speeding up time or slowing it down, zooming in on microevents, or tracking energy. We could operate our own power of ten camera. We could add or subtract pedagogical layers on top of the oceans or the earth's mantle.

A learner could talk to Copernicus, arguing with him about his theories of planetary motion . . . or enter in a debate with some detractors.

MATH Students could exist in a world of pure math. They could play around with calculus. Fractions with common denominators could flow together. Angles could be bifurcated. Graphs and charts could be manipulated.

Squeak (www.squeakland.org), from Alan Kay's Viewpoints Research Institute, is a place to start. Squeak is distributed free, runs on multiple platforms, and is supported by an open source community.

Or math could exist as a pedagogical layer on top of the world. As a car drives, the graph of acceleration shows the relationship. Looking as a ball is flung into the air would invoke layers of graphs and charts. Pool tables could teach angles. This would be similar to taking a walk with a doctoral student in physics and listening to her describe the world she sees. Students could challenge themselves to create equations to match outside activities, either visually or sequentially.

ENGLISH Some people like to talk of simulations of great plays or novels. There will be some spectacular attempts that may just prove the case, and the best creative works will thrive on re-interpretation, not be insulted by it. The 3D simulation could be of participating in Huck Finn's world or of being a fly on the wall as Samuel Clemens wrote the book.

NEW OUTPUTS As simulations play out, doctoral students will create not just long research papers (linear content), but complex dynamic models (systems content) and a better, almost anthropological understanding of discrete steps in a current or historical process (cyclical interface). Homework output for all grades will just as often be in the form of mathematical spreadsheets and then artistic renderings of interface mock-ups and visualizations of interactions, not just a string of words.

One has to especially be excited for young boys in this new world. So many that I have seen seem hardwired to learn kinesthetically.

The Real Revolution

Various intellectual movements, such as Marxism and feminism, have sparked re-analysis of traditional material through new lenses. Now imagine the intellectual revolution as we pour through our collective annals and look at content through these new lenses.

New classes of scholars, scholarly works, and world-class institutions will be minted that successfully unpack, no, reconceive our libraries. Huge and gaping holes will be discovered in our views of our history to be filled by new waves of cutting-edge researchers (Figure 27.2). Imagine the energy and appeal of departments around the world that flourish in this area. Imagine their output. The waiting lists to get into these places will dwarf the Brown Universities of the world.

Linear content alone will become suspicious, the language of charlatans. The question will be "Why weren't the other content types considered?"

TEACHING NEW THINGS

The bigger revolution, however, will be when we use simulations to teach new things altogether, tasks that were previously unteachable. We will go from hunting, gathering, and evaluating critical skills (the role of HR and teachers today) to deliberately growing them. We will surface those new classes of professional skills that are neither vocational (such as woodworking, keyboarding, cooking) nor academic (existentialism, comparative literature). Or perhaps the most important skills will actually be both.

Figure 27.2. Rethinking Our Libraries' Content Through New Lenses.

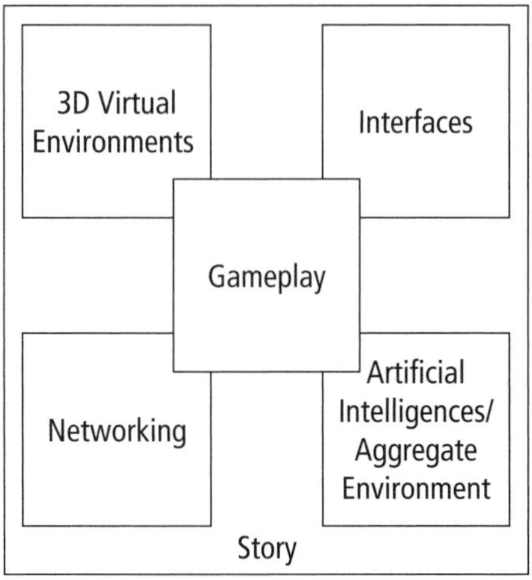

The technology clusters around the world spend billions to tweak infrastructures to increase productivity by 5 or 10 percent. Good educational simulations, as we are seeing, will increase productivity by 20 or 30 percent. Think of the corresponding bump in the standard of living.

At a personal level, right now, self-help books are a successful category, even though they probably don't do much good. Simulations will allow anyone to participate in *real self-improvement,* actually making themselves more productive, valuable, and in control. Personal areas for *self-improvement* that will become transferable include:

Communication	Creating and using boards and advisors
Creating new tools	Decision making
Innovation/adaptation	Negotiation
Nurturing/stewardship	Project management
Relationship management	Researching
Risk management	Security
Solutions sales	Sourcing/contracts
Teamwork	Turning around a bad situation

Simulations will also teach individuals how to better impact entire organizations (private, government, religious, non-profit, military), including how to better use strategies. *Enterprise strategies* that will now be transferable include:

Communication	Creating and using boards and advisors
Creating new tools	Decision making
Innovation/adaptation	Negotiation
Nurturing/stewardship	Project management
Relationship management	Researching
Risk management	Security
Solutions sales	Sourcing/contracts
Teamwork	Turning around a bad situation

TEACHING A LOT OF THINGS AT ONCE

"Hey wait," you may be thinking, "the individual and business skill lists are the same!"

At a strategic level, individual and business skills *are* the same. I will give you a few examples in a moment. But here's a much bigger thought: *Most of our cultural literacy, the hard-earned knowledge of the people who lived before us, if it hadn't been distorted by generations of the application of the incomplete lens of linear content, would also look like the lists of personal skills and business strategies.*

In fact, the destiny of next gen sims is to teach these professional skills, and to do so by simultaneously teaching content at three previously distinct layers (Figure 27.3).

Active Self-Improvement

Through well-thought-out interfaces and cyclical content, simulations deal with our *day-to-day activities* as both a microcosm and an analogy to bigger skills. A critical (and as we have said, under-appreciated) piece of any genre is the interface. Future simulations will tackle huge issues. But the interfaces will be inspired by some of the most common tasks:

- Write a letter or email.
- Conduct a one-on-one conversation
- Plan a meal
- Buy from the shelves of a supermarket or office supply store

Figure 27.3. Aligned, Recursive Skills.

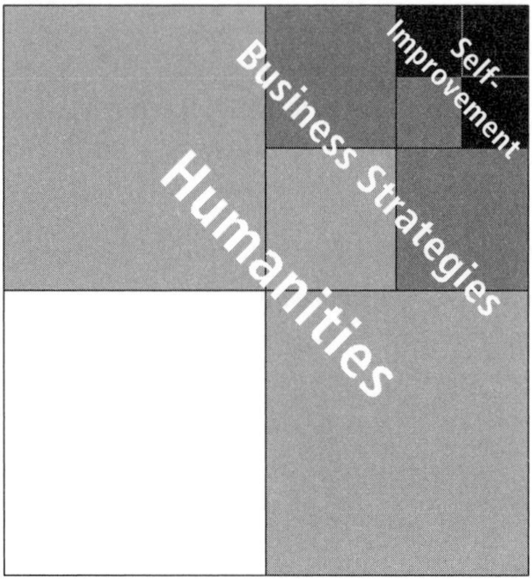

- Draw on a whiteboard
- Set goals for a team
- Decide to intervene or not in a situation
- Write a budget
- Plan one's day, week, or month
- Set up a home office

The good news is that this will eventually train us to add a layer of cognition on top of our daily tasks. When we go shopping for clothes, a computer, or dinner, we will be considering a lot more variables and impacts than we do today.

In the words of master genre creator Will Wright, "The interface is what makes the simulation accessible." He used a dollhouse interface for *The Sims*™ and a model railroad interface for *SimCity*™. This did not restrict the simulations (*SimCity*™ does not behave like a model railroad); it just produced an entry point.

The Systems of Enterprise Strategy

The interface will often focus on *individual skills*. But the *systems* that next gen sims will represent and teach are relevant for *enterprise strategies* as well.

As two examples, from a systems perspective, the activities of leadership (gaining influence, moderating tension, generating ideas, and getting work done) and branding (developing a consistent value proposition and emotional hook, reflecting the value and hook across all activities, updating as necessary) are the same for an organization as for an individual.

The Humanities

Finally, next gen sims will effectively tie to the greatest issues of academics, *The* Humanities, and that makes for a good and rewarding life by tapping the experiences of those who came before us.

BREAKING DOWN THE BARRIERS

In other words, *Life's Little Instruction Book* and *The Rise and Fall of the Roman Empire* might be closer relatives than we think.

Corporations, universities, even countries are starting to shift their perspectives. I have witnessed senior conversations from the Coronado Club to the Charles Hotel over the last fifteen years. Ever so slightly, I have seen the conversations move, from a point where this kind of thinking was impossible, to where it is beginning to seem inevitable. What we think of as content, education, and training is finally, and permanently, changing.

Breaking down the artificial barriers between what we learn and what we do, between business and academics, and between understanding history and controlling our future, simulation development will be a defining 21st century industry.

SECTION FIVE

APPENDICES

APPENDIX I

ALIGNING THE RIGHT INSTRUCTIONAL SOLUTION FOR THE RIGHT PROBLEM

The genre is the content.

—With apologies to Marshall McLuhan

LET'S MORE SURGICALLY UNDERSTAND where and why simulations fit. To do this we will need to zoom out and look at characteristics of most teaching and training programs. Here are some lists to treat like a walk around Idaho's Coeur d'Alene Lake. For the sake of time, you will have to move briskly past most spots, but stop now and then and really look around.

Sources of Training Initiatives (from Tactical to Strategic) (and a Good Place to Skim)

Every training program was started for a reason. Here are typical reasons why enterprises do educational programs, from least to most strategic (this is most assuredly not theoretical—I have worked in at least two cases with each of these):

- *Legacy:* The program has always been done.
- *Cut Budget/Consolidation:* One educational program is meant to cover five previous programs. Or cheaper online versions replace more expensive, classroom-based models.
- *Employee Survey:* Employees are unhappy about the training they receive.

- *Enabled by IT Infrastructure:* An organization has finished a rollout of computers and bandwidth, and now, because they *can* offer courses using technology, they *do* offer courses using technology.
- *Rolling Out a New Internal Offering:* A new application requires adoption by employees to be successful, and the training department is asked to make that happen (by the way, and I am sorry if this is out of line, but it really bugs me when the training department is called a *partner.* In this case, the use of *partner* means under-funded and overly responsible. Unless the training people were involved from the start making decisions, they are not partners but *subcontractors.* They should be able to negotiate for price, not just be stuck with what budget the developers didn't spend).
- *Customer Survey:* External customers are unhappy, confused, or not happy enough with their use of core offerings.
- *Merger:* Employees of the new, merged organization need to understand the new directions and begin to work productively with their new counterparts.
- *Weak Enterprise Results:* The enterprise cannot continue doing business as usual.
- *Rolling Out a New External Offering:* The enterprise is exposing salespeople, customers, and the service departments to dramatically new offerings, the successful adoption of which will significantly impact the bottom line.
- *Changing External Conditions:* Something happened, either by a competitor, public perception, or government mandate that changes the way we do business.
- *Long-Term Skill Gap:* The enterprise has realized that it does not have, nor will it bring in exclusively from the outside through consultants, new hires, and outsourcing, the skills it needs to compete and excel.
- *New Enterprise Direction:* The organization wants to proactively change its core offerings or value proposition.

Training Processes (in Order of Implementation) (Keep Skimming)

Different training programs require different processes for success. Here are some of the important processes to consider:

- *Project Management:* Fully track inputs, time frames, and outputs.
- *Alignment with Enterprise Strategy:* Develop a program to increase the success of an enterprise strategy through new employee behavior.
- *Needs Assessment:* Understand the skill gap between where the audience is and where the audience is expected to be.
- *Infrastructure Assessment of Mandatory Audience:* For everyone who needs to engage the program, understand their highest common denominator in terms of technology, availability, and geography.
- *Content Creation or Procurement:* Acquire the least expensive content that fully meet the needs.
- *Pilot Delivery:* Test the deployment of the experience with small groups representative of the training audience.
- *Pilot Assessment:* Use the pilot delivery to improve the deployment process.
- *Rollout Delivery:* Deploy the experience to all of the necessary participants.
- *Rollout Assessment:* Understand how successful the program was at cost-effectively meeting the requirements of the sponsors.

Training Results (from Tactical to Strategic) ("Miks" Is Skim Backwards)

Training initiatives and experiences are launched to accomplish results. Here are some of the typical possible results, from least to most strategic:

- *Completion Rate:* Increase the percentage of those who start the course and finish the course.
- *Cost Reduction:* Lower the cost of deploying educational experiences.
- *One Contact Point:* Decrease the places that people wanting educational experiences have to go to meet their needs.
- *Increased Access:* Increase the number of people in the enterprise who have access to educational experiences.
- *New Simple Process Behavior:* Enable participants to successfully and appropriately use new linear skills.

- *Customer Satisfaction:* Increase the satisfaction of target customers.
- *Lower Turnover:* Reduce the unwanted turnover of target employees.
- *Employee Satisfaction:* Increase the satisfaction and motivation of target employees.
- *New Intuitive Behavior:* Enable participants to successfully and appropriately use new dynamic skills.
- *Organizational Alignment:* Enable target employees, contractors, and vendors to better match their skills with each other, and against organizational goals.

e-Learning Content (from Tactical to Strategic) (Skiiiiiim!)

Content defines the educational experience. Here are some broad categories of e-learning content, from least to most strategic:

- *Course Libraries:* Hundreds of generic online workbooks.
- *Online Communities:* Bulletin boards set up to facilitate and organize conversations from users (Figure A1.1).

Figure A1.1. A Bulletin Board to Support an Online Community.

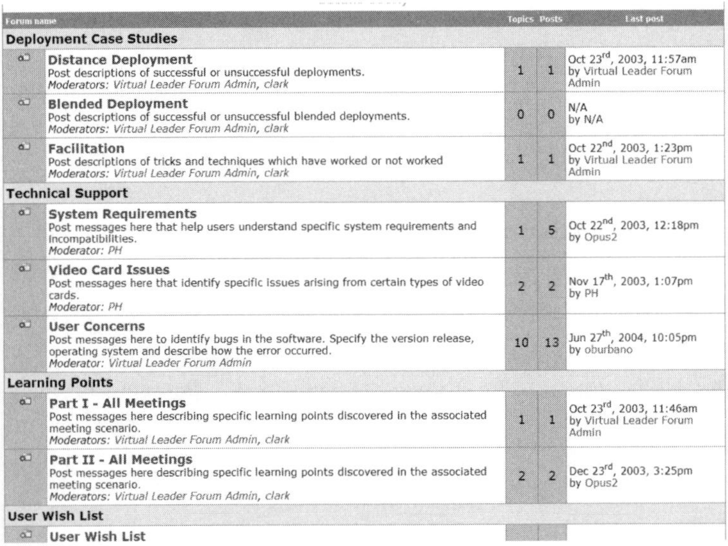

Forum name	Topics	Posts	Last post
Deployment Case Studies			
Distance Deployment Post descriptions of successful or unsuccessful deployments. *Moderators: Virtual Leader Forum Admin, clark*	1	1	Oct 23rd, 2003, 11:57am by Virtual Leader Forum Admin
Blended Deployment Post descriptions of successful or unsuccessful blended deployments. *Moderators: Virtual Leader Forum Admin, clark*	0	0	N/A by N/A
Facilitation Post descriptions of tricks and techniques which have worked or not worked *Moderators: Virtual Leader Forum Admin, clark*	1	1	Oct 22nd, 2003, 1:23pm by Virtual Leader Forum Admin
Technical Support			
System Requirements Post messages here that help users understand specific system requirements and incompatibilities. *Moderator: PH*	1	5	Oct 22nd, 2003, 12:18pm by Opus2
Video Card Issues Post messages here that identify specific issues arising from certain types of video cards. *Moderator: PH*	2	2	Nov 17th, 2003, 1:07pm by PH
User Concerns Post messages here to identify bugs in the software. Specify the version release, operating system and describe how the error occurred. *Moderator: Virtual Leader Forum Admin*	10	13	Jun 27th, 2004, 10:05pm by oburbano
Learning Points			
Part I - All Meetings Post messages here describing specific learning points discovered in the associated meeting scenario. *Moderators: Virtual Leader Forum Admin, clark*	1	1	Oct 23rd, 2003, 11:46am by Virtual Leader Forum Admin
Part II - All Meetings Post messages here describing specific learning points discovered in the associated meeting scenario. *Moderators: Virtual Leader Forum Admin, clark*	2	2	Dec 23rd, 2003, 3:25pm by Opus2
User Wish List			
User Wish List			

Source: SimuLearn.

- *Template and Documentation Libraries:* Repositories of custom tools and information to help employees and customers help themselves.
- *Virtual Classrooms:* Technology to facilitate same-time, different-location sessions, including an instructor, possibly an assistant, and a geographically dispersed class.
- *Stand-Alone e-Learning Modules:* Repositories of custom learning objects to help employees and customers help themselves, accessible through search engines.
- *Four Traditional Simulations:* Branching stories, interactive spreadsheets, game-based models, and virtual products and labs.
- *Embedded Help:* Learning objects proactively delivered at the point of need.
- *Strategic "Must-Take" Course:* Even a badly designed course, if taken by enough people with enough motivation, becomes unifying and relevant (partially explaining Dr. Phil). Great courses can leverage the network effect of content to significant advantage.
- *Next Gen Sims:* Highly interactive educational simulations that have the IT footprint of a modern computer game.

Education Infrastructure (from Tactical to Strategic) (Read This List Carefully—Just Kidding—S-K-I-M))

e-Learning content needs to be supported by some form of back-end infrastructure. Here are some broad categories of e-learning infrastructure, from least to most strategic:

- *Search Tools:* The ability to find the wanted content.
- *Portal:* The one place that links to all relevant content and infrastructure (Figure A1.2).
- *Authoring Tools:* The ability to create and modify content.
- *Learning Content Management Systems (LCMS):* The ability to organize and deploy content in learning objects.
- *Learning Management Systems (LMS):* The ability to enable the right person to take the right course in the right way, and to track the results.
- *Document Management Systems Integration:* The ability to draw from and write to an organization's document management system.

Figure A1.2. A Learning Portal with Classes, Progress, Tools, and News.

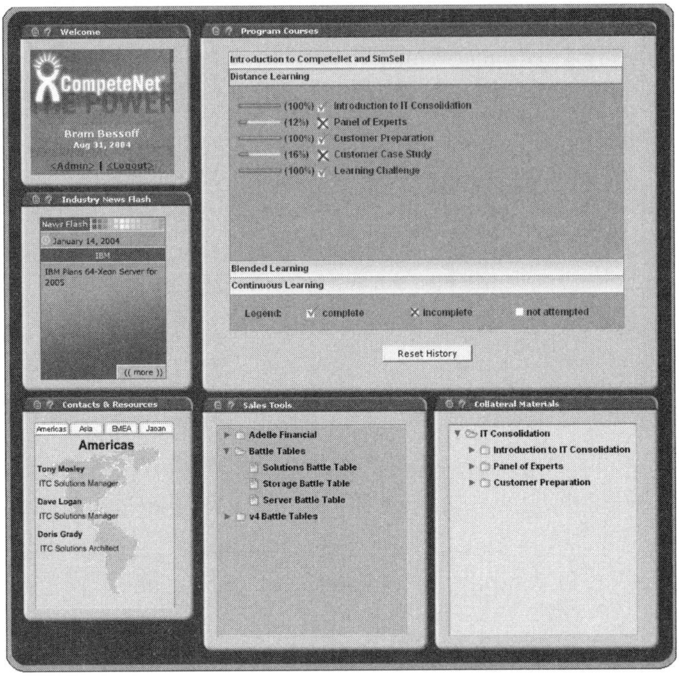

Source: CompeteNet. Used with Permission.

- *Enterprise Resource Planning (ERP) System Integration:* The ability to draw from an organization's ERP system, which tracks individuals and assets.
- *Customer Relationship Management (CRM) Systems Integration:* The ability to draw from an organization's CRM system, which manages the end-to-end customer experience to know which customers to train, and track their success.
- *Logistics Net Actuator (LNA):* Actually, I just made that one up.

Other Educational Content (from Tactical to Strategic) (Either Skim or Scan; Your Choice)

e-Learning is not the only relevant content, of course. It is not even the most powerful tool an organization has in this area. Here are some broad categories of non-e-learning content, from least to most strategic.

- *Magazines:* Well-illustrated, hype-focused publications that align people by professions, not organization.
- *Manuals:* Well-researched, but linear and confusing reference documents.
- *Videos:* Linear, visual, and scalable lectures or case studies.
- *Job aids:* Short, highly accessible, well-designed documents that provide quick access to frequently asked questions and procedures.
- *Lectures:* Live or recorded instructor-presented material.
- *Help Desk:* Accessible experts able to give personalized assistance in a narrow problem space.
- *Conferences:* Networking and information-sharing sessions, often live, but increasingly online as well (Figure A1.3).
- *Workshops:* Experts working with small groups in a traditional hands-on style to solve some real business problem.
- *Personal Action Plans:* Individual commitment and steps to improve one's skills and control to achieve an often pre-determined higher organizational status.

Figure A1.3. The Digital Detroit Conference.

Source: Author.

- *New Compensation:* Paying employees based on how well they meet very targeted and measured objectives.
- *Coaches:* Personal advisors who proactively challenge and upskill high-ranking or high-potential individuals.
- *Apprenticeships:* A lower-level employee works closely with a higher-level employee to understand how his or her job and the organization really work. In exchange, the apprentice is willing to take on menial tasks.
- *Skunk Works:* A group of people come together to solve a problem in a new way, drawing from a diverse and untraditional skill set. Skunks are optional. From conversations and personal experience, I would say that this represents the purest learning experience. Don't take my word for it. Try this experiment. As those who have done it know, riding with CEOs or politicians in private jets (or even a limousine) for more than fifteen minutes creates the inevitability for awkward dead time. This is all the more salient because even in the roomiest cabins, you are a mere few feet from your client for hours. If conversations go from business to chitchat, here's what I suggest. After weighing in on the obligatory vacationing comparisons (Rio de Janeiro versus Bangkok, blah, blah, blah), bring up the topic of what were *his or her* most intense learning experiences. Ten times out of ten, he or she will say it was some new project that no one had ever done before, or the revamping of a distressed group.

ACCORD (SKIM TIME IS OVER)

When I am air dropped in to evaluate any e-learning implementation, the most important thing I look for is accord. Given the results desired, are the right processes, content, and infrastructure being involved (Figure A1.4)?

For example, say an enterprise is rolling out a new internal offering; perhaps a benefits enrollment application. Let's call this, relatively speaking, a tier-two level of training. The goal is to teach a new simple, process-driven behavior, a tier-two result (Figure A1.5). Vice presidents care about this (by the way, not executive vice presidents, or even senior vice presidents, but plain ol' "we-used-to-call-them-directors" vice presidents).

Just putting out new templates and perhaps a chat room (tier-one e-learning content) would probably not be robust enough do the job.

Figure A1.4. Teaching Options (Super Jumbo Edition).

Results
e-Learning Content
Infrastructure
Other Content
Source
Process
End-Learners
Organizational Alignment
New Intuitive Behavior
Lower Turnover
Employee Satisfaction
Customer Satisfaction
New Process Behavior
One Contact Point
Increased Access
Completion Rate
Cost Reduction
Next Gen Simulations
Strategic "Must-Take"
Core Four Simulations
Embedded Help
Stand-Alone E-learning Modules
Template and Documentation Libraries
Virtual Classroom
Knowledge Management
Course Libraries
Online Communities
Search Tools
Authoring Tools
Portal
LCMS
CRM Integration
Learning Management Systems
Document Management Systems Integration
Manuals
Standards
ERP Integration
Magazines
Conferences
Job Aids
Videos
Workshops
Help Desk
Lectures
Skunk Works
Personal Action Plans
Apprenticeships
New Compensation
Coaches
Rollout Assessment
Rollout Delivery
Pilot Assessment
Project Management
Pilot Delivery
Content Creation or Procurement
Audience Assessment
Needs Assessment
Cut Budget/Consolidation
Alignment with Enterprise Strategy
Employee Survey
Enabled by IT Infrastructure
Customer Survey
Tactical
Weak Enterprise Results
Merger
Rolling Out New Internal Offering
Rolling Out New External Offering
Tier 2
Changing External Conditions
Long-Term Skill Gap
Tier 3
New Enterprise Direction
Strategic

Figure A1.5. A Tier-Two Solution.

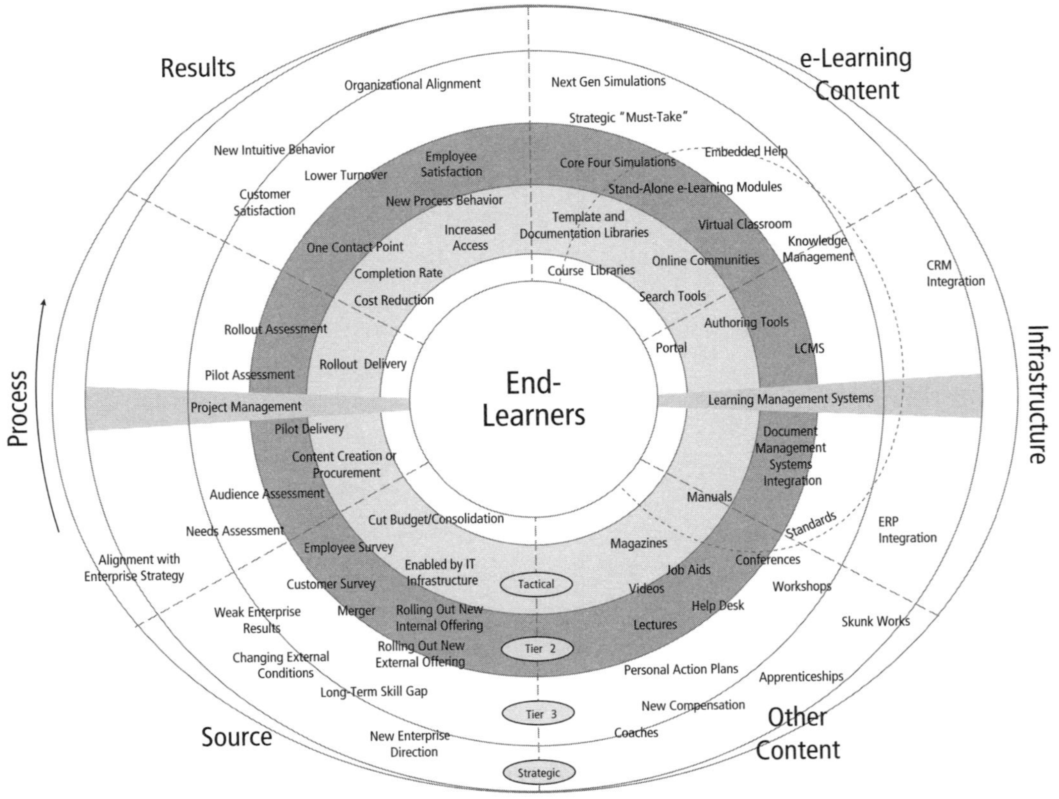

Results
e-Learning Content
Infrastructure
Other Content
Source
Process
End-Learners
Organizational Alignment
Next Gen Simulations
Strategic "Must-Take"
New Intuitive Behavior
Lower Turnover
Employee Satisfaction
Core Four Simulations
Embedded Help
Customer Satisfaction
New Process Behavior
Stand-Alone e-Learning Modules
Template and Documentation Libraries
Increased Access
Virtual Classroom
One Contact Point
Knowledge Management
Online Communities
Completion Rate
Course Libraries
CRM Integration
Cost Reduction
Search Tools
Authoring Tools
Rollout Assessment
Portal
LCMS
Rollout Delivery
Pilot Assessment
Learning Management Systems
Project Management
Pilot Delivery
Document Management Systems Integration
Content Creation or Procurement
Manuals
Audience Assessment
Cut Budget/Consolidation
Standards
ERP Integration
Needs Assessment
Magazines
Employee Survey
Conferences
Alignment with Enterprise Strategy
Enabled by IT Infrastructure
Job Aids
Customer Survey
Tactical
Videos
Workshops
Weak Enterprise Results
Merger
Rolling Out New Internal Offering
Help Desk
Lectures
Skunk Works
Rolling Out New External Offering
Tier 2
Changing External Conditions
Personal Action Plans
Apprenticeships
Long-Term Skill Gap
Tier 3
New Compensation
New Enterprise Direction
Coaches
Strategic

We would not expect to see the new simple, process-driven behavior catch on.

On the other hand, doing a detailed needs assessment, and using simulations and coaches (tier three), would be overkill. It would both cost too much for what we wanted to accomplish and take too long. A better response would be to use tier two and below across the board: a pilot to practice, virtual classrooms and lectures for content, supported by tier ones, such as new templates and chat rooms.

After you have identified the right tier, look at the processes, e-learning content, and infrastructure in that tier and the lower tiers. A tier-three problem will involve all processes from tiers one, two, and three. You may not want to waste your time on processes from higher tiers. The primary content (both e-learning and other) should be from the same tier as the results, but use lower tiers for support.

APPENDIX 2

E-LEARNING ARCHITECTURE CONSIDERATIONS TODAY

IN MOST CASES, implementing enterprises will have to assemble their own e-learning pieces, rather than buy one complete solution. They will have to painfully integrate different content (including simulations), different management systems, and manage the experience of a vast diversity of students. Furthermore, they may want to integrate their e-learning application architecture to the existing enterprise resource planning (ERP) and customer relationship management (CRM) applications.

CONTENT

Most content is delivered directly to the student. There are different types, and successful programs will involve more than one type of content, including traditional learning events (Figure A2.1).

The two most common types of e-learning content today are still workbook-style Web pages (Figure A2.2) and virtual classroom sessions.

Off-the-shelf content providers supply generic business and IT skills workbook-style courses. This allows companies to give up customization for lower price.

Custom content is workbook-style material built specifically for a given organization. It can be built externally, internally, or originally designed externally and updated internally. Custom content is also necessary when e-learning is used to support the strategic deployment of a new skill across an organization.

Off-the-shelf and custom content tend to have the same characteristics as other web-based content. It increasingly uses off-the-shelf plug-ins (although there are some exceptions).

e-Learning content creators can use virtually all general-purpose authoring tools, from PowerPoint® to Flash®. This is getting easier with every new release.

Figure A2.1 e-Learning Content.

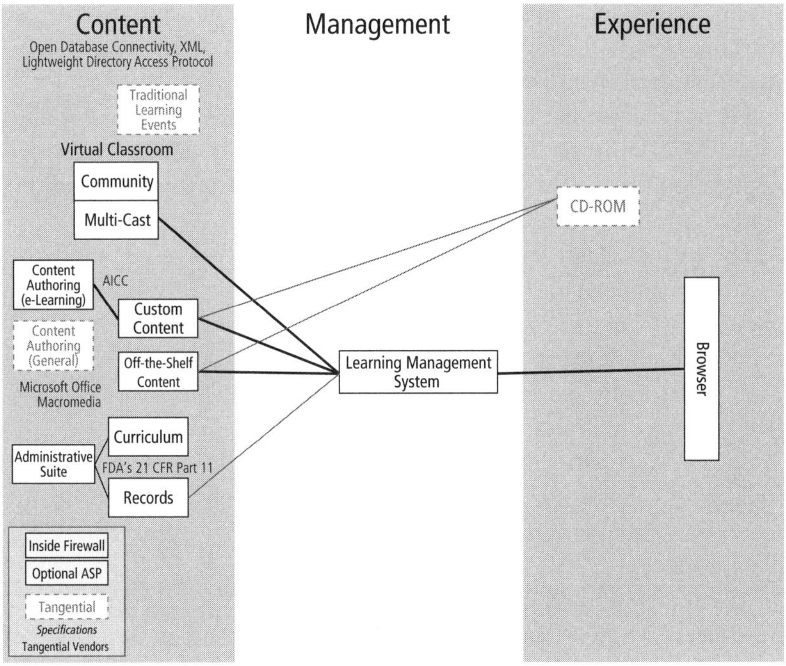

Figure A2.2. Linear Workbook-Style Content.

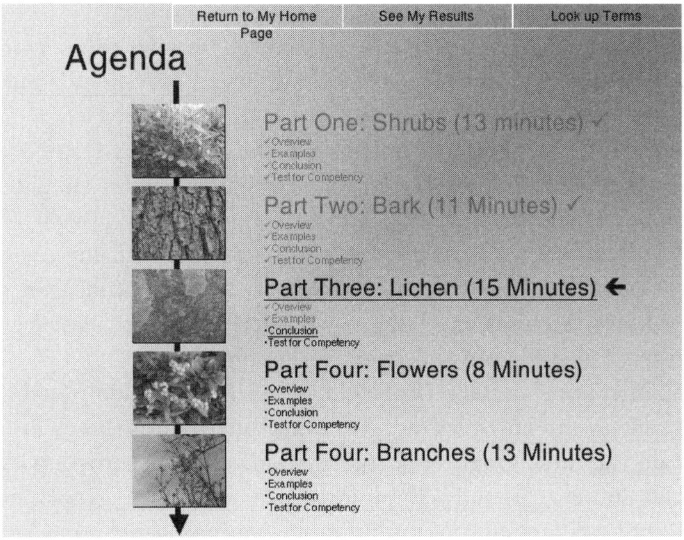

Source: Author.

However, e-learning has some specific elements, including testing and tracking, not found in general authoring products. Therefore, e-learning specific authoring tools may be necessary. Or organizations that use learning content management systems (LCMS) can add this functionality to standard web-delivered content instead.

Virtual classroom tools provide infrastructures for synchronous (same time, different location) courses integrating voices, slides, and application sharing, as well as authoring tools for capturing and editing sessions for future use.

The virtual classroom capability can be seen as both a multi-cast capability (to push the lecturer presenting to a group of students) and a community tool (for the students to talk and work among themselves). It is the vision of many of the virtual classroom vendors to expand both capabilities to become both a more productive telephone and interactive broadcasting medium.

At the same time, other tools, specifically in the community area, such as AOL's Instant Messenger and Microsoft's Messenger, are increasingly adding capability to compete head on with the virtual classroom vendors.

All content should be able to be launched and tracked through a third-party learning management system (LMS). And at least some of the content should be able to be edited and reassembled by learning content management system (LCMS) tools.

Often forgotten, there is another type of content, not designed for students. e-Learning also requires administrative content.

Curricula present, suggest, demand, or even prohibit courses for specific students. This meta-content can be changed directly by a member of HR or at the manager level.

One part of an enterprise curriculum can be a skills map—a database that specifies which positions in an organization should have which competencies in which skills. Skills maps can be bought off the shelf, but they will invariably need customizing. For many organizations, this effort of customization is a politically harrowing one, as all affected business units must weigh in and come to some agreement on necessary skill levels and collection methodologies.

Administrative content also includes records, including who took what courses and how they did. Any e-learning records should be automatically captured from the learning event. Other records inputs can include 360-degree and job-performance reviews, personal action plans, and satisfaction forms from non-e-learning-based content, such as conferences.

MANAGEMENT ISSUES

If the content is the cars, the management structure is the roads (Figure A2.3). In the e-learning space, there are two primary types of management systems: content management and everything else.

To handle everything else is the learning management system (LMS). Learning management systems have two big goals: to get the right content to the right person at the right time and to record the event.

Beyond that, they can be responsible for integrating and optimizing different learning channels and vendors, keeping track of costs, allowing students to search for content, and contributing to a successful skills management program.

Dedicated, content independent LMSs range from between $12 and $50 per user, with a minimum investment of around $20,000 and a cap at about $1,000,000 per year for most enterprises.

One decision is whether to use an application service provider (ASP) or to bring the LMS within the firewall. According to IDC, for issues of control and security, the majority of LMSs still reside on customer

Figure A2.3. e-Learning Management.

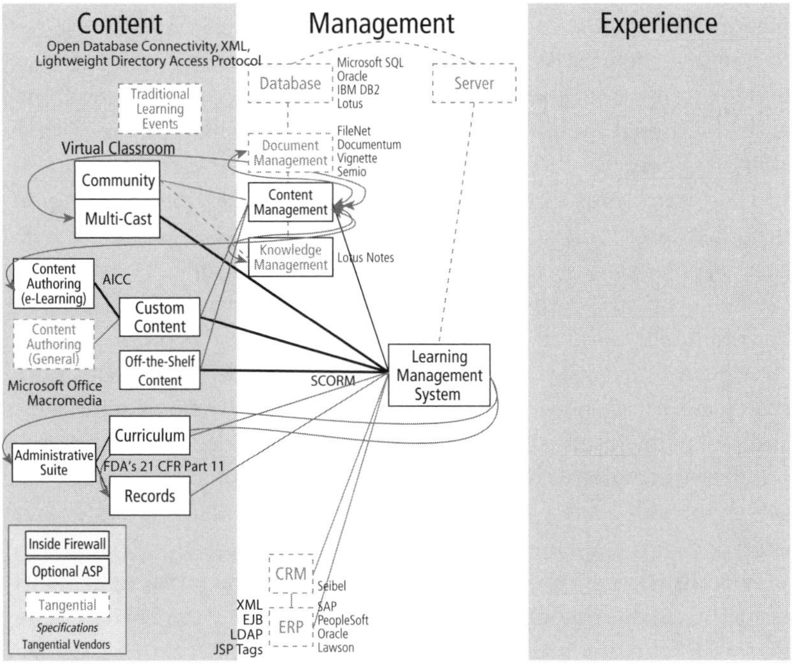

servers. The trend over the past two years, however, is that hosted systems have taken a significant share away from installed systems, a trend that is likely to continue.

One factor in this decision, and one of the biggest requirements (and costs) of an LMS, is integration with the rest of an organization's systems. There are many aspects to consider.

Unlike, say, an instant messenger-type application, e-learning has lost the battle for the desktop. Because so much content is Internet-based, e-learning has to be sought out, rather than be "in a user's face." To make content more immediate, using Outlook or any other calendar/mail program to schedule and link to content is critical.

Enterprise resource planners (ERP) vendors, including SAP, have been in and out of the LMS space since before there was an LMS space. The ERP vendors' original position was that an enterprise didn't need LMSs at all, since an ERP could handle all of the functionality. They were wrong, although they are getting less wrong every day.

Having said that, LMSs still need to integrate tightly with any ERP. Often, LMSs build a mirror database to the ERP, and synchronize it on a regular schedule.

While customers have always had to be trained, e-learning has allowed it to be ramped up and a strategic advantage. Customers can cost-effectively be trained before rather than after a sale, for example. Integration with a customer relationship management (CRM) tool streamlines the process.

e-Learning, to be effective, must be designed and coordinated with traditional training events. And even in an environment with no e-learning content at all, LMSs can play a critical support role.

Therefore, LMSs should manage classrooms and class times and certify classroom-learning events. For example, if a class is cancelled because of weather, the LMS should automatically reschedule the event, alerting the participants and reserving the appropriate space.

Traditional learning events (with associated LMS functions) include classrooms (manage certification, update attendee lists, send email reminders to attendees, manage resources); conferences (track times and costs); magazine subscriptions (track titles); videos (provide library functions including check-in, check-out); skunk works (track new skills); job aids (fax or send images on request); and help desk (provide contact information and frequently asked questions).

In contrast, learning content management systems are significantly more focused (although ironically can be more expensive). They store e-learning content to maximize its reuse. Many LCMSs also have additional (and inconsistent across vendors) other features, including:

- Easy-to-use search tools
- Easy authoring tools with extenders to Microsoft Office®
- Very powerful authoring tools for experts to build sophisticated content flows
- Links to material on peers' hard drives
- The capability to import, edit, and tag virtual classroom sessions
- Collaboration capacity
- Associated off-the-shelf libraries with editable content
- Capability for simultaneous web-based, paper-based, and CD-ROM/DVD output
- The ability to deploy content without the need for a specific LMS system

The hardest part about all management tools is that they need to be fluid. Some organizations spend resources to purchase and integrate everything as if they are building a permanent electronic edifice, the virtual equivalent of a brick-and-mortar university. A better mental model is closer to a television news crew, ready to set up at a moment's notice wherever new critical learning has to happen next.

LEARNER EXPERIENCE

Nothing matters until the student engages the content (Figure A2.4). This traditionally has happened through a browser.

Content that is accessed through the Internet tends to travel through a portal. The basic functionality of a portal has been to provide students with a verification process, a list of courses they can or should take and links to sign up for or launch the appropriate learning event. The LMS typically manages the portal.

Portal integration is expanding in at least two different directions. Within e-learning, portals are increasingly being able to launch an e-learning event without leaving the portal wrapper. For example, virtual classrooms and chat rooms can be initiated within a smaller window in the portal page. Outside of e-learning, portals are becoming more universal. In some organizations, learning data has to be imported into a third-party portal, where it is only one of many features.

Figure A2.4. e-Learning Experience.

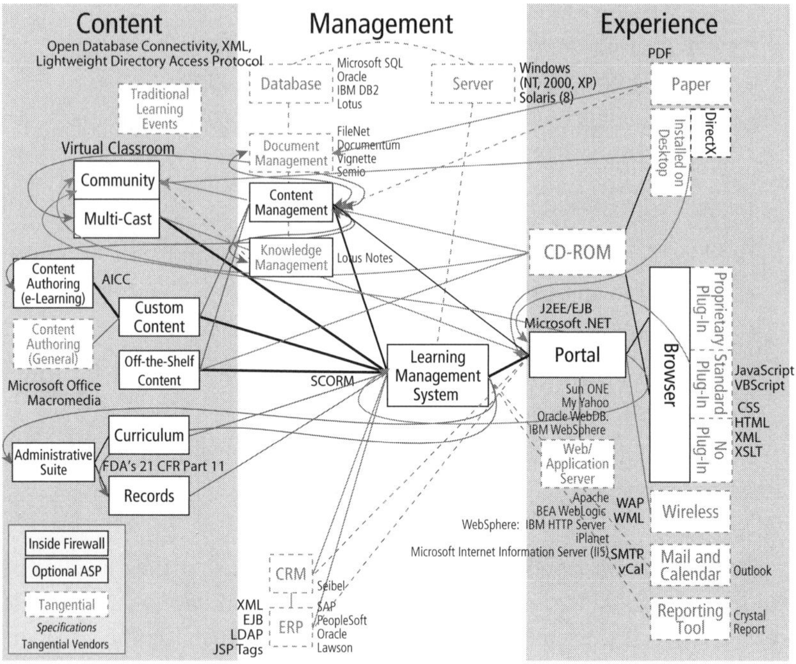

Portal security is often a bottleneck for the potential users of e-learning. e-Learning data is among the corporation's most valuable. It can contain lists of all employees, reporting structures, employee scores on tests, 360-degree review comments, and employee job ambitions. Meanwhile, for e-learning to be a factor in skills management, including hiring, firing, certification granting, or promoting, the results have to withstand scrutiny. Was the person who took the test actually the person who was supposed to take the test? Did cheating occur? Passwords provide some security, but biometrics and Web cams may be the next level. Without such tools, only tests taken in proctored environments can be trusted and legally defended.

For all e-learning content, many IT organizations have a goal of zero plug-ins. But the quality of content often falls below the threshold of effectiveness for most applications.

e-Learning applications that use industry standard plug-ins (such as Macromedia's Flash® or Apple's QuickTime®) can contain the best of both worlds. The interactivity is high enough to make the content relevant, and the burden on IT is minimal. Enterprise IT groups should consider making critical plug-ins standard (part of the enterprise image) to decrease variability and end-user frustration.

During the late 1990s, when the Internet was seen as a universal content and application distribution system, and network pipe capacity seemed to be growing exponentially, any software installed on a desktop was prohibited by the IT organization. Lock-down was thought to be the secret to effectiveness.

Tools such as Palm software have proven the business case for modifying that policy, especially with high-performance individuals. While still not preferred, installing e-learning content and applications at the desktop level can provide a richer student experience while freeing up networks for other business-critical applications.

With a messenger tool, such as those offered by AOL or Microsoft, the learning application resides on the desktop, although the content comes through the network. Dynamic help files, tightly integrated with a specific application, are installed with the application.

With simulations, the content resides directly on a desktop (even if the desktop is in a lab somewhere). Simulation with any kind of dynamic three-dimensional graphics will use the DirectX API. DirectX is a Microsoft API to access many of the graphic and sound capabilities of a desktop computer. It has to be installed separately on earlier operating systems, but Microsoft has finally included it natively in their XP operating system.

Even for content that can be streamed over the enterprise network, with the deeper understanding of bandwidth limitations, CD-ROMs are returning as a preferred method for distribution. This is especially powerful for content that does not have to be updated that often.

Finally, and ironically, paper remains a key output of e-learning. This is increasing as document management and learning content management are converging in some organizations.

THE CRITICAL ROLE OF CONTENT

e-Learning provides scale. But the desire to force every employee to only access dumbed-down content aimed at the least powerful computer and network connection assures bland content. It is much better to carefully segment your audience and do the most for each constituent, not the least (Figure A2.5).

Figure A2.5. Bonus: e-Learning Architecture Considerations Today Suitable for Framing.

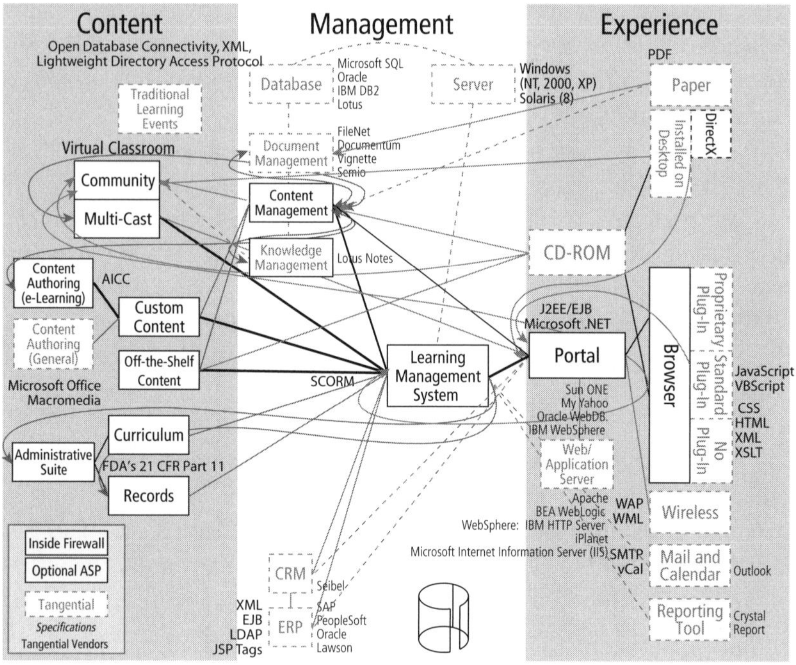

APPENDIX 3

TRADITIONAL CORPORATE SIMULATION VENDORS

MANY EARLY SIMULATIONS GREW out of a general introductory B-school curriculum, which themselves came out of military paper-and-pencil simulations. Business school professors authored them. Their use in corporations was similar to executive education programs. They were often for designated, "high-potential" managers. In most cases, the task is not to learn how to perform a specific business function, but "just in case," and to gain a better understanding of the entire organization.

Others, however, are designed for practitioners who will need to use the skills directly and even brush up or re-certify old skills. There is a higher premium on fidelity, at both the interface and functionality levels. This second segment is currently growing more robustly.

The simulation vendors look in many ways like the LMS vendors in 1995. They tend, with a few notable exceptions, toward smaller companies (Figure A3.1). They often are stronger in deep technical expertise than in marketing. They have, more than the broad libraries vendors, evolved around very specific vertical and horizontal segments. Any organizations looking at simulations should start as specifically as they can.

The X-axis in the figure organizes the vendors by vertical industries. The Y-axis organizes the vendors by horizontal experience and strengths. Square boxes represent branching stories; ovals represent interactive spreadsheets, and diamonds represent virtual labs.

Game-based simulations tend not to have a significant horizontal or vertical focus. They include:

- EGames Generator (http://egames.carsonmedia.com/online/default.asp)
- Games2Train
- LearningWare's Gameshow Pro Web (www.learningware.com/)

Figure A3.1. The Simulation Market Map (with Vendors Organized by Traditional Strengths).

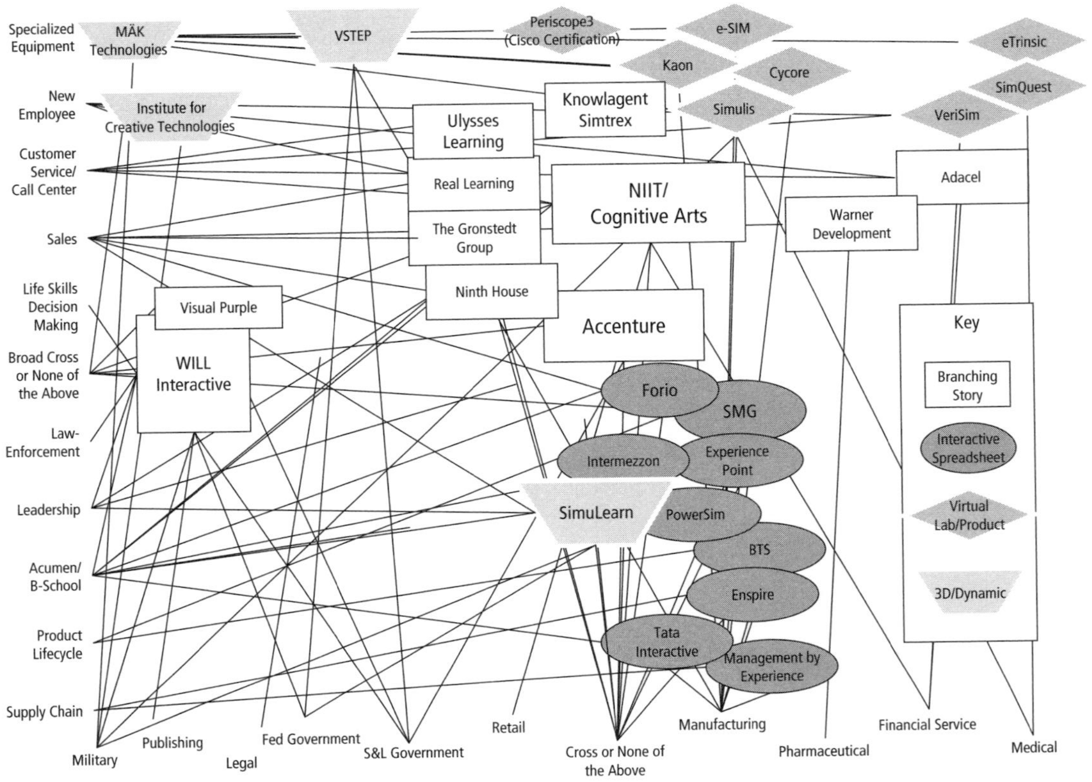

- Half-Baked Potatoes' Hot Potatoes (http://web.uvic.ca/hrd/halfbaked/)
- Interactive Games (www.oswego.org/staff/cchamber/techno/games.htm)
- QuizGame Master (http://cybil.tafe.tas.edu.au/~capsticm/quizman/qmhome.html)
- QuizStar (http://quizstar.4teachers.org/index.jsp)

Development questions to determine horizontal and vertical experience include:

- How many projects has the vendor accomplished in similar vertical industries in the last three years? What metrics were used?
- How many projects has the vendor accomplished in similar horizontal segments in the last three years? What metrics were used?

APPENDIX 4

ADVANCED TECHNIQUES FOR BRANCHING STORIES

WITH EXPERIENCE, clever designers are developing methods to increase the diagnostic properties and flexibility of the student's experience. Here are just some of the options.

Branching Stories to Generate Scores

Some, including developers from the University of Virginia's Darden School, have added score values to each of the nodes on the tree (Figure A4.1). That way, by the end of the journey, the students have not only arrived, but the simulation can also give them a score.

Some designers have added a timer, so that instead of being infinitely long at each branch, a default decision is made after, say, thirty seconds, unless the student inputs another option. This tempers one more significant criticism, the jilting start-stop that breaks up the ability to see patterns longer than one turn.

A Maze Piece

Some designers may introduce an *infinite maze* concept (Figure A4.2). The students have to maneuver their way through a highly defined, say, conversation. The students ask one wrong question, the onscreen character might say something like, "I am not following you. Let's start over again," and they are back to the beginning. The students have to keep trying until they get it right.

I have used this technique when I have had to reinforce:

- Applying defined processes
- Giving highly specific responses

Figure A4.1. Adding Scores to Branching Stories.

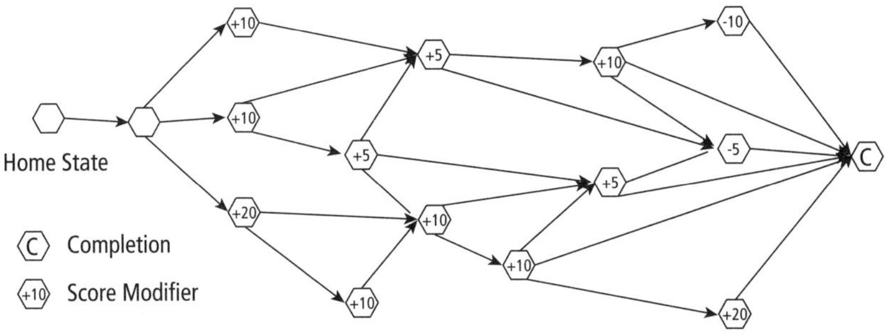

Figure A4.2. A Maze Branching Story Piece.

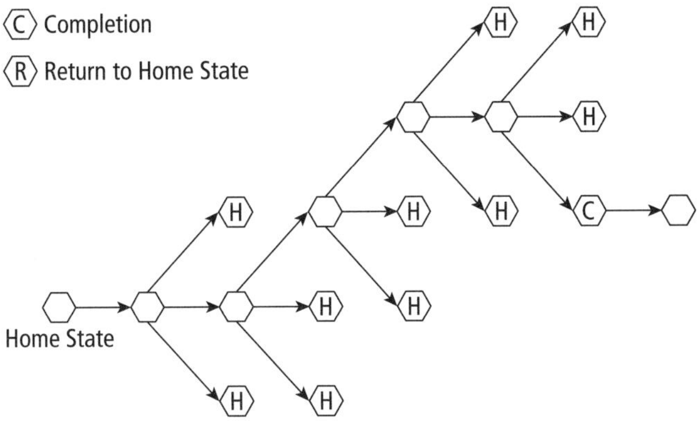

Gradual Feedback

Branching stories can give general performance trends as well. Figure A4.3 is an example that uses a persist "litigo-meter" to give students a longer-term feeling for how close they are to avoiding a lawsuit.

Saying Things in Your Voice

Some tricks are quite simple, but effective. Each branching option does not have to go to different locations. Sometimes, two or more options can lead to the same response (Figure A4.4). This can be used to increase the impression that the student is saying things exactly (or at least more closely) to how he or she wants. This can also keep the student involved during some longer information-dumping stretches.

Figure A4.3. The Persistent Meter (Upper Right) Gives Learners a Bigger-Picture Sense of How They Are Doing.

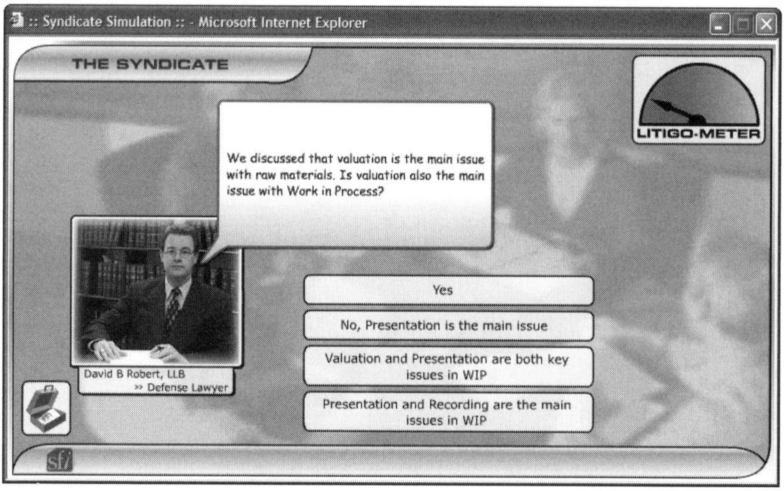

Source: SmartFirm Inc. Used with Permission.

Figure A4.4. Your Own Voice.

Another technique is not to give the student exact quotes from which to choose. Instead, they choose the strategy and the intent (Figure A4.5) and let the simulation pull the quote. This makes sense when, and only when, the learning objectives are around ideas, not key phrases.

Really Saying Things in Your Own Voice

Of course, one way for the students to really say things in their own voice is to record themselves through a connected microphone. In Gitomer's sales training simulation, rather than given a multiple-choice question, the salespeople have to record themselves. Then they are given multiple-choice options to identify which of the quote most resembled theirs. The salespeople in training next receive feedback as to the relative strengths and weaknesses of their approach.

They can redo their quotes if they want and also drill down further through a branching structure organized not as an ongoing story but as specific coaching. Finally, the sound of the voice is saved for their managers to review.

Figure A4.5. Chose Intent, Not Quote.

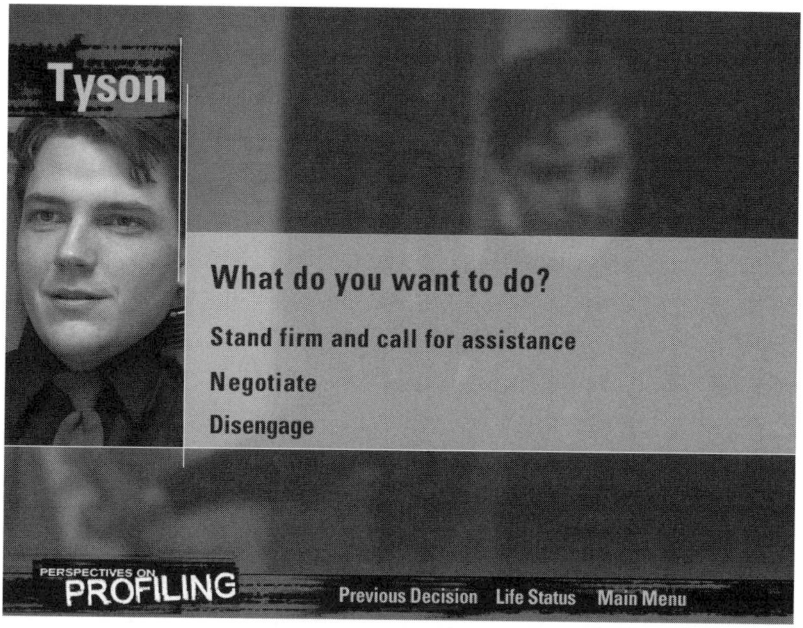

Source: WILL Interactive. Used with Permission.

Getting the Back Story

Another technique is to allow students to get more back story/background if they want, but to forge right on ahead if they don't (Figure A4.6).

This might look like:

> You clear your throat and Chester looks up at you. You say:
> (A) "How long have you been smuggling Ossetra caviar?"
> (B) "Never mind."

Figure A4.6. A Background Information Branching Story Piece.

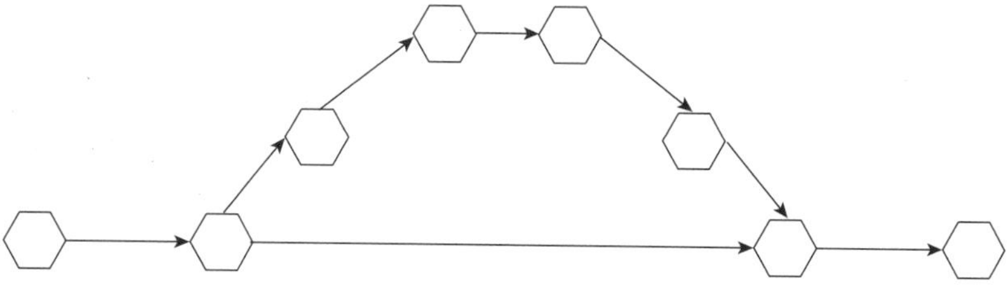

Shades of Gray

It is more art than science to get the options right. Branching story designer Matthew Sakey gives a good example of the necessity for and the power of subtlety. "Our target was systemic, recidivist felons who had expressed genuine desire to reenter society in a law-abiding capacity," he explained. (I later found a dictionary that actually had the word *recidivist* in it, and learned that it referred to a repeat offender.)

In the simulation, the inmate, upon his virtual release, would check in with his parole officer and get an apartment. Then he had to find a job.

Mathew and his team wanted to avoid the limited and obvious choices far too common in branching stories. For example, when asked, "Why do you want to work in my restaurant," the student is too often presented with blatant choices such as:

(A) Because I love the fast-food business.

(B) Because I want money.

(C) I don't. And I think I'll kill you!

"But if the potential answers are too discrete," Matthew notes, "you're not 'role playing' at all; you're choosing the answer that is most likely to return a favorable result."

Matthew explained, "Our challenge was to force the users instead to seriously consider several reasonable answers. Then they could choose the one that they felt was most suitable in both the context of the situation and of their own nature."

Thus, when asked by a work-release manager. "Why do you want to work in my restaurant," Matthew's available responses looked more like this:

(A) I worked in the kitchen during my time in prison, and I became comfortable with the process. Since I already know a great deal about volume food service, it seemed like a good choice to begin my career after parole.

(B) In an environment like this, employees generally have a variety of tasks and responsibilities. I prefer that method of working to others. I'm more comfortable doing a number of things than I would be, say, operating a single machine all day.

(C) I like the flexible hours and the wage that's being offered. I'm so used to a strict routine that I think it would be helpful to try something that is more flexible, so I can get used to the way life works outside of prison.

(D) My parole officer gave me a test and recommended this business for me based on its results. I just want to get started doing something, and this seems like a fine opportunity and pretty good pay.

(E) I can walk here from where I'll be staying, and it's also convenient in other ways: I already know how to use some of the equipment, I've worked in food service before, and some of my friends already work here.

Now, of those five, there are some responses that are clearly inferior to others, but none are wrong answers. Or rather, none are so blatantly wrong that they'd be dismissed out of hand by a serious player and chosen as a way to devalue the experience by a player who had lost interest in the game. There are also no answers so obviously superior to others that only a fool would choose something else.

The Answer Changes

One of my history professors, Dick Jeffers, said that over his twenty years of teaching American history, his test questions always stayed the same. But, he added, the right answers changed every year.

Jacob Stahl, a director of sales training and development at Purdue Pharma, put that observation to better use. His task was to teach salespeople *to be aware of the different expectations of the doctor* with whom they are trying to communicate. For example, their approach had to be different whether the doctor wanted a bottom-line approach or wanted details of trials or benefits to the patient.

So *the salespeople encountered the same ten choices of conversation starters* for each doctor they encountered. But which four or five were right depended on which doctor, with clues to their personality being suggested by his or her dress, office style, reading material, and other clues.

The Long Interview

CompeteNet and other branching story designers use an extensive series of interviews as the organizing structure of their branching stories. Also aimed at the sales process, CompeteNet presents students with a series of conversations with individuals, pairs of people, and full industry panels, ranging from decision makers to merely useful (Figure A4.7).

Critically, the learners start with only a limited number of questions to choose (they might initially be allowed six questions out of the possible nine showing). These questions become a type of currency.

Figure A4.7. Interviewing a Panel, Choosing the Right Questions.

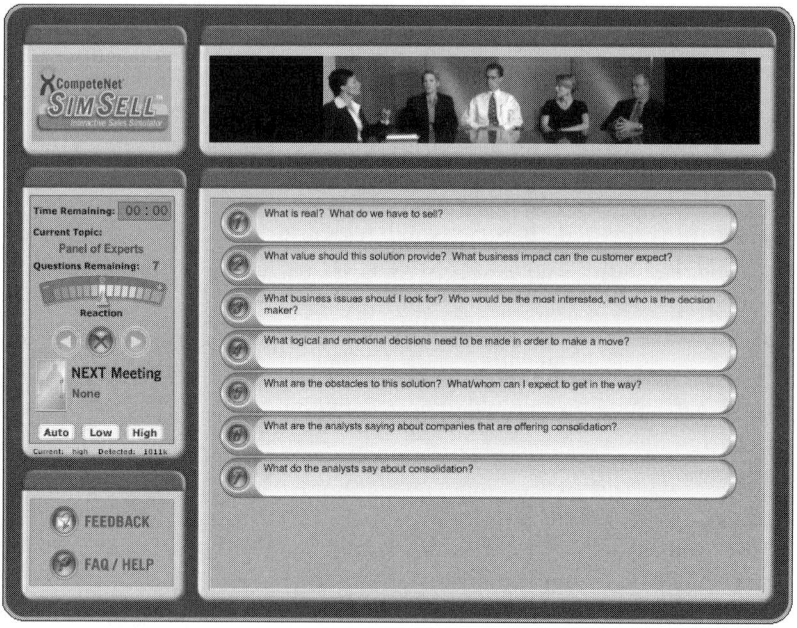

Source: CompeteNet. Used with Permission.

Each question reaps a response from the individual or panel that can:

- Give key information that will be important in this or subsequent conversations
- Add or subtract hidden points from categories like *trust, respect, and likeability* that will, when certain culminations are reached, unlock new questions and/or change the responses to existing questions
- End the meeting abruptly
- Open up or close down subsequent meetings with other key individuals (Figure A4.8)
- Open up or close down other questions
- Increase or decrease the number of allowed questions
- Make the sale

Or, of course, the question can be useless. Rather than giving just a few options at a time, CompeteNet's Bentley Radcliff likes to give most

Figure A4.8. Wisely Choose One of Five Potential Conversations on the Path to the Sale.

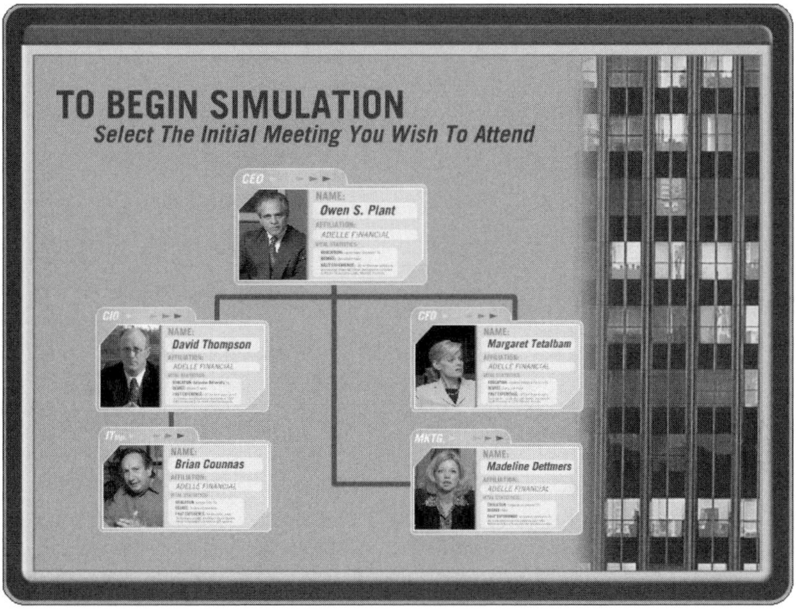

Source: CompeteNet. Used with Permission.

of the options up-front and have the learners organize and prioritize the options themselves.

There is also an assessment module. The onscreen characters turn the table and ask the student pointed questions. Their responses can again change the tone of the conversation, as well as opening up and closing down options.

APPENDIX 5

ADVANCED TECHNIQUES FOR INTERACTIVE SPREADSHEETS

THE ORIGINAL INTERACTIVE SPREADSHEETS STARTED very simply. They were often created on a text-only CRT mainframe node by a tenured professor using only a handful of relationships they might have programmed in using FORTRAN or (heaven help us) BASIC (again, if any of these terms are unclear, ask your parents or grandparents).

The relationships that the professors chose to model, and the actual values ascribed, were originally designed to rigorously simulate existing case studies. Invariably, the relationships were modified a bit over time to make the experience more engaging or exaggerated.

The Beer Game, developed by MIT in the late 1960s and described decades later in Peter Senge's *The Fifth Discipline,* may be the most famous multi-player example. Even today there are multiple online versions available, including at Forio and Darden's School of Business. In it, students play the roles of manufacturers, distributors, and retailers of a brand of beer. Inevitably, because most players think linearly, small bumps in demand are magnified and potentially bankrupt two or all three of the roles. (The system is nicely modeled in Figure 7.1.)

Today, innovators are still adding layers of thinking and new mechanics to this medium to increase their power. Richer diagnostics, deeper turns, and alternative allocations, described below, are just some of them.

Richer Diagnostics

Some designers, including myself, have added even more diagnostic capability by adding not just a one-dimensional trigger at a given interval, such as described above, but a two-dimensional *table-based trigger.* The simulation looks up not only *where the player is,* but also *where the player was a few turns ago.* For example, if number of customers is much lower than number of customers three turns ago, then the simulation would play a message carefully and delicately, always politically correctly, saying something like "Wow, your number of customers has really tanked in the last two weeks. You are a loser. Yeah, A LOSER! No, you are. No, YOU ARE!"

A Deeper Turn

Bjorn Billhardt is the soft-spoken CEO of Enspire Learning. He sees each turn as an opportunity to include multiple elements, and force more student thinking.

"The first part of a turn," he explains, "is reviewing the results from that last turn. This can include the obligatory charts, and possibly a media clip. Next comes a strategic decision. Do you hire candidate A, candidate B, or candidate C? Do you produce model X or model Y of a new product?

"Then the allocation decision comes, made in the context of the strategic decision. How do you want to compensate your new hire? How much of model X or model Y do you want to produce? Finally, there is the production room. Here the student get a series of updates, every week or every month, depending on the simulation" (Figure A5.1).

The students can make slight changes, based on feedback they are getting. But any change, and especially a big change, will cost a lot. At that point it is extremely expensive to reverse course.

The purpose is to let students make mistakes and get into a trajectory that is not what they wanted. That is where a lot of the very painful lessons are learned.

Alternative Allocations

The decisions in interactive spreadsheets traditionally are around allocating money and inventory. Bjorn also describes other allocation decisions.

FINITE RESOURCES "Anything that is a finite resource is a candidate," he commented. "For a sales simulation, the precious resource is time. You only had so many hours. You could not pursue all of the customers you want to. You could also meet with more customers and be less well prepared, or fewer and be more prepared. And even if you have a lot of potential customers, you still might want to get more, or better ones."

Figure A5.1. The Production Room from Enspire's Global Supply Chain Management Interactive Spreadsheet.

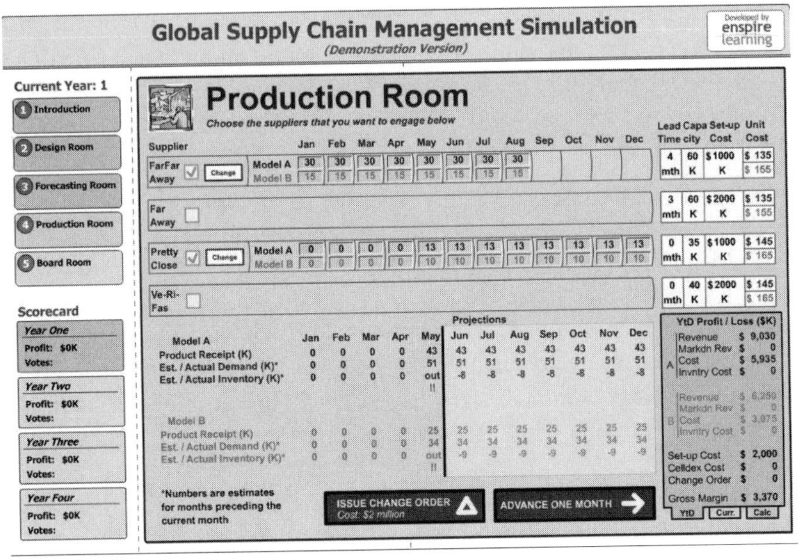

Source: Enspire Learning. Used with Permission.

EMPHASIS A good example of a non-traditional resource is *emphasis.* A CEO of a nonprofit organization could put emphasis on fundraising *or* networking *or* building a volunteer base.

Feedback Moments

Another opportunity for enrichment is the feedback moments. Rather than just showing a graph or static media clip, some interactive spreadsheets, like a good Cuban cigar, force deeper opportunities for reflection.

In Enspire's *Global Supply Chain Management* simulation, you have to worry about board votes. Every year, the board members either vote for you or against you, depending on your performance in areas that they care about.

In some points, if a member is on the fence, he or she might ask the learners some pointed questions. Support hangs in the balance, based on the responses. Bjorn explained, "One board member might be risk-adverse. You can decide to pursue a risky strategy, accepting the fact that you will not have that person's vote."

VARIATIONS

As with branching stories, there are some interesting variations on interactive spreadsheets worth noting. And this list is by no means complete.

Airline Financials

One airline used interactive spreadsheets in a novel and highly appropriate way. They were faced with having to cut benefits after 9/11. As part of their communication plan, they built and distributed an interactive spreadsheet of their organization's financial condition. They asked their employees to play around with the numbers and see if they could figure a way out of their financial crunch without taking such drastic actions.

The airline did in fact cut the salaries. Nobody was happy about it, but through the distribution of the financial spreadsheet, there was more of a feeling that everybody was in this together, looking for solutions.

Board Games

Paradigm Learning has captured many elements of interactive spreadsheets into a board game model. This simulation-that-looks-like-a-game uses cards, facilitators, look-up tables, and playing pieces to replace the numbers and computations of their onscreen counterpart.

Paradigm compresses the programs into one-day sessions. The morning is spent engaging the simulation, and the afternoon is spent tying it to real life. While dice and event cards may seem like *game elements,* they can be just as appropriately used as *simulation elements.*

APPENDIX 6

GETTING WHAT YOU WANT

The Black Art of Customizing the Four Traditional Simulation Genres

READY? ANY SIMULATION, including branching stories, interactive spreadsheets, game-based models, and virtual products and virtual labs, must be able to be efficiently customized. There.

That is a very easy statement to make. And we all have a pretty good intuition about the concept of customizing, right?

But here's the tricky part. Our instinct around customizing content is genre specific.

Let me explain. Because believe it or not, dozens of very smart chief learning officers (CLOs) and chief information officers (CIOs) completely miss this point.

Consider these offensively obvious examples:

- We know what efficiently can be customized in a car: sound systems (Bose with speed-sensitive noise compensation), seat materials (pebbled leather), or color (titanium gray metallic), as examples.
- We know what efficiently can be customized in a new suit: buttons (horn), material (hopsack), pleats (not), cuffs (yes), and dressing (to the right).

So understanding what can be efficiently customized in a simulation genre is *sine qua non* to understanding the simulation genre. It both opens up and restricts what the simulations can do and how we can use them well.

TOOLKITS AND REUSABLE LEARNING OBJECTS

In some circles (especially in the Bay Area, parts of Seattle, and a certain hotel bar in New Delhi), it is impossible to talk about any type of e-learning content without putting it in context of two concepts: *toolkits* and *reusable learning objects.* Amazingly, when in Tampa, these issues are not so important.

Toolkits

Generically, *toolkits* are authoring environments for effectively building specific types of content. They tend to span from enabling you to quickly build relatively generic content to enabling you to more slowly build more customized material.

A common example of an easy-to-use *toolkit* is Microsoft's PowerPoint®. The good news is that if you only have four minutes to create an hour-long presentation, you can do it. The bad news is that most PowerPoint presentations tend to look pretty much the same.

Macromedia's Flash® *toolkit* trades off less ease of use for the ability to create content of higher variety. It strikes a perfect middle ground for many developers. Visual Basic® is another great compromise for fast development.

At the other extreme of toolkits is the concept of *programming languages.* These enable you to very slowly (very, very slowly) build highly specialized content (Figure A6.1).

Figure A6.1. From Authoring Toolkits to Programming Languages.

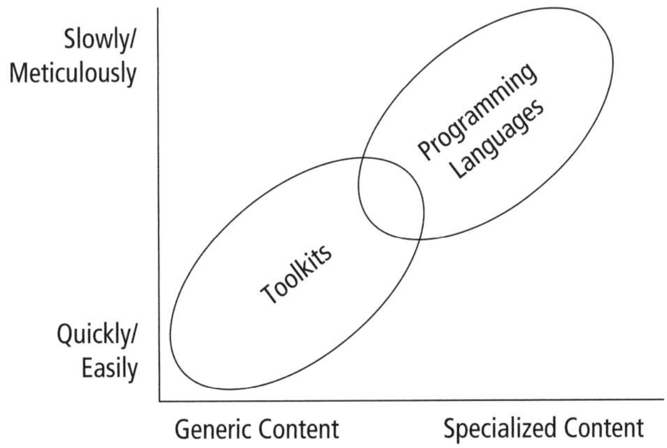

Programming *languages* include Pascal, C, C++, and the perennial favorite of bit-flippers everywhere, Assembler. They add even more flexibility, at a much greater cost of specialized knowledge and time (Figure A6.2).

Here's a rule of thumb: The easier a toolkit is to use, the less flexible and more genre-specific it is.

Toolkits as a Business Lever

In the real world, the word toolkit conjures up the image of using real tools to build real things. For example, if you were building a watch, you would use a broach to enlarge the tapering holes, or a bench key for fitting the arbours.

In the computer world, however, toolkits and programming languages are closely associated with specific environments. You can build a presentation in PowerPoint, but it can only be accessed, viewed, and edited in the PowerPoint environment.

As a result, from a vendor perspective, toolkits go beyond allowing you to build something. They are powerful business models.

If all of the moons align, a great toolkit can give the vendor near-total control of the standards around an entire category of content. Look again at Microsoft with Office® documents.

Having said that, it does not always work. There are numerous examples of toolkits reaching the market too early, such as the artificial

Figure A6.2. From Authoring Toolkits to Programming Languages: Examples.

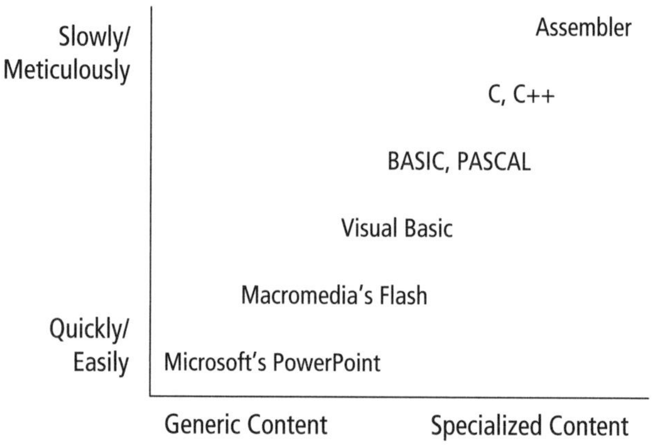

intelligence toolkits of the 1980s. Businesses didn't have the skills to use them effectively (imagine a room full of staffers or doctors trying to figure out how to train a neural net), and the vendors disappeared.

Reusable Learning Objects

Reusable learning objects are small pieces of reusable e-learning content. The term learning objects comes to us from two places.

First, learning objects can be two- or three-minute mini-courses. This simple premise had vast implications for all formal learning.

- People learn primarily how to do specific, well-defined tasks.
- Users could test out of pieces of courses they already knew.
- As systems evolved, users did not even have to bother with signing up for a formal course. They could search for and find only the mini-courses they needed.
- With a bit more evolution, learning portals could proactively serve up a customized dynamic curriculum that varied significantly by the activities of the day.
- Finally, the course objects themselves could be embedded into the point of need, merging seamlessly with the interface of an application or a PDA.
- They can line up to learning objectives. Thanks to the early and far too influential work of Robert Mager, almost every book on designing instruction and curriculum states: "Clearly identify the outcomes or actions participants can expect to demonstrate as a result of the educational experiences. Use an action verb at the beginning of the objective and don't EVER use the word 'understand' because it can't be demonstrated."

Second, learning objects are *elements* within a course. For the sake of customizing simulations, we will use this second definition. They could be logos, video clips, text from speeches, XMLs, addresses, graphics, or 3D objects, as long as a course designer could easily reuse them between courses.

They could also be so designed that once a change was made in one place, the new information would cascade to all content that used it. If the marketing people could change the color of your corporate logo to a slightly darker blue, you would only have to change it in one place to change it in all of the courses.

The *technology* of the learning objects comes generally from the move to object-oriented programming, and specifically from expatriates from Oracle and Sybase that flooded into e-learning in the late 1990s to form companies that produce learning management systems and later learning content management systems (so named to hopelessly confuse industry outsiders).

Architecture

Both e-learning-specific and broader authoring tools create learning objects. They are often stored in some type of content management database (Figure A6.3). Ideally, they are assembled as they are being delivered to the user.

Breaking Free of our Default Genre

So what's the problem? What is the rare insight that so many learning professionals have missed?

Here it is. *The Web has become e-learning's default genre, whether you wanted it to or not.* This is so pervasive that e-learning toolkits are

Figure A6.3. Learning Objects Architecture Considerations.

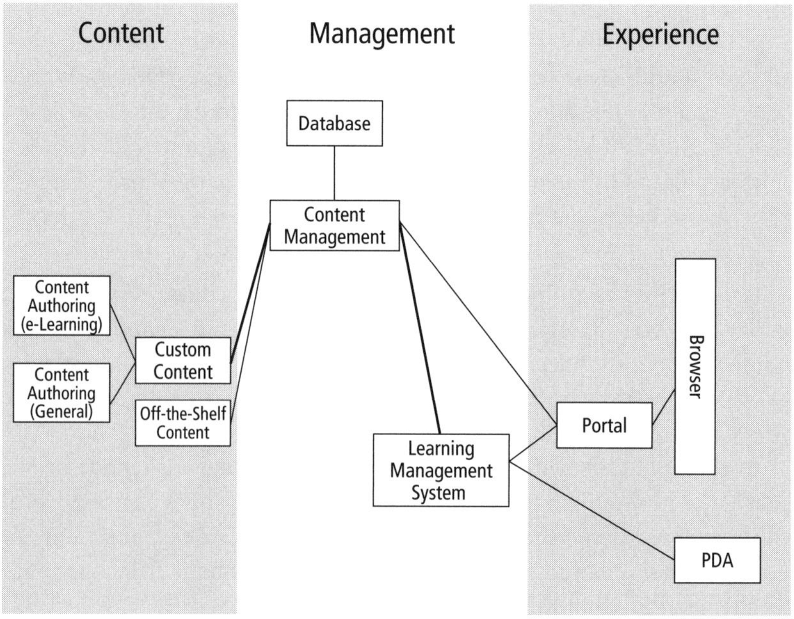

thought of as specialized variations of web-creation *toolkits* (with the browser being the environment), and *learning objects* are thought of as being interchangeable with Web objects.

This is not accurate, and the epicenter of significant confusion. In fact, the phrases, the very concepts of, *toolkits* and *learning objects* have different and specific purposes and implications to impact different simulation types.

ADVANCED TECHNIQUES

Different Examples of the Roles of Toolkits and Reusable Learning Objects to Customize Different Simulation Types

The four traditional simulation types have different levels of ease of use and flexibility (Figure A6.4). All are easier than building from scratch, of course.

Branching Story-Based

Recall story-based simulations (Figure A6.5). They consist of nodes, branches, media, and help files.

Let's use an example of a branching story focused on a topic critical to most CEOs. It's called "How to Avoid a Speeding Ticket."

TOOLKITS If we wanted to edit our "How to Avoid a Speeding Ticket" branching story, we would probably use a toolkit. They can be used to

Figure A6.4. Toolkits for the Four Traditional Simulation Types.

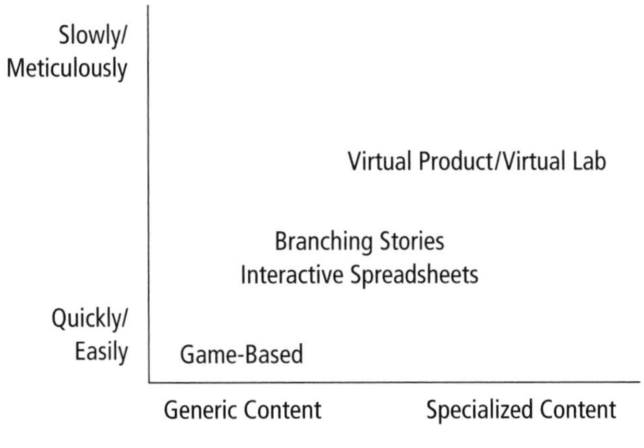

Figure A6.5. Pieces of a Branching Story.

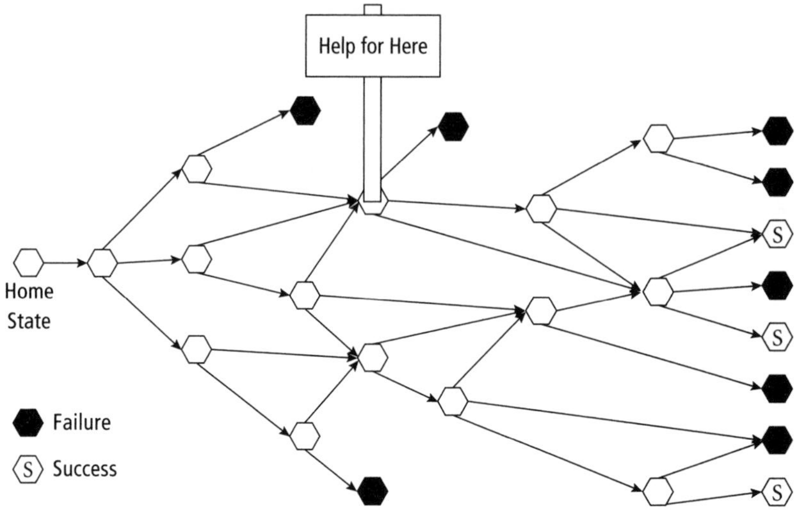

restructure branching points to change the connections between nodes. They can even add new segments.

Say our simulation had begun with the officer approaching our parked car. But further research suggested that there are opportunities for success or failure well before that moment.

So we would be adding a few earlier decisions, say pulling over quickly versus leading the officer on a bit of a chase; pulling as far over on the shoulder as possible versus pulling over but still exposing the officer to the traffic; turning on blinkers; turning on your interior light at night; even positioning your hands on the steering wheel where they are clearly visible to lower the tension of the officer.

New customized media (pictures or video) can be inserted. A series of generic police vehicles and officers could be replaced with Georgia state troopers.

Words in the learner's options, including the possible answers, could be changed. Imagine the text started as: "Well, I guess I was speeding."

It could be easily changed to: "When I saw the lights, I looked down and looked at the speedometer and saw that you were right. I was speeding."

If scoring is used, toolkits can change the relative influence of any given node. Consider one statement the player could make: "Hey, did you realize that speed guns could lead to sterility?"

If this originally had a –10-point impact to the "likeability" score, that could be changed to a –5.

REUSABLE LEARNING OBJECTS (RLOs) Reusable learning objects are also genre-specific. In the speeding examples, the RLOs could include pictures and video clips. This might be the logo of the company or the program, or specific pictures, such as of the police car or the inside of the dashboard. In some situations, the reusable learning object is the branching architecture itself, void of any content.

Interactive Spreadsheets

Recall interactive spreadsheets (Figure A6.6). They consist of equations and feedback.

Let's imagine a course also aimed at an issue that keep CEOs up all night: What to do with their paychecks. We can imagine that it might include categories such as:

- Primary residence (mortgage vs. outright purchase)
- Summer residence (mortgage vs. outright purchase)
- Winter retreat (mortgage vs. outright purchase)
- Residential golf course community (Somerby vs. Punta Cana)
- Schools and camps
- Boats (large vs. very large)
- Taxes (shelter?)
- Investments outside of the company
- Lawyers on retainer
- Investments in the company (including stock options)
- Alimony and child support
- Charities
- Living expenses
- Vacations

Output variables include portfolio; status of family; quality of life; reputation; and status of organization.

TOOLKITS Toolkits change the values associated with each interdependent relationship. They could increase or decrease the appreciation on

Figure A6.6. Triggers in an Interactive Spreadsheet.

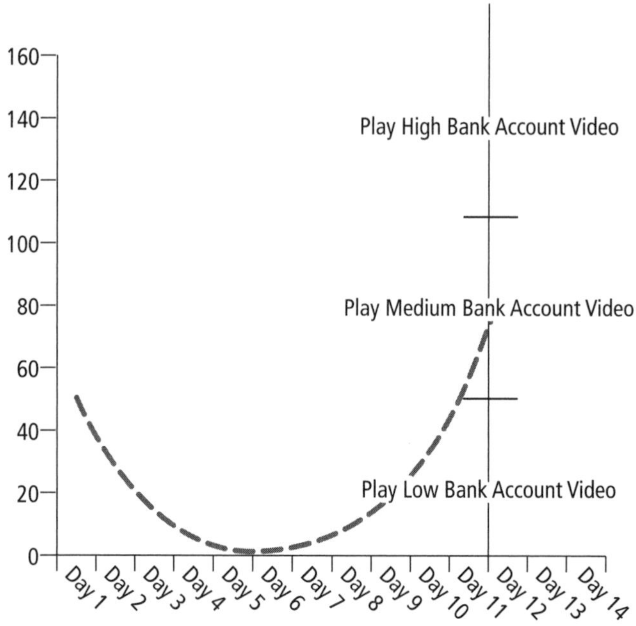

the houses, or change the impact they have on status of family. They could change the relationship between charities and quality of life (the charities can be very grateful). With a toolkit, a designer could hide certain variables and make visible others. A designer could add new variables that can change gameplay.

They can also import linear content and identify triggers and trigger ranges. For example, if taxes are too low compared to legal obligations, one might receive a letter from a certain government agency that shall remain anonymous (although the initials are Internal Revenue Service).

REUSABLE LEARNING OBJECTS Other than a few logos, perhaps, and maybe a few equations, there are few reusable learning objects in interactive spreadsheets. Some would argue that the shell of an interactive spreadsheet is a reusable object.

Game-Based

Of the four traditional genres, most game-based follow the typical Web philosophies of both toolkits and reusable learning objects.

TOOLKITS Toolkits are used to quickly import new text-based questions. Toolkits can also allow the game template to be swapped out with another corresponding one.

REUSABLE LEARNING OBJECTS Reusable learning objects include text, pictures, and video, often in the form of questions and answers.

Virtual Products/Virtual Labs

Recall virtual products and virtual labs (Figure A6.7). They have an underlying state based and light calculation model.

TOOLKITS Toolkits for virtual products and virtual labs are on the opposite side of the spectrum from game-based models. They are relatively difficult to use, yet allow tremendous flexibility. Everything can be changed, but not much can be changed easily. Toolkits from Macromedia include Director®, Shockwave®, and especially FlashMX®.

REUSABLE LEARNING OBJECTS Reusable learning objects include algorithms and other pieces of code, graphic elements, complete and working finished products, and text.

Figure A6.7. Pieces of a Virtual Product with Analog Controls.

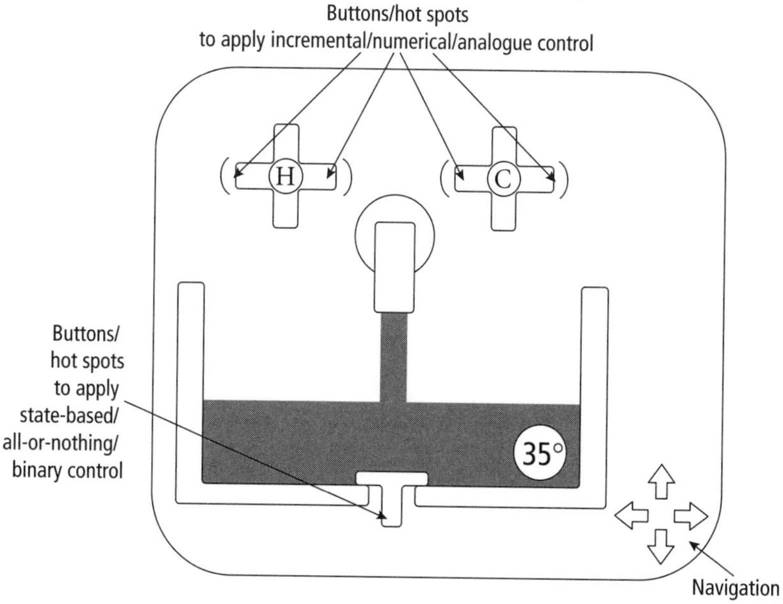

Some well-designed virtual objects draw XML sheets to finalize their presentation to the learner. Therefore, significant changes can be made to a text file, not the Flash code, to alter the simulation.

Development questions around customization include:

- Given the difficulty of simulation design, what help will the vendor provide these services, and how will they be charged?
- Given a need, what percentage of the solution is already created that can be reused?
- What elements of a finished simulation are easy to change? Able to be changed? Are toolkits available so the changes can be done at the client site?
- How long is there between when the project is approved and when the first student will engage the first simulation?

OTHER RESOURCES

- Polsani, P. (2003). Use and abuse of reusable learning objects. *Journal of Digital Information, 3*(4).

APPENDIX 7

E-LEARNING AND COMPUTER GAME MILESTONES

HERE ARE SOME MILESTONES in the development of e-learning and computer games.

1910—The first flight simulator is patented.

1958—Physicist William Higinbotham creates *Tennis for 2* on an oscilloscope.

1961—MIT student Steve Russell creates *Spacewar,* the first interactive computer game, which becomes popular on college campuses.

1963—Control Data and the University of Illinois, using a grant from the National Science Foundation, develop the technology and content for a computer-assisted instructional system that would become known as PLATO.

1971—Nutting manufactures the first arcade video game, called *Computer Space.* But the public finds it too difficult to play.

1972—Will Crowther writes *Colossal Cave Adventure,* the first interactive fiction computer game, on a Digital Equipment Corporation PDP-10.

1972—The first flight simulators to use computer-rendered scenes are built by General Electric for the U.S. Navy.

1972—Atari is launched.

1973—*Pong* is launched.

1976—Atari is sold for over $25 million to Warner Communications.

1977—Atari branches out into the home video game arena and releases VCS (what would later be called the 2600).

1978—Atari releases the arcade game *Football.* The game features a revolutionary new controller called the trackball.

1978—Midway imports arcade game *Space Invaders* from Taito. *Space Invaders* displays the current high score, adding a sort of asynchronous multi-player aspect.

1978—The University of Phoenix is accredited; new university models will not be coming from Harvard or Wharton.

1979—Atari releases what was to be their best-selling arcade game, *Asteroids.*

1979—Roy Trubshaw and Richard Bartle create *Multi-User Dungeons* (MUDs), and the advent of online multi-player adventuring.

1980—Atari creates the arcade game *Battlezone,* the first three-dimensional first-person game. The U.S. Army Tank Corps use a version in tank training.

1980—Namco releases *Pac-Man,* the most popular arcade game of all time. *Pac-Man* becomes the first video game to be popular with both males and females.

1980—Atari releases its exclusive home version of *Space Invaders* for the VCS. Sales of the VCS skyrocket.

1980—Mattel Electronics introduces the Intellivision game console. The first serious competition for the VCS, the Intellivision has better graphics and a steeper price—$299.

1980—Williams releases popular arcade game *Defender,* its first video game. *Defender* extends beyond the boundaries of the computer screen.

1980—*Zork,* a genre-defining text-based adventure game from Infocom, is released on the Apple II.

1981—Nintendo® creates popular arcade game *Donkey Kong.*

1982—Atari releases the 2600 version of *Pac-Man,* which is so bad that it shakes public confidence in the company.

1982—Coleco releases the Colecovision, a cartridge-based game console.

1982 (1983)—Commodore releases the Commodore 64, an inexpensive but powerful computer that outperforms any video game console. It has a $600 price tag.

1982—*ET* is a spectacular failure as an Atari 2600 video game.

1983—Cinematronics releases *Dragon's Lair,* the first arcade game to feature laser-disc technology.

1983—Computer game industry crashes under weight of hundreds of bad games.

1983—DataBeam is founded; real-time collaboration had started.

1983—Electronic Arts releases M.U.L.E. (Multiple-Use Labor Element) computer game for the Atari 2600. This pushes the multi-player capabilities of the Atari, allowing four players at once.

1984—CBT Systems (before it became SmartForce, later merging with SkillSoft) was founded, introducing and solidifying workbook-style content.

1985—Commodore launches the Amiga computer, with dedicated sound and graphics chips.

1985—Nintendo® test-markets its Nintendo® Entertainment System (NES) in New York. Nintendo® requires games to earn their seal of approval, avoiding earlier third-party quality control problems, and opening up avenue for hardware to be subsidized by software.

1985—Russian programmer Alex Pajitnov designs *Tetris.*

1986—Apple includes hypercards with its MAC operating system, making authoring low-end e-learning easy for non-authors.

1986—Nintendo® releases 8-bit NES console worldwide. In the United States it retails at $199, including *Super Mario Brothers* game.

1988—Coleco files for bankruptcy.

1989—Maxis releases PC game *SimCity*™.

1989—Nintendo® releases its handheld Game Boy® ($109). The system comes with *Tetris,* and despite a tiny monochrome screen, it begins to build an historic sales record.

1989—SEGA® releases the 16-bit Genesis in the United States for retail price of $249.

1989—Authorware introduces as the first e-learning icon-based authoring system.

1989—Control Data spins off PLATO.

1991—Capcom releases *Street Fighter II* and brings new life to arcades.

1991—Neal Stephenson publishes cyber-punk classic novel *Snow Crash.*

1991—S3 introduces the first single-chip graphics accelerator for the PC.

1991—id releases *Wolfenstein 3D* that defines the first-person shooter and returns relevancy to PC computer gaming.

1992—Midway launches arcade game *Mortal Kombat,* with unprecedented graphic violence.

1993—id releases *Doom,* a groundbreaking and genre-defining PC-based first-person shooter.

1993—Westwood releases *Dune II* on the PC, a groundbreaking and genre-defining real-time strategy game.

1993—ILINC was founded, a significant virtual classroom company.

1993—PC game *Myst* was released, eventually selling over five million copies. It is one of the first games to take advantage of the extra capacity of CD-ROMs.

1993/1994—The Entertainment Software Rating Board (ESRB) is established to rate video games.

1994—Maxis, the creators of *SimCity*™, publishes PC game *SimHealth,* challenging players to reform a city's health care system.

1994—The SEGA® Saturn™ and Sony PlayStation® launch in Japan.

1995—Centra was founded, a significant virtual classroom company.

1995—Sony releases the PlayStation® in the United States for $299. (It was launched in Japan one year earlier.) PSX hardware brings 3D graphics cost-effectively to the home.

1996—GartnerGroup launches e-learning: e-learning is a hot new market.

1996—Sony drops the price of the PlayStation® console to $199.

1996—Nintendo® 64 console launches, provides 64-bit processing to home console games.

1997—Arizona proposes a new bill that makes it a misdemeanor for retailers to display violent material.

1997—Docent and Saba are founded, defining the new LMS marketplace.

1997—Tamagotchi is introduced to the United States. Other electronic pets are subsequently introduced.

1997—Ultima Online officially opens its doors to players. This was the first huge MMORPG effort in 3D format.

1998—GartnerGroup gets out of e-learning: e-Learning is harder than it looks.

1998—Google is founded: e-Learning's first killer application is not e-learning.

1998—KnowledgePlanet is formed from KnowledgeUniverse and KnowledgeSoft: Portals are hot.

1998—Nintendo® 64 console price is dropped to $129.95.

1998—Sony's PlayStation® console price is dropped to $129.95.

1999—Asymetrix become Click2Learn: Portals are hot.

1999—EverQuest® launches for the PC: Massively multi-player online role-playing games go big-time.

1999—Infogames releases PC game *RollerCoaster Tycoon.*

1999—Microsoft launches their competition to AOL's Instant Messenger: e-Learning's other killer application is also not e-learning.

1999—Ninth House launches: Many think that broadband will be widely available and change e-learning.

1999—SmartForce is the new name of CBT systems: CD-ROM is dead; online content is critical; the perception is that this is the right time for an all-in-one vendor.

2000—Accenture spins off Indeliq: Branching simulations are hot.

2000—Sony launches their 64-bit PlayStation® 2 (PS2).

2000—Columbia University launches for-profit Fathom.com: e-Learning is seen as a growth opportunity.

2000—DigitalThink gets out of off-the-shelf content: They believe the market for libraries is sewn up.

2000—WBT Systems realizes that it is (and always had been) an LCMS vendor not an LMS vendor: Content management as a segment is born.

2001—Click2Learn divests custom content: The market is trifurcating into technology, services, and content.

2001—KnowledgePlanet acquires Peer3; Centra acquires MindLever; Docent acquires gForce. Saba launches authoring: Learning content management systems (LCMS) are critical, but can't stand on their own.

2001—Macromedia launches the Flash MX Suite; content is getting better.

2001—Microsoft includes DirectX as part of XP operating system: 3D graphics and sound capabilities are built into every desktop computer.

2001—Microsoft officially launches the Xbox® console. Based on PC architecture, the $299 console comes equipped with a 733Mhz CPU, Nvidia GPU, 10GB hard drive, and built-in Ethernet port.

2001—NYU Online disappears: Can traditional universities make it in e-learning?

2001—Plateau 4 LMS is launched: J2EE/EJB architecture pushes e-learning into the portal world.

2001—Riverdeep acquires Broderbund: The early learning content market is consolidating.

2001—SmartForce and Centra to merge: The time might be right for an all-in-one vendor.

2001—SmartForce and Centra call it off: Services, technology, and content are still very different.

2001—Thomson acquires NETg and drops the NETg name; e-learning assets are more important then e-learning.

2001—Thomson brings back the NETg name; e-learning is critical to content.

2001 (2002)—Nintendo®'s GameCube™ console is released. Nintendo® reports that $98 million worth of systems, games, and accessories were sold in the United States on launch day.

2002—Indeliq is absorbed back into Accenture: Branching simulations still have major market issues.

2002—MIT makes its university course content open and free to the public: Has content been Napstered?

2002—The United State's Army releases a free first-person shooter PC game called *America's Army,* as either a high-level training simulation or a recruiting game.

2002—SmartForce and SkillSoft merge: Content libraries are mature enough for consolidation.

2002—The price of the PS2 console in Japan falls twice in 2001, from a starting price of $320 to $281.70 to $240.

2002—The price of the SEGA® Dreamcast® console begins the year at $149.99 but has its price reduced to $99.95, $79.95, and finally $49.95 at the end of November.

2002: PeopleSoft acquires Teamscape: The enterprise players blur the line between human resources systems and learning systems.

2003—Columbia University closes for-profit Fathom.com: e-Learning is seen as a high risk.

2003—Google acquires Blogger.com: Weblogs go mainstream.

2003—Microsoft acquired Placeware: Line between e-learning and infrastructure continues to blur.

2003—NIIT acquires CognitiveArts: India increases influence and brand awareness in U.S. e-learning.

2003—Second Life launches. Their EULA will assign property rights to the creators of in-word objects, not the game creators, Linden Lab.

2003—There.com launches.

2004—SimuLearn's *Virtual Leader* wins "Best Online Training Product of the Year" by *Training Media Review*/American Society for Training and Development, the first time a simulation wins against more traditional e-learning content.

2004—Learning management system pioneers Docent and Click2Learn merge to form SumTotal Systems: More mergers to stabilize marketplace and compete with growing threat from ERP systems.

2004—*Full Spectrum Warrior*™ is launched: Xbox® console is used as an e-learning platform; the U.S. military invests in soft-skills simulations; commercial game version becomes a big hit.

APPENDIX 8

FULL INTERVIEWS WITH JANE BOSTON, WARREN SPECTOR, AND WILL WRIGHT

A FEW YEARS AGO I had a chance to interview three gaming experts for a column I wrote for *OnlineLearning* magazine (and yes, this being the training industry, that was back when there was an *OnlineLearning* magazine).

The three people were

- Jane Boston from Lucas Learning Ltd.
- Warren Spector from Ion Storm
- Will Wright from Maxis

I had to brutally edit the piece to meet my eight-hundred-word limit, and then again for the introduction to this book. Here are all 3,500 words, the super-extended director's edition, for those who speak DVD.

CLARK: What ideas (and types of ideas) are best taught through simulations? What ideas (and types of ideas) should never be taught through simulations?

JANE BOSTON: From my perspective, simulations are best used in four ways.

First, they are ideal for developing an understanding of big ideas and concepts—those things for which experience alone can deepen understanding. It is one thing to memorize a definition of nationalism or to read a passage describing the brittleness or fragility of an ecosystem; it is quite another to enter into an environment where those ideas play themselves out based on your own actions and ability to identify and solve problems.

Secondly, I believe simulations are great for dealing with time and scale. The computer gives us an opportunity to speed up results of an action that might actually take several lifetimes to play out. This allows players to see the potential impact of decisions made now on the future. Dire warnings about issues like the finite amount of drinkable water on the earth rarely impact people's behavior, yet a simulation has the potential of creating an emotional connection to the information that may have at least some small influence on both understanding and behavior.

I think simulations are good for situations where it is important to give people practice in decision making before it is faced in a dangerous or critical, real-life situation. Some of the simulations used for emergency personnel provide an opportunity to experience "life-like" situations and react to unexpected and challenging problems.

Finally, simulations are wonderful resources for taking us to a time or place that we are unable or unlikely to experience directly.

Simulations are not appropriate for teaching discrete bits of information ("facts") or for rote drill and practice. Because they are an immersive experience, they are better suited for those things that need to be learned in context and require active problem solving. There are some topics that are controversial, and until we understand better what is taken away from the experience, we need to be cautious in implementing. Is a simulation of a WWII battle an immersive history lesson or a lesson in combat techniques? A simulation should never be treated lightly as "only a game." Good simulations have the capacity to generate very strong thoughts and feelings in their participants, and anyone using a simulation should be prepared for that possibility.

WARREN SPECTOR: I'm no expert when it comes to training and/or education, but common sense tells me that simulations are best-suited to dealing with matters of the mind rather than matters of the body. I think there are two reasons for this. First, our simulations are still pretty rudimentary—we typically simulate only a few forms of sensory input, making genuine immersion in the sim a hit-or-miss proposition. Also, we interface with current simulations in ways that are radically different from the ways in which we interface with the real world—I mean, there's no real-world analogue of a mouse and keyboard or a game pad! Simulations that utilize more realistic interface elements (cockpit mock-ups, bobsleds, skis, and so forth) are few and far between.

Simulations, then, seem best-suited to teaching concepts, tactics, general approaches to situations, rather than specific actions. And the limited depth of our simulations today means that, even when we have real-world analogue interfaces, it's imperative that the people operating the simulation provide appropriate context and additional instruction to those who might mistake the partial simulation for an accurate re-creation of a real situation.

WILL WRIGHT: Simulations are great for understanding processes that are outside of our experience. You can play with time or scale. You can interact with molecules and planets. Many designers tend to map them into instinctive structures that we already have, either through analogy, or through gut feel. And for a lot of things, of course, the human mind is better than any computer.

CLARK: Can games change the behavior of players outside the game? How could you maximize the transferability of game-learned experiences to life?

JANE BOSTON: Because behavior is based on what we know and have done before, games become part of our overall experience. The degree of impact they have is much like the rest of life and is dependent on what the player brings to the game in terms of knowledge, skills, and attitudes; the context and circumstances in which the game is played; and what happens before and after the game. I've facilitated "off-line" simulations in which some participants exhibited extreme forms of emotion and carried feelings from a simulation into their relationships with others throughout the course of a two–week institute and again months, even years, later on in follow-up workshops.

I believe the transferability of game-learned experiences can be maximized by being clear about the purpose of the simulation before using it and by thinking of it as one tool in an overall learning experience. Setting an appropriate context with the players in advance is important, as is making sure that the players understand the rules and roles. In some simulations, guided practice may be needed before starting the actual game.

From my perspective, the most critical elements of a simulation come after the game itself. Debriefing what has happened—what a player experienced, felt during the simulation, and is feeling afterward, what strategies were tried and what happened, what other strategies might have been applied, what else the player needed to know or be able to do, analogies to real-life situations, how the players' own values and experience influenced their actions—are all important items for discussion.

WARREN SPECTOR: I think the most anyone can say about the effect games may have on player behavior is that some people will be affected in some ways at some times by some games. Not much there on which one could or should base an educational program (or public policy!). I think the key to using games to influence behavior and/or learning is to put specifically conceived and implemented games in an appropriate context (a classroom, for example) and use them to teach very specific, targeted things. In general, I've seen very little evidence, anecdotally, that game playing has any more influence on behavior than any other entertainment medium or social situation.

CLARK: How accurate does a simulation have to be to be a valid teaching tool?

WILL WRIGHT: In most interesting fields, like weather modeling, predictive simulations are very difficult or impossible. However, the property of weather being unpredictable can be a property of a good descriptive simulation.

Let me give you an example. Say you put the ball on the tip of a cone and let it go. A perfect predictive simulator would tell you exactly which side of the cone the ball would fall on for the exact condition set-up. A descriptive simulator, like *SimCity*™, would probably use a random variable to decide down which side the ball would fall. While that simulation would fail at being predictive, it would teach both the range of possibilities (that is, the ball never falls up), and also, from a planning perspective, it teaches that you can't rely on predicting the exact outcome and how to deal with the randomness.

I have seen a lot of people get misled. I see a lot of simulations that are very good descriptive (like *SimCity*™), but a lot of people use them predictively (like a weather model).

CLARK: How do you research topics for a new product? What is the role of subject-matter experts? A person from what perspective (academic, practitioner, consultant) has the most useful information and perspective for making a simulation?

JANE BOSTON: Our ideas come from many places. With George Lucas as our creative director, they often come directly from him. He has a great interest in simulations and their potential as a learning tool. We also research commonly taught topics in schools and think together about which ones can be done better using computer technology. It is important to us to connect our work to those things being taught every day in classrooms.

Subject-matter experts play a key role in making and creating simulations. We like to put people from lots of different perspectives around the same table when we're working on a high concept. We'll bring together academic experts, practitioners, and others with interesting backgrounds to help us identify the most important themes and ideas for us to convey through the simulation. For example, when we were creating *Star Wars® The Gungan Frontier™*, our ecology simulation, we worked with teachers, population biologists, ecology and science center staff, zoo educators, and so on. You need a mix of those whose work focuses on the big ideas and concepts, those who are working directly in applying that knowledge in everyday work, and those who are translating that into educational experiences for others. None of these alone is sufficient. I also love to add to the mix that person who brings an unusual connection to the topic to the table.

WARREN SPECTOR: You research topics for a game project pretty much as you would any other kind of media artifact. You figure out what you're trying to achieve—what you hope players experience as they play—and start digging up books, magazines, movies, Web pages, and anything else that can help you get where you're trying to go. I hate to sound mysterious or mystical, but there's no one answer to this question. If you're making a game set in real-world locations, go find information about those locations. If you're making a fantasy game, you might want to read every fantasy book you can get your hands on so you understand the genre's conventions well enough to represent them well (or undermine them, depending on your intent!). In making the kinds of games I do, "experts" really don't enter the picture much. (It'd be tough to find an illuminatus who'd admit to being one and orcs and elves don't talk to humans much.) But if you were making a game about the LAPD or the Navy SEALS, you better talk to some real LA policemen or some SEALS. But really, where games are concerned, experts and real-world information sources are only so valuable. Making a successful "real-world" game involves knowing where to deviate from reality in the interest of fun more often than it does knowing reality inside out so you can cleave to it religiously.

WILL WRIGHT: That is my favorite part of a game. I usually do a game that I am interested in. I find someone who is either controversial, or between two fields. I will use content experts as canaries in the mine. I did *SimEarth* based on Lovelock's *Gia*.

CLARK: Gaming is starting to reach the masses. What lessons can e-learning learn as it tries to do the same?

JANE BOSTON: Stay close to the learner (your customer)—understand his or her needs, interests, and context. Be very clear about what you're trying to do and don't try to do everything. Use the computer in ways that take advantage of its unique capabilities. Get good at doing each thing well before spreading out to other things. Just because things are possible to do, doesn't mean you should do them—especially when it comes to the high-end stuff. It's important to create the highest quality possible product with tech specs that match the installed base. And to develop products at a cost that keeps the price point appropriate for the budget realities of schools or other customers and allows developers to sustain themselves financially.

WARREN SPECTOR: As developers try to reach larger and larger audiences (to offset larger and larger development budgets!), we have to focus on a few critical points, I think Any time we think something is too simple, we have to make it simpler. We absolutely must streamline our interfaces and make them so intuitive users forget they're even USING an interface. We have to make sure users know exactly WHAT they're supposed to do at all times and challenge them to figure out HOW. We might even want to consider leaving the fantasy ghetto behind and giving people subject matter they're already interested in—in other words, make games that have built-in appeal to a larger audience.

CLARK: What is the budget and development time of today's computer games?

JANE BOSTON: A game with high production values can range in cost from several hundred thousand dollars to over four million in development costs alone. Development time also ranges broadly. Depending on size and complexity and art load, a complex game can take years to complete. I usually think of a range between twelve and twenty-four months as typical.

WARREN SPECTOR: Development budgets vary widely from studio to studio, publisher to publisher, and country to country. In the United States, for a triple-A title, you're talking anywhere from a couple million dollars to over ten. In Europe, I think budgets tend to be somewhat lower and, in Asia, lower still.

WILL WRIGHT: Ten million is closer. Online stuff is even worse. To make the game 10 percent more polished it costs twice as much. If you are a gamer, you might notice. You are still talking millions. It is one of those NASA things—the space shuttle was three times the complexity of Apollo, but ten times harder to build. You should be able to spend a hundred thousand, half million, three million.

CLARK: What are the elements that make a simulation immersive (that is, to make someone who is playing the game buy into the illusion)? What happens that breaks people out of "immersiveness"?

JANE BOSTON: There are many factors that affect this. Perhaps the most important is what I've heard George Lucas call the "immaculate reality." Attention to the detail and cohesiveness of the simulated environment is crucial. One discordant factor breaks the illusion. Likewise, the choices and actions the player faces must fit within that universe and its internal "rules." One of the important tasks a player faces in a simulation is making sense of the world he or she has entered and figuring out its internal rules—both its consistencies and its intentionally designed inconsistencies. It is important not to break into a simulated experience with peripheral information. For example, you wouldn't want to interrupt an ecological simulation with something flashing questions about your experience at you. Save the questions for later.

WARREN SPECTOR: At the most fundamental level, making a simulation immersive involves removing as many obstacles as possible between player and belief in the reality of the depicted world. Obstacles take many forms—shifting camera position during play (for example, third-person conversations in a first-person game); forcing players to switch from real-time gameplay to separate interface screens; dialogue presented in text, rather than spoken, form; objects that don't behave and/or can't be used like their real-world analogues. I'm not saying you want to recreate the real world, but certainly you want to strive for internal consistency, at least, so players aren't reminded they're "just playing a game" any more than necessary. What you want to do is (and I'm about to reveal a boatload of prejudices here!) create a game that's built on a set of consistently applied rules that players can then exploit however they want. Communicate those rules to players in subtle ways. Feed back the results of player choices so they can make intelligent decisions moving forward based on earlier experience. In other words, rather than crafting single-solution puzzles, create rules that describe how objects interact with one another (for example, water puts out fire, or a wooden box dropped from sufficient height breaks into pieces and causes damage based on its mass to anything it hits) and turn players loose—you want to simulate a world rather than emulate specific experiences. OK, I'm officially failing to get my point across, so I'm going to stop.

WILL WRIGHT: The more creative the players can be, the more they like the simulation. This might be giving them a lot of latitude. People like to explore the outer boundaries. There is nothing more satisfying than solving a problem in a unique way. Another derivative: being able to describe yourself to the game, and the game builds around you. It also helps if a player can build a mental model of what is going on in the simulation. This has more to do with the interface. All it takes is one weak link in the chain to blow this. Have them think they understand it enough to start testing their theories. At this point they are reverse engineering your program. You want to give them an entry path. People will say, "Oh wow, my mental model was way off." Most of my games use an obvious metaphor and a non-obvious metaphor. They think it is a train set, but they come to realize it is more like gardening. Things sprout up and you have to weed.

CLARK: How do you reward or penalize a player within the context of a simulation?

JANE BOSTON: I'm a strong believer that logical consequences are the best and only reward or penalty for a player in a simulation.

WARREN SPECTOR: I'm not sure penalizing players is ever appropriate in a game. Well, that's an overstatement. Obviously, there are inevitable penalties associated with failure but, when you can just load a saved game and try again, how severe do you want those penalties to be? Basically, game development is about presenting players with genuine challenges and then providing sufficient rewards to keep them feeling good about themselves and eager to tackle the NEXT challenge. Reward schedules are critical. But penalties? Punishment? Sounds like entirely the wrong tack to take. But maybe games are different from more educationally motivated sims in this regard.

WILL WRIGHT: With a game, you need some kind of reward structure. I try to have several goal paths; I try not to force them down any. In *SimCity*™, you can go for happiest people, or biggest city.

There is never one way. One way kills creativity. New ways of solving problems drive people in wanting to share experiences.

The photo albums in *The Sims*™ are important. We have to create new ways for users to share. Otherwise people used to feel as if they wasted the time they spent playing a game. So it is important to have an artifact that they take away from the game. They can show people. Getting people to engage other people with what they learned is critical. If you can get people to talk about something, it creates a snowball effect. You have to create glue. The community becomes the effective tool for learning.

CLARK: Any ideas at how to measure the effectiveness of a simulation? Please?

JANE BOSTON: All of us who work with these powerful tools realize how complex and difficult it is to measure their effectiveness. Subjective tools such as pre/post discussions, interviews, and writing activities can capture some of this. Rubrics have been developed to look at actual participation during the course of a simulation, but I tend to oppose that approach. Test performance on measurable items may be used, but it is impossible to separate what combination of things contributed to the learning measured and to account for any learning not covered by the test items. If you figure this one out, let me know!

WARREN SPECTOR: I haven't a clue. The measure of a game's success is in sales or, possibly, in critical acclaim. If players tell me they played *Deus Ex* for twelve hours straight without eating or going to the bathroom, the team succeeded; if they stop playing after five minutes, we've failed. Similarly, great reviews tell us one thing, bad reviews tell us another. From a slightly different standpoint, if players describe the way they solved problems in a game and, in doing so, describe situations the team didn't preplan and didn't anticipate, well, that's a big win. But in terms of measuring the effect of a simulation or determining what was learned by a player, in any specific way? Beats me. You'd have to talk to an educator or a psychologist about that. And even then I'm not sure I'd believe the answer. But maybe I'm just a cynic!

WILL WRIGHT: You first have to develop intent. The most interesting things to use simulations for are the hardest to measure. Teaching creative problem solving is very difficult to measure. A simulation is more like on-the-job experience. It is a broader element. You have experienced a larger landscape of possibilities. How you measure that, I wouldn't want to hazard a guess. It almost feels to me that the forces that demand tight metrics would not co-exist with simulation users. They may be incompatible ecosystems.

INDEX

I

J

K

L

M

X

Y

Z

ABOUT THE AUTHOR

CLARK ALDRICH is an internationally acclaimed e-learning analyst, consultant, and simulation designer, serving dozens of Global 1000 clients. He has been identified as an "e-Learning Guru" by *Fortune* magazine, "Visionary of the Industry" by *Training* magazine, and a member of "Training's New Guard" by the American Society for Training and Development.

He was the lead designer of SimuLearn's *Virtual Leader* (Best Online Product of the Year, *Training Media Review/Training & Development,* 2004) and has authored hundreds of articles, chapters, keynotes, reports, and columns, as well as the book *Simulations and the Future of Learning* (Pfeiffer, 2004)). Mr. Aldrich has been a subject-matter expert on e-learning and simulations for almost every major news source, including *The New York Times, Wall Street Journal,* CNET, *Business 2.0,* CNN, and *U.S. News and World Report.* Previously, he was the research director who created and was topic leader for Gartner Group's e-learning coverage. He can be reached at clark.aldrich@att.net.

Pfeiffer Publications Guide

This guide is designed to familiarize you with the various types of Pfeiffer publications. The formats section describes the various types of products that we publish; the methodologies section describes the many different ways that content might be provided within a product. We also provide a list of the topic areas in which we publish.

FORMATS

In addition to its extensive book-publishing program, Pfeiffer offers content in an array of formats, from fieldbooks for the practitioner to complete, ready-to-use training packages that support group learning.

FIELDBOOK Designed to provide information and guidance to practitioners in the midst of action. Most fieldbooks are companions to another, sometimes earlier, work, from which its ideas are derived; the fieldbook makes practical what was theoretical in the original text. Fieldbooks can certainly be read from cover to cover. More likely, though, you'll find yourself bouncing around following a particular theme, or dipping in as the mood, and the situation, dictates.

HANDBOOK A contributed volume of work on a single topic, comprising an eclectic mix of ideas, case studies, and best practices sourced by practitioners and experts in the field.

An editor or team of editors usually is appointed to seek out contributors and to evaluate content for relevance to the topic. Think of a handbook not as a ready-to-eat meal, but as a cookbook of ingredients that enables you to create the most fitting experience for the occasion.

RESOURCE Materials designed to support group learning. They come in many forms: a complete, ready-to-use exercise (such as a game); a comprehensive resource on one topic (such as conflict management) containing a variety of methods and approaches; or a collection of like-minded activities (such as icebreakers) on multiple subjects and situations.

TRAINING PACKAGE An entire, ready-to-use learning program that focuses on a particular topic or skill. All packages comprise a guide for the facilitator/trainer and a workbook for the participants. Some packages are supported with additional media—such as video—or learning aids, instruments, or other devices to help participants understand concepts or practice and develop skills.

- *Facilitator/trainer's guide* Contains an introduction to the program, advice on how to organize and facilitate the learning event, and step-by-step instructor notes. The guide also contains copies of presentation materials—handouts, presentations, and overhead designs, for example—used in the program.
- *Participant's workbook* Contains exercises and reading materials that support the learning goal and serves as a valuable reference and support guide for participants in the weeks and months that follow the learning event. Typically, each participant will require his or her own workbook.

ELECTRONIC CD-ROMs and web-based products transform static Pfeiffer content into dynamic, interactive experiences. Designed to take advantage of the searchability, automation, and ease-of-use that technology provides, our e-products bring convenience and immediate accessibility to your workspace.

METHODOLOGIES

CASE STUDY A presentation, in narrative form, of an actual event that has occurred inside an organization. Case studies are not prescriptive, nor are they used to prove a point; they are designed to develop critical analysis and decision-making skills. A case study has a specific time frame, specifies a sequence of events, is narrative in structure, and contains a plot structure—an issue (what should be/have been done?). Use case studies when the goal is to enable participants to apply previously learned theories to the circumstances in the case, decide what is pertinent, identify the real issues, decide what should have been done, and develop a plan of action.

ENERGIZER A short activity that develops readiness for the next session or learning event. Energizers are most commonly used after a break or lunch to stimulate or refocus the group. Many involve some form of physical activity, so they are a useful way to counter post-lunch lethargy. Other uses include transitioning from one topic to another, where "mental" distancing is important.

EXPERIENTIAL LEARNING ACTIVITY (ELA) A facilitator-led intervention that moves participants through the learning cycle from experience to application (also known as a Structured Experience). ELAs are carefully thought-out designs in which there is a definite learning purpose and intended outcome. Each step—everything that participants do during the activity—facilitates the accomplishment of the stated goal. Each ELA includes complete instructions for facilitating the intervention and a clear statement of goals, suggested group size and timing, materials required, an explanation of the process, and, where appropriate, possible variations to the activity. (For more detail on Experiential Learning Activities, see the Introduction to the *Reference Guide to Handbooks and Annuals*, 1999 edition, Pfeiffer, San Francisco.)

GAME A group activity that has the purpose of fostering team sprit and togetherness in addition to the achievement of a pre-stated goal. Usually contrived—undertaking a desert expedition, for example—this type of learning method offers an engaging means for participants to demonstrate and practice business and interpersonal skills. Games are effective for team-building and personal development mainly because the goal is subordinate to the process—the means through which participants reach decisions, collaborate, communicate, and generate trust and understanding. Games often engage teams in "friendly" competition.

ICEBREAKER A (usually) short activity designed to help participants overcome initial anxiety in a training session and/or to acquaint the participants with one another. An icebreaker can be a fun activity or can be tied to specific topics or training goals. While a useful tool in itself, the icebreaker comes into its own in situations where tension or resistance exists within a group.

INSTRUMENT A device used to assess, appraise, evaluate, describe, classify, and summarize various aspects of human behavior. The term used to describe an instrument depends primarily on its format and purpose. These terms include survey, questionnaire, inventory, diagnostic, survey, and poll. Some uses of instruments include providing instrumental feedback to group members, studying here-and-now processes or functioning within a group, manipulating group composition, and evaluating outcomes of training and other interventions.

Instruments are popular in the training and HR field because, in general, more growth can occur if an individual is provided with a method for focusing specifically on his or her own behavior. Instruments also are used to obtain information that will serve as a basis for change and to assist in workforce planning efforts.

Paper-and-pencil tests still dominate the instrument landscape with a typical package comprising a facilitator's guide, which offers advice on administering the instrument and interpreting the collected data, and an initial set of instruments. Additional instruments are available separately. Pfeiffer, though, is investing heavily in e-instruments. Electronic instrumentation provides effortless distribution and, for larger groups particularly, offers advantages over paper-and-pencil tests in the time it takes to analyze data and provide feedback.

LECTURETTE A short talk that provides an explanation of a principle, model, or process that is pertinent to the participants' current learning needs. A lecturette is intended to establish a common language bond between the trainer and the participants by providing a mutual frame of reference. Use a lecturette as an introduction to a group activity or event, as an interjection during an event, or as a handout.

MODEL A graphic depiction of a system or process and the relationship among its elements. Models provide a frame of reference and something more tangible, and more easily remembered, than a verbal explanation. They also give participants something to "go on," enabling them to track their own progress as they experience the dynamics, processes, and relationships being depicted in the model.

ROLE PLAY A technique in which people assume a role in a situation/scenario: a customer service rep in an angry-customer exchange, for example. The way in which the role is approached is then discussed and feedback is offered. The role play is often repeated using a different approach and/or incorporating changes made based on feedback received. In other words, role playing is a spontaneous interaction involving realistic behavior under artificial (and safe) conditions.

SIMULATION A methodology for understanding the interrelationships among components of a system or process. Simulations differ from games in that they test or use a model that depicts or mirrors some aspect of reality in form, if not necessarily in content. Learning occurs by studying the effects of change on one or more factors of the model. Simulations are commonly used to test hypotheses about what happens in a system—often referred to as "what if?" analysis—or to examine best-case/worst-case scenarios.

THEORY A presentation of an idea from a conjectural perspective. Theories are useful because they encourage us to examine behavior and phenomena through a different lens.

TOPICS

The twin goals of providing effective and practical solutions for workforce training and organization development and meeting the educational needs of training and human resource professionals shape Pfeiffer's publishing program. Core topics include the following:

- Leadership & Management
- Communication & Presentation
- Coaching & Mentoring
- Training & Development
- E-Learning
- Teams & Collaboration
- OD & Strategic Planning
- Human Resources
- Consulting